CAUGHT

IN THE SPIN

Book two in the CAUGHT series

Sharleen Scott

Out West Press
Yakima, Washington

Sharleen Scott/ Out West Press
PO Box 185
Naches, WA 98937

www.sharleenscott.com

Publisher's Note: This is a work of fiction. Names, characters, places, and incidents are a product of the author's imagination. Locales and public names are sometimes used for atmospheric purposes. Any resemblance to actual people, living or dead, or to businesses, companies, events, institutions, or locales is completely coincidental.

Edited by Dori Harrell at doriharrell.wix.com/breakoutediting

Cover design by Kelly A. Martin www.kam.design.com

Caught in the Spin/ Sharleen Scott. -- 1st ed.
ISBN 978-0-9915890-2-9

To my mom, Marylyn McMahan, for always saying I could do anything I put my mind to. And so I have.

To my grandmother, Irene McMahan, for sharing her love of reading.

Many thanks to my editor, Dori Harrell, who stuck it out through the many revisions and offered encouragement when my confidence faltered.

Life gives everyone scars—
some people just wear them more openly than others

1

The hair on the back of Tom Black's neck stood on end. Nomadic shivers roved his spine. He braced his hands against the windowpane and stared into the night, his thoughts spinning from the smash of déjà vu that woke him and left him wondering if it was real. His common sense argued otherwise. The logical assessment: His dreams had taken him for a nocturnal joyride. He inhaled and scrubbed his palms across his unshaven cheeks but couldn't shake the sensation she'd been there.

He'd tangled his hands in her strawberry-blonde hair and kissed her warm lips. In the glow of the summer moon, he'd held her and swore he wouldn't let her go. Not this time. But wanting wouldn't make it happen. As tendrils of light peeked through the blinds, she'd touched his cheek and whispered, "Good-bye, Tom. I'll always love you."

And he knew it was only a dream. When Jolie left, she

didn't say good-bye.

He lay back on the bed with his hands clasped behind his head and looked at the woman sleeping beside him. Not strawberry-blonde but brunette, just as she should be. It was only a dream. There was no other rational explanation. But if it was, why did he feel this pleasant exhaustion, this physical contentment? He doubted a dream, even a great one, could produce such a high level of satiation. Unsettled, he pulled the sheet up and drifted into a restless sleep where Jolie's sweet laugh punctuated his dreams.

At daylight, Tom slapped blindly to stop the alarm's irritating screech, yawning wide. With one eye open a narrow slit, he checked the time and groaned. The short hours he'd slept hadn't left him rested. He exhaled and rubbed his gritty eyes. A to-do list waited in the office and he had to get up. A hay truck was coming this morning. The vet would check the bulls and administer inoculations, the crew had fences to repair in the south pasture, and there was a paperwork mountain to tackle. And that was only the beginning. If yesterday was anything to go by, today would be hot and humid. He hated Nashville in the summer.

He stared at the ceiling, delaying the start of his work day. Female fingers teased the dark hair on his chest as she leaned against him. Her warm breath tickled his skin. Tom frowned. Normally, he couldn't think of a better way than sex to start the day. The problem was, he felt as if he'd already done it and wasn't in the mood for another round. She looked at him and licked her full lips. Tom gave her credit for trying, but he had to get moving. Undaunted, she drew circles around his navel with her finger.

"Make love to me, Tom," she said, smiling as her questing hand headed south.

He stopped her progress and chuckled. "That's enough of that. I need to get up."

"Aw, come on. You were sound asleep when I got here last night." She wiggled to free her hand from his grasp. "Why do you think I come over here? To listen to you mumble and moan in your sleep?" she said, confirming he hadn't made love with her during the night.

Tom tensed. "I don't talk in my sleep."

She laughed. "Yeah, you do. Nothing understandable most of the time. Last night you mumbled a lot. Smiled, too. It must have been a good dream." She licked her lips again and gave him a look that normally caught his interest. "I love making love with you," she said. She kissed her way up his chest and looked in his eyes. "I love you."

She waited for a reply, but he didn't give her one.

"Tom, did you hear me?"

"Yeah."

She rose up on her elbow and stared at the unresponsive man. "Don't you have anything to say?"

He contemplated her statement.

"Tom! I said I love you."

"I heard you."

"Well?"

"Well what?" He dodged, rolling from under her and out of bed, stretching to work the kinks from his stiff knee. The early morning sun cast sufficient light through the blinds for Tom to see he was in trouble. She sat in the middle of his bed, eyes narrowed and jaw clenched.

"When someone says 'I love you,' the proper response is 'I love you, too.' We've been together nearly two months now."

He muttered, "Can't say it if I don't feel it." Besides, he didn't consider what they'd been doing "being together," not in a lasting sense anyway. They'd gone out for a while and settled into a nice routine. Several nights a week she came by after work at the local watering hole. They'd grab a bite to eat on her night off. To his thinking, that didn't constitute a left-hand-ring relationship. Apparently, he'd miscalculated. He looked for socks in a dresser drawer, found his jeans in a chair, and slipped them on.

"Now look, Shelly. I like you and we've had a good time, but let's not read more into it than there is." He riffled through the clothes in his closet for a chambray work shirt. Locating it, he turned and found her blocking his path to the bathroom, stark naked and ready for battle like some kind of Greek warrior goddess.

"You like me? That's it?"

Tom stared at her, feeling bad he couldn't offer her more. "Yeah. That's it."

She stared back. "You cold, unfeeling, cynical bastard!"

He shrugged. "I'm not arguing with you. It's probably true." As he slipped his arms in the sleeves, her hand connected with his cheek. He clenched his teeth and finished buttoning his shirt, tucked it into his jeans, and looked at her with a frown. "I think you should leave now and..." He paused, feeling like the callous bastard she thought him. "I don't think you need to come back. I'd say we've taken this about as far as it can go."

She bit her lip.

"If you think about it, you'll see I'm right. I can't give you what you want." Her lip quivered and Tom was afraid she'd cry. If she did, he'd need to comfort her and this whole breakup thing grew more difficult. It just wasn't decent to send a crying woman out the door. An angry one pretty much wrote her own invitation to leave, but a distressed woman required special handling.

"You..."

She tightened her fist and Tom corrected his evaluation of her emotional state. She wasn't planning to cry—she was going to hit him again.

"...jerk!"

Tom prepared to duck or cover sensitive body parts, but he stayed silent. If he couldn't say what she wanted to hear, keeping his mouth shut seemed best.

"Humph." She spun and hunted for her clothes on the floor, glaring over her shoulder as she stalked into the bathroom.

Tom wandered into the kitchen to brew a pot of coffee, not waiting to see what mood she'd be in when she came out. A few minutes later, he watched from the kitchen door as she stomped across the living room, pausing to slide into her purple cowboy boots without bothering to pull her jeans legs over them. The front door stood open, giving a straight shot to the porch. With one last glare at Tom's impassive face, she huffed and shoved the screen hard enough to hit the wall and snap the spring. On the porch, she yelled, "Get out of my way!"

Tom moved to the window to see his best friend and foster brother walking up the steps at the wrong time and laughed at the shocked expression Clay Masterson wore as he jumped aside, barely stopping his backward momentum into a yellow rosebush.

"Morning, Sherry," Clay said, rubbing his butt.

Since Clay hadn't done anything to earn the departing woman's animosity, Tom stepped out on the porch to provide a more worthy target. The tires of her red Toyota threw gravel when she gunned the engine and sped down the driveway. She appeared done with him, probably for good.

"Where's Sherry going so early this morning?" Clay asked, unperturbed by her treatment of him. "She usually hangs around awhile." He bent and retrieved the door spring, reattaching it.

"Leaving," Tom said. "Sherry?" He laughed. "Damn. I think I called her Shelly."

"Not in the middle of—"

Tom stopped laughing and scowled. "No. Give me a little credit."

"Is that why she's pissed off?" Clay adjusted the well-worn Stetson Sherry nearly knocked from his head.

"Among other things. Want some coffee?"

Clay nodded and followed Tom into the kitchen, taking a seat at the table. He tossed his hat to the empty chair and looked at Tom with anticipation.

Cornered, Tom figured he'd have to confess or Clay would sit there all day, waiting. "She called me a cold, unfeeling bastard...oh, and cynical too. I didn't argue and I guess that made her mad. Up to now, her opinion of me was somewhat higher." He set a mug of steaming coffee in front of Clay and sat down with a mug of his own.

"From the look of the welt on your cheek, I'm thinking you'll need to take her name off the security list."

Tom rubbed his cheek, hoping the mark would fade before anyone else saw it and asked questions. "Suppose so. I doubt she's coming back anyway. She wants more from me than I have to give her."

"You know, Tom, at the rate you're going through the women here locally, you'll run out soon." Clay smiled at Tom's scowl.

"There aren't that many. A few here and there..."

"They say the memory is the first to go," Clay said with a laugh.

Tom shrugged. He could count on one hand the number of women he'd looked at in recent years. They came on to him like bugs to a zapper, but that didn't mean he hooked up with them all. He knew his shortcomings in the relation-ship department and his buddy did, too. But that didn't stop the guy from razzing him. "Jealous, are you?"

"No, and you know it. I'm married to the only woman I'll ever want. I don't need variety. Never have."

"Yeah, I know. I'm the one who should be envious." And if he thought about it enough, he would be. Clay's marriage two years earlier had been the best thing to happen to his friend. Clay had with Harlie what Tom could've had with Jolie if he hadn't screwed up years before.

His thoughts drifted to the late-night Jolie incident, and now, in the daylight, he was convinced it was only a dream. He wasn't superstitious like a lot of cowboys. He'd never en-tered a rodeo arena with a good-luck charm in his pocket, and he didn't believe in creepy stuff like ghostly visitations. Although, if it was only a dream, it was the most vivid he'd ever experienced, complete with scents. He didn't think dreams could involve olfactory senses, but last night might prove otherwise. Maybe he should have paid more attention in his college psych classes, but dream interpretation was phony crap, and as far as he was concerned, Freud could keep his wish-fulfillment theories. Like most of the male students, he'd been more interested in the human sexuality part of the curriculum. Now he wished—

"Tom?" Clay leaned across the table, waving his hand in front of Tom's face. "Are you okay?"

Tom shook free of his thoughts. "Yeah. Fine." He frowned into his coffee cup. "I'm thinking I might look for Jolie again." Clay's eyebrows shot up, and Tom regretted blurting it that way.

"Jolie? Why would you do that?"

"I don't know…just thought I should give it another try."

"But it's been what, twelve years? I know what she meant to you, but don't you think…" Clay leaned back in his chair, shaking his head and frowning. "Wouldn't it be a mistake? I mean, look what happened last time you two were together."

"It wasn't the relationship that caused that. It was the accident—"

"I know. And it was her leaving after that mess that sent you over the edge. Why risk it?" Clay blew out a breath. "If you're set on this, I'll help you look. But give it some serious thought before you do anything."

Tom debated telling Clay about his dreamland rendezvous with Jolie. Maybe it did mean something. He'd pulled her into his dreams before, but not like this, and he didn't understand why he'd have such intense thoughts about her now. She was part of his past—a past he tried to forget.

No, it was better to keep his nocturnal festivities with Jolie to himself. Clay would think he was a nutcase if he told him. Heck, he thought he was a nutcase at the moment. "I know," Tom said. "She's probably married by now anyway, and if she'd wanted me, she'd have come back on her own. It's just—"

Clay gave him a sympathetic smile. "You have to move on, Tommy. That's all there is to it. You need to stop torturing yourself with what could have been."

"I know." Tom shrugged. "You're right. It's a stupid idea. So," he said, changing the subject. "Are you leaving for Oregon today?"

"No, that's what I came to tell you. We won't be going. Harlie doesn't want to fly right now."

"Why?"

"Morning sickness. Flying makes her puke." Clay grinned.

Tom returned the smile. "Well, look at you grinning like you were the first guy to figure out how to do that. Pregnant again, huh? Congratulations, stud. When's she due?"

"December. Looks like you'll be stuck with us this summer."

"I can live with it." Tom glanced at the wall clock. "If you aren't leaving, why are you out so early this morning? I haven't even had breakfast yet."

"Your door was open, so I figured you were up." He rubbed his eyes. "Abby's teething and kept me up all night. The only thing that calmed her was a cold teething ring and me singing. I went through my entire song list, every baby song I know, and rocked us both silly." He yawned and ran a hand through his sandy-blond hair, causing odd strands to stick out. "She just went to sleep, so I thought I'd sneak out before she started again."

"But you love it."

"Not the crying, but it's something to have her put those

little arms around my neck when she's hurting and know I make her feel better. I hope you get to experience it someday, pal."

"Not likely." Tom snorted. "Fatherhood isn't in the cards for me. I'm content with hugs from your little rug rat."

"I'm trying to talk Harlie into getting some help," Clay said. "It took some convincing, but she's agreed to talk to a few people from a nanny service. I hope she'll hire one of them."

Tom moved from the table and rummaged around in the cupboard, found a loaf of bread, and dropped two slices in the toaster. "I'm surprised she isn't recruiting from the local homeless shelter," Tom said with a chuckle. A former street kid, Harlie was hell-bent on helping every down-and-out she encountered. "Besides, I thought she wanted to do the supermom thing." He opened the refrigerator and located butter and apricot jam.

"She does, but with Abby running all over, she'll have a hard time keeping up soon. I don't want her wearing herself out when it isn't necessary." The bread popped up from the toaster. Tom handed the slices to Clay and dropped in two more.

"If you were up all night, why didn't you sleep in?" Tom asked.

"Couldn't relax, and you said you expected a hay truck this morning. I thought I'd help."

"The crew can do it."

"I know, but I need the exercise." Clay spread jam on his toast and took a bite.

"I've got a great little bull that needs riding if you want a workout," Tom offered, smiling.

"Spitfire? No thanks." Clay laughed and shook his head. "Too old for that bull-riding stuff. I'll help with the truck. You have a buyer for him yet?"

"Maybe. Gib Sanborn will come soon to take a look at him."

"Spitfire is a good bucker," Clay said. "Mean, too."

"He has potential. His daddy is a rank bugger and it looks like he inherited it. We'll see what Gib thinks of him." Tom took a bite of toast and frowned. "Maybe Sally would whip up some pancakes when she gets here this morning." Clay's housekeeper was a pancake genius.

"Probably better than toast." Clay glanced at the toast with disdain.

"Let's see if the truck is in and head over to your place if it isn't." Tom grabbed his hat and walked toward the door, wanting a change of scenery. If he and Clay yakked over coffee long enough, Tom was bound to tell him about the dream, and he wasn't sure what Clay would think about a ghostly visit from a woman who shouldn't be dead.

2

Nashville summers were traditionally hot and humid. To-day's weather report was traditional in every way. Tallie Peters didn't care. She was cruising on a wave of excitement impossible to tamp down with sticky air. On the stereo in her company sedan: Jason Aldean's "She's Country."

"You've got that right, baby," Tallie said with a laugh as she pounded the guitar beat on the steering wheel. The miles flew by. Rolling hills, blanketed in bluegrass, sugar maples, and oaks filled the landscape. If the stereo volume wasn't cranked to ear blasting, she might consider it serene.

She followed the directions given by her boss, a map hastily drawn on scrap paper. One last glance at his scribbles and Tallie pulled into a broad driveway, stopping at the security entrance. Multiple cameras gawked at her like starving vultures, making her feel alternately like an unwanted gate-crasher or a paparazzi-hounded movie star. She considered waving or sticking out her tongue but thought better of it. Whoever watched might not find her silliness amusing, and goofy wasn't her image selection for the day.

She glanced around for an indication of how to gain access to the estate. There wasn't a call button she could see. Maybe visitors were expected to pole-vault over the fence. The call button was probably concealed. If not, how many times a day would overeager fans push that button hoping Clay Masterson might respond? She scanned for the obvious, like a fake rock, but didn't see any possibilities. No fake rocks. No real ones either. What was she supposed to do— send up smoke signals?

While she inspected the entrance area, a large emblem across the gate caught her eye and had her wondering: MB? A sign to the side of the gate answered one question but introduced another: Masterson-Black Ranch. Tallie corrected herself: ranch, not estate. Okay. Masterson was easy to figure out. But who, or what, was Black? If she paid attention to celebrity gossip, she'd probably know. Most likely, it wasn't important, but she did like to have all her ducks lined up and saluting in advance.

She rolled down her window and spotted the call box tucked inconspicuously in a sheared shrub and pushed the button. Moments passed, leaving Tallie time to mull over the gate, fences, and security cameras. They screamed wealth and self-importance. Been there, done that. Not impressed. At least the shrub wasn't a guitar-shaped topiary. Some celebrities were gooney for that sort of thing.

"Yes?" A female voice said, startling Tallie.

"I'm Tallie Peters from Stockton Management. Mr. Stockton sent papers for Mr. Masterson to sign," Tallie said with a professional tone she hoped concealed her sudden anxiety. Until seeing the reality of Clay's Masterson's super-star existence, she'd looked forward to meeting him. Now, her nerves jumped like crazed toads.

"Harv called and said he was sending someone out. I'll open the gate. Come up the driveway and turn left. You'll see the house."

No doubt the house was a megamansion, considering the Fort Knox safety precautions. After a brief wait, she heard a click and the large gate swung wide, inviting Tallie to enter

Clay Masterson's inner sanctum. The long driveway was flanked on either side by lush pastures dotted with horses and cattle. A distinctive hum brought her attention to the electric wire atop the perimeter chain-link fence. Fort Knox, indeed.

After the turn, she found a white farmhouse with a wraparound porch and multipeaked roof, surrounded by ancient willows and imposing oaks. She stared at the classic house and retracted her first assessment. Clay Masterson was one of the wealthiest country music stars and he lived normal. But she wasn't ready to concede her opinion entirely. This was only the house, not the man.

Before climbing from the car, she took one last look in the rearview mirror. Her lipstick wasn't smeared, but the toads in her stomach were jumping. She stepped out and adjusted her skirt and tucked in her blouse. After grabbing the briefcase from the passenger seat, she slammed the car door and headed to the house.

An attractive brown-haired woman answered the door, carrying a baby on her hip and wearing a friendly smile. The nanny, Tallie assumed. She wore denim shorts and a tank top but no shoes. Surprisingly casual.

"Hello. I'm Tallie Peters to see Mr. Masterson," she said. The equally dark-haired baby blew a raspberry and giggled. Tallie fought to retain her professional demeanor, though the corner of her mouth attempted to rise.

"Stop that, Abby," the woman scolded. "Come in. He's out back somewhere. I'll get some shoes and we can walk out and find him." The woman turned and left the room only to return a moment later without the shoes. "Where are my manners? I didn't even introduce myself. Must be lack of sleep or something," she said with a laugh. "This runt is teething and kept us up half the night. Luckily, the tooth broke through this morning or she'd still be fussing." She held out her free hand. "I'm Harlie Masterson. Sorry I didn't mention that earlier. It's nice to meet you, Tallie."

Tallie shook the offered hand and stared at Harlie Masterson in wonder. Not the nanny, but the wife. Another Clay Masterson character reassessment was in order. His wife appeared, well, normal. So far so good. No whacked-out, arrogant celebrity types here. Her stomach jitters receded to mild tadpole quivers. "It's nice to meet you too, Mrs. Masterson."

"Just Harlie works for me. I'll get those shoes now and we can go out back." She left the room again, returning in a pair of plaid Converse All Star sneakers. She opened what must be the kitchen door. "Sally? Can you keep Abby for a minute? I need to find Clay. Any idea where he is?"

A petite gray-haired woman came out, arms outstretched. "Of course. Come here, dumplin'. He's with Tom in the hay barn. Tell them lunch is almost ready."

"Will do. Mama will be right back." She leaned and kissed the little girl, who giggled and grabbed her mother's shoulder-length hair. Harlie untangled it from the baby's fingers and gave her a loving pat. "Bye-bye. Let's go, Tallie," she called as she pushed open the kitchen door. Tallie rushed to keep up as they walked outside and down a paved driveway, passing several barns, shop buildings, and corrals. Her heel caught in a hole, nearly twisting her ankle. What a day to wear spike heels. Hiking boots would've been more appropriate, but who knew she'd be mucking around a cattle ranch today. She'd imagined a knock on the door, a quick collection of signatures, and back to the office in time for her sack lunch.

"Have you worked for Harv long?" Harlie asked while they walked.

"I've been with the company for three months, in accounting, but have been Mr. Stockton's assistant for only two weeks." They turned from the driveway and walked into an alleyway between two barns. "I'm enjoying it so far. I have to tell you, Harlie, this is my best day yet. Meeting your husband is...exciting." Exciting, terrifying, and what if she said something stupid and made the man angry? Celebrities were so unpredictable, or so she had heard. Her exposure so far was limited to financial records, and she was beginning to reconsider the wisdom of accepting this new position. The jitters returned and Tallie nearly lost her hard-won composure. Mr. Stockton should have allowed her to cut her professional teeth on a minor star, but no, the man throws a superstar her way.

Harlie laughed. "I hated Clay the first time I met him."

"Seriously?" she said, eyes wide.

"It's tough to like a guy who threatens to have you arrested," she said. "But once he figured out I wasn't a psycho fan, it all worked out." Harlie gave Tallie a reassuring smile. "He's freakishly normal, so relax. It'll bother him if you make a fuss. This is his home, and around here, he's just Clay."

They rounded the end of the barn and stopped in a huge pole building bursting with activity. A flatbed hay truck sat alongside the building where a man on a boom truck operated a motorized hook swinging hay bales between the truck bed and barn. Men on top of the haystack caught the bales against their chaps-covered legs using large hooks and set them in place. Tallie watched the hay fly through the air and cringed as the empty hook swung back, sure someone would get hurt. Several moments passed before she realized one of the guys on the stack was the man she needed to see. Clay Masterson was bucking hay.

Despite the shed's open-air construction, the space inside was stifling and Tallie fanned herself. The truck was almost empty when she caught sight of another man working the stack. With an effortless toss and a push with his thigh, he stacked a bale weighing a hundred and fifty pounds or more, flexing well-formed shoulder muscles. The job completed, he chucked his leather gloves aside and ran his hands through his straight, midnight-black hair, pushing it from his face. Even though he was sweaty and covered in chaff, Tallie couldn't stop staring—maybe even because of it. His damp shirt stuck to the angles and lines of his body. The temperature around Tallie jumped a notch and she couldn't blame the weather.

Clay grabbed a handful of hay and dumped it on the man's head, causing him to utter a few good-natured expletives. Clay laughed and dodged before his smiling victim could retaliate.

"That is the finest-looking man I've ever seen," Tallie said with an appreciative sigh. Harlie laughed and Tallie covered her red cheeks with her hands. "Did I say that out loud?"

"You did. Which one are you talking about?"

Tallie looked up, her eyes drifting back to him. "The dark-haired one. Not that I don't think your husband is handsome," she quickly added. "But I'm not ill-mannered enough to drool over him when I'm standing next to you."

"It's okay if you did," Harlie said with the smile of a confident woman. "I'm getting used to it. And I agree with you that both of them are enjoyable to look at. I've often wondered if Montana produced any ugly boys." She laughed. "It looks like they're done with the truck. I'll introduce you."

Tallie watched the darker man, unable to take her eyes off him. Not only was he something to see but, for some reason, was also familiar. She ran down the list of possibilities and nothing clicked. Before she could ask Harlie his name, Clay Masterson walked toward them. As he drew nearer, Tallie tried to ease her cavorting nerves. She wasn't starstruck in the scream-and-pass-out sense, but this was Clay Masterson, after all. She tried to control her willful gaze and failed. If pressed, she'd say it wasn't entirely her fault. The guy held multiple sexiest-man titles for a good reason. What woman in her right mind wouldn't take advantage of male eye candy when presented at close range?

And also en route was the man who could give the crowned king of male perfection a challenge for the title. Even unshaved and scruffy from physical labor, she found him disturbingly attractive. His untamed good looks and the deep resonance of his voice—low, unhurried, and mind-boggling sexy—turned Tallie's brain to mush. With a mental shake, she reminded herself she was on the clock and her job description didn't include libidinous ogling of gorgeous men. She swallowed hard and forced her attention to her boss's number-one priority.

෨෩

Tom could've done without the hay in his shirt and was contemplating suitable revenge when he noticed a pretty woman watching them. Or more accurately, she was watching him. A friend of Harlie's, he assumed. He didn't remember meeting her before, and he was sure he'd remember this one and her pale-blonde hair. It was also hard to miss those lovely legs stretching out from under her white skirt.

"You know, Clay, if it weren't for those two attractive women standing over there, I'd stuff a handful of hay in an uncomfortable place just for the thrill of watching you squirm. But since we have company, I'll let you off the hook this time." Tom shrugged his shoulders, trying to dislodge scratchy pieces.

"What women?" Clay looked around and smiled when he saw Harlie. The work finished, he jumped to the ground and made a beeline for his wife.

Tom grabbed his black Resistol cowboy hat from the bale he'd tossed it on, knocking it against his leg to remove the clinging hay before sliding it on his head. He followed Clay off the stack, instantly regretting the impulsive move when his stiff knee began to throb. Intent on getting a closer look at the eye-catching blonde, he hadn't taken time to judge the drop to the ground. Now he'd pay for it the rest of the day. Nothing new in that. The knee had plagued him for years and always would. He rotated his shoulders, trying to remove hay from under his collar while watching the blonde. Clay hung all over Harlie, as usual, and the other woman needed someone to talk to. Forgetting his knee discomfort, he sauntered her way to volunteer for the job. As he stepped up to the group, he rubbed his neck, causing a hay flurry to fall, and remembered, too late, he hadn't shaved that morning. Had he even combed his hair? Luckily, he'd thought to grab his hat. With a quick motion, he ran his fingers through his hair and replaced the hat.

"Looks like you have a problem, Tom," Harlie said as she brushed stray pieces from his sleeve.

"That blond moron you're married to better watch his back," he said with a smile.

"Moron?" Clay said with mock indignation. "That's the best you can do? I'm disappointed in you. Last week you called me a—"

"I could think of something better, but I don't want to embarrass Harlie's friend." Tom interrupted before last week's creative insult to Clay's character was repeated. It wasn't intended for mixed company then and it sure wasn't appropriate now. He looked at Harlie's friend, waiting for an introduction.

"Who's your friend, darlin'?" Clay asked, still holding Harlie tight in his arms.

"She's here to see you. Tallie Peters—my husband, Clay."

"Here to see me? What can I do for you?" He looked at her with knitted brows.

"I'm from Harv Stockton's office. He sent papers for you to sign," she said with unbending professionalism Tom found amusing. If she thought to impress Clay with it, her sexy little train was on the wrong track. Clay was as down to earth as a guy could get. Tom, on the other hand, found her rigid manner fascinating and wondered what it would take to loosen her up.

"Ah. The new assistant," Clay said. "Harv's been raving about you."

Tom cleared his throat and tipped his head toward Tallie.

Clay snorted. "I suppose you want an introduction or something?"

"Well, I'm standing here." Tom glared at Clay.

"Sorry, Tom," Harlie said. "Tallie Peters, this is our friend, Tom Black."

Tallie's eyes went wide and an unprofessional squeal escaped her. "Tom Black? The Tom Black? Oh my gosh! I thought you looked familiar, but I couldn't figure out why. Tom Black. Wow," she said with enthusiasm.

Tom looked at her warily. "Have we met?" If they had, he was certain he'd remember her soft blue eyes and spectacular legs. But he didn't. Clay said the memory was the first to go. Maybe he was right.

"Oh no. We've never met, but I remember you."

She grinned at Tom, dropping the severe facade. Apparently, meeting him was the thing to unwind her, though he didn't understand why. He stared at her in bewilderment but wasn't puzzled enough to miss her sweet dimples when she grinned. "Why?" he asked. Maybe she'd seen him in the bar, but she wasn't the type to hang out at Lefty's. He couldn't imagine her at the stock auction either. This woman had string-quartet and evening-gown class, even if she did squeal when excited. But he could overlook that if she'd smile again.

"If you are who I think you are, you're only my favorite bull rider of all time. I loved watching you ride."

"Oh." Tom grimaced. "That was a long time ago."

"I know, but you were wonderful," she said. "The way you made it look so easy, like you were superglued to the bull's back."

"Yeah, well, I don't do that anymore." He frowned and

looked at Clay. "I have some calls to make, so I'll see you later. Nice meeting you, Tallie." He turned and limped to his pickup, his uneven gait more pronounced after the morning on the haystack.

"Hey, Tom," Harlie called after him. "Lunch is ready. Are you coming up to the house?"

"No, thanks. I have some stuff at home, and I need to change my shirt." He waved and climbed into his pickup truck, unsettled by the reminder of who he wasn't anymore. That guy died years ago, and the new Tom Black didn't care to hear about how great he'd been back in his glory days.

◦◈◦

Tallie watched Tom Black drive away. "Was it something I said?"

Clay frowned in the direction of his departing friend and shook his head. "Don't worry about it," he said with a quick smile. "You must be hungry. Have lunch with us." With his arm draped across Harlie's shoulders, they walked toward the house.

Tallie followed along, wishing again for stout hiking boots. With Harlie in sneakers and Clay in cowboy boots, they walked at a quick clip, leaving Tallie to hobble along in her absurdly inappropriate heels. "Lunch? Oh, I couldn't do that. I need to get back to the office."

"Harv lets you eat, doesn't he?" Clay asked with an amused smile.

"Well, yes. Of course. I usually have a sandwich at my desk."

"Stay and have lunch with us. Sally always fixes more than we can eat anyway."

"I'd better not. I'll get back late." The invitation was generous, but she was sure Mr. Stockton would be upset if she returned late. This little foray had already run longer than expected.

"Harlie, darlin', grab that cell phone out of my pocket there by your hand. Easy though. I had a run-in with a rosebush this morning." She stuck her hand in his pocket. He jumped and laughed. "She can't keep her hands off me."

Harlie handed him the cell phone, rolling her eyes. "Knock it off. You'll embarrass her."

Tallie smiled. "I'm not embarrassed." She may be envious of such an obviously happy couple but not uncomfortable. She did wonder what it would be like to have a man dote on her the way Clay doted on his wife. She'd never experienced it and probably never would. All she had to do was talk to a man and he ran from her as if she'd sprouted a second nose. Clay told her not to worry about it, but she knew she'd said something to anger Tom Black. She saw the cloud cross his face before he excused himself.

Clay selected a number on his cell phone. "Hey, you slave driver. What's this I hear about you forcing your employees to eat lunch at their desks... Your new assistant, Tallie. She says you chain her to her desk and make her eat lunch there. There're probably labor laws against that, you know."

Brought back from her mental side trip to Tom Black, Tallie was horrified to hear Clay's half of the conversation. "Mr. Masterson!" Tallie said, shocked. "You'll get me in trouble!"

Clay winked and continued. "We'll send her back after lunch. We like her, so we're keeping her for a while... Sure, she'll be back today. Don't worry about it. Talk to you later, Harv." He disconnected the call.

"Come on. Let's eat," he said as he opened the kitchen door for the women. "Sally! Tom isn't eating but Tallie is. I need to get cleaned up and I'll be back." Clay left the farmstyle kitchen. Tallie washed in the kitchen sink and sat at the table already set with plates and silver, gnawing her lip.

"Is something wrong?" Harlie asked as she took her seat.

Tallie pursed her lips. "I'm concerned about getting back to work so late. Mr. Stockton might be upset with me, and I can't afford to lose this job. I have a son to support."

"You don't have anything to worry about. Harv won't be upset and you won't lose your job."

"How can you be so sure?"

"Because Harv works for Clay, not the other way around. If Clay says it's all right for you to have lunch with us, Harv will be okay with it. If Clay is happy, Harv is happy. Cool, huh?" Harlie squeezed Tallie's hand, and it reassured her. "You have a son? How old is he?"

"Eleven." Tallie smiled at Harlie's lifted eyebrow. Everyone gave a double take when she mentioned it. "I know I don't appear old enough to have a child that age. I was young and naïve. You know how teenagers can be." Tallie wasn't sure why she told a stranger her deepest secrets, except she'd been locked in basic survival mode for so long, she was starved for female friendship. Women understood things, and it was nice to have someone to talk to.

"You must have been young," Harlie said as Sally poured iced tea. "Thanks, Sally."

"I made a few mistakes back then, but I'm glad to have my son." Tallie sipped her tea, watching Harlie for signs of disapproval, and was pleased the other woman didn't comment. If Harlie had an opinion, she kept it to herself.

"We're expecting our second child." Harlie placed a hand on her stomach. "Abby is only a year old, but I have the opposite problem. I'm thirty-two and my biological clock is heading into meltdown. Clay wants to fill the house with kids. And speaking of Abby, there's my little angel girl."

Clay walked in carrying Abby, buzzing her around like an airplane. She giggled, pouting when the ride stopped. Tallie watched as he placed his daughter in her high chair and kissed her hair before taking his place at the table.

"So Tallie," Harlie said as she trickled dressing on the salad Sally brought to her, "you saw Tom ride bulls? I just met him a few years ago, so I missed all that."

Tallie nodded. "I was a huge rodeo fan, and I loved to watch him ride. The meaner the bull, the better he rode. I watched every competition on TV and always went to the arena when they came to town. He was so intense."

Clay laughed. "That's a good word for him. He was intense, type A to the core, and passionate about the sport. He wanted to be a champion bull rider from the time we were little kids and wasn't letting anything stop him."

Tallie nodded. "I saw the last competition on TV, when he was going for the world championship. After that bull was done with him, they talked about his injuries, but he disappeared from the news quickly."

"He finally found something that could stop him," Clay said. "That bull busted him up bad."

"You were there, weren't you?" Tallie said. "You running through the stands to the arena was almost as big of news as Tom Black getting hurt. I wondered about it at the time."

"Tom is my foster brother." Clay said, his voice low. "I had to make sure he was okay and when he wasn't, it about killed me." Harlie moved her hand to clasp his. "It was touch and go there for a while." Clay leaned back in his chair, Harlie's hand still nestled in his. "It was like that bull wanted to kill him..." He stared off into space a moment, obviously remembering. "Anyway, he had a head injury he recovered from all right, some broken ribs, his nose...the worst was his knee. It's what finished him. Even with all the surgeries, they couldn't get the smashed knee anywhere close to normal." Clay frowned. "Later on, they tried talking him into doing TV commentary, but he refused to enter the arena if he couldn't compete." Clay's frown turned into a grin. "Tom doesn't like to talk much either. So, I bought this place and talked him into moving to Nashville and running it for me. He's the college boy with all the business degrees." Clay sipped his iced tea. "Business wise, it paid off. He's done a great job with this place, and I couldn't have a better partner. If you still like bull riding, you'll have to come out sometime when he has riders testing the bulls in the practice arena. He can't get on them anymore, but he enjoys raising the bulls."

Clay finished his iced tea and glanced across the room at a disheveled young man, in low-slung jeans and shirtless, walking slowly toward the sink, oblivious to the group assembled at the table. "Morning, sunshine," Clay said to the new arrival, though it was clearly afternoon.

"What's for breakfast?" the kid asked with one eye closed against the light streaming through the window. As if that short question had fatigued him further, he stretched, yawned wide, and ran his fingers through his sleep-gnarled, nearly black hair.

Clay shook his head with amusement. "You missed it, pal. We're having lunch if you want something. Salad and chicken sandwiches." The kid, who Tallie estimated at roughly twenty years old, wrinkled his nose and shook his head.

"Nah. Not hungry yet. I ate some nachos and stuff around three."

"Very nutritious. I won't tell your parents how far your eating habits have deteriorated since you've been here," Clay said, though it was clear he was teasing. "Long night, huh?"

"Sat in on three sets in two clubs. It was good." The kid blinked hard, trying to focus. His eyes landed on Tallie and he raised an eyebrow.

Clay laughed. "Not on your life, but I'll introduce you anyway. Tallie Peters, this is the newest member of my band, Jax Talbot. He's a houseguest too. He wandered in here last winter and hasn't left yet. I'm not positive, but I think we may have adopted him or something."

Jax lifted his unshaved chin toward Tallie in acknowledgement. "Hey," he said.

Tallie smiled. "Hey. Nice to meet you, Jax. What instrument do you play?"

Since it appeared Jax had difficulty concentrating on the conversation and keeping his eyes focused at the same time, Clay stepped in. "This kid is an exceptional guitarist." He turned to Jax, who leaned solidly against the kitchen counter, bracing his hands in either side of the sink as if he'd fall down without its support. "Will you be around Saturday night?"

Jax shrugged and rubbed his bicep where an intricate three-cornered Celtic knot tattoo resided.

"We're having a barbecue, if you are."

"We are?" Harlie said, clearly surprised.

"We're home for the summer. Why not? Johnny called and said the guys want to come out and jam. They can bring the wives and kids Saturday and make it a party. Maybe Jax will get some sleep between now and then so he can sit in with us. I have a couple of new songs to try out."

Jax nodded. "Sounds like a plan." With another joint-popping stretch, he ambled from the room, mumbling, "Nice to meet you, Tallie."

Clay watched him depart with an amused smile. "I suspect there may have been some tequila with those nachos last night, but I'm sure he'll survive it." He turned to Tallie. "Can you come out for the barbeque?"

Shocked by the invitation, she wasn't sure what to say. Tallie Peters invited to a barbeque at Clay Masterson's house. "Can I bring my son?"

"Sure. Bring your swimming suits. What do you think, Harlie? Four o'clock?"

She shrugged. "You're planning it."

Over lunch, they discussed picnic plans and after pie was served, Tallie stood to leave.

"I'll get those papers for you to sign and be right back." Tallie strode through the house and returned with the briefcase she'd set by the front door. If Clay was going to act like a hotshot superstar, now would be the time. Tallie steeled her nerves and prepared for the worst.

Clay glanced at the papers she handed him and signed at the bottom.

"You don't need to read them?" Tallie asked, surprised.

"No. We went over them on the phone. Harv's been my manager for over twenty years and I trust him implicitly." Clay handed the papers back and she tucked them neatly away.

"I'd better be going. Thanks so much for lunch."

"It was fun," Harlie said with a warm smile. "You'll come out on Saturday?"

"I will. See you then."

In the car, Tallie thought about the Mastersons and what a loving couple they were. Warm glances passed between them frequently, and they took every opportunity to touch each other. Tallie wondered what it would be like to have an emotional bond like that. Her only relationship started bad and ended worse, and she hoped to never see Roy Peters again.

She left the Mastersons' driveway and headed back to town. On the radio: a string of advertisements. She scanned for an alternative and found it on a classic-rock station: George Thorogood and the Destroyers' "Bad to the Bone."

It was the most fitting description of Roy Peters she'd ever heard.

3

Tom wished Clay had left for the summer after all. The guy couldn't stay home without planning barbeques and forcing him to attend. Clay was the fun, outgoing, good-natured one. Tom wasn't exactly a social butterfly. Rodeo-contestant camaraderie back in the day, sure, but party small talk wasn't his thing. People said opposites attract, and he supposed his friendship with Clay proved it. Since they'd been like brothers practically since birth, he'd go to the barbeque, do his part, and escape as fast as possible.

This barbeque probably wouldn't be too bad—less painful than a bull's hoof to the head anyway. He liked Harv and Marcy Stockton, and the guys in the band were always a kick. So what was his problem? He suspected it had something to do with that pretty blonde reminding him of things he didn't want to think about anymore.

A good-sized crowd had gathered by the time he parked his Ford four-by-four pickup in Clay's driveway. As he entered the yard, he glanced around, noting the crew had done a satisfactory job stringing the yard lights. They'd also opened the doors leading to the indoor pool. Buffet tables were set up on the porch and guests milled around, filling plates. He took a place in line, filled his plate with ham and potato salad, and found an empty seat at a picnic table. Too late, he realized it was the wives' and significant others' table. The gals always seemed to congregate at the parties and for a guy like him, it would be small-talk hell and he was trapped. The drummer's wife started it by telling stories about her kids—every one of them more precocious than the last. Johnny's wife added her amusing anecdotes about their son's preschool class and tried to draw Tom into a conversation where he was as out of place as a tumbleweed at the opera. When they started comparing potty-training nightmares and looking at him like he should have something to add, Tom excused himself and crossed the yard to dispose of his dishes. Halfway, he noticed the cute blonde at a picnic table, talking to Marcy Stockton. Tallie Peters' light-blue eyes sparkled when she laughed and her dimples appeared with her smile. But he hadn't been friendly to her the other day and was sure she wouldn't want to talk to him again. It was probably better that way. She was the kind of woman a guy eventually made a commitment to, and since Tom wasn't into commitment anymore, there was no point in thinking about her.

"Go talk to her," Clay said from behind him, nudging Tom with his elbow.

"Why?" Tom turned toward Clay.

"I have to tell you why you need to talk to a pretty woman? You're in worse shape than I thought." Clay looked at him like he was an idiot. "I saw you looking at her. Couldn't help but notice those dimples. Wow."

"She's nice to look at," Tom said, trying to keep his gaze from turning Tallie's direction.

"I think she's interested in you, pal. You were the chosen topic of conversation at lunch the other day." Clay teased and Tom frowned. "And you can bet I wasn't the one who brought up the subject."

"Don't push at me, Clay. She's interested in who I was

years ago, not who I am now. What is it with you happily married people that you can't leave the rest of us alone?"

"The key there is happy. You could stand some of that in your life. You're getting kind of sour in your old age."

"I'm only thirty-eight, same as you." He knew Clay was trying to help, as he always did, but Tom didn't need it. He figured it had something to do with the discussion of finding his former fiancé again. Clay was right. That was a nest of rattlers that didn't need poking. But he didn't need women shoved at him either. When he was interested, he did fine on his own.

"Jax was checking her out," Clay said.

"Who?"

"Tallie Peters. He met her at lunch and was checking her out, big-time," Clay said with raised eyebrows.

"Jax?" Tom scowled. "That pup is only twenty. What is he doing checking out Tallie?"

"He's almost twenty-one, and that's old enough to look."

Tom was surprised by the sudden nudge of jealousy. Jax had no business gawking at Tallie Peters. She was too old for him. It was more appropriate for Tom to check out Tallie and he certainly had been. Jax looking at Tallie wasn't right. He was a scrawny kid who should date girls his own age. Not older women like Tallie.

Clay chuckled. "Tallie didn't pay him a bit of notice, so cool your temper."

"Cool my—" Tom said with annoyance, ticked off Clay read him so easily. "What are you getting at? I just thought Jax was too young for her, that's all."

"If you say so."

Uncomfortable with the conversation, Tom shifted course.

"Where's Harlie? I haven't seen her yet."

"Upstairs getting Abby dressed. She hired a gal to help her. She's supposed to start on Monday." Clay glanced at the house as Harlie walked their way carrying the baby. "Her name is Gail Fremont and she'll stay in the room by Abby's."

"I should run a security check on her." Tom worried about a stranger living in the house. He was in charge of Clay's security on the ranch and took the responsibility seriously.

"That shouldn't be necessary. She has good references from the nanny service and Abby seems comfortable with her. She's kind of mousy." Clay laughed. "I think Harlie did that intentionally."

"Did what intentionally?" Harlie asked as she joined the men.

"Hired a mousy nanny," Tom said with a smile, making Clay squirm. He enjoyed getting Clay back on occasion.

"Did you tell him that?"

"I didn't—" Clay glared at Tom. "Okay. I said she was a little mousy—"

"She has excellent qualifications and is quite sweet. I didn't even consider..." Harlie frowned. "Oh, dear. I hadn't thought of it...but...no, I wouldn't have...okay. I may have subconsciously picked her for her lack of, uh...she is a timid girl." She looked uncomfortable at the thought.

"Why?" Tom elbowed Clay. "You've got this guy panting after you like a sheepdog. I don't think you'd need to worry about him straying with the nanny." He laughed and noticed Harlie's gaze had traveled across the yard to Jax coming from the house with his electric guitar in hand. The newest member of the band already had a swarm of female fans attracted to his aloof onstage persona and rough-around-the-edges good looks. Clay's website was flooded with comments from Jax's legion of admirers, either offering to trim his shaggy hair or wanting to tangle their fingers in it. "What? He's after the nanny too?" Tom said with alarm. The kid was a testosterone-filled menace.

Harlie laughed. "No, he isn't, but he does live with us, and the nanny will live with us too." She raised a brow.

Tom nodded, understanding. "And two young people living under the same roof for an extended period of time—"

"Things will go bump in the night," Clay added with a laugh. Harlie slapped his arm and glowered. Clay winked and stepped out of hitting range. "Have you eaten yet, darlin'?"

"No. I was hoping Tom would keep track of Abby so I could. She already ate and has been changed. Do you mind, Tom?" Harlie said with a hopeful smile.

Tom was glad to know the diaper situation was under control and wouldn't involve him. "No problem. Come here, sugar." Tom held up his hands and Abby squealed with delight. He smiled and took her from Harlie.

"Thanks," she said. "I'll relieve you soon."

Tom wandered around with Abby until he found an empty cedar lawn chair and sat with the squirming baby. Abby grabbed his nose, squealing. Tom laughed and tickled her, making her squeal louder. His loud raspberry on her neck had them both giggling.

"Excuse me. Do you mind if I sit here?"

Tom looked up, saw the pretty blonde standing by his chair, and choked. His cheeks flamed red and heat crawled up his neck. Tallie smiled and pointed to the empty chair next to his.

"Uh no, help yourself."

"You're good with her. Most men wouldn't watch a baby alone." Tallie dropped into the chair and crossed her legs.

Tom forced himself to look away. Wow was a fitting response. He turned his attention to the baby, a much safer place for his thoughts. "Abby and I spend a lot of time together, don't we, sugar?" Abby responded by grabbing his nose. "She's a sweet little thing," he said. Abby held her hands out to Tallie. "Want to hold her?"

She smiled. "I'd love to. It's been a long time since my son was a baby. Come here, sweetie." Tallie held out her hands and Tom passed the baby to her, their hands brushing during the exchange.

"Is your son here with you tonight?" Tom asked as he watched Tallie play patty-cake with Abby, grinning and laughing. Those dimples just drove him crazy.

"Yes. He's by the pool. The skinny blond in the blue swimsuit."

Tom picked the boy out of the crowd of wet kids and was surprised he wasn't younger. "He looks like you. How old is he?"

"Eleven."

Tom raised an eyebrow. Eleven. Well, that confirmed she was too old for Jax. He was tempted to ask about the kid's father, but Harlie arrived.

"There's my angel girl. Has she been good?" Harlie held her arms out to take Abby.

"Ma ma ma," Abby chanted.

"She's okay if you want to leave her," Tom said.

"No, you've been held captive long enough, Tom. Clay says the guys will play some music soon and Abby will probably fall asleep anyway. Thanks for watching her." Harlie waved to someone across the yard and left Tom alone with Tallie.

Without the baby distraction, they fell into an uncomfortable silence.

"I think I owe you an apology," they said in unison and laughed together.

"Why?" They spoke at the same time and laughed again.

"Wait a second." Tom held up his hand. "What do you have to apologize for?"

Tallie looked at him from beneath long lashes. "Well, I must have said something to upset you the other day, and I'm sorry if I did."

Tom winced. "I'm the one who owes you an apology. I was rude. It wasn't your fault."

"Okay. We have that settled." Tallie smiled and relaxed.

Mercifully, Clay chose that moment to play a loud guitar riff that ended their stilted conversation. It started as a jam session with musicians jumping in at random. There was a lot of joking and hollering over the music. Jax was hot on his sleek black Ibanez, keeping up with Clay and his Stratocaster. Both were phenomenal guitarists.

Tom listened to the music and glanced at the woman next to him. He wasn't sure what to do about Tallie Peters. She wasn't the kind of woman he'd been involved with in recent years. She wasn't someone he could get caught up in for a while and brush off when it got complicated. There was an innocence about her that scared him. Too bad he couldn't stop looking at her.

The impromptu band was set up near the edge of the crowd, leaving an area in the lawn where guests danced. After a few warm-up songs, they burst into a fast tune that left the dancers breathless. Clay waved at Tom and Tallie to get up and dance, but Tom shook his head.

"It's not that I don't want to dance with you, Tallie," he explained when he saw her disappointment. "I can't do the fast stuff with my bad knee." He hoped the explanation would keep him in his seat. But his hopes were dashed when Clay asked the guys to play a slow song so he could dance with his wife. Clay snuggled sleepy Abby against his shoulder and held Harlie with the other arm. They danced near Tom.

"Come on, Tom," Clay called. "It's a slow one. No excuses."

Someday, he was going to have to kill that man, Tom thought when Tallie gave him an encouraging smile. He'd all but told her he'd dance with her and now he was stuck. Tom stood, held out his hand, and led her into the crowd.

"I'm not good at this," he apologized, knowing he couldn't move smoothly with his flawed knee. Dancing was something he avoided since he tended to lurch. He placed a hand on her lower back, held her hand in his, and moved as evenly as possible.

"I haven't danced in a long time, so I think we're even." Tallie smiled and moved in step with the music until the song ended.

As if to torment Tom, the next song played was even slower. Again, there was no valid excuse to sit. She raised her eyebrows, questioning. He shrugged—why not? She moved closer. He shifted his hand on the small of her back and inadvertently moved her tank top. Soft skin teased his fingertips and had him wondering what the rest of her was like. Warm and silky smooth, he imagined. She swallowed and stared into his eyes. A feeling ran through his body, and not the usual lust for a good-looking woman he could satisfy in a night. No, this was a tingling of excitement, a wondering about possibilities he hadn't felt in years.

Tom tried to push down his unease. For years, he'd thought he wanted to find a special woman to take Jolie's place in his heart. Tallie was that sort of woman, but Tom felt compelled to step away. He didn't need permanent entanglements anymore. He did fine with an occasional, casual hookup—like Sherry. Didn't he? Yes, that had worked out fine. He and Sherry had their fun and when it got complicated, he broke it off clean. She might have hurt feelings for a while, but knowing Sherry, she'd get over it soon enough and move on. She'd been in and out of love half a dozen times since he'd known her. But a woman like Tallie was different. Women like her had expectations guys like Tom Black couldn't live up to. The song ended and Tom managed to make it back to his chair without committing to another dance. The music remained loud. Conversation with Tallie grew difficult and was limited to shouted comments and eye contact. The eye contact did him in.

A few songs later, Jax set his guitar aside and walked straight to Tallie. He bent down, said something in her ear, and held out his hand. After a nearly imperceptible glance toward Tom, Tallie smiled at Jax and let him lead her to the dance area.

The moon began its ascent through the graying sky. A cool breeze tickled Tom's cheek and tossed the party lights from side to side, not cold but noticeably more comfortable than earlier in the evening. He relaxed, stretching his long legs to ease his disagreeable knee. The crowd had grown in number as the sun went down. Friends of friends arrived with snack foods and beer in hand. Additional musicians, hearing of a jam session, joined the party and gave the original players a break and a chance to dance with their spouses. Tom estimated at least seventy people filled the yard and pool. With Abby in bed, Harlie worked her way through the crowd and settled into an animated conversation with Marcy Stockton. Clay had reclaimed his guitar and led the group of musicians through a soulful blues ballad that enticed more dancers from their chairs. Jax and Tallie danced in perfect step.

Tom tried to ignore the dancing pair but found them in the crowd and tracked their movements. The music was unhurried and Jax held her close, talking in her ear and laughing when Tallie responded. He wasn't sure what they had in common. Tallie was a single mom who was a good eight to ten years older than that scrawny kid. Tom looked away, watching the children in the pool splashing and yelling to one another. They were a motley bunch: a couple of chubby ones, a short girl with freckles, the drummer's auburn-haired twins, and Tallie's towheaded, skinny son. The boy was lean, roughly five feet tall, but he'd fill out soon enough. Tom glanced from Tallie's kid to Jax and realized Jax had filled out some since he'd arrived in Nashville eight months earlier. He'd shown up on Clay's doorstep hungry from low-paying bar gigs and needing a job. Clay added him to the band and kept him as a permanent houseguest they thought of as their own kid. Tom had sort of adopted him too. He was a great kid.

And the kid certainly had filled out; his bony shoulders were more muscular, probably thanks to Clay's home gym. Now, he had those more mature arms wrapped around Tallie and Tom didn't like it. Jax wasn't a kid anymore but a fairly large man who rested his hand in the same place Tom had enjoyed pressing his hand earlier. He narrowed his eyes and stared at them, turning away when Jax looked his way and grinned.

If Tallie was interested in Jax, there wasn't much Tom could do about it. It was probably for the best anyway. Tallie dragged emotions to the surface Tom didn't want to acknowledge. His experience with serious relationships was flawed, and he knew he'd end up hurting her. No matter how he looked at it, this was for the best. He relaxed, relieved he'd dodged a bullet. Tallie deserved a whole man, not a gimpy old bull rider like Tom Black, and with Jax, she would have that. The kid had two good legs and, as far as Tom knew, didn't carry the relationship baggage Tom did. And if it came to a fight over her, Jax had already proved his mettle by showing up on a superstar's doorstep asking for help. That took a lot of guts and Tom wasn't sure he could compete with that sort of thing anymore.

He wasn't the man he used to be.

⁂

Jax leaned and spoke in Tallie's ear.

"I'm what? Are you flirting with me?" she asked with a laugh. "If you are, I should let you know I'm old enough to be your...much older sister."

He laughed. "Yeah, right. I can't say the idea hasn't crossed my mind, Tallie." He looked at her with appreciation. "You're a hot woman."

Tallie was amused by his candor. "But?"

"But I'm not ready to die, and I think flirting with you would end my time on this rock too soon."

"What are you talking about?"

"Well," he said, "if looks could kill, you'd be dancing with a corpse."

Tallie looked around. There wasn't anyone paying noticeable attention to them. Tom was the only single man she knew in the crowd, and he was watching the kids in the pool. "Who do you think wants you dead, Jax?"

"You didn't see the looks Tom gave me when we started dancing?" He spun her around. "Don't look. He'll see you."

She did anyway. Tom was looking their way now but the expression he wore didn't indicate he wished Jax dead. He seemed bored to her. "I don't see—"

Jax turned her again so he faced Tom. "Well, he's doing it now. He's clenching his jaw," he said with a laugh, certainly more pleased than worried. "And his right fist."

"You're paranoid. Tom isn't interested in me." Tallie had hopes but didn't seem to gain ground.

"Oh, come on. You don't see it? That guy is seriously interested in you. Oh...there he goes again, staring at me and clenching his fist. He's pissed off."

"Jax—"

"I'll bet if I kissed you, he'd fly right out of his chair and beat the crap out of me." Jax looked at her mouth and bent forward.

"Jax! No!" she said with alarm.

"I won't," he said with a sly smile, straightening up. "I asked you to dance so I could apologize."

What was it about her? Everyone wanted to apologize for something tonight. "Why?"

"When we met the other day, I was a little out of it." He looked abashed and Tallie held back a smile.

"Clay mentioned tequila."

"He thought that?" he said with concern. "No, nothing like that. I don't drink the hard stuff. I was tired."

"From club hopping?" she asked, remembering the conversation about his three sets in two clubs.

"Yeah, that and, well." He blushed. "I met someone and she..."

Tallie raised a maternal eyebrow at him.

"Not that! Jeez, I just met her," he said. "How do you women do that eyebrow thing anyway? My mom does it and she freezes me every time."

Tallie laughed. "What about the girl?"

"Girl? No, no. A woman. She's at least twenty-two. And hot. Like you." He grinned when Tallie blushed. "We started talking and didn't stop until the sun came up. That's why I was tired."

"Why are you telling me all this, Jax? You just met me."

He shrugged. "You're easy to talk to. And well," he said with a comic leer, "if things don't work out for me with Sasha, and Tom keeps acting like you aren't the hottest woman he's ever seen, I might give you a call."

Tallie was amused by his assumption. He was an adorable kid with those chocolate-brown eyes and long lashes, but too young for her. "So, you and Tom are...what? Not friendly?"

"Tom? We're cool. He has a big TV and stuff. And when Clay and Harlie, you know," he said and raised his eyebrow suggestively, "want to be alone, it's a place to go if I don't have plans." Jax glanced over his shoulder. "But if I keep dancing with you, I doubt he'll let me hang out anymore. He may not let me breathe much longer."

The song ended and Jax walked Tallie to her chair. Tom still sat with his long legs stretched and his arms folded across his chest, giving no indication her dance with Jax bothered him. With a wink to Tallie, Jax disappeared into the crowd and surfaced a moment later among the impromptu band with his guitar in hand. Before Tallie could say anything to Tom, Jax played an earsplitting lick and the band was off and running again.

It wasn't long before Cody found his mother. Tallie took his hand and pulled him into the chair with her. Tired from his evening swim, he laid his head against her shoulder and closed his eyes. She loved these moments, the feel of her son's warmth against her arm and his rhythmic breathing while she brushed her fingers through his blond hair. He was growing up fast and wasn't her little boy anymore. Eight more inches and he would look his mom in the eye.

"I'm tired," Cody said with a yawn.

Tallie patted his leg. "We'll go soon." She turned to the man seated next to her, wanting to resume some sort of conversation. "So—"

"I wanna go home now, Mom," Cody said. "All the kids left already." He looked at Tallie, his eyelids drooping. She smiled and rubbed her hand across his head. He did look exhausted and a bit bedraggled wrapped in a beach towel, and his chlorinated hair was sticking up in odd clumps. Tallie hated to leave the party but had to consider her son. Cody always came first in her life and tonight, in Tom's arms, was the first time in years she hadn't thought of Cody first. The circles under her son's eyes brought him to the forefront and she had to take him home. Reaching into her pocket, she found her business card with her home number on the back and handed it to Tom.

"Maybe we can get together for coffee sometime," she suggested.

Tom smiled. "I might be able to do that."

Might. Disappointed by his noncommittal response, Tallie stood, pulling Cody to his feet. "Let me know," she said.

Tom stood. "Yeah. Okay. I'll give you a call...sometime...when I'm in town." He glanced around, apparently looking for an escape route. "Thanks for the dance, Tallie. It was nice seeing you again."

She nodded. "You're welcome. Good-night, Tom." Cody grabbed her hand and pulled.

"Come on, Mom."

"Okay, okay."

"Tallie!" Harlie called to her as she moved across the yard. "Are you leaving?"

"Yes. Cody needs to go to bed. Thanks so much for inviting us. We had a great time."

"I'm glad you came. Drive home safely." Harlie smiled and waved as Tallie was pulled by her eager child. Tallie glanced around, but Tom had disappeared.

It was just as well. She'd practically thrown herself at the man all evening and thought they'd connected. So why didn't he ask her out? She left him her number so the ball was in his court now.

If he was interested.

4

If he could figure out a way to skip Mondays altogether, he would. Everything that could go wrong did. Tom spent most of the morning up to his knees in mud from a busted main line, had to call the vet about a sick calf, and the bank misplaced his last deposit. When he thought it couldn't get any worse, Sally called to tell him he had a visitor at the gate.

"Who is it?"

"All I know is he's a lawyer. He says it's personal, and he needs to talk directly to you," she said. "Should I let him in?"

As much as he'd like to keep attorneys on the other side of the fence, he supposed he'd better see the guy. "Send him in. I'm at my house." One look at his muddy jeans and he headed inside, shed the grubby clothes, found fresh Wranglers and a shirt, and was pulling on his boots when the car drove up. He watched the man climb from a rented sedan and wondered what a slick-looking out-of-town lawyer wanted with him. Tom pushed open the screen door and stepped out on the porch, waiting for his guest, a tall, lean man in his midthirties with brown hair and wearing an expensive suit.

"Tom Black?" the man called from the driveway, shielding his eyes from the glare of the midday sun. "Thomas Michael Black?"

"Right. What can I do for you?" Tom eyed him with suspicion and noticed the lawyer doing the same.

"I'm Jason Gardner." The man held out his hand as he joined Tom on the porch. Tom shook it.

"What can I do for you?" Tom asked again.

"I'm an attorney, here on the behalf of my client."

Jeez, he was getting sued, he was sure of it. "And who might that be?"

"Jolie Morgan."

It felt like the world's largest Brahma had kicked the wind from Tom's lungs. He gulped. "Where is she?"

"She asked me to bring this to you." The lawyer handed him a DVD.

"Where is she?" he asked again

"Watch that and I'll answer any questions I can," Jason said, obviously unprepared when Tom lunged at him and grabbed his shirtfront.

"Where is she?" he said, his nose inches from Jason's face. "I've searched for years for her. I want to know where she is."

"Back off or I won't tell you a damned thing," Jason shot back. "I'm required to follow her instructions."

Tom released the man's shirt and paced near the door, taking a deep breath to calm his surging emotions.

"She made this video for you and said it would explain everything. I'm not allowed to answer your questions until after you see it." He handed Tom a card. "I'll be in town for a few days. Call me when you're ready to talk." He backed away, straightening his shirt while he walked to his car. "Call me," he called out as he climbed in.

Tom watched as Jason drove out, turning the disc in his hands. "What the heck?" He wandered into the living room and popped in the DVD. As he waited for it to begin, his stomach churned.

The first image was blurry. When the picture focused, what he saw made his heart stop. Jolie. He dropped hard onto the leather couch. She sat in a bed, thin and pale, wearing an oversized blue T-shirt and a scarf tied on her head. Despite her changed appearance, she was still the woman he'd loved with his heart and body all those years ago. He could still remember the feel of her tender skin beneath his hands, the gentle sweep of neck to shoulder, and how she would lean her head back when he kissed her in just the right spot. He'd never forget the feel of her mouth on his, the sweetness of her breath, the rise and fall of her laugh.

When she spoke, her voice was weak and breathless, startling him from his reunion with the past.

"Hi, Tom." She inhaled, her breath jagged. "This is so hard. I know you probably hate me and I'm sorry for that. I have some things I need to tell you, so please don't turn this off until I'm done. It's been twelve years, and I've thought of you every day." Tears pooled in her eyes. She paused and wiped at them with her hand. "Leaving you was the hardest thing I've ever had to do, but I couldn't stay and watch you destroy yourself. And us." She stopped to take another deep breath. "You're wondering why I've decided to contact you now." She paused. "I found out six months ago I have cancer and it was found too late. I've had every treatment there is, but the prognosis is the same. I have limited time and a lot of things to settle before I...go."

It felt like a weight pressed Tom's chest, heavy and suffocating.

"I'll start at the beginning, twelve years ago." She swallowed. "I want you to know, I've never loved anyone the way I loved you and when you almost died, I thought I'd die, too. I was so proud of the way you fought to come back, to walk when they said you wouldn't, to fight for the chance to compete again. Bull riders are tough, and you were tougher than most. I was so impressed with your dedication, your drive to get back into what you loved. And when they said you couldn't, I thought it was a bad break, but we still had each other. We could still have our life together. But it wasn't enough for you. I wasn't enough for you. Competition was what you lived for and when the dream was gone, you gave up. You were there physically, but emotionally, you left me when the drinking started. I begged you to stop. Do you even remember it? I know you were depressed, and I tried to be supportive. I did." Jolie bit her lip and blinked back a tear. "Okay. Back on track. This is all old news." She blew out a breath. "I'm assuming you found the note on the fridge."

Tom grunted in disgust. Oh yeah, he'd found her note all right. It was the most heartless kiss-off he'd ever seen. "By the time you find this, I'll be gone," she'd said. "Don't look for me. I don't want to be found." Well, he'd looked anyway. Searched everywhere, called everyone, and no trace of her could be found. She'd disappeared.

Jolie continued. "After I left our house, I stopped by my parents' house to tell Mama good-bye. She said she couldn't let me go alone, so she packed a bag and left with me. Her life with my dad was horrible and she'd had enough. We moved around for a few months, sure you were looking for me, even though I asked you not to, and decided to stay in

Denver. We found jobs and settled in. Five months after arriving," she said, looking directly at the camera, "I gave birth to our son."

"What the?!" Tom stopped the video and replayed it to make sure he'd heard it right, listened, and replayed it a second time and a third. A son. He had a son. She was pregnant when she left. How could she keep something like that from him?

"Now you know why I had to leave and why I chose to hide. I grew up in a house with an alcoholic father and there was no way I would allow that to happen to my son. You wouldn't stop drinking, no matter how much I begged you. So I decided to raise our baby alone." Jolie looked down, inhaled deeply, and continued with tear-filled eyes. "Next to leaving you, sitting in the hospital alone was the next most difficult thing I've ever done. I wanted you there so badly, wanted you holding me, holding our son. I almost broke down and called you, but I couldn't trust you anymore. I've never been able to hate you though. You're still in my heart as firmly today as you were twelve years ago." Jolie started to cry and there was a break in the video where it had been shut off and restarted. Jolie was sitting in the bed again, but the oversized T-shirt was pale green.

"I hate to say this, but when I found out I was running out of time, I dreaded contacting you. I was sure you'd be an alcoholic with no future, if you hadn't killed yourself already, and I couldn't bear the thought of my son living with you. So, before I made my decision, I hired an attorney to do some research on you." She smiled. "I'm so happy to know you're healthy and doing well. Jason tracked you down in Nashville and tells me you're with Clay raising horses and butt-kicking bulls. I'm sorry I didn't believe in you, but I also wonder if you would have accomplished so much if I'd stayed. He tells me there is no reason to think you're still drinking, which is a relief because...I want you to have your son. He's a wonderful boy. Healthy, happy, loves sports and video games. I've kept him away from rodeo, and I'm ashamed to say I haven't told him much about you. I'll leave it to you to make your own impression on him." Jolie took a deep breath, her ill health obvious in her tired eyes. "I know you'll be a good father if everything Jason tells me is true. Please love him for both of us. Losing his mom will be difficult for him. Please be kind and help him through it. I'm entrusting you with the most valuable person in my world. Love him, please."

The look in her eyes tore Tom apart. She was begging him to love his own child. He would have if he'd known about him. He thought of the feelings he had for little Abby, and she wasn't even his.

The video ended with Jolie holding her hand to the camera as if to touch him. "Good-bye, Tom. I'll always love you." He was tempted to hold his hand out to her but stopped when he realized he'd experienced this before.

And maybe it hadn't been a dream after all.

It was the sort of shock that could send a guy back to the bottle. But Tom hadn't touched a drop in eleven years and wasn't into mindless oblivion anymore. That was the coward's way out. Once an alcoholic, always an alcoholic, they said, and choosing not to drink took strength. He had a child to think about now, and Tom needed to prove he had the strength to be a father to his son. He had to prove he deserved Jolie's trust. Instead of reaching for a bottle, he grabbed his cell phone and called Jason Gardner. The attorney arrived promptly with a manila envelope in his hand. The two men sat at the kitchen table drinking coffee. Jason patiently waited for Tom's questions to begin. The previous night had been hellish for Tom, and Jason seemed to respect his misery.

Tom took a shuddering breath and asked the most difficult question first. "She's already dead, isn't she? That's why you're here." Tom looked at Jason.

Jason nodded. "Yes."

"When?"

"Three weeks ago—"

Tom swallowed hard and asked a question he didn't want answered. "The tenth?"

"Yes, how did you—" Jason asked, startled.

"What time?"

"Why does it matter?"

"It matters. What time?" Tom took a gulp of his coffee to still the tremor running through him.

"One thirty-three a.m."

The coffee caught in Tom's throat and he coughed, unable to catch his breath. He swung from his chair, knocking it across the floor in his rush to move away. He couldn't breathe. "Holy shit," he gasped and moved to the sink, filled a glass with water, and gulped it down.

"Are you all right?"

Tom braced his hands on the counter and swallowed air. It was a coincidence she'd died the night of his weird dream. It was only a dream, damn it, a dream, not some freaking visitation from a dying woman.

But, if she did visit, why would she do it? To torment him with his failure? The DVD had already done a good job of that. He closed his eyes and tried to settle his rattled nerves. No, he had to be wrong. Jolie had never been vindictive. She had a sweet and nurturing spirit.

Spirit? What made him think that? Maybe he was buying into it. He refilled the water glass and drank. No, Jolie wasn't malicious.

"Mr. Black? Tom? Are you all right?" Jason Gardner asked again.

Tom nodded his head. "Yeah. Fine. Just needed a moment..." He retrieved his chair and sat, ignoring Jason's knit brow and puzzled stare. He'd better get it together before this lawyer thought he was a raving loon. At that moment, Tom thought he was losing his mind.

Jason stared across the table, shuffled his papers, and returned to business.

"Why are you here now? Why not earlier?" Tom asked.

"It was Jolie's request I not contact you until after she was...gone."

"I'd have taken care of her if I'd known." Tom's voice was ragged. "Why wouldn't she at least let me say goodbye?"

"She was well cared for. And as for seeing you, she was afraid you hated her for leaving, and she wanted to think of you as you'd been before the accident."

"I never hated her. I love her as much today as I did then." He closed his eyes and took a deep breath. "What about the boy?"

Jason slid the manila envelope across the table. Inside, Tom found a birth certificate for Michael Thomas Black

Morgan. Thomas Michael Black, father. Jolie Ann Morgan, mother. There it was in black and white. He swallowed hard when he pulled out the hospital copy and saw the tiny footprint. He touched it with his shaking finger before laying it down. He'd missed so much.

"Is he with Jolie's mother?"

"No. Mrs. Morgan passed away two years ago. Mike's been staying with me. Right now he's with my sister and her family until I get back."

Tom narrowed his eyes. "So she never married?"

"No. She was asked frequently but always said no." Jason locked his eyes on his coffee cup.

"How would you know that?"

Jason looked him square in the eye. "Because I did the asking. This is as hard for me as it is for you, Tom. You aren't the only one grieving for her. I loved her as much as you must have, but I couldn't have her because she wouldn't let you go. How do you think I feel meeting the man who held her heart? I had to be content with friendship because of you. She wouldn't marry me, but I was the one holding her hand when she died."

"That was her choice." Tom almost smiled. Gardner may have had her hand but Tom had her. Nope, can't go there.

"Yes, it was. And it was also her choice to give Mike to you. I'll be honest with you. I tried to talk her out of it. He doesn't know you and it will be hard on him. I've known him for five years and am the closest thing to a father he's ever had."

"I'm sorry for that, Jason. If I'd known about him, I'd have been a father to him. But Jolie didn't give me that option. Now I know he exists, I want to know him. He's my son." Tom looked at Jason with narrowed eyes. "He is mine, isn't he?"

"As much as I'd like to tell you no and keep him with me, I can't. When you see him, you'll know whose son he is. There isn't any point in arguing about this. As Jolie's attorney, it's my obligation to see her wishes carried out. My personal feelings and opinions don't matter."

"So what do we do next?"

"I can bring him here to you or you can come to Denver. Your choice."

Tom thought about it. "I'd like to see where he's been, and maybe it will be easier for him if I meet him on his turf. How much time does he need?"

"I can have him packed and ready to travel this weekend if it works for you," Jason said.

"That's fine. I'll make the arrangements and give you a call."

After the attorney left, the weight of it hit him. He was the father of an eleven-year-old boy and didn't have a clue how to handle it.

5

Clean sheets, new pillows, a Nintendo Wii with games, and a freezer full of pizza and ice cream were in place and ready for Michael Thomas Black Morgan's arrival. Tom was in a nervous panic for four days trying to anticipate what an eleven-year-old would like, and he hoped he'd hit a few things the kid would appreciate. Jolie hadn't encouraged an interest in rodeo, so thinking back to what he'd wanted at that age didn't help. He doubted Michael would appreciate a saddle or a new pair of chaps. A bull rope would confuse the kid.

He asked Harlie for advice, thinking a woman would have a better handle on it. She suggested the pizza and video games. Clay was useless and couldn't get over the shock Tom was a father. Tom wasn't over that jolt either, but he was dealing with it. Sally said her grandsons liked baseball cards and bubblegum, so he bought a few packs and set them on the dresser in Michael's room. She also suggested Tom should relax or he'd scare the kid half to death. That was easy for her to say since she'd been acquainted with her children since birth.

At the end of it all, he called his parents with the news of a new grandchild who probably wore size ten sneakers. His mother cried. Happy tears, she said. His father, as expected, made comments about Tom's knowledge of birth control and wondered how many other grandkids he didn't know about. Then he laughed and congratulated Tom on his impending fatherhood and offered what advice he could. Set the rules, follow through, and show as much love as you can. That's pretty much it, he'd said. Tom had smiled at the description of his own childhood.

Early Saturday morning, Tom boarded a flight to Denver, picked up a rental car, and drove to the cemetery. He wandered the paved walkways, stopping to read an engraved marker, moving on when it wasn't what he sought. Near a maple tree on a gentle slope, he found it. The stone, gray, cold, and freshly installed, stared at him, yelling its truth: Jolie was gone. With his hands clasped together to control a sudden shake, he stared at the memorials to the woman he'd loved: one of stone and the other handmade. Someone had visited shortly before him, leaving a fresh rose bouquet. Next to the flowers sat a photo of Jolie, framed in pink. A note, written in childish scrawl, said, "I love you, Mom." Jason said Tom wasn't the only one grieving her loss and here was raw proof. Somewhere in Denver was a heartbroken kid who would never hug his mom again. Their kid.

Tom stared at her smiling face, a face he'd seen in vivid detail nearly four weeks ago. A face he'd kissed and touched as if she had been there. The fact he knew the date and time of her death indicated something weird, but he still didn't want to believe it. Ghosts didn't exist. If he admitted they did, next thing he knew he'd be like those gooney-eyed people on TV talking about their brushes with ghosts and poltergeists. Maybe he'd play along for a bit, pretend it was real, and get some of this out of his system. It couldn't hurt.

"So," he said to the smiling picture, "what am I supposed to think, Jolie? Am I supposed to believe you came to see me that night? Am I crazy if I think you did?" He cleared his throat. "Okay, we'll work with the assumption I'm not crazy and shit like this does happen." He looked over his shoulder, making sure he was still alone. "I, uh, hmmm," he glanced around again. "I have some things to say and now seems like the time. If you're still hanging around here, I'd appreciate it if you'd listen to what I have to say. I understand now why you left. I was a mess and I admit it. I fell apart and if it wasn't for Clay and my family, I wouldn't be here talking to you now. I straightened out though. I stopped drinking and haven't touched a drop since. If you'd come back, you'd have seen that." Tom's anger crept to the surface and he tried to smash it down. "All you had to do was come back and see. I spent years building a new life, hoping you would share it with me. Everything I did was for you, to prove to you I wasn't the loser you thought I was. I bought a house for us to live in, but I live there alone. Always have. But you never came back to see."

Tom paced the grass beside the grave. "And when you do come back, it's as some kind of ghost or something. What the hell was that about anyway? One last screw for old time's sake? Is that all I was to you? I loved you with everything I had. But let me tell you something, Jolie Morgan." He stopped pacing and pointed at her picture. "I will not be some kind of afterlife boy toy for you. If you plan on making a habit of this, you can forget it right now. Don't you come around in the middle of the night thinking you can do that again, because it's over. You didn't want me in life, and I'll be damned if I'll let you have me now. No matter how good it felt. It's done." He closed his eyes and tried to calm his rage. Years of frustration poured from him, shocking him with its ferocity. Now that it was unleashed, he couldn't stop it. He had to let it out or choke on it. "Since it was like a dream," he continued, "I don't know in real time how long you were there...or if you were. What I'm wondering is, all that time you spent whispering in my ear that night, why couldn't you give me a hint of all this? Why do I have to find out about my son from a stranger? Do you know how it made me feel? Gardner looked at me like I was some sort of deadbeat dad, and I didn't even know I had a kid." Tom gritted his teeth and paced away from the gravesite, unable to look at her face. He walked the cemetery trails, avoiding people where possible.

When he returned, his anger receded and grief took over. With tears dampening his eyes, Tom touched the cold stone. "Damn it, Jolie, I don't know... I'm just trying to come to terms with this. Knowing I'll never see you again...it hurts. Knowing it's my fault I missed the last twelve years with you...well, the ache is a lot worse when I know I did something stupid to cause it." He dropped to the grass and leaned against the closest maple tree, stretching his long legs and wiping his eyes with a handkerchief. Other than chirping birds and distant traffic, the cemetery was quiet. Tom closed his eyes and relaxed, contemplating what he wanted to say next.

"Since you left, I've been with a few other women. Okay, more than a few. Twelve years is a long time, you know. They were great gals, but mostly, they kept me company and filled my time. None of them ever took your place." Tom watched a plane flying overhead, its contrail striping the sky. "I was afraid to let them get close, afraid of failing again and hurting another woman the way I hurt you." He let out a derisive snort. "I'm not so tough after all, Jolie.

Not anymore. I used to go after stuff like I had a right to it, but I don't have that drive anymore. It's all gone. I go through the motions, that's all." The contrail dissipated, leaving a wide swath of white. He glanced around, making sure he was still alone. "I want you to know, I'll always love you. There will be a place for you in my heart forever, but it's time I moved on. I can't keep going this way, caught halfway between you and living life the way it should be lived. I'm tired of being alone." He plucked a piece of grass and tossed it aside. "I met someone who could be good for me. She's a lot like you. Not in looks or anything, but she's sweet and pretty. Like you were." He pinched another grass blade and twisted it absently between his fingers. "She's classy. A real upper-crust type but she doesn't act like it. Not snooty or anything like you might expect from someone who comes from money. There is just something about her, something special that hit me between the eyes the first time I saw her." He smiled and relaxed into the one-sided conversation. "She's interested in me. I don't know why a washed-up bull rider with a bum leg would interest her, but she gave me her phone number and suggested we get together. When things settle down with Michael, I may give her a call. I'm not sure yet." A warm breeze whispered across his skin. Tom closed his eyes, imagining the soft stroke was Jolie's and she agreed it was time he moved on. He knew it was.

"I also want you to know," he said, "I'll raise our son right. I'm not sure I know how yet, but I'll do my best. I promise." He sat in silence for a while, checked his watch, and stood, ready to leave. "I'm supposed to get Michael in an hour, so I guess this is it. I'm serious about the nocturnal visitations. If that's something you can do, I prefer you didn't. This is good-bye." Tom returned to his rental car, his back straighter, shoulders thrown back, and his stride purposeful, thinking the past hour weird but oddly therapeutic. He'd had his chance to say good-bye to Jolie and the sense of limbo that had plagued him for years lifted.

No, Jolie hadn't tried to torment him.

She set him free.

An hour later, Tom sat in front of a large Victorian-style house, wondering if Jolie had lived there with the lawyer. Just because she refused Gardner's proposals didn't mean the relationship was platonic. It didn't matter anymore; he hoped she'd found some happiness. Bolstering his courage, Tom dragged himself from his rental car and walked up the sidewalk to meet this stranger who was his son.

Jason Gardner greeted him at the door in jeans and a faded Napa Valley T-shirt, his eyes bloodshot and haggard. He led Tom into an office on the lower floor. Closing the door, he motioned for Tom to take a seat in the chair opposite an antique cherry desk.

"There are a few things I need to mention before you take him," Jason said as he shuffled papers into order. "Jolie made a few provisions regarding Mike. He has an out clause, I guess you could say."

"What kind of out clause?"

Jason leaned back in his chair. "If Mike isn't happy, he doesn't have to stay with you."

Tom let out a snort of disbelief. "So this could be a waste of time. I'm taking a boy who I've never met away from the only home he's ever known, and he decides if he wants to stay?"

"He doesn't know anything about it, which is why we're talking in here. Jolie was afraid you wouldn't want him, so it's as much for you as it is for him. If it doesn't work out, you can bring him back. Papers are prepared for custody transfer, just in case."

The guy had nerve to tell him he expected him to fail, and that ticked Tom off. "Jolie and I talked about having children when we decided to get married. Why would she think I wouldn't want him? He's my child, and I'm not going to return him like a pair of ill-fitting boots," Tom said with disgust. "And who would I return him to? As far as I know, I'm his only blood relative other than Jolie's father, and I'm sure she wouldn't want him to raise Michael."

"He would come back to me. If you decide you don't want him, he can live with me."

"It will work out," Tom stated bluntly.

"We'll see," Jason said. "He's upstairs packing the last of his stuff. There wasn't room for everything in the suitcases, so I'll ship the rest." He picked up a manila envelope and handed it to Tom. "Here are his school transcripts and medical records." Jason stood and walked to the door.

"After what I said earlier, I know you won't believe me, but I want this to work out for him. Mike deserves to know his father. But if it doesn't pan out, he has a place to go where he's loved." Jason opened the door. "If you'll wait in the living room, I'll get him." Jason pointed to a doorway and turned to climb the stairs.

Tom sat uneasily in the elegantly furnished room and wondered what Michael would think of his house outside Nashville. It wasn't decorated in fine antiques and fussy gewgaws requiring lots of dusting. His house had practical furniture, and occasionally, a saddle tossed on the porch rail. A workingman's house. Footsteps in the hall indicated Michael's arrival, and Tom heard low voices he wished he couldn't hear.

"I don't want to go, Jason," a quivering young voice said. "Why can't I stay with you?"

"It'll be okay, Mike. He's a nice guy, and you'll like him," Jason said. "He's a cowboy, and he lives on a ranch with horses and cattle. You'll like it there."

"Don't make me go." The boy sniffled. "Mom's gone and now I'm losing you, too."

"You aren't losing me. You know my phone number. Call me if you want to talk. Shh, Mike, it's okay."

Tom could hear the strain in Jason's voice and the crying boy. It tore at his heart, and he cursed Jolie for doing this to them. He should have known he had a son when Michael was born so he could be a part of his life. This was unfair to both of them.

"Are you ready, Mike?" Jason asked. "Be brave. This is what your mom wanted. She wanted you to be with your dad, with Tom. He's nervous too. Come on. He wants to meet you."

Tom watched the doorway, standing slowly when he saw Jason enter with his arm around a terrified boy in baggy shorts and a Denver Broncos T-shirt. His heart almost stopped. It was like looking in the mirror, and he knew without a doubt he'd fathered this boy. He judged him close in height to Tallie's son, but where Cody Peters was fair, Michael was as dark as his father. Wavy jet-black hair, cut short, and familiar green eyes stared back at him. He wasn't sure if the look Michael gave him was fearful or belligerent, but either way, it was unsettling to have his own eyes glaring at him.

"Mike, this is your father, Tom Black." Jason guided him near Tom.

"It's nice to meet you," Tom said, trying to smile, wishing he could think of something to say to wipe the fear from his son's face. At closer inspection, he was sure he saw fear in Michael's eyes.

"Let's have a seat so you two can talk." Jason waved his hand toward the furniture.

Tom took a seat on the sofa. Michael sat on the edge of Jason's chair, leaning into him.

"Tom, maybe you can tell Mike a little about your home and the people there," Jason said.

Tom nodded. "Well, it's a two-story house and your bedroom is upstairs. You can see the fishing pond from your bedroom window. We have a boat on the pond in the summer. Do you like to fish?" Tom asked. Michael nodded. "Good. I do, too. I own and run a ranch where we raise cattle and horses. Do you like to ride horses?"

Mike shrugged his shoulders.

Tom took a nervous breath. "We have two border collies named Cookie and Clyde. They like to sleep on the foot of the bed if you let them. They're nice dogs." He looked at Jason for help.

"What about the people, Tom?"

"Well, my buddy Clay Masterson lives next door. You might recognize the name. He's a famous country music singer. He's married to a terrific lady named Harlie, and they have a one-year-old daughter, Abby. They have a swimming pool at their house we can use anytime."

"You know who Clay is, Mike. Your mom bought you some of his CDs," Jason added. Mike nodded, never taking his wide eyes off Tom.

"Clay is more like a brother than a friend. We grew up together. So, I guess he's like an uncle to you," Tom said with a shrug. He was sure he babbled, but he wanted to fill the quiet spaces.

Jason glanced at his watch. "I guess you two need to leave if you're going to make your flight." Michael tensed and leaned harder against Jason.

"Michael." Tom leaned forward. "I know you're scared, and to tell you the truth, I am too. This is all as new to me as it is to you. I didn't even know you existed a week ago, and I'm working real hard to make this easier on both of us. I want to get to know you, and I'll do my best to take care of you." He took a deep breath. "I'll probably make some mistakes, but I'll try my best. Are you willing to try, too?"

Michael was silent for a moment. "Yeah, I'll try. It's what Mom wanted. She said I had to give you a chance."

"That's all I ask for, a chance." Tom stood. "I'll take your stuff to the car if you two want to talk." Jason nodded and Tom left the room to retrieve the bags from the hall. When he returned, Michael had straightened his shoulders and said he was ready to leave. They walked from the house together. Jason hugged Michael before opening the passenger door, saying his good-byes as the boy closed the door, looking like he was close to tears again. Jason shook Tom's hand.

"Remember what I said. He always has a place here with me if things don't work out."

"I'll keep it in mind," Tom said and climbed into the car. He put the key in the ignition and turned to Michael, who stared straight ahead as if facing a firing squad.

"Ready to go, Mike?"

"My name is Michael," he said without looking at Tom.

Tom started the car and headed for the airport. Apparently, he had to earn the right to call his son Mike. He could see a lot of himself in this boy and he almost smiled. Stubbornness was a genetic trait in the Black family and this boy had it tenfold.

Michael barely uttered a word on the way to the airport, spoke only to the flight attendant on the plane, and walked silently through Tom's house to his new room upstairs. Tom tried to talk to him until he realized he wasn't getting anywhere and let the boy settle in his own way. He reminded himself Michael recently lost his mother and had been taken away from everything familiar. It would take time for him to adjust, so he let him be.

Sunday morning. Tom woke early. Not excited about the idea of spending the day with the silent boy, he lay in bed staring at the ceiling, contemplating the day. Maybe he'd take Michael for a tour of the ranch and they would spend the afternoon fishing. He'd let him run the boat. Boys usually liked stuff like that. First, he'd figure out some breakfast. Rolling from bed, he worked a kink from his travel-weary knee before finding fresh Wranglers and a PBR T-shirt. He rubbed his rough cheeks but decided a shave could wait. He wandered into the kitchen and made coffee. He searched the freezer for sausage, tossing it into the microwave to defrost. He'd shopped before the trip to Denver, so there were plenty of eggs to scramble and bread for toast.

Breakfast prepared, Tom climbed the stairs and rapped his knuckles on Michael's door.

"Breakfast is ready." No response. "Michael? Are you okay?" Tom tried the doorknob but found it locked.

"I'm okay," Michael said, his voice flat.

"Come have some breakfast."

"Not hungry."

"Michael, you need to—"

"Go away!"

Tom took a deep breath. "I'll put your plate in the refrigerator and we can heat it up later." He returned to the kitchen, wishing he'd thought to change the doorknob on the bedroom to one that wouldn't lock.

Tom tried the door again at noon and found it still locked. Worried the kid would starve, he warmed up his breakfast plate and set it on a tray in front of the door, telling Michael it was there. Several hours later, the empty plate returned to the tray in the hall.

By Tuesday afternoon, Tom was concerned. Michael wouldn't come out of his room. He continued setting trays of food by the door and they reappeared empty hours later. Michael was sneaking to the bathroom. Tom hadn't figured out when and resorted to spying on the bedroom door hoping to catch him. He didn't.

At dinnertime, panic set in. Other than breaking down the door, he couldn't think of a way to get him out of there. While pacing the kitchen, he noticed Tallie's business card on the refrigerator and decided to call for help. If a single mom of an eleven-year-old couldn't help him, he was sunk.

The evening air was thick. Sweat dripped from Tallie's brow and neck, tickling her skin. Nashville was a miserable place in the summer. She filled her watering can from the corner spigot and let the cold water run on her bare feet before shutting it off. No, that wasn't true. Phoenix had Nashville beat. Months of hundred-plus temperatures were wretched too. But it was a dry heat, everyone said. As if that made the sweltering southwest more bearable. It had been an adjustment, from dry to muggy, but after eleven years, Tallie couldn't make the distinction any longer. Heat was heat. With a sigh, she poured the cool water into a pot of petunias and returned to the spigot for more. She needed a garden hose, but the money couldn't be wasted when she had a good watering can.

It had been a long day at the office. Mr. Stockton conducted meetings and Tallie was required to hover in case he needed her. She filled her time with busywork at her desk, mind-numbing busywork, leaving her thoughts free to meander all over Tom Black. Weeks had passed since the barbeque where she'd made such an incredible fool of herself. When she thought of that night, she realized Tom had tolerated her like he would an overbearing child. What she'd taken for possible interest was politeness on his part. He'd been strained, the conversation forced.

Heat rose in Tallie's cheeks. Not from the muggy air but embarrassment. She hadn't flirted with a man since she was a teen and obviously didn't know how. Tom would have called by now if she'd done it right.

The watering can was empty again. Tallie set it on the table, a white resin circle with four chairs and a partially burned cinnamon-scented candle in the middle, and glanced around for the next gardening duty. A healthy crop of weeds practically waved to her from their flower bed next to the postage-stamp-sized patio behind her duplex. Not wanting the weeds to strangle the snapdragons, she dropped to her knees on a purple foam pad and yanked out the unwanted grass. When she'd covered her hands in dirt, the phone rang.

"Great timing." Tallie scrambled to her feet and brushed dirt from her hands as she ran for the phone. She caught it on the third ring and answered, breathless and irritated.

"Yes?"

"Tallie?"

"What?" she said, plugging her ear against the WWIII racket coming from Cody's bedroom. "Cody! Turn that darned thing down! I can't hear on the phone!" She waited for the volume to go down. When she could hear, she returned to the call.

"Sorry about that," she said. "Who did you say this is?" There was a moment of silence and Tallie thought she heard a low chuckle.

"It's Tom," he said. "Tom Black."

Oh god. Tom Black, and she just screamed in his ear like a shrew. Not good, not good at all. She laughed uncomfortably and grimaced. "Sorry to yell in your ear that way. Cody has this new video game. Well, it isn't new new, but new to him. We were at a second-hand store yesterday and he saw a Nintendo game he didn't have...you can't buy them new anymore, they quit making them, so we find them at yard sales and stuff like that...so anyway, he saw one and just had to have it and it's, well, a loud one. Too loud." Sheesh, she was babbling like an idiot and couldn't stop herself and was that another chuckle she heard on the other end of the line?

The man was laughing at her, doggone it all. This was not good at all. She closed her eyes, searching for control, and pinched the bridge of her nose, scattering dirt across her face. When she opened her eyes, dirt flew in, and she tried to blink it away. "Oh crap," she said, blinking. Temporarily forgetting the call, Tallie wiped the dirt from her eye with the back of her hand.

"Tallie? Are you still there?"

"Just a sec...I can't...hold on..." Tallie set the phone on the counter and ran to the sink, splashing cool water in her eyes. "Ow ow ow!" She sucked in her breath and wiped her eyes with a towel. When she could see, Tallie returned to the phone and contemplated ending the call. With luck, Tom would think the call had been disconnected. Maybe he would think he'd dialed a wrong number.

"Tallie?"

"Yes."

"Are you okay?"

"Fine. I was pulling weeds before you called and wiped dirt in my eye." Don't laugh or I will hang up on you. "So, Tom," she tried a normal voice tone and a carefree chuckle. "How are you?" Right, say something inane. The man was probably wondering why the heck he called. Before he could answer, she apologized again. "I'm so sorry I screamed in your ear. I usually don't do things like that, and well—"

"Tallie—"

"I'm embarrassed—"

"Tallie—"

"Maybe you want to hang up and forget you called me. I'm not doing well here—"

"Tallie!"

She resisted the urge to pound her foolish head into the wall. "What?"

Tom chuckled. "If this is a bad time, I could call back. But I need to ask you something."

Tallie swallowed. "No. Don't. I'm okay." She took a deep breath. "How are you, anyway?" she asked once more, trying to sound casual when she felt anything but that. She'd made an idiot of herself again and didn't know how to recover the situation.

"Okay, I guess." He sighed. "No, I'm not."

"What's wrong?"

"I've got a problem I'm hoping you can help with."

"I'll try," Tallie offered, wondering if this was some cute way of asking her for a date. Okay, she hadn't blown it. Yet. "What's the problem?"

"My son locked himself in his bedroom Sunday morning and I can't get him to come out."

"Your son? I didn't know you have a son." So much for the date. This was turning into a parent support group. But parenting was something she had a handle on and could discuss with a modicum of intelligence.

"I didn't know I had a son until a week ago either. I just brought him here from Denver on Saturday. He locked his bedroom door Sunday morning and hasn't come out since. I've been setting food outside the door for him, so he isn't starving."

"How old is he?"

"Eleven. That's why I thought you could help me. What would you do if your son did this?"

Tallie heard a ring of desperation in his voice. She was disappointed he wasn't asking her out, but at least he thought to call her when he needed help. "I can't remember Cody ever doing anything like that, but if he did, I'd bake cookies."

"You'd what?"

"Bake cookies. But first I'd stop putting food by his door. When you think he's good and hungry, bake a batch of chocolate chip cookies."

Tom laughed. "That's devious."

Tallie smiled. The situation might be salvageable yet. "I'll bet you it works. If you don't bake, they sell cookie dough at the grocery store."

"I think I can manage it. I have chips in the freezer. That's an excellent idea. I'm glad I called you, Tallie."

Warmth spread across Tallie's cheeks. "I'm glad you called too. Let me know if it works."

"I will. Thanks."

Tom disconnected the call and located the chips. An hour later the delicious cookie aroma wafted through the house. Tom thought he heard Michael's door open and smiled. Tallie Peters was a smart woman. Smart, good-looking, and great legs—what a combination. He pulled the pan of cookies from the oven and glanced around to see Michael standing in the doorway. His stomach growl echoed across the room.

Tom worked at removing the cookies from the pan, acting as if Michael's presence in the kitchen wasn't unusual. "Dinner is on the table. Have you washed your hands?" He nodded at the table set with two plates.

"Can I have a cookie?" Michael stared at the pan and licked his lips.

"After we eat. They're too hot now."

Michael nodded and sat at the table, eyeing the steaming dishes. "What's that?" He pointed to a covered dish.

"Pork chops, baked potatoes, and green beans," Tom said and waited for a reaction.

"Pork chops and potatoes were my mom's favorites."

"I know. I thought you might like them too." Tom moved to the table and sat down. Michael looked away, wiping his eyes.

"Sorry. I didn't mean to upset you. But you know, it's okay to let out a few tears, Michael," Tom said.

He shook his head. "No, it's not. Only babies cry." He turned his head to hide his quivering lip.

"I must be a great big baby because I had myself a couple of real good cries lately." Tom lifted the lids off the dishes and placed food on Michael's plate.

"Nuh uh. Guys aren't supposed to cry. You're just saying that so I won't feel like a wuss." He looked at Tom with large, doubt-filled eyes.

Tom let out a breath and contemplated what to say next. The truth was a good start. "I loved your mom, Michael. I don't know what she told you about us, but we were supposed to get married. That's how much I loved her. When she left, I was heartbroken and spent years looking for her, always hoping I'd find her or she'd come back to me. When Jason came last week to tell me she was gone, I cried. Maybe it's not considered a manly thing to do, but I cried for her. This past week I've had to get used to the idea she'll never come back and that makes me sad." He looked at Michael, and even though he bore no physical resemblance to his mother, he was still part of her. "Having you here helps.

We both loved her and maybe we can help each other get through the pain of losing her."

Michael bit his lip to stop a quiver. "I cry a lot for her," he admitted, sniffing. "I miss her."

"I do, too." Tom stabbed a potato and set it on Michael's plate. "We'd better eat so we can have some of those cookies."

"Did you make them?" Michael looked doubtful again when Tom nodded. "Have you ever done that before?"

"No. But I tasted one and they're not bad."

Michael smiled. Jolie's smile. "I guess if they didn't make you sick, I'll try one."

Tom laughed. "I'm feeling pretty good."

After Michael went to bed, Tom lay on his bed and called Tallie again. When she answered, her groggy tone had him glancing at the clock.

"I woke you," he said, trying to sound remorseful when his mind was contemplating images of Tallie lying in bed. Pajamas or T-shirt? Possibly she slept nude. Yeah, he liked that idea. Nude worked for him...maybe a little too well.

"Tom? I must have fallen asleep. What time is it?"

"Ten. I didn't notice it was so late."

"That's okay. Are you still having problems with your son?"

"I just wanted to tell you, the cookies worked. You're a genius." He laughed, trying to keep his mind on the conversation when all he could think of was what she might not be wearing.

"I'm glad to hear it. What's your son's name?"

"Michael Thomas Black Morgan. How's that for a name?" Pride filled him. He had a son and was darned pleased about it.

"It's great. It's none of my business, Tom, but why didn't you know you had a son?"

"It's a long story. How about if we come over to see you tomorrow night, and I'll tell you all about it? Unless you and Jax have something going on that night."

"Jax? Why would... Jax is an adorable kid, but we aren't... Why are you asking me about Jax?"

Why did he bring up Jax? He didn't know and wished he hadn't. Jax, with his incredible musical talent and two healthy legs, wasn't who he wanted Tallie thinking about. But he'd boxed himself into a corner. "Well, you two got along pretty well at the barbeque, dancing together and all, and I thought..." He let out a frustrated breath. "I thought maybe you'd given him your number too."

Tallie laughed and Tom wished he hadn't brought this up. "No, Tom. I gave my phone number to one man and hoped he'd call me."

"Oh. Okay." Relieved, Tom decided to kick this insecurity bullshit in the butt. It was killing him and his chances with Tallie. "So tomorrow night works for you? I thought it would be good to introduce the boys. Michael could use a friend his age."

"Sure," she said. "We don't have anything planned. Is seven okay?"

"Perfect. I'll pick up pizza on the way and bring cookies."

"That sounds great. I'll see you tomorrow." She paused but didn't hang up. "Oh, Tom?"

"Yeah?"

"I'm sorry I babbled like an idiot earlier. I don't know what came over me."

Tom smiled. He knew what it was because he was feeling it too. When he thought of Tallie, he babbled like a freaking idiot. "It's okay. I think you're cute. Good-night, Tallie." He hung up before she could respond.

⚜

Tallie set the phone on the nightstand. Cute? Cute made her sound like a gerbil or something. Cute made her sound like a kid who should be dating a twenty-year-old like Jax Talbot, not a woman Tom Black would date. She shut off the light and closed her eyes. He didn't say he wanted to see her, just introduce the boys. If she wasn't careful, she'd be Michael's friend's mother in Tom's mind and she wanted more than that.

She just wasn't sure how to go about it.

⚜

The next night, Tallie stopped on her way home from work to buy salad fixings and wondered if she should get some beer. No, Tom drank Pepsi at the Mastersons' barbeque. She grabbed a six-pack of pop instead.

It was hot and sticky again. As soon as she arrived home, Tallie jumped in the shower, yelling at Cody on her way to the bathroom to straighten his room. With limited time until Tom and Michael arrived, she dug through her laundry pile on the bed, finding clean white shorts and a navy-blue tank top. The air conditioning wasn't keeping up with the rising temperatures and the house was too warm already. She hoped her guests wouldn't roast.

The knock at the door had her sprinting barefoot through the living room, leaving her a little breathless. She'd planned to find her sandals but didn't have time.

"Hi," she said to the two males standing on her step. The

man looked freshly showered in Wranglers and a black T-shirt, the boy in baggy gray shorts and a Colorado Rockies baseball T-shirt. She hoped her stare wasn't too apparent. Michael looked like his father but with wavy black hair. And his father was looking too sexy for words. "Come in." She waved them in, taking a last look around to make sure everything in her threadbare home was neat. At times like this, she wished her sofa wasn't orange.

"Cody!" she called as they walked in. "Our guests are here."

Cody walked from his room, eyeing their visitors. His eyes narrowed when they landed on Tom.

Tom made introductions as the boys looked at each other, assessing. Cody relaxed somewhat. "Where should I put the pizza?" Tom held up the steaming boxes. "There's one cheese and one Hawaiian. I didn't think to ask what you'd like." He looked apologetically at Tallie.

"What you have sounds delicious. Bring it in the kitchen and I'll get the plates."

Tom followed Tallie into the cozy kitchen and set the pizza boxes on the stovetop. When he turned, he almost stepped on her toes.

They smiled shyly at each other. "Sorry," he said.

"It's fine. I should put on shoes," she said, trying not the stare at him. Her kitchen was so small and he filled so much of it. "I have a table outside. Maybe it would be cooler out there."

"Whatever you want," Tom said. He helped her collect the dishes, salad, and pizza and walked out the kitchen door to the small patio. Fortunately, a breeze moved the air. The two timid boys wandered out, sat at the table, and filled their plates with pizza and salad.

"Can we eat in my room, Mom? I want to show Michael my new video game," Cody asked.

Tallie nodded. "That's fine. Don't spill anything," she warned as the boys took their food into the house.

Tallie helped herself to a piece of Hawaiian pizza, sighing with pleasure at the sweet pineapple taste. She leaned back in her chair with her bare feet propped up on an empty chair and crossed at the ankles. "Thanks for bringing the pizza. I'm starving." She took another bite. "Michael looks like you."

Tom smiled. "It shocked me when I saw him. I hadn't even seen a picture of him."

"I know it's none of my business, but I'm dying to know. Why didn't you know about him? Where is his mother?"

"She died recently. Cancer." He frowned. "I hadn't seen her in almost twelve years."

"Poor Michael. No wonder he looks so sad."

"He's having a rough time. His mom died, and he doesn't know me. We talked a little bit last night and I think it helped." He looked down at her legs, swallowed hard, and looked away. "And about the first question, why didn't I know?" He blew out a breath. "She said she didn't trust me anymore, didn't trust me to be a father to my son."

Tallie reached for his hand, giving it a gentle squeeze.

He laced his fingers with hers. "And the sad part is, at the time, she had every right to feel that way. I let her down in every possible way."

"Tom, you don't have to…"

He shrugged. "It's okay. Maybe talking about it will help. But maybe it's more than you want to know about me."

"If you want to talk, I'll listen," she said, enjoying his strong hand holding hers. He could talk for days if he would keep hold of it.

He gave her a long, considering look and continued. "The night before the world finals twelve years ago, I asked Jolie to marry me. Best day of my life when she said yes. The next day, a bull named Devil's Spawn tried to kill me, and I woke up in a hospital room with a concussion, broken ribs, broken nose, and a smashed knee. The doctor said I could be back in competition if I healed well, so I worked hard to get back in shape. But it was too much for my knee and I tore it apart. After the second surgery, the doctor told me to take it easy or I'd mess it up again. At that point it was doubtful I'd make it back into competition, and I got depressed. Jolie stuck it out, encouraged me to get healthy, and took care of me." He closed his eyes. "I paid her back by drinking. Just like her dad." He opened his eyes and stared across the yard. "The funny thing is, I never drank much before. An occasional beer was all, but I drank so heavily, I can't remember much about it. I lost about eight months. Woke up one day and she was gone. Her note said she didn't want to be found, but I looked anyway. I haven't touched a drop in eleven years, but it didn't matter. She never came back, and I couldn't find her."

"You didn't know she was pregnant when she left?" Tallie asked.

"No. About two weeks ago a lawyer came from Denver with a video she'd made telling me why she left. My alcoholism...my depression...my son. If it wasn't for the cancer, I doubt I'd know about him now." He frowned. "I know I screwed up, but not telling me about Michael was wrong. If you could have heard him the day I picked him up, it would've broken your heart. He didn't know I could hear him, and he was crying and begging Jason Gardner to let him stay with him in Denver. And I couldn't blame the kid. He doesn't know me. It's so unfair what she did to us. This could have been an easy transition if I'd known about him before. I'd have been there for him."

Tallie squeezed his hand. "I know it's hard, but you'll have to forgive Jolie for Michael's sake. If he knows you have bitter feelings toward his mom, it'll make him angry."

"I don't think I'm bitter. Just confused."

He made circles with his thumb, sending an electric jolt through her system.

"I straightened out my life, and she didn't give me a chance to show her. She just assumed I would always be the loser she left." He blew out a breath and stared down at their joined hands. "Nothing to do now but start from scratch and hope Michael and I can connect. It's time to get on with something new." He looked at Tallie and smiled. Their eyes held. "Enough about me." He laughed. "This is why I was rude to you the day we met. I haven't wanted to think about any of that for years. Now I've been able to close that chapter of my life and start a new one with my son. He's talking to me some, but it's going to take time."

"Kids bounce back pretty fast. Keep him busy, and he won't have as much time to think about it. When Cody is upset about something, I don't let him sit around moping." Tallie was tempted to close her eyes and just enjoy the feelings he stirred. She'd never had a man hold her hand so gently.

He let go to grab another piece of pizza and didn't take

her hand again. When they finished eating, Tom offered to help clean the mess.

Tallie stood, brushing her leg against his arm as she stacked the boxes and plates. "Sorry," she said.

Tom stood and smiled one of those seductive too-gorgeous-to-be-true smiles. Their eyes locked. Tallie's knees went liquid, and she wondered if he would try to kiss her. She hoped he would, but her neighbor wandered into her yard with a watering can and the moment was broken.

Tallie waved to the older woman before collecting the dishes and returning to the house. Tom was close behind. After depositing the pizza, he retrieved a bag from the counter and handed it to Tallie.

"You brought my cookies?" She grinned, took one from the bag, and bit it. "Mmm. You're good at this. I'm impressed." She set the bag on the counter along with the half-eaten cookie, saving it for later.

"First effort," he said with obvious pride. "I got lucky. Michael liked them too." His gaze moved from her eyes to her mouth and lingered. "Just a second. You have a crumb right here." He rubbed his thumb across her lower lip. "And here." He brushed another crumb. "And...oh, hell, I'll get them all at once."

He bent and brushed his lips across her mouth, a seductive little sweep. He kissed and nibbled her lips as his hands slid around her waist, pulling her closer. She wrapped her arms around his neck and laced her fingers through his soft black hair. She'd never been kissed so sweetly. She'd never wanted a kiss to last forever until now. His tongue slid between her lips, teasing hers, building heat. She gasped with surprise. His hands found their way to the skin revealed by her raised arms, and he pushed her shirt up for more, stopping when young voices interrupted from the other room.

"Die, sucker, die!" Cody yelled. Michael laughed.

Releasing her from his kiss, Tom leaned his forehead against hers and smiled. "I have to keep reminding myself I can't do what I want when I want anymore." He closed his eyes and swallowed hard.

Tallie blushed at the implication. She thought they were merely kissing and was embarrassed by her naïveté. Apparently, she'd led him to believe she was willing to take things further than a kiss. And the shocking part was, she wanted to take things further, but not this quick and not in the kitchen with the boys so close. "I, ah, had better get the dinner mess finished up." She backed away from him.

Tom relaxed against the counter and helped himself to a cookie. "What's the story on Cody's dad?"

Her shoulders tensed. She grabbed a dishrag and scrubbed the kitchen counter. "He's not around."

"Does Cody ever see him?" He took another bite of his cookie.

"No, and if I have my way, he never will."

"Where does he live?"

"I don't know." She turned her back to Tom, not wanting him to see how the subject upset her. She'd never been a good liar and didn't want to tell him the truth. What would he think of her? Of Cody? Cody never told anyone where his father was, preferring to think him dead. "I don't know. And I don't care. He's never seeing Cody again, so it doesn't matter."

"Is that fair to him? To either of them?"

Tallie closed her eyes and let out a frustrated breath before turning to him, her eyes flashing anger. "It's not the same thing, Tom."

"If you're keeping the kid away from his father, it sounds like you're doing exactly what Jolie did."

"He knows he has a son. I'm not denying Roy anything. His son doesn't want to see him, okay? Just let it go. I don't want to talk about it." She glared, trying to calm her nerves and her shaking hands.

"Fine." Tom backed off. "I'm sorry. It's none of my business." He turned to leave the kitchen, but she stopped him with an unstable hand on his arm.

"No, I'm sorry. Maybe someday I'll feel like talking about it but I'm not there yet, okay?" She held his arm with her trembling hand.

"You're shaking. Come here, honey." Not waiting for her approval, he took her in his arms, holding her close. Tom pressed his cheek into her hair. "When you want to talk about it, I'll listen. And if you don't, I won't pry."

The tension left her shoulders as he held her and stroked her hair. She fit there, tight in his arms, like she belonged. She didn't make a move to disconnect, enjoying the comfort his strong presence offered. She looked up at him and wordlessly invited him to kiss her again. He dipped and touched her lips with his, sweet and slow. He took the kiss deeper but stopped.

"What am I doing? I shouldn't have kissed you, but there is just something about you that makes me want to kiss you over and over again. I can't stop."

Tallie gnawed her bottom lip. "There's something about me that doesn't want you to stop," she said, wondering where she'd found the nerve to say something so suggestive.

She'd never been this way. In fact, she hadn't let a man near her in years and here she was panting in the kitchen with Tom. But she could tell he was different. She was sure he was accustomed to getting what he wanted from a woman, but he had a gentleness that said he wouldn't press her if she wasn't willing. Her quickened pulse and the gooey feeling throughout her body told her willingness wasn't a problem. Oh boy, was she willing.

Tom rubbed his thumb across her cheek, tried for another kiss, and found easy success. Tallie found her back pressed against the kitchen counter with Tom tight against her, the heat of his body warming hers. Tallie had a glimpse of Tom's intensity level, the driven competitor going for a goal. She should be shocked by his abrupt behavior but wasn't. She couldn't think, only lose herself in the feel of his broad shoulders beneath her hands, the way his muscles bunched and relaxed as he held her. Her senses filled with him, his taste on her lips—sweet from the pineapple and cookies they'd eaten—the soapy scent on his skin, and the rhythm of his breath. His hands roamed her back before settling on her butt. She let out a little squeak of surprise when he gave a gentle squeeze, but she didn't push him away. They were over the edge, reason slipping away fast, when the boys let out another whoop from the other room. The reality slam forced them to break their kiss.

"Sorry, I forgot." He glanced toward the ruckus coming from Cody's room. "I'd better go home." He sighed into her hair. "I think the boys are getting along well."

"Sounds like it. There's nothing like a video game to cement a friendship."

At the sound of the bedroom door opening, they stepped

apart, and Tom walked to the sink. "How goes the war?" He found a glass in the cupboard, filled it with water, and drank.

"That game is so cool. Can I come back and play with Cody again?" Michael asked.

Tom looked at Tallie for a response.

"Of course you can come back, Michael. Any time your dad wants to bring you."

Happy grins passed between the boys. "Come on, Mike. We have some Huns to destroy!" Cody ran from the room with Michael close on his heels.

Tom bristled.

"What's wrong?" Tallie asked.

He frowned. "He won't let me call him Mike. Everyone else can but not me. It's like I have to earn what he gives everyone else for free."

"Does he know the circumstances leading to him not knowing you? Does he blame you?"

"I don't think he knows much of anything about me at all. Jolie said she wanted me to make my own impression on him." He ran his fingers through his hair. "How am I sup- posed to do that when he hardly talks to me?"

"What did he do today?"

Tom shrugged. "I'm not sure. I had work to do. I imagine he watched TV and played some of his games."

"Do you want some more cookie-baking advice?" she smiled at his skeptical look. "Take him to work with you tomorrow. Let him see what you do. Let him help. Take him fishing, just the two of you. I bet he'll start talking to you."

The corner of his mouth lifted into a smile. "You know, Tallie, I feel stupid when I'm around you." He laughed.

"You have all these great common-sense ideas I should be able to think up on my own."

"I've been at this parenting thing a lot longer than you. My mind works differently."

"I'm glad. Otherwise, I'd still be putting food trays in front of his bedroom door. It's late. I should take Michael home." He stepped across the kitchen, stopping in front of Tallie. "If Michael comes back to play with Cody, can I come play too?" He leaned in close, bent to give her a little kiss—followed by a sly smile.

Tallie bit her lip, knowing exactly what the look meant. She wasn't that naïve. "Are you busy Friday?" she asked, hoping her voice didn't sound as husky as she thought it did.

"No."

"I'll fix dinner. Does six work for you?"

"We'll be here." He nipped her lips one last time before leaving the kitchen to rap on Cody's bedroom door. "Come on, Michael. We need to go." He smiled at the expected response.

"Ah, man! We aren't done with the game yet!" Michael wailed through the door.

"We're coming back Friday night. Let's go."

"Friday! All right!" Michael opened the door, grinning.

They said their good-nights at the door and Tallie waved as the truck pulled away from the curb.

☙

"You had a good time?" Tom asked Michael as he drove onto the street.

"Great. Cody's cool. I can't wait to go back Friday."

Tom smiled as they traveled through the graying evening

light. The song on the radio: The Zac Brown Band's "Whatever It Is."

Tallie had *it.*

Tom didn't have a handle on it any better than the guy singing the song, but he looked forward to figuring it out on Friday night.

6

Tom nudged the bedroom door with his boot, peeking in to see why Michael hadn't responded to his call upstairs. He smiled at the sight of the sleeping boy on the bottom bunk, his wavy black hair flopping over his brow. The dogs were snuggled against him. Cookie and Clyde wagged their tails and wiggled. The boy stirred but didn't wake.

"Michael, it's time to wake up." Tom laughed when Cookie nuzzled Michael's chin and licked him. "Wake him up, pup."

Clyde licked Michael's nose and he came awake with a start. "Blech! Dog slobber!" He shoved the border collie away and looked up to see Tom laughing in the doorway.

"What?"

"It's time to get up. I have things to do and you can help me."

"Why do I have to get up?" Michael grumbled.

"You aren't going to laze around all summer. Come on. I need to get some work done and those dogs need out." Michael dragged himself from the bed, adjusting his boxer shorts. As he headed out the door, Tom grabbed a T-shirt from a dresser drawer and tossed it at him. "See you downstairs."

When Michael emerged, Tom waved him out to the porch, stopping him near the dogs' dishes and a large sack of dog food. "It can be your job to take care of the dogs. They belong to Clay, but he's never home, so they adopted me.

Did you have a dog in Denver?"

"We couldn't have pets in our apartment." He watched as Tom measured the food, two scoops in each bowl.

"Feed them morning and evening and make sure the water bowl is full. Okay?"

Michael nodded.

"Run upstairs and get dressed and we'll take off."

"I'm hungry," Michael grumbled. "Can I eat first?"

"That's first on the agenda. Sally is cooking pancakes this morning. Get going. I'm hungry too."

"Who's Sally?" Michael asked as he headed inside.

"Clay's housekeeper. She makes terrific pancakes. Get moving."

Michael ran upstairs, returning in shorts, T-shirt, baseball cap, and tennis shoes, running as Tom hustled him to the pickup. As they drove through the ranch, Tom pointed out the barns, corrals, and the boat at the dock.

"You get to meet Clay and his family this morning," Tom said as they pulled into the yard.

"Clay Masterson, the singer, right?" Michael asked wide-eyed.

"Yeah, that's him. But around here he's just Clay. We slap his ego down so he doesn't get obnoxious." He laughed at Michael's shock. "He's like my brother, Michael. We've known each other since we were born. I can say just about anything to him."

At Clay's house, Tom ushered Michael into the busy kitchen.

"Morning!" Clay called, giving Michael an easy smile. "Come in and have a seat, Michael. Sit here." He pointed to the chair next to him, which Michael took with reluctance.

Tom settled into the chair at the end, calling "Good morning" to Harlie at the other end of the table. Abby sat in her high chair next to Harlie, munching a bite of sticky pancake. Tom made the introductions while Sally poured batter on the griddle.

"Man!" Clay exclaimed as he studied Michael like a bug under a microscope. "This takes me back. You look just like your dad did when we were kids."

Tom smiled and nodded thanks to Sally when she brought him a cup of coffee.

"I have some pictures to show you after breakfast, Michael," Clay said. "You'll see what I'm talking about."

Harlie added, "Clay, be sure to show him the one on the wall. Would you like some juice, Michael?" Michael nodded and Harlie passed the pitcher down the table.

"What have you been doing since you got here?" Clay asked.

Michael shrugged his shoulders and looked like he wanted to hide under his cap, not answer questions.

"Does he talk, Tom?"

"Some. I think you're scaring him. Let him eat. He woke up starving."

Sally placed a steaming stack of pancakes in front of Michael, smiling. "Healthy boys are always starving, Tom. I'll get you some bacon, sweetie. Would you like an egg too?"

Michael nodded.

Tom handed him the syrup. "Dig in."

"The picture Harlie is talking about was taken right after your dad was thrown on his butt by a bull." Clay laughed. "What a temper. I'm surprised the bull lived through it."

Michael looked owl-eyed at Tom. "What were you doing

with a bull?"

"Riding the sucker, or at least trying to." Tom poured syrup on his newly arrived plate filled with a stack of pancakes, bacon, and eggs.

"Why?"

Tom saw his son's amazement and realized there were more than a few holes in his paternal knowledge. It was apparent now Jolie hadn't told the kid anything about his father. There was no way she could have talked about Tom Black without mentioning rodeo and bull riding.

"I was in a rodeo and riding bulls was one of my events," he said, embarrassed to explain such a basic concept to his son in front of his friends. Until the accident that shattered his knee, Tom had devoted his life to rodeo and Jolie knew it.

"Oh, yeah. Jason said you were a cowboy. I didn't know he meant a real rodeo cowboy. I thought he meant you wore a hat and boots and raised cows." Michael shrugged.

Clay gave Tom an astounded look. Tom shook his head at Clay when he started to speak. "I guess we have a few things to talk about," Tom muttered. "You've never seen a bull rider, have you?"

Michael shook his head.

"We'll take care of that today," Tom said. "I have a couple of guys coming this afternoon to practice on Spitfire. Want to watch?"

"Yeah! I've never seen a rodeo," Michael said with uncharacteristic enthusiasm.

Tom was glad to finally hit something to bring the boy out of his shell. "We'll see if these guys can beat him. But first we have some work to do as soon as you finish eating."

"Can I see the pictures first?" Michael asked.

"Sure, if Clay has time."

They sat around the table, with Sally refilling the plates before she sat down to eat. Michael listened to the adult conversation, answering when asked a question, but for the most part, he was a fascinated sponge.

"Done?" Clay asked him.

Michael nodded.

"Come on then." Clay waved the boy into the living room and pointed to a picture on the wall of two boys on horseback. Tom was dusty from his earlier tangle with the bull.

"See what I mean? Could be twins," Clay said. Michael stared at a boy who could be him. Clay pulled a photo album from the shelf and handed it to Michael. "Take a look in there, sport. There are pictures of your aunt and grandparents too."

Michael sat on the sofa. "I have an aunt and grandparents?" he asked as he leafed through the pictures, stopping when one caught his eye.

Tom couldn't believe Jolie hadn't told the kid anything, and yet she claimed she hadn't hated Tom at all. Why not tell him? Had it hurt that much? "You have a grandpa and grandma in Montana who are eager to meet you. I have a sister who is your aunt. She was your mom's best friend when they were kids. She has some kids close to your age. That's why there's a bunk bed in your room. They stay with me once in a while."

"I have cousins too?" Michael flipped through the pictures, frowning. "Mom never told me. She said our family was me, her, and Grandma Morgan."

"You have family, Michael," Tom said.

"Where were you off to in such a hurry last night, Tom?" Clay asked and pointed out a picture of Tom's dad.

"Tallie's."

"Peters?" Clay grinned.

Heat rose in Tom's cheeks. "I wanted Michael to meet Cody," he said, knowing that was only part of why he went. "They got along great."

"Cody's cool," Michael said

"So is Tallie." Clay needled, causing Tom to bristle. "Pretty, too."

"She's okay," Michael said. "Who's this?" He pointed to a dark-haired woman.

"Your grandma, my mom. Are you about ready to go, Michael? We need to do a few things." Tom stood and headed to the door.

"Yeah, okay." He laid the photo album down. "I get to play with Cody again Friday night."

"Playing at Tallie's Friday night?" Clay raised his eyebrows at Tom.

"Shut up, Clay, before I say something I shouldn't." Tom decided he'd better leave before Clay embarrassed him more. Funny thing was, he couldn't figure out why he was embarrassed. He'd been with women over the years, put up with a ton of Clay's teasing, and usually laughed right along with him. But he'd never had the urge to smack the guy before and that worried him.

Why was Tallie Peters different?

⟡

They spent the morning checking on the work crew and completing repairs where needed. Tom spent time in the office returning phone calls, with Michael looking bored and commenting on his lack of entertainment prospects. His Nintendo DS sat on his nightstand at home. The security monitors held his interest for a few minutes, but he soon grew restless when nothing moved on the screen but horses. After lunch, they met the bull riders at the practice arena. Tom hoped it would wipe the uninterested look off the boy's face. This day was tanking fast.

"It's hotter than hell today, Tom," one of the cowboys, a wired-up redhead, said in greeting.

"You think it's hot now, Rusty—wait until you're on that bull. You think you can take him?" Tom grinned at the cowboy's cockiness.

"Damn right I will, but I'll bet you a buck he'll toss Henry in the dirt." Rusty elbowed his buddy.

"Shit," Henry said.

Tom laughed at the expected response. Henry never said much about anything. "Get your gear and I'll have the guys bring him in. You're wearing helmets." Tom pushed back his hat, wiped the sweat from his brow, and resettled the hat. He called to his foreman to get Spitfire and noticed Henry's scowl. "You aren't getting that pretty face smashed here, Henry. Wear the helmet or don't ride. Your choice." After getting his own head busted up, he'd decided helmets were the best idea. They were more acceptable in competition, but some guys thought the extra weight and vision restriction caused problems and wouldn't wear them. With no money to win in his practice arena, Tom made the guys wear helmets. They could piss and moan all they wanted and it did no good. Tom was firm on it.

"You used to do this?" Michael leaned on the corral rail

with Tom, watching Rusty prep his rope and strap on spurs. Tom noticed the gangly boy attempted to mimic his stance: bent knee, cocked hip, and elbows on the rail. It amused the heck out of him. But Michael's question didn't. It was a question his son shouldn't need to ask. He should know.

"I didn't just do this, Michael. I lived for it." He tipped back his hat to get a good look at his son. "Just what did your mom tell you about me?"

"Your name," the boy said with a shrug. "It was on my birth certificate so she had to tell me."

"That's it? My name? She never told you what I did or that you look like me or anything?" His anger swelled and Tom worked to push it down. He didn't want Michael to know his father's feelings toward Jolie weren't charitable at the moment. If he wasn't careful, she'd get evicted from that promised place in his heart. He wanted to keep her there, for Michael's sake, and his own.

"No, nothing. I asked about you. Everybody else had a dad and I wanted to know about mine, but she always looked sad, so I stopped asking. I thought maybe you were a spy or something, and she wasn't allowed to talk about you." He looked away. "That's what I used to tell the other kids, that you were away on a secret mission in Afghanistan or Iraq and we didn't know when you'd come back. Some of my friends' dads were there, so they believed it."

"A spy?" Tom shook his head in disbelief, not that Michael made up stories, but because Jolie had shortchanged the kid in the father department. "Even when she got sick and knew you would come to live with me, she didn't tell you anything at all?"

Michael shook his head.

"Hell," Tom muttered. "If you want to know anything, just ask. I'll start by telling you I was not a spy but a professional bull rider. I won a lot of gold buckles in my career and was a hair away from the world championship and a nice chunk of change."

Michael's bored look was gone, so Tom continued. "You've noticed I limp, right? It's kinda hard to miss."

Michael nodded.

"I got stomped real bad at the world finals and it finished me off for riding. Now, I raise bulls for other guys to ride. Watch this." He pointed to the chute. Rusty nodded. The gate opened and Spitfire burst out like a volcanic eruption. Twisting, bucking, and swinging his head, the bull gave it everything he had. Rusty kept his seat until four seconds into the ride when Spitfire changed direction abruptly. The surprised rider hit the dirt with a thud, jumped to his feet, and sprinted to the fence. Michael watched with wide-eyed fascination.

Rusty walked around the corral to Tom and Michael, brushing dirt from his Wranglers. "Hell of a bull, Tom. Will he be in competition?"

"Gib's coming to look at him soon. You may get another chance at him. You were looking good until he dumped you on your butt." Tom laughed at Rusty's scowl.

"Henry is getting ready. I doubt he'll take him either," Rusty said with a trace of hope in his voice.

Spitfire was again loaded in the chute. Henry nodded and the bull did his job a second time. Henry landed on his back in three seconds. One of the hands played bull fighter and distracted the bull while Henry ran for the chutes. Rusty laughed when his friend dove to safety.

"If you want to try again, Rusty, I'll have them load him up. Or you can try a few of the others," Tom yelled.

"Might do that. Thanks. I'll tell your guys when I'm ready." He wandered back to the chute, hitching up his jeans. "Hell of a bull, man!" he called over his shoulder.

"What do you think, Michael?" Tom asked.

"You're crazy if you did that."

"A lot of people thought so." He laughed. "Want to take the boat out for a while?"

"Can I drive?"

"Sure. Let's grab some poles and see if we can catch a few fish for dinner."

"I'm not cleaning them," Michael said with disgust.

"You catch 'em, you clean 'em." Tom laughed when Michael made a sour face. "Come on."

Back in the truck, Michael gave Tom a thoughtful glance and looked away.

"You have something on your mind, Michael?"

"I was wondering what I should call you." Michael looked at Tom, mental wheels obviously churning. "I mean, double-o-seven is out, right?"

Tom smiled and shook his head. "Yeah, I'd say so. It's up to you. I don't expect you to call me Dad unless you want to, maybe when you know me better. My name is Tom. I'll leave it up to you."

Michael nodded and appeared to contemplate what he'd said. He was a quiet, thoughtful kid, Tom mused. A lot like his father and grandfather.

"Tom?"

The disappointment at hearing his name was like a stone in his gut. "Yeah?"

CAUGHT IN THE SPIN

"Can I have a cowboy hat and boots like yours? I like that black one you wear. It's..." Michael looked at Tom from the corner of his eye. "Cool."

Tom felt a rattle of emotion but stared straight ahead. The request was almost as good as calling him Dad. "Sure. We can go shopping Saturday if you like."

It was a step, anyway.

7

Friday night. Tallie rushed in the door, arms heavily laden with grocery bags, trying to reach the phone before the caller hung up. She hoped to afford a cell phone one of these days. She'd stopped at the store on the way home and picked up spaghetti ingredients, garlic bread, and chocolate ice cream. Something cool was called for since the temperature hovered in the nineties. After setting the bags on the kitchen counter, she grabbed the phone.

"Tallie? This is Sid Merrill."

Tallie cringed. A call from her attorney never meant good news. "Hi, Sid. What's up?" Tension collected between her shoulder blades as she braced herself.

"There's a parole hearing scheduled for Roy. They're considering his release."

"What?" Tallie froze. "Release? No," she said. The phone wobbled in her hand. "They can't."

"They can and they're thinking about doing it."

"They can't let him out." She closed her eyes tight and swallowed. "He said he'd finish it if they let him out."

"Then we need to do what we can to keep him in there. You need to attend the hearing and tell them he's threatened you."

"No! I can't do that." She paced the kitchen on unsteady legs.

"You have to, Tallie. Otherwise, they'll let him out. He's been a good boy and they're releasing him early because of it."

"I can't do it, Sid. He terrifies me."

"You have to. Be at my office at nine Monday. We have to do this. I'll see you then."

She slammed down the phone. It was unbelievable. He shouldn't be released for years. She'd be gone by then, hiding somewhere Roy couldn't find them. It was too early now, and she didn't have enough money to run. At least, not for long. Numb, she walked into her room and dropped on the bed, staring into space. What was she going to do now?

The knock on the door an hour later woke her from an unplanned nap and had her trembling. Tallie looked at the clock, surprised to see it was six and Cody wasn't home. Panic hit her like a vicious slap until she remembered she'd neglected to call his friend's house and tell him to come home. The knock on the door became more insistent. She wandered out to open it.

"Tom?" She blinked and her hand flew to her hair. It was probably standing on end.

"We said Friday night, didn't we?"

"Yeah. I'm sorry. I got distracted and forgot. Come in. I need to call Cody and tell him to come home." She walked into the kitchen and made the call. Tom followed.

"Are you all right?"

"Yeah, fine." She shook her head to clear the fog. "I'll just put some water on for the spaghetti. It won't take long." She unloaded the groceries on the counter, upset when she found the melted ice cream in the bottom. "Oh, I forgot about this." Tears welled in her eyes. She blinked them away.

"Hey, it's okay, honey," Tom said. "We don't need it. How about if we go out for ice cream after dinner?"

She nodded.

Tom looked at her with obvious concern. "I'm assuming this is about more than melted ice cream? Want to talk about it?"

She shook her head. "No, I'm okay."

"I'll help with dinner. Tell me what to do," Tom said. They cooked the spaghetti and fixed a salad. Cody came home in time to eat, and the boys disappeared to the bedroom to play video games.

Tom helped clear the dishes, and Tallie could feel him watching her. With the mess cleared away, he cornered her.

"Something is bothering you."

"It's not your problem, Tom."

"If you're upset, you can talk to me. Maybe I can help."

Tallie shuddered when she thought about her problem. Tom led her to the table and pulled a chair out for her. He set one opposite hers, sat, took her hand in his, and waited. She looked at him, blinking. Typical man. Present him with a problem and he tries to solve it. She sighed.

"What is it?" he asked.

It was clear he planned to sit there until she spilled it. She looked at him, debating. How much did she want him to know? She was so afraid of how people would judge her and Cody once they knew. Oh heck, why not tell him? She and Cody would leave town soon anyway. There was no way she could go to the hearing, and if Roy was freed, she couldn't stay in Nashville. What did it matter if Tom knew about Roy? Either way, she'd lose him. Lose him? She didn't even have him. She huffed out a breath. "Just a second." She walked across the room and turned the radio on to cover their voices. "I don't want Cody to hear." She returned to her chair, bit her lip, and took a deep breath. She looked into Tom's concerned eyes, uncertain where to start. Tom apparently mistook her delay for an emotional breakdown.

"Come here," he said and pulled her into his lap and wrapped her in his arms.

It felt good there, held close to him, his hand brushing her hair. His strength gave her the confidence she needed. "They're letting him out."

"Who? Out of where?"

"Roy, my ex-husband. They're letting him out." She turned her face into his chest and sniffled. She felt like such an idiot, but now that she was on his lap, wrapped in his comforting arms, she had the desire to cry. It had been years since she'd allowed herself the luxury of tears and now, with a strong man to lean on, she couldn't stop the impulse. If he hadn't dragged her onto his lap, if he hadn't wrapped those strong, reassuring arms around her, she might have controlled the embarrassing waterworks pooling in her eyes. Too late now, she pressed her head to his shoulder, breathed deeply, and basked in the comfort he offered. Oh, he smelled good too. If she had it her way, she'd sit right where she was forever and never think of Roy again. She'd just lean into Tom and sniff that terrific guy scent, all freshly showered and masculine, and...

"Letting him out of where?"

So much for the fantasy. She exhaled. "Prison. They are letting him out of prison."

"Cody's father is in prison?"

She nodded.

"Why?"

"Oh, just a little thing like trying to kill me. He's been in prison for years and now they want to let him out early. He'll kill me if they do."

He was obviously dumbfounded by her confession. Of all the things he expected her to confide, her potential murder apparently wasn't one of them. Tom's arms tensed around her.

"Oh." He blew out a breath. "I wasn't expecting...why does he want to kill you?"

"He wants our son and I won't let him have him. Cody is terrified of him and doesn't want to see him. So, I have to leave here. If I stay, he'll kill me and take Cody."

"How did you find out about this?" Tom asked, running his fingers through her hair, attempting to soothe.

"My attorney called and said there is a parole hearing on Monday. He wants me to testify that Roy has threatened me, but I can't do it."

"If you testify, will they keep him longer?"

"My attorney thinks so."

"Then you need to do it."

She sat up, looking at Tom like he was an escapee from a loony bin. "No. I'm packing our stuff and leaving. I've been saving money so we could move somewhere and hide. I thought I had more time."

"Honey, you can't run away. You need to testify and keep him locked up. I'll go with you to the hearing if you want me to."

"You will? Why?"

"You shouldn't face this alone. I'll go with you."

She shook her head. "No. That's kind of you, but I can't do it. It's not your problem. I'll pack what I can in my car and leave tonight or maybe first thing in the morning. If I drive straight through without stopping, I can put a couple of states between us before they let him out. I can deal with this..." She nodded, the decision made, and moved to leave his lap. There were so many things to do, she needed to get moving. Bags to pack, groceries in the ice chest, the phone service canceled. He put a hand on her hip and stopped her.

"Where will you go?"

She shrugged. "I'll just drive until I get tired and stop. Maybe a big city. I could hide easier..." She gnawed her bottom lip and thought it might work. Roy wouldn't have any idea which direction to look. Maybe she'd go north to Boston or New York...change their names...

Tom was scowling now. "Tallie honey, you need to think about what you're saying. You're talking about uprooting your son and living on the run. Do you have any idea what it would cost to relocate to another city? Your lawyer may be right. If you go to the hearing, you may be able to stop this. Maybe you should try."

He looked so sincere and he said it with such conviction, she starting thinking he could be right. "You'll go with me?"

He nodded. "I'll stay with you through the whole thing."

"I don't know..."

"Maybe I should have some details about what happened," he said. "With Roy?"

She had a feeling he didn't want to hear the story, but he needed to hear it. Maybe sitting on his lap wasn't the best place for confidences. She shifted her weight and he grimaced. No, this wasn't the best place for serious conversation. Tallie bit her lip, raised a brow, and swallowed. Their eyes locked. She knew where this was going. They couldn't be near each other without touching. And touching led to kissing.

She looked at him through long lashes. "It's a long story. You sure you want to hear it?"

"If it concerns you, I do."

"Maybe we should sit somewhere else?" She gave him a knowing smile and shifted her weight, making him groan.

"Good idea."

They moved to the sofa and sat with a respectable distance between them. Tom leaned on pillows near the end and Tallie perched on the edge of the cushion, clasping and unclasping her hands. She paused for a moment, debated what to tell him, and decided to trust him.

"I grew up in Scottsdale. That's where all this mess started."

"Ah," he said. "I didn't think you sounded like a Southerner."

"Southwest." She paused. "It started with my dad's rodeo obsession. He'd take my brothers and me to rodeos whenever he could. When I was sixteen, I saw Roy working at a rodeo. He asked me out, and my mother had a fit when I told her about him. He was eighteen and too old for me. I was forbidden to see him. Of course, that meant I wanted to see him that much more. I climbed out my bedroom window at night to meet him. Stupid, I know." Tallie leaned back on the sofa. "Anyway, I kept sneaking out to see Roy for months. At this point, it becomes a cliché teenager-gets-pregnant story. I was incredibly naïve." She sighed. "My mother insisted I abort the baby. She said I was too young and 'it' would ruin my life. Cody was always 'it' to her, never her future grandchild. So, 'it' would ruin the life she had planned for me: Ivy League university, husband from Ivy League, and so forth. I wanted to marry Roy and live happily ever after. Mother said if I married Roy, I wasn't welcome in her house again, and I haven't seen my family since." Tom reached over and took her hand in his. She moved nearer. "We moved in with Roy's dad. He told me every day Roy shouldn't have married a slut like me, and he hoped the baby died." She smiled ruefully. "His son gets me pregnant and I'm a slut because of it..." She shrugged it off. "We couldn't afford a place of our own on what Roy made working for a stock contractor, so we were stuck there. When I was seven months pregnant, he found out his mom was real sick, and we moved here to take care of her. She was nice, nothing like his father. She was so happy to have a grandchild, and she seemed pleased to have us with her, so I was glad we came here. When Cody was a few months old, her health failed and she died. We stayed here, living in her house, and I thought we were doing fine. But Roy changed, started to act more like his father. He was working nights in a gas station and couldn't find a better job. I stayed home with Cody and couldn't work. He blamed me for our lack of money and got mean. About five years ago, I decided I'd had enough, packed mine and Cody's stuff, and left." She gripped Tom's hand tighter. "Roy found out—I think one of his friends saw us—and he chased us down before I could get out of the area. I wouldn't stop my car, so he rammed us with his pickup. He shoved us off the road and into a tree. Cody..." She paused, closing her eyes. "Cody screamed and screamed every time Roy hit us. He knew what his daddy was capable of and was so scared. Thankfully, I had strapped him into the backseat of the car. The paramedics said he could have died when we hit the tree if he hadn't been in the back." She took a deep breath to calm her nerves, but her leg vibrated. "The car was totaled. The front end crushed. I was trapped under the steering wheel and couldn't move. When I looked out the window, Roy stood there with a handgun pointed at me. Another driver stopped to see if we were okay and called 9-1-1, or I'm sure Roy would have killed me on the spot and taken Cody. He promised he'd finish the job when he got out, and I know he will."

Tom put his arm around her shoulders and pulled her to him. She hugged him tight, her head on his chest.

"We'll go to the hearing and they won't let him out, Tallie. They need to know he's still a threat."

Her voice shook when she spoke. "You're right. I know you are. I'll go, but I'm not telling Cody. His father terrifies him and I don't want him worried."

"That's understandable. I'm sorry I said what I did the other night about Cody's father having the right to see him. He hasn't any rights." He kissed the top of her head. "I'm sorry I upset you."

"You couldn't know, and your nerves are still raw from your situation. I'm not doing what Michael's mother did. Cody isn't safe around his father."

"Thanks for telling me," Tom said.

Though finished with the story, Tallie still trembled. She snuggled tight against him, feeling safe. His hands moved across her skin in soothing sweeps, settling her agitated nerves but stirring her in other ways. Something was going to happen, she was sure of it. She looked into his eyes. His gaze flicked to her lips. A long silence stretched between them, and she figured something had to happen to break it. In the other room, Michael laughed.

Tom stretched his arms over his head, locking them behind his neck. "I've been to Arizona a few times."

If he yawned, she was going to hit him. Where was the kiss she expected? The boys were busy in the other room and wouldn't interrupt. She wanted to throw herself into a mindless kiss and forget Roy ever existed. "I know."

His lips twitched into a smile. "Were you there?"

"Yes."

"And?"

"It was okay."

"Oh. When were you there?"

"The last one, before the world finals." She turned and sat on her knees. "You rode an ugly Brahma. I can't remember his name."

"Breaker," he said.

"Yeah, that was him. You did pretty well on him," she said. "I think you scored high, but I can't remember." He frowned. She laughed and leaned into him. "It was one of the most exciting things I've ever seen. You were amazing. You were always amazing."

Tom laughed. She pressed against him, her soft breast against his arm. He cupped her cheeks in his calloused hands and pulled her into a kiss, his mouth moving languidly across hers. He deepened the kiss and she followed along, her breath skimming his skin. She swung her leg across him and straddled his lap. He groaned and intensified the kiss. She shouldn't do this, shouldn't kiss him this way. He pushed her blouse up...kissed her neck and nibbled her ear. She knew where it would lead, where she wanted it to lead. They needed to stop, but she was so willing to let him do what he wanted. He slid his hands beneath her blouse and up her back; his fingers deftly unhooked her bra. She startled a bit but didn't stop him from touching.

She was out of control and knew it. Doing something to stop herself was another matter entirely. Tom was such a good kisser. He made her feel cherished and wanted. Reckless, too. She knew what she wanted and was pretty sure they were on the same path. His hands skimmed her back. Her bra hung loosely, his hands roamed freely across her back, and oh my, they were cupping her butt. She thought she would explode from the pressure building inside her. If they kept going this way, they would end up in bed together. And that could be difficult because the boys might hear. The boys...

Tallie pulled away from Tom's mouth and grabbed his hands. Her lips were swollen and her body throbbed. "Okay. Reality check." She took a deep breath. "The boys—"

As if on cue, Cody laughed, reminding them they weren't alone.

Tom laid his head back and blew out a breath. "Yeah, sorry. I shouldn't have—"

"Me either." Tallie ran her hands through her hair. "I shouldn't be sitting here like this." She slid from his lap, perching on the edge of the sofa. Tom caught his breath before leaning forward to place a tender kiss on her neck and snuggle her. She shivered when his warm breath grazed her ear.

"It was my fault," he said. "I should have more self-control, but I seem to lose it when I'm around you." He pressed his lips to her neck. "I'm thinking..."

"What?" she said, breathless.

"Maybe I could talk Harlie and Clay into letting the boys hang out at their house some evening." He wrapped his arms around her waist.

"And why would you do that?"

"Because they have a pool."

"And why do the boys need to hang out at Mastersons' when we both have houses?"

He shifted his weight behind her. "I'm thinking I'd like to take you out for a nice dinner, maybe a little of that slow dancing you like so much. I'm kind of clunky at it, but if you don't mind, I'll give it a shot."

Tallie swallowed hard. "Umm...okay. That would be nice. I don't mind clunky." He tightened his arms around her and nuzzled her neck.

"Maybe," he said, "Harlie would keep them for a sleepover..."

"Why would she need to do that?"

"I'm thinking, after all that slow dancing, you might consent to some kissing and, well, we'll see where it goes from there."

"Oh."

"So it's a date?"

"Okay." She couldn't catch her breath with Tom holding her that way. Especially since his lips kept finding new places to torment. "Tom?"

"Hmmm?"

"I think now is a good time to go for ice cream."

He nibbled her shoulder and laughed. "I think you're

probably right."

She wiggled from his arms and called for the boys. "Cody! Michael! Let's go get ice cream!" She pounded on the bedroom door and barely moved away before two excited boys ran out.

"I want sprinkles!" Cody said.

"Me, too!" Michael agreed and they ran out the door to Tom's truck.

Tallie made a dash to the bathroom for a quick hair brushing and bra adjustment before following the boys out the door.

"Hey, Tallie," Tom said.

She stopped at the door.

"I'm taking Michael shopping tomorrow for boots and a hat. Want to go with us?"

"Boots and a hat?"

"His request. He wants boots and a hat...like mine." He smiled.

"Oh, Tom, that's terrific. If Michael doesn't mind, I'd love to go." She put her arm around his waist and headed for the truck, thankful for the wonderful distraction to take her mind off Roy.

8

Roy Peters sat in his cell, flicking playing cards into the sink, his nerves tingling. He'd stared at these gray walls for years now, thinking about when he'd get out. He leaned against the wall, his long legs stretched across the floor. Six feet tall and well-muscled thanks to the prison system, he was strong and in excellent shape, his blond hair cut short. He wondered if Tallie would recognize him. He dreamed of that moment.

He'd met people inside. He knew who to see about fake ID if he needed it and how to get some money. He figured it would be easy to find her and get things settled. Now, he just waited for word the parole board agreed Roy Peters was a model prisoner who deserved early release. He almost laughed when he thought about it. He deserved an Oscar.

"Ya think they're gonna do it, Roy buddy?"

Roy looked at his cellmate, not seeing him at first. Over the years, he'd conditioned himself to ignore the guy. Too much time together in a cramped space and Roy was sick of looking at him. He was blond and thinner than Roy but similar in height. Roy stared, not speaking.

"Let ya go, I mean," Eli said, looking at Roy with hope-filled eyes. "They let you go and you can set stuff up, just like we talked about. You'll help me out, just like you said." He swallowed. "I been in here so long, I don't know nothin' about livin' outside anymore."

"I know, Eli," Roy said.

"I'm supposed to be out in six months."

"I'm aware of that, Eli—"

"And I don't know nothin'. You're gonna help me. You promised, Roy—"

"Shut up, Eli. Your yammering is giving me a headache. I said I'd help you. I'll help you. Just shut the hell up," Roy said, tossing another playing card into the sink.

Eli's eyes flew open wide. "You said H-E double toothpicks, Roy."

Roy grinned. "Yes, I did."

"But Preacher says that's a bad word, Roy."

"Yes, it is."

Eli was speechless a moment. Roy wished he'd figured out how to do that earlier. Usually, Eli talked himself hoarse.

"So, um, Roy, whose gonna look out for me if they spring you early?" He wrung his hands. "There are some of those guys that scare me. Scare me a lot. Whose gonna—"

"You'll be all right, Eli. I talked with the chaplain, and he says he has a job for you. He'll take care of you."

Eli smiled. "Promise? Just like you promised to help when I get out, right?"

Roy nodded. The chaplain would take care of Eli in here, but after his release, Eli would find out soon enough what kind of help Roy would be to him. Zippo. Zilch. Eli had served his purpose for Roy just as he had for the friends who'd gotten the guy locked up. They sold Eli out and got him sent up for ten years. The guy wasn't too smart, and Roy used Eli's limited brainpower to his advantage by becoming his best friend. Nobody messed with Eli when Roy was around. He went out of his way to be helpful, especially when the guards watched, and the effort paid off. Roy Peters was considered a model prisoner, a do-gooder who looked after the simpleminded. Although, there were days he wondered if Eli was playing him false, too. Occasionally, there was a glimmer in Eli's eyes, like the guy was more intelligent than he let on. Maybe Eli wasn't as innocent as he wanted Roy to believe. Roy smiled at the thought. Most likely, he and Eli used each other. Eli had had Roy's protection from the other inmates and Roy might be getting out.

Everything was working out just fine.

9

Tuesday morning. The Stockton Management Nashville office was a madhouse, and Tallie hardly had a moment to sit back and contemplate her possible success at the hearing. She hadn't received official word yet but was confident her testimony about Roy's threats to her and Cody would out-weigh the prison officials' fantasy Roy was repentant and reformed. She knew better. Roy's mean streak had carved a Grand Canyon-sized channel through his heart and a few years in prison would have deepened the abyss.

He'd complete his sentence eventually and they'd let him go, but for now, Tallie had the necessary time to plan her relocation. With the job at Stockton Management, she'd put a little away every month. Not a lot, but enough to move later.

On her way home from work, she stopped for a few gro-ceries, having decided to invite Tom for dessert. She'd like to have Tom for dessert but settled on baking a peach pie. The pie would have to do until Tom Black a la mode could be added to her menu.

She juggled her grocery bags as she slid the key in the front door and barely caught them when the door swung open. Concentrating on balancing the bags, she maneuvered into the kitchen and slid them on the counter. A large hand clamped over her mouth and a well-muscled arm grabbed around her waist, squeezing like a boa constrictor until she couldn't breathe. Her first thought: rape. She tried to scream but the hand held tight. She squirmed and kicked, trying to get away.

"Hello, Tallie, long time no see," he said in her ear.

Tallie fought for freedom, screaming, but no sound escaped from behind his hand.

"Is that how you greet your loving husband? Seems like you'd want to give me a kiss hello after all these years. Maybe more than a kiss."

She struggled against his grasp but couldn't break free.

"I have a question for you. I'm going to take my hand off your mouth so you can answer me. If you scream, I'll snap your scrawny neck. Where is my boy?" He moved his hand from her mouth but slid it down her throat, his fingers digging into her flesh.

"I don't know. I just got home." Tears filled her eyes as Roy tightened his hold on her neck.

"You're lying. Don't try to tell me you don't know where he is while you're at work. Try again. Where is he?" He slid his hand to clasp her jaw, bruising her skin. Tallie sucked in her breath when the pain ripped through her jaw. It felt as if it would break from the pressure.

"Don't hurt me, please, Roy. He isn't here. He's staying with a friend out in the country. They'll bring him home soon."

"I should snap your neck right now. If you're lying to me, I don't have a problem finishing this. I'll be back in a while. He'd better be here." Roy tightened his hold on her waist as he squeezed her neck. Tallie gasped. "Call the cops and you're dead tonight. Try to play games with me, and I'll kill you both." Tired of the sport, he shoved her against the wall, knocking the wind from her lungs. She crumpled to the floor. "I'll be watching you."

Tallie curled up on the cold floor, waiting for the kick she knew would come. Roy always finished with a kick, kind of a sadistic trademark. He stood over her clenching his fists but turned and stomped out without a final blow. Tallie covered her head with her arms and tried to breathe.

She had to pull herself together. Time was running out, and she needed to act fast. She stumbled to her feet, wincing at the shock of pain through her shoulder. She grabbed a sack from under the sink, ran to the bedroom, and stuffed clothing in. If she could get to the car, there was a small chance she could flee. But she had to reach the neighbor's house and retrieve Cody without Roy seeing her.

Suddenly, the futility of it hit her.

He said he was watching. Roy would follow her and grab Cody as soon as he saw him, and petite Mrs. Tinker couldn't stop him any better than Tallie could. It was another of Roy's little games she'd nearly forgotten. He'd played with her this way during their marriage. He'd taunt and poke at her until she lost her temper, and it was anyone's guess how he would respond to her anger. Usually, it was the excuse he needed to teach her a lesson. Tonight was just another example of Roy's favorite game. Make a threat and retreat. Just when she thought it was safe and could relax, he'd come back full of accusations. She knew he was watching. He always did. Taking a deep breath, she tried to steady herself and think. Her gaze landed on the ingredients for Tom's pie. She needed help and there wasn't anyone else to call. She dialed his cell with shaking hands, praying Roy wasn't watching her that closely. Tom answered immediately.

"I need help," she whispered into the receiver, trying to control her fear. "I don't know what to do, Tom. Can you come?"

"Tallie? What's wrong?"

"He's out, Tom!" Something moved on the street and she screamed. Just a neighbor's dog. She turned from the window, afraid to look any longer.

"Tallie? What's wrong? Who are you talking about?"

"Roy. They let him out, and he was here. I'm so scared. He wants Cody and says he'll be back." She tried to control it, but her voice shook. "I'm scared. He said he'll kill me if I don't give him Cody."

"How did he get out? I thought the board recommended he stay locked up."

"I don't know," she said, her voice shaking harder. "But he was here, and he's coming back."

"I'm on my way. Call the police. I'll be there as quick as I can," he said.

"I can't call them. He's watching me and said he'll kill me tonight if I call them. I'm so scared."

"Okay. I'll figure something out. Where's Cody?"

"At his friend's house down the street."

"Can you call him and tell him to stay put and out of sight until I get there?"

"Yes, but hurry, Tom, please. I can't stop shaking."

"I'm on my way. Stay out of sight until I get there."

Tom disconnected the call, grabbed a rifle from the bedroom gun rack, and rummaged through a dresser drawer for ammo. He wouldn't use it, but Roy Peters didn't know it. Adequately armed, he sprinted up the stairs.

"Michael, I'm dropping you off with Harlie and Clay for a while. I need to run into town and I'll be back as soon as I can and no, you can't go." Tom headed downstairs with Michael on his heels.

"What's with the gun?"

"I don't have time to explain now. I'll tell you later. Come on." He rushed Michael to the truck and had it started and moving before the driver's door slammed shut.

Running as fast as his knee would allow, Tom burst into Clay's house. "Clay!" He ran through the kitchen and found his friends snuggled on the sofa in the living room.

Clay sat up straight and asked, "What's wrong?"

"I need to talk to you. Michael, stay here with Harlie." He motioned for Clay to follow him back to the kitchen.

"What's up?"

"Tallie called. They released her ex-husband from prison today. He's been to her place and threatened her. If she calls the cops, he said he'll kill her. He wants Cody. I'm on my way there to get her and I need Michael to stay here."

"Sure, no problem. I'll come with you."

"Like hell you will. I can't be worrying about you too. I'll call the cops when I get there." Tom started for the door.

"You can't do this by yourself, Tom. I'll call Phil and Stuart and have them meet you there. Give me the address."

"Good idea. Your bodyguards would make a good show for the creep to see." He wrote the address down and ran out the door. "I'll be back for Michael as soon as I can," he called over his shoulder.

"Don't worry about him. He's okay here," Clay said from the open doorway. "Be careful!"

CAUGHT IN THE SPIN

Tom jumped in his truck and spun gravel down the driveway.

࿇

Tallie made the call to the neighbor and told her to keep Cody out of sight. That done, she hid behind her bed, gripping a baseball bat. Her nerves were frayed. Her jaw throbbed and had turned a sickening purple. At a knock on the door, she almost screamed but realized it couldn't be Roy. He wouldn't knock. She managed to control her fear long enough to crawl into the living room. Peeking out the window, she saw two bulky men standing at her door. Both tall and solidly built, one with brown hair, the other blond. She doubted they were Jehovah's Witnesses or selling Avon. Both had an air about them that scared the heck out of her. Something lethal.

"Who is it?"

"Tallie Peters?" the darker of the two said.

"I know who I am. I asked who you are!"

"Clay Masterson called and said we needed to come over here until Tom arrives."

"How do I know you're telling the truth?" She gripped her baseball bat tighter and peeked out the window again. They were huge, muscled bodybuilders who looked like they could break her in half. No way would she trust them and give them the chance. They could easily be friends of Roy's.

"Call Tom. He'll tell you."

"Okay, I will." Tallie crawled into the kitchen and dialed Tom's number. "Did you send some men over here?"

"Are they there already? Let them in, honey. They're Clay's bodyguards, Phil and Stuart. They'll keep you safe until I get there."

"Okay. Are you coming now?"

"I'm almost there. Stay calm. You're safe with them."

Tallie hung up the phone and ran into the living room to open the door. "I'm sorry, but I didn't know what was going on." She felt foolish to have doubted their word. How would they know to mention Clay Masterson and Tom if he hadn't sent them himself? Fear had shocked her into imbecility.

"No problem. Has your ex been back yet?" Phil pulled his handgun from the holster and perused the street.

She shook her head. "No, he hasn't."

"Why don't you relax for a minute and I'll look around." Phil stalked around the house like a panther, glancing out windows and checking behind doors.

"Are you okay, Tallie?" Stuart asked, studying the bruises on her neck and jaw.

"I'm better now you're here. Roy said he would come back tonight to get my son. We need to get him without Roy seeing us."

"Tom will be here soon, and we'll figure it out." Stuart stepped to the window. A few minutes later, tires screeching to a stop signaled a new arrival. "I'd say that's him." Stuart opened the front door.

Tom ran in, rifle in hand. "Thanks for coming, Stu. Where is she?"

Stuart pointed to Tallie standing in the kitchen door. Tom leaned the gun against the sofa, rushed to her, grabbed her into his arms, and held her tight. She gasped, and he loosened his hold. Shock registered across his face when he saw the bruises on her neck. "He hurt you. How did he get out? They said they wouldn't let him go."

Tallie clung to Tom, needing an anchor. She shook her

head and whispered, "I don't know."

"It's okay,' he said. "We'll call the cops and report this and get Cody."

She reared back. "No! We can't call them. He's watching. He always watches me." A shudder ran through her, and she clung tighter to Tom. "He's out there...waiting somewhere." Her breath came in gasps as the panic took hold. It was just like before...Roy would be back and she would pay for this.

Tom gently cupped her face in his hands, mindful of her darkening bruises "Tallie, you aren't alone anymore. There are three armed men in this house. If Roy wants to try something, I'll blow his head off." Tom wrapped his arm around Tallie's shoulder, keeping her close, while he dialed 9-1-1.

Stuart met the police officers on the sidewalk, showed his ID, and explained the situation. Tom paced across the living room, tension radiating from him in waves. Tallie made coffee to keep her mind occupied.

When the first officer entered the room, Tom came unglued. "How did that guy get released? I want to know right now!"

"We don't know yet," the officer said, unruffled by Tom's outburst. "I need to talk to Miss Peters first." The officer nodded to her as she came in from the kitchen. "Miss Peters? Can you tell me what happened?"

"Yes." She nodded, wincing at the sudden movement. She took Tom's hand, leading him to the sofa to sit next to her. She began at the beginning, explaining the parole hearing and ending with Tom arriving. "We need to get my son now, please. He isn't safe."

"I'll send a couple of officers to get him. What's the address?"

Tallie found a piece of paper, jotted it down, and handed it to the officer. "It's only six houses down. I'll call and let them know." Tallie took the cell phone Tom offered her and made the call.

"We'll do some checking on his release and see what we can find out. Where will you be, Miss Peters?" the officer asked.

"I guess I could take Cody to a motel." She looked from one man to the other, a frantic feeling growing within her.

Tom pulled a card from his wallet and handed it to the officer. "She'll be here if you need to call her."

"The Masterson-Black Ranch? Clay Masterson's place?"

Tom nodded.

Tallie shook her head. "No. I can't impose on you, Tom. We'll go to a motel."

"No, you won't. He'll follow you and take Cody. You can stay with me."

"It's a safe location for you, Miss Peters. From what I've heard, Clay Masterson's place is one of the most secure estates in the Nashville area."

"Get your stuff packed, Tallie. I'm not leaving you anywhere. I have an extra bedroom and Cody can have the other bunk in Michael's room." Tom gave her a gentle hug, careful not to squeeze too tight. "Go get your stuff."

She nodded numbly and went into her room to pack.

"Where's my mom?" she heard Cody say as the front door slammed. "What's wrong?"

"She's in the bedroom, packing some stuff. Go give her a hand and she'll explain it to you," Tom said.

When Cody was inside the bedroom, Tom lowered his voice and spoke with the officer. "I want some answers. Roy Peters has been threatening to kill her for years. He's been out less than one day and has already assaulted her and threatened to take her son. I want to know how he got out when the parole board recommended he serve his full sentence. As long as he's free, she's in danger."

"I'll check it out and let you know. I have officers in the area, but they haven't seen him yet. When he's found, he'll go back in on assault charges for what he did tonight. Stupid, isn't he?" The officer shook his head in amazement.

"Stupid and extremely dangerous," Tom said. "I need to help Tallie. Will you be here for a while?"

"We'll make sure he isn't close by and leave when you do."

"Thanks." Tom shook the officer's hand and went to find Tallie. He stood in the bedroom doorway listening as Tallie talked to Cody, and he found another reason to despise Roy Peters. Tallie sat with her arms around the crying boy, trying to ease his fears.

"They have to find him, Mom. They have to. He'll hurt us like he did before." He sobbed into Tallie's shoulder. "Why does he want to hurt us?"

"I don't know, Cody. But I won't let him near you again. He won't have a chance to hurt you. I promise."

"He'll come back, Mom. After everybody leaves, he'll come back tonight."

"We aren't staying here tonight. That's why I'm packing some clothes for us. Tom is taking us to his house to stay. We'll be safe there." She wiped his tears.

"Tom has a gun. Is he going to shoot Roy?" Cody asked.

"I don't think that will be necessary. Not with the police, Clay's bodyguards, and Tom here. Roy wouldn't dare come here now."

"I wish Tom would shoot him right between the eyes."

Tom winced. This was his own father Cody wanted dead. "Do you need some help, Tallie?" Tom asked from the doorway, trying to calm his rising anger. How could a man damage his own family this way? Tom felt ill at the thought. He wanted to hug them and keep them safe. "The police are waiting for us to leave."

Tallie stood, looking sad and shaken. "I have a pile of my stuff ready. Come on, Cody. Let's get yours. The suitcases are in your closet." She guided her son from the room and Tom collected her clothes from the bed.

The last of the clothes were packed and loaded into the backseat of Tom's truck. Tom asked Stuart to drive Tallie's Chevy Celebrity to his place. They were on their way out when Tallie paused and ran into the kitchen, returning with a grocery bag.

"What's all this?"

"I'd planned to bake a pie tonight and invite you over. I'll do it tomorrow. You really deserve a pie now." She tried to smile but winced.

He put his arm around her and walked her to the truck.

On the road, Tom called Clay. "I'll pick Michael up on the way," he said.

"Don't worry about him. He and Harlie are playing Monopoly and he's winning." He laughed. "Harlie keeps telling him they should turn some of the hotels into homeless shelters, and he's having a good time trying to figure her out. Get Tallie and Cody settled in, and I'll run him home."

"Thanks, I appreciate that. And thanks for calling Stu and Phil. I was relieved to find them there when I arrived." Tom pulled into his driveway and stopped. "We're heading in. I'll see you in a bit."

As Cody climbed from the truck, Cookie and Clyde barked and jumped on him, demanding attention. Tom smiled as he watched the boy drop to his knees and hug the dogs. It was the most normal thing he'd seen all evening. He and Tallie followed Cody to the porch.

"Let's go in, Cody. You can bring the dogs. They sleep in Michael's room upstairs." Tom opened the door, directing Cody in. Tallie stood on the porch, looking around. The sun had set and the sky was gray.

"Tom," she said. "Thank you. If it weren't for you..." She bit her lip and swallowed hard.

"Hey, don't do that. You're safe now. He can't get to you here." Tom guided her in the door. "Come on, Cody. I'll show you and your mom where your rooms are."

He led them upstairs, stopped at Michael's room, and slid his hand over the light switch. "You can bunk here with Michael. Dogs, too." He gave Cody what he hoped was a reassuring smile. "Tallie, your room is down here." He opened a door further along the hall. The room was decorated in soft, feminine hues: an apricot quilt, matching curtains, and striped wallpaper.

Tallie stepped in and glanced around. "This is nice, Tom."

"My sister did it when she came to visit. She thought the guest room should have a few girly frills. I'll bring your stuff up." He hesitated to leave her when she looked so wilted and defeated. "The bathroom is across the hall. How about if I run some bath water for you? A hot soak might make you feel better."

She gave him a slight smile, wincing. "That sounds wonderful."

"I'll take care of it." He left, stopping at Michael's room on his way by. Cody sat on the floor, hugging the dogs. "You okay, Cody?" The boy nodded. "I'll get your clothes and you can get ready for bed. Michael will be here soon."

After several trips, the truck was emptied. He stopped in the kitchen to fix a mug of tea and went to check on Tallie, who met him at the bathroom, refreshed and wrapped in a large terry robe.

"Better?"

"Much. Is that for me?" she asked when she noticed the hot steaming mug smelling of chamomile.

"I thought it might calm your nerves. It's that sleepy-time stuff. My sister left it." He shrugged.

"You are calming my nerves. Thanks so much."

"You don't have to keep thanking me. I'm glad I have a safe place for you." He heard the hum of Clay's pickup in the driveway. Moments later, the downstairs door opened and closed. "That's Michael. I need to talk to him. Go on to bed, and I'll get Cody settled in." He handed her the mug and went downstairs to find Clay and Michael. "You have a roommate for a while, Michael."

"Who?"

"Cody. He's upstairs."

"Cool!" he said and ran up the stairs without waiting for more information.

"Thanks for keeping him, Clay. I wouldn't have wanted him there tonight."

"Did you see the guy?"

"No, I'm sure he ran as soon as we got there. He's the type that likes to beat up on women and kids. Grown men are more than he wants to tangle with. Tallie is calmer now. She looked pretty wild when I got there." Tom frowned. "He hurt her. Bruised her around the neck and I'm not sure where else. She's favoring her shoulder, so I think he slammed her around some. The cops are checking to see why he was released and should be calling tomorrow."

"It's good she called you. Keep us posted, okay? I gotta go or Harlie will wonder what happened to me. Night," he called as he walked out the door, shutting it quietly behind him.

Tom let out a breath, debating if he should go upstairs. Michael would help Cody settle in and he'd be fine, but Tallie might need something. He went upstairs and found he was correct about the boys. Michael helped Cody put his stuff away and they were talking. He tapped on Tallie's door, peeking in when she called to him.

"Come in." She patted the spot next to her on the bed. She wore a big pink T-shirt and was tucked under the covers, looking at a romance novel. Tom noticed the book cover and blushed. It was an erotic romance and the cover art went beyond suggestive.

He frowned. "I don't... My sister again..." he said, pointing at the book. Tallie smiled at his discomfort and patted the space next to her again. He sat and brushed his fingertips across her bruised neck. His frown deepened. "I hate it that he got his hands on you, Tallie. Are you hurt anywhere else?"

"My jaw is sore and my right shoulder is bruised where

he threw me against the wall."

Tom grimaced when she mentioned the abuse. If he ever got his hands on that bastard...

"The hot bath helped ease the soreness. I know you won't want to hear this, but it isn't any different than what he did when we were married. Roy said I had lessons to learn."

She was right. Hearing about Roy Peters' brutality against his family made him sick. "He hit Cody too, didn't he? I heard him talking to you in your bedroom."

She nodded. "I decided I had to get away from him when he started hitting Cody. He thought I was making him soft, so he hit him to toughen him. Cody was only four years old when he started hating his daddy."

"He won't touch him again, Tallie. I promise. You can stay here as long as necessary." He rubbed his hand across her cheek, so tempted to lay down with her and give her what comfort he could. But he knew where it might lead and he wasn't planning to do that. He'd offered her a safe place to stay and the offer didn't hinge on her sleeping with him. He wouldn't have Tallie feeling pressured to be with him. "I'll get you some pain reliever." He left the room to find what he needed in his bathroom and returned with the tablets and water. After she'd swallowed them, he kissed her on the forehead and wished her good-night. It was the last time he planned to touch her while she stayed in his home.

Michael let Cody and the dogs settle into the bottom bunk, while he took the top. They lay quietly in the dark until Cody broke the silence.

"Mike? You awake?" he whispered.

"Yeah."

"Can I ask you something?"

"Yeah."

"Does Tom ever hit you?"

"No. Why?" Michael leaned his head down over the side of the bunk, but he couldn't see more than an outline of Cody in the dark.

"Cause my dad hit me a lot. I thought maybe all dads did."

"No. Never. Why did Tom bring you and your mom here tonight?" Michael asked. "He took his gun with him. How come? Nobody would tell me anything."

"Cause my dad beat up my mom. He got out of prison today and wanted to take me away from her."

"Did my dad...Tom," he said, correcting himself, "shoot your dad?"

"No, he came with two other big guys with guns and they called the cops. It was so cool, Mike!" Cody sat up in bed. "Two cops came to get me at my friend's house and I rode in their patrol car. When I got to my house, Tom and these other guys were there with guns. It was just like a western movie. Tom is so cool."

"You think so?"

"Yeah. Tom is the coolest. You're so lucky he's your dad. I wish he was mine." Cody lay back on his pillow.

"He is kind of cool, isn't he?" Michael said, more to himself than to Cody. "We better go to sleep. Tom makes me get up in the morning and work with him sometimes."

"Can I go to work too?"

"Yeah, you can work too. Night."

Tom heard the boys' voices as he walked by but decided

to let them talk. Cody needed to talk to someone and Michael was his best buddy now. He thought of all the times he and Clay had talked about things and was glad the boys had each other. It started when Clay was two and his mother died. Shortly after, his father abandoned him and the Blacks became his foster family.

As if they kept an imaginary balance sheet, Clay helped Tom when Jolie left, giving him a chance to make something of his life after he fell apart. Tom repaid the gesture and did what he could to help Clay and Harlie get back together after they blew apart. They always picked each other up from one thing or another. He couldn't have a better friend than Clay and hoped the boys upstairs would have that too.

He walked through the house, checking door locks and turning off lights. Before climbing into his bed, he worked the kinks from his knee as he did every night and thought about Tallie upstairs. It would be difficult to stay away from her; just thinking about her laying up there alone drove him crazy. As he drifted off to sleep, his last thoughts were of her and how good her soft skin felt under his hands.

10

Tom woke early. He showered, shaved, and dressed for work in Wranglers and a green chambray shirt before heading to the kitchen to start the coffee and listen to the morning news on the kitchen TV. He needed to go to the office and brief the guys on his guests and wanted an early start.

Not only did his crew work the ranch, they were also the security force. Most of them lived off the ranch but used the bunkhouse when on security detail. One of the single guys stayed in the bunkhouse full time. In all the years Tom had handled the security for Clay, no one had come on the property who shouldn't. That included vandals, thieves, and whacked-out fans who plagued Clay Masterson everywhere he went. And the guy had millions of them.

Each night, one crew member took a shift watching the security monitors and driving the ranch. All employees underwent thorough security checks and were fired immediately if found untrustworthy. No one was allowed on security until they'd been on the payroll for a while and had proven themselves. Problems seldom occurred because Tom personally handled the employment issues on the ranch. Occasionally, he delegated some duties to his foreman, Lon Taylor, but not often. Because of his diligence, he was confident Roy Peters wouldn't get near Tallie or Cody as long as they stayed within his security gates.

Hearing footsteps behind him, Tom turned to see Tallie in a sky-blue dress and high heels. Sexy wasn't adequate to describe her. Devastating was a better description. He gulped. "You are the prettiest thing we've seen around here for some time." He couldn't help but stare at her legs. "But aren't you a little overdressed for this neighborhood?"

"Thank you for the compliment." She grinned until her dimples drove him wild. "I may be overdressed for here, but I won't be when I get to work." She grabbed the coffee cup Tom set out for her and poured a steaming cup.

"Work?"

"Yeah, as in my job. Cody can hang out with Michael today, can't he?"

Tom had the feeling he'd landed in some alternate universe where Roy Peters hadn't assaulted her last night. The bruises on her neck and jaw had turned purple, reminding him of every detail of the previous evening. She'd tried to cover the bruises with makeup, but they were still visible. "You can't go to work, Tallie."

"I have to. I can't afford to lose my job." She sipped her coffee and stared at him through the steam.

Tom scowled and rubbed the back of his neck. "You're telling me you're driving into the city today after your ex-husband threatened to kill you and steal your son?"

"I'll be okay. He won't bother me at work," she said.

"No!" He paced across the kitchen. "You aren't leaving! Didn't you hear the cop last night when he said this was the safest place for you?"

"Tom, I'll be okay."

"Tallie, he may not get to you in the building, but what about walking to and from your car? You aren't leaving."

She set her jaw and glared. "I can't afford to lose my job, Tom. I have to risk it."

"No, you don't. I'll call Harv and explain it to him."

"He's in meetings all morning." She looked at the clock. "In fact, he's already started. You won't get through to him, and I'll get fired for not showing up."

Tom pulled his cell phone from the charger and hit a speed dial number.

"Harv? Tom." He leaned on the counter, glaring at Tallie.

"Just a second, Tom," Harv said. "Can you gentlemen excuse me for a moment while I take this call? Thanks. What's up?"

"I have a situation here. Tallie Peters' ex-husband assaulted her and tried to kidnap her son last night."

"Are you kidding? Is she okay?"

"Not kidding, and other than some bumps and bruises, she's fine. She called me. I went in with Phil and Stu and brought her here to the ranch."

"Did the cops get the guy?"

"No. That's the problem. They're looking for him and recommended she stay here," he said and gave Tallie a pointed stare, "where she's safe until they get him back in custody."

"Good idea. I wouldn't want anything happening to her."

"So that brings us to her job. She won't be able to come in until this is over. The guy is still after her." Tom kept his eyes on Tallie while he talked. Her annoyance with him was obvious, but he didn't care. She wasn't leaving if he had anything to do with it.

"I understand. Tell her to take as much time off as she needs. We'll survive."

"She's worried you'll fire her. I didn't know you were

such a hard ass, Harv." Tom chuckled.

"I didn't know I was either. She doesn't have anything to worry about. She's a good employee. I don't want to lose her and I don't want her hurt. Take care of her, Tom."

"Will do." Tom disconnected the call and stared at Tallie. "He won't fire you."

Tallie crossed her arms and scowled at Tom. "How did you do that? His secretary never interrupts Mr. Stockton's meetings."

"Secretary? I've never talked to one. I have Harv's personal cell phone on speed dial. I talk to him all the time." He smiled. "Honey, I handle the security for one of the biggest stars in country music, a guy Harv depends on for his livelihood. When I call, Harv Stockton talks to me."

"Oh." She blushed.

"Why don't you change into something more..." He gave her an appreciative once-over and swallowed. "Casual, and I'll take you on a tour of the ranch after breakfast. Do you think those lazy boys will want to go with us?" He hoped so. No telling what he'd be tempted to do if they were alone all day. He could see their tour including Clay's bus, or maybe the little cabin on the other side of the pond, or any number of secluded places where one thing could easily lead to another.

"I'll check while I'm upstairs." She walked from the room, turning back to see him watching her.

She returned with two sleepy boys who were dressed but grumbling. Tom wondered if Tallie owned any clothes that wouldn't put his senses on high alert. He hadn't figured out yet how he would keep from touching her. And her wandering around in low-cut Levis and a close-fitting T-shirt was going to drive him insane. The effect those jeans had on her butt was the stuff of dreams. He jammed his hands in his pockets to keep from grabbing her.

He made it through breakfast and started his tour in the office, where he introduced Tallie and Cody to Lon and the ranch hand on duty. The security monitors and the gun cabinet fascinated Cody. Michael had already seen it and wanted to move on.

Tallie enjoyed sitting next to Tom as he drove the ranch, pointing out corrals, the practice arena, old barns topped with antique weathervanes, and the bunkhouse. The boys were allowed to explore but a few places were off-limits. The bullpens were at the top of the prohibited list. He also pointed out the perimeter fence was electric on the top and the jolt could cause serious damage, like death. And much to the boys' dismay, the boat required an adult presence. But they could fish the bank if they wanted.

While they drove, Tallie reached for Tom's hand. He gave hers a squeeze and moved his hand to the steering wheel. He parked the truck near the boat dock and turned the boys loose to run the path around the ten-acre pond. Tallie and Tom followed, their pace a romantic stroll. Or it would be if Tom removed his hands from his pockets. He did, but only to indicate a scenic spot.

"Clay and I dug this pond," he said. "It was a bitty stock pond when he bought the place. We dug it out, stretched it to about ten acres, and stocked it with fish." As punctuation, a trout leapt from the water and returned with a splash. The path meandered along the perimeter, winding through tall grasses and trees. A slight breeze slapped water against the bank. The boys were at the head end, racing. Tallie heard their occasional shouts. A blue Herron stood on the opposite shore, a sentinel watching their progress. Otherwise, she and Tom were alone. Tallie left the trail, stepping beneath a willow whose branches hung low. She could hear birds rustling in the leaves. Tom didn't follow her detour.

"Tom?" she called from beneath the willow canopy.

"What?"

"Can you come here, please?"

"Why?"

"There's a bird I want you to look at."

"It's probably a sparrow."

Tallie let out a huff. "Or maybe it isn't. Hurry, before it's gone."

The willow branches parted and Tom gingerly stepped in, looking up into the branches, his head cocked, listening to the birds' twittering. "Where is it?"

"Here," she whispered. Tallie leaned against the tree, pointing up. "Come closer, you'll see it." Tom stepped near her, still staring up.

"I don't see——"

"It's right here." Tallie grabbed his shirt front and pulled him against her. Her mouth was on his before he could argue or move away. He didn't appear inclined to do either. She wrapped one arm around his neck, while the other hand remained fisted in his shirt, holding him tight. Her kiss was steaming hot and he sunk into it. He tasted of the butterscotch Lifesavers he had in the truck, decadent and sweet. She wanted more and not from the candy package.

The day was hot and muggy, but beneath the willow, the

air was cool, contrasting with the heat emanating from Tom's rock-solid body. He braced his hand against the tree, careful not to smash her against the trunk, taking the kiss deeper, taking control. The man's lips were medicinal. While he kissed her, she forgot about her achy jaw and the pain in her shoulder. To heck with pain medication—Tom's kisses were the best pain reducer she'd ever experienced. She could easily overdose.

She released the fabric fisted in her hand and caressed his chest. He moaned. "Tallie." His lips trailed from her mouth to her neck. She tipped her head back, wincing as she stretched. But she didn't care. He nibbled her ear, tenderly kissed her bruised jaw, and returned to her lips. His hand pressed against her lower back, his fingers venturing into her jeans waistband, lower, lower. Tallie gasped, thrilled by his intimate caress, wanting more.

He pressed against her. "Tallie, I want—"

"MOM! Where are you? MOM! Come here."

Tom groaned and muttered, "Damn." He looked into Tallie's eyes, his stare heated and his breath heavy. His focus drifted to her bruises. He touched her sore shoulder and frowned.

"MOM!"

"TOM!"

"Just a sec," he yelled. He stepped away from Tallie, attempting to catch his breath. "I'm sorry."

"Why?"

"I shouldn't have..."

"Tom!" Michael yelled again. "Where are you?"

"Shouldn't have what?" she asked.

He shook his head. "Never mind." He gave her a long

stare before parting the branches for his retreat. Tallie swallowed hard and pressed her fingers to her lips.

"Tom! Come here. You gotta see this!" she heard Michael yell to his father. Tallie waited for her heart's return to normal rhythm and followed Tom through the branches.

Partway down the trail, Cody, Michael, and Tom stood in a hunched circle, looking at something dark in the path. Cody saw Tallie and ran to her, grabbing her hand.

"Come on, Mom. You gotta see this. Tom says it could be old."

Tom looked up as Cody pulled his mom to where they stood. His eyes held none of their earlier heat. But something else lingered there. Remorse. He was sorry he kissed her. Why? Most likely, it was the bruises. She was another man's punching bag and it bothered him.

Cody dropped to his knees and looked the black-and-orange critter in the eye.

"It's a box turtle," Tom told him. "We have a dozen or so around here." Michael had a leaf and tried to interest the turtle in a snack. He wasn't buying it. "They don't eat leaves, Michael. Snails, bugs, salamanders, that kind of stuff. They like some greens but not the leaves. This guy is probably on his way to the water to hunt, so let's let him get to it. He needs to get out of the hot sun. We need to go too."

Michael and Cody were reluctant to leave but Tom didn't offer a choice. As they drove to the house, Tom's cell phone rang.

"Tom Black...Yeah, Detective, can you hold on a second?" Tom pulled up to the house and parked. "Michael, why don't you and Cody head in the house for a snack? There are Oreos in the can if you want them." The boys jumped from the truck and ran inside. Tallie stayed, wanting to hear the conversation. Tom put the cell phone on speaker.

"Any news on Roy Peters?" Tom asked.

"Yes, sir."

"What is it?"

"Well, I'm afraid this is one of those 'Does this shit really happen?' stories that happen all too often. The parole board did recommend they keep ol' Roy locked up for the duration of his sentence."

"We were at the hearing and thought it amazing they let him go."

"It's unfortunate, but this situation isn't amazing but normal. You see, it's a money thing. Bad economy, budget cuts, and such. Some state bean counter decided they needed to empty a few prison beds, so a handful of prisoners got a lucky break. Roy was one of them." He sighed. "From a law-enforcement viewpoint, it's a frustrating thing. We work our tails off to lock them up and accountants let them go."

Tom shook his head. "But why Roy? He has a violent history and has made threats against Tallie and her son. They had to know he was a risk."

"What I'm hearing is, the prison chaplain made quite a case for Roy."

"The chaplain?" Tom frowned.

Tallie looked at him with a questioning look. "Roy's never been to church in his life."

"Well, ma'am," the detective said, "it appears Roy found religion."

"He WHAT?" she said, astounded.

"Yes, ma'am. The chaplain says Roy had an 'experience'

and was born again. They spent many hours together, discussing theology and good works Roy could accomplish while incarcerated." He paused. "Roy even ran a prayer group and was the star pupil in the anger management class. They said he was a master at role-playing."

"Oh, good grief," Tallie said. "And they believed he changed so dramatically?"

"Yes, ma'am. It's been known to happen, and in many cases, the inmates are quite sincere. In Roy's case, the chaplain bought it hook, line, and sinker. The poor man is quite shocked over Roy's behavior these past days. Before his release, Roy told him he planned to go to seminary and preach when he got out. Said he wanted to help those like himself avoid the mistakes he made. It's obvious now it was just a ruse. We'll keep looking for him. He's been to his house but didn't check in with his parole officer. We'd have grabbed him there if he'd shown up. Let us know if you see him out your way."

Tom sighed. "Yeah, if a guy wearing a warped halo comes to the ranch, I'll give you a call. Thanks for the update, Detective." He disconnected the call and looked at Tallie.

She shook her head. "Well, that's just dandy, isn't it? I'm the victim of a bad economy." She wanted to hit something or someone. After the way Tom looked at her when he walked away earlier, he was as good a candidate as any. But when he looked at her with those concerned green eyes, she melted. The man turned her to goo.

"They'll find him, Tallie. And until they do, you're safe here." He gave her thigh an impersonal pat, almost brotherly. Tallie waited for more, a comforting hug or even a warm kiss on the cheek, but Tom pulled the keys from the ignition and climbed from the truck.

Tallie watched him retreat into the house. She wasn't sure how it happened, but somewhere along the way, she'd gone from potential lover to freeloading roommate, and she was confused as to what brought on the change. But a change had certainly occurred.

She climbed from the truck and slammed the door. Well, it could sure as heck change back, and Tallie planned to use every weapon in her arsenal to turn him from the indifferent path he was on.

After dinner, the boys played on the porch with the dogs, leaving Tom and Tallie alone to clear the dishes. Until she'd shanghaied him into that incredible kiss under the willow, Tom thought he'd handled the no-touch state of affairs quite well. But he lost his willpower when she locked her mouth on his. It wasn't going to happen again. Unfortunately, it appeared she intentionally did things to drive him crazy. Or maybe he was hypersensitive. When she loaded the dishwasher, he swore she bent over further than necessary and when she rinsed the dishes, she had a way of scrubbing the plates that made her breasts sway. He had to stop his head from swinging along with the motion. He hoped they found Roy soon before he dragged her into his bedroom.

The dishes finished, Tallie left the kitchen, her hips swinging like liquid swishing in a glass. Tom covered his face with his hands and groaned.

"Did you say something?" she asked from the door.

"No." He looked up from his hands and shook his head vigorously. "I have something in my eye."

"Oh." She sighed with sympathy. "Come over in the light, and I'll see if I can get it out."

"It's okay. I think it's gone now." Tom blinked a few times to prove it. He tried to back up, but she caught him and led him to the light over the sink.

"Oh, come on, tough guy. I'll look at it for you." She pulled on his eyelid, trying to see.

He felt like such an idiot.

"I guess it is gone. I don't see anything."

She was so close he could feel her warm breath on his skin; her lips were close enough to kiss.

"Blink your eyes," she said.

"What?"

She giggled. "Blink your eyes and see if it's gone."

"What's gone?"

She giggled again. "The thing in your eye."

The only thing in his eye was an eyeball. Oh, yeah, the dust or whatever was supposed to be there. "It's fine now. Thank you." He backed up and walked from the kitchen.

In bull riding, there was a name for this tricky maneuver. It was called bailing out.

⊙❧

Roy Peters had seriously screwed up. If he'd controlled the urge to confront Tallie, he'd have grabbed Cody by now and been long gone. Now, he lay low, using his prison contacts for a place to stay. The cops were crawling all over the place, including his house. He'd started working on the fake ID. The mustache he'd started growing and the glasses found in a costume shop completed the new look. "Gives you a choirboy look," the salesgirl said.

The night Tallie took off, Roy followed at a distance and

found where she was staying—a fortress with security guards, an advanced security system, and a high-voltage electric fence. He wondered who lived there and how Tallie had connected with them. The gate was marked MB Ranch, but that didn't mean a thing to him. Masterson-Black meant even less. Some rich asshole was all he knew. Tallie's kind of people.

The following day, he drove the area and found a spot near a neighbor's barn where he could watch the ranch entrances to see who came and went. His anger spiked when he spotted Tallie and Cody riding in a pickup with that black-haired guy and another kid. Roy hoped to get a shot at the guy when he finished with Tallie.

By early afternoon, he thought he'd hit pay dirt when a young woman drove out. Thinking she looked more like an employee than a resident, he followed her into town. She made stops at the drugstore and the bank before visiting a sandwich shop.

Roy grinned when he thought how easy this would be. The girl would be flattered if he talked to her. With his looks, well-toned body, and charm, she'd be putty in his hands. They all were.

He watched her enter the shop, order food at the counter, and find a seat. The shop wasn't full but held enough patrons she wouldn't think it odd he wanted to sit with her. He glanced her way as he walked in and ordered an iced tea. She noticed him, just as he'd counted on. Women always did. Roy paid for his drink and stood back from the counter, pretending to search for a seat before approaching her table, wearing a smile guaranteed to have her panting for him.

"This place is real full today. Mind if I share your table?"

he drawled, turning on his southern charm.

"No, not at all." She visibly swallowed.

"Why is a pretty girl like you sitting alone?" he asked and wasn't disappointed when she blushed.

"I'm just doing errands for my boss."

"Are you now? I'll bet a pretty thing like you must be a personal assistant to some important executive or something." He sipped his tea and kept his demeanor serious.

She laughed shyly. "Oh no, I'm a nanny. I take care of a little one-year-old baby."

"I'll bet you're real good at that. There's just something sweet about you." He gave her a look that would melt a woman more seasoned in seduction and decided to tone it down a bit before they had to carry her out. "Do you work close by here?"

"No, out in the country, at Clay Masterson's place." She offered the information innocently.

"Clay Masterson? The country singer?"

She nodded.

That explained the security. "That must be a great place to work," he said. "They have a cattle ranch, don't they?"

"Yes, they do. Cattle, horses, and bulls."

"Hmm. You know, I've been thinking I'd like to change jobs, and I heard they are good to work for there. Would you know if they're hiring?"

"Yes, I think they are. I heard Mr. Black talking to Mr. Masterson about needing a few more ranch hands."

Roy tried to contain his elation at hearing that welcome disclosure. "You wouldn't happen to have the phone number where I could call this Mr. Black, would you?"

"No, I don't, but I can get it." Her face lit up.

"What's your phone number, sweetie? I'll call you. Here, write it and your name on this." He handed her a napkin. "I'll call you tomorrow. Maybe you and I can go out sometime." He looked at the napkin she handed him. "Gail. A pretty name for a pretty girl. I'll be calling."

"Okay." She sighed. "Oh, wait a minute. You can't call tomorrow. I'll be busy all day."

"Oh?" Roy feigned interest even though he had the needed information. She'd probably be up to her ears in baby drool and he didn't care to hear about it. There was only one kid of interest to him. Cody.

"Yes. It's so exciting." She grinned. "There will be a film crew on the ranch all day filming Mr. Masterson's video for his new song. They want Mrs. Masterson and the baby in it, so I have to be there while they film to help with the baby. I've never seen a film crew before."

That piqued Roy's interest. "Well, that does sound exciting. They'll be there all day, you say?"

"Mm hmm. I have to have the baby ready by eight in the morning, and they'll be there until evening. They're bringing caterers and everything."

"I'll bet it takes a lot of people to film a video." Roy worked the angles, figuring out how he could use this situation to his advantage. If he could sneak in with the film crew, he could get his kid and be gone by tomorrow night.

"I think so," Gail agreed with a nod. "There will be lots of people from his manager's office, and security will be pretty tight, from what I hear."

"Oh?" Roy sat back in his seat and tried to conceal his excitement. This girl was a gold mine of information.

"Mm hmm. Mr. Black is having all the ranch hands on

security detail for the day."

"Well, that does sound like an exciting day for you. I'll bet you love your job." Roy wanted to bolt and make plans for the morning, but he didn't want Gail getting suspicious.

"Oh, I do. I love babies and Mrs. Masterson is so nice to work for." She sighed as a dreamy look entered her eyes. "And Clay Masterson is so handsome and nice, too."

"What about this Mr. Black? What's he like?"

"Oh, he's handsome too. Like you are." She blushed and looked away. "He's nice too. The ranch hands say he's good to work for. And his girlfriend is so pretty."

Roy tensed at the mention of Tallie. "Probably not as pretty as you." He smiled and winked as Gail blushed again. "He'd probably have his girlfriend there to watch the filming, wouldn't he?"

"Oh, I'm sure of it. Tallie works for Mr. Stockton, Mr. Masterson's manager, so she'll be there for sure. And I'll bet her son will want to watch too. It's so exciting. He won't want to miss it either."

Roy almost jumped from his seat and danced a jig. This was just too easy. "I'd best be getting along." On impulse, he leaned across the table and kissed her on the lips. She nearly stopped breathing. "It was nice meeting you, and I'll be calling."

Gail stared at him in amazement. "Okay."

He winked at her, walked out of the sandwich shop, and made a beeline to the MB Ranch.

11

"Come on, boys! I need to be at Clay's before the film crew gets here!" Tom yelled up the stairs. "Hurry up or walk!"

"Let them walk, Tom. It's not far and I need to go too," Tallie said from the front door. "If you don't hurry, you may be walking."

"We need both vehicles anyway, Tallie. Go on. I know you're excited to get to work. I'll bring the boys." He started up the stairs. "Tell Harv and Clay I'll be there in a minute."

"Okay. They'll have things for me to do, so I'll see you there." She stepped through the door with a skip in her step, happy to do something other than sit around. If Tom would pay her a bit of attention, it wouldn't be so bad, but she had begun to feel like an unwanted houseguest. She still hadn't figured out what happened to cool Tom off.

She wound her way through the ranch, parking her car near Clay's shop. As she walked into the yard, Harlie hailed her.

"I'm glad you're here." Harlie walked up to her, looking relieved. "I'm so freaked out about this."

"Why?" Tallie said as Harlie fell into step with her.

"I've never done this before. Clay says, relax. Harv says it's no big deal." She shook her head and sighed. "It is a big deal and I can't relax."

"Would it make you feel any better if I said I'd feel the same way? I've never been in front of a camera before, and I think it would scare me to death."

Harlie stopped and gave Tallie a relieved smile. "Thank you. I knew you'd understand. I'm terrified. What if I screw up? What if I make Clay look bad?"

Tallie set her hands on Harlie's shoulders and looked up into her fretful eyes. "You'll be great. And if you aren't, there is such a thing as editing. This isn't live television." She released Harlie with a reassuring squeeze. "Let's go get some coffee. Maybe that will help." Harlie nodded numbly and followed along.

The caterers had arrived early and erected a breakfast table in the backyard. Tallie and Harlie helped themselves to steaming cups of coffee and were joined by Harv Stockton. Tallie did a double take when she saw her boss in shorts and a George Strait concert tour T-shirt. She'd never seen Mr. Stockton in anything other than an expensive, well-tailored suit.

"Mr. Stockton?"

"Morning, Tallie." Harv greeted her with a smile. "You know, you've worked for me for months now. I think you can call me Harv. Everybody else does."

Harlie laughed. "You don't look like a 'Mr. Stockton' in those shorts anyway. Nice legs. All that tennis pays off."

He grinned at the compliment. "It's too hot for a suit." He looked at Tallie. "Call me Harv, all right?"

"Okay." Tallie agreed.

"So how are things? Any word on your ex-husband?" he asked.

Tallie shook her head. "Nothing." Not wanting to talk about her unpleasant personal life, she glanced around at the assembled crew. "What would you like me to do today?"

"Not sure yet." Harv looked around. The film crew was just arriving and getting organized. "For now, you can keep Harlie from having a panic attack." He smiled and Harlie glared. "I know you are, Harlie. It's not that bad. Clay's done a bunch of these. Just follow along and you'll do fine."

Harlie appeared doubtful.

"After the crew gets set up," Harv said, "I may need you to do a few things, Tallie. I'll let you know. Until then, enjoy the shoot and try to keep Harlie from disappearing."

Tom sat in his pickup at the main gate, watching as the rest of film crew filed in. A cloud of uneasiness hung over him. They'd done this before, but this time he had the added responsibility of Tallie and Cody. He scrutinized every vehicle and each occupant until he was confident every person belonged with the crew. There was a moment at the end of the line when he'd taken a second look at the last car, and he made a mental note to check out the vehicle and the guy, though the man did appear to belong. After he closed the gate, he drove to the house and parked near Tallie's car.

He wandered into the yard, stopping to introduce himself to the director, Joe Barnett, and took a closer look at the crew while they unloaded equipment. He looked again at the guy who had driven in last, but he grabbed some boxes from the truck and followed the others to the backyard.

The shoot began with Clay, Harlie, and Abby near the swing set. The song "Good Life" was about family and the happiness found there, so the director started with Clay playing with Abby. The little girl hammed it up and the director applauded her performance. After the swing set scene, they had Clay and Harlie walk around the ranch with Abby until she tired. Gail was called in to take her to the house for a break.

The next scene called for Clay and Harlie to lie on a blanket in the grass. Tom leaned against a tree where he'd have a good view. Harlie had obsessed about this scene all morning and he didn't want to miss it. When they began to shoot, Tom understood why she was nervous. The director instructed Clay and Harlie to talk up close and kiss while lying on the blanket. Clay shrugged his shoulders and gave her a kiss.

"No, no," the director said. "Is that how you kiss your wife, Clay? The poor woman must feel terribly unloved."

Clay laughed. "Just how much reality do you want, Joe?"

"I want the real thing. Look in her eyes and show us how much you love her."

Clay smiled slyly. "I thought this was a G-rated video."

Joe laughed. "Keep your clothes on but show us how you feel."

Tom scanned the crowd as Harlie and Clay made out on the blanket. When Clay decided to put on a show, he did a fine job, but it was a little embarrassing to watch. As he scrutinized the onlookers, his eyes fell on Tallie. She, too, gazed through the crowd. When her eyes landed on his and locked on, his heart raced. They stared across the yard until the director spoke to Clay and broke their concentration.

"That's great, Clay. I think we'll move things to the front porch and get a shot of you two on the swing." Clay and Harlie remained on the blanket. "Clay? Ready?"

"Give me a minute." They'd rolled across the blanket, caught up in each other, apparently forgetting about the camera crew, and now he lay on his back with his wife draped across him.

"Are you okay?" Joe asked.

"Fine. I just need a second." Clay smiled at Harlie. "Stay put."

"What's wrong?" Joe asked.

"Well," Clay laughed with discomfort. "There is a good reason why this woman keeps getting pregnant." Harlie turned red and hid her face in his shirt when everyone laughed.

"Okay, everybody, take a break," Joe called out to the crew and walked away, laughing.

Tom walked over, stopping near the blanket.

"Got a problem, stud?" he asked with a grin.

"Nothing I can't handle. But I think Harlie may die of embarrassment. Are you okay, darlin'?"

"Yeah," she said. "Has this ever happened before?"

"Uh, no. I've never been in this sort of position in a video before."

Tom couldn't help laughing. "Should I get a bucket of cold water to dump on you?"

Clay glared at him. "Just go away. I'm fine now. You can get up, darlin'." Clay and Harlie climbed to their feet.

Tom wandered off, chuckling. Not paying attention, he ran into Tallie and had to step back.

"What's so funny?" she asked.

"Clay had a bit of a problem, but he's says he's better now." He couldn't contain his amusement.

"What kind of problem?"

"Oh, you missed it?" He wondered how to explain it, and considering he'd been on the verge of having the same problem, he didn't want to get into it. Not with the woman who was the source of his difficulty. "Well," he thought for a moment, trying to phrase it for the least embarrassment. "Um, see, Clay got a little wound up rolling around on the blanket and well, he, um..." He frowned.

Tallie smiled and laughed. "I think I get it." She moved closer and looked up at him. "I got a little warm myself."

Tom gulped at the implication. "I need to check on a few things." He turned to leave.

"Tom!"

He stopped and looked at her. "What?"

"I've almost finished that book," she said with a dimpled smile. He gave her a blank stare. "You know, the one your sister left in the guest room..."

The erotic romance. "Oh?" His brow shot up.

"I just wanted you to know how much I enjoyed it—"

"Good. I'm glad—"

"And how educational I've found it."

Tom gulped again. Erotic romance. Educational. Oh god.

She stepped to him and whispered in his ear. "Chapter Six, page one-fifty, sounds...interesting." She stepped back and winked.

"I'm sure it is." Tom gave her an uncomfortable smile and wandered in the direction of the front porch, wondering how he would survive having Tallie around. It was the most frustrating experience of his life. Not only did he want to kiss the daylights out of her, but now he needed to get a hold of that book and see what was going on in Chapter Six.

Tallie sat at a picnic table with the boys, eating pasta salad and ham with a plastic fork, her eyes scanning the crowd for a glimpse of Tom. She wasn't sure why she looked for him but couldn't stop herself. He could try to ignore her all he wanted, but she was sure he felt something when their eyes met earlier that morning, and she needed to get him to act on it. She smiled to herself. Mentioning the book did something to him. He looked like he'd swallowed sour milk.

"What do you guys think so far?" she asked between ham bites. Both boys shrugged.

"The cameras were interesting for about five minutes," Michael said, his tone bored. "Why do they want a video of Clay and Harlie rolling around on a blanket?"

Tallie contemplated an answer. "Clay's song is about how good his life is and Harlie is a big reason for that. It's about love and finding happiness."

"What does wrestling on a blanket have to do with happiness?" Cody said, his brow furrowed in confusion. "Nothing great about wrestling a girl."

Tallie couldn't help but laugh. Oh, the innocence of preteen boys. "Well, they weren't wrestling. They were hugging and kissing."

"Oh, puke!" Michael grimaced. "It wasn't so bad when I thought they were wrestling."

"That's just gross." Cody agreed.

"Wait a couple of years, guys. You'll think kissing is a good thing."

"Blech, never!" Cody added as he finished his pasta salad. "Is my DS still in your car, Mom?"

"Yes, Michael's too. If you'll dump my plate in the garbage, I'll get them for you." She took her last bite and handed Cody the plate. Before walking to the car, she stopped at the buffet table and grabbed a pop from the ice chest and wandered down the driveway, sipping the cold drink. As she neared her car, she felt another presence, as if she was watched, but shook it off. The ranch burst with people, and any one of them could be close by and not a threat. She set the pop can on Tom's truck hood and dug in her pocket for her keys. The key was almost in the lock when she sensed movement near the garage and swung around to have a look, her heart pounding.

Nothing there, but she gave more than a cursory glance in the direction of the garage, just in case. The afternoon shadows could offer a miscreant the perfect hiding place. She tapped her key in the palm of her hand and took a breath before turning back to the car door. An overactive imagination could be a distracting thing. Tom had checked every car entering the ranch that morning and she trusted him. She opened the car door and bent to move a pile of clothes, trying to locate the boys' game players, when she heard slow footsteps behind her, crunching in the gravel. She jumped at the thunk and fizz of her pop can hitting the gravel and turned, but not quick enough to see who or what had bumped the pop.

"Tallie! You're needed out front," Harv called from the yard.

"Okay, Harv!" She paused, debating if she should look around the vehicles for the pop-dumping culprit. To her relief, a large tabby cat rubbed against her leg, purring loudly. Tallie laughed and scratched the cat's ears. "Silly thing," she said. "You scared the daylights out of me." She didn't have time to dig the video games from the pile on the floor now and ran back to the house before Harv had to call for her again.

CAUGHT IN THE SPIN

Roy crouched out of sight, watching as his darling ex-wife retreated to the yard, smiling when she directed Cody to walk right into his father's path.

"Cody!" she called. "They need me over there. You'll have to get the games." She tossed the keys and continued on.

"Oh man!" Cody grumbled and caught the car keys. "I'll be right back, Mike." He slid from his chair and wandered across the yard to the car, pretending to play basketball as he went. "He shoots, he scores, and the crowd goes wild." Cody dribbled an imaginary basketball, spinning and jumping.

Roy tensed, listening as Cody moved closer to his hiding spot. He was afraid to peer around the garage too soon and alert Cody, but he had to see what was happening. Tallie had almost seen him. Luckily, that cat arrived when it did or she might have looked around more. Roy hung back, gauging the distance from him to Tallie's car. Cody dribbled his imaginary ball and cheered as the ball went through the hoop in his mind. He even stopped and did a victory dance by the car. After the imaginary crowd finished cheering, Cody dug the keys from his pocket and studied them. He tried a few without success. A square one wouldn't fit. A round one went in a little but not all the way.

"Oh, man," he groused after each failed attempt.

Roy watched as Cody fiddled with the keys, trying one, then another. Taking advantage of Cody's turned back, Roy crept around the corner to the hood of Tom's truck, stepping gingerly over the spilled pop. He figured it couldn't be any easier to grab the kid, toss him in Tallie's car, and sneak out the gate with him. The runt even brought him the keys. He took another step, kicking a rock that drew Cody's attention. The boy glanced around and went back to testing the keys. Roy took a handkerchief from his pocket to use as a gag, tested it for strength, and stepped to the edge of the truck. He itched to grab the kid but took it slow, not wanting to startle him. As soon as Cody had the door open, Roy would make his move.

"Cody!" a male voice called. Footsteps crunched in the driveway gravel. "You over here?"

"Yeah, Tom. By Mom's car." Cody jingled the keys.

Roy snuck back around the garage corner, cussing under his breath. Tom came around the end of the truck.

"I can't figure out which one it is," Cody said.

Tom looked at the keys and pointed. "Try that one."

Cody stuck it in the door and it fit. "Cool," he said with a grin and climbed in the backseat. He rummaged around, found the Nintendo games, and crawled out.

"You can set those in the house for a while. If you're interested, the director wants you and Michael in the video."

"Us? Why?"

"Come on. I'll tell you on the way." They locked the car and walked down the driveway.

Roy blew out a frustrated breath and cursed Tom Black.

◦◈◦

"What do they want us for?" Cody asked Tom again.

"He thought it would look good to have you boys fishing with Clay on the pond. Abby isn't old enough, so Clay suggested you and Michael." Tom increased his pace as they drew closer to the house.

"Sweet. I don't have to wear makeup or anything, do I?"

Cody appeared horrified at the thought.

"I have no idea. But if they need it, I don't think a little makeup will hurt you." Tom laughed. "They dabbed a bit on Clay and it didn't seem to damage him any. He's still a guy."

Cody frowned. "Okay. If Clay can do it, I guess I can. I don't have to kiss anybody, do I?" He looked up at Tom, obviously revolted at the idea.

Tom tried to keep a straight face. "I don't think so. Why?"

"Cause they made Clay do it, and I don't want to be rolling around on no blanket kissing girls. That is just disgusting." Cody visibly shuddered at the thought.

Tom ruffled Cody's hair. "Don't worry, pal. I think they want you wrestling bait and fishing poles, not girls."

"Good." Cody sighed with relief. "I guess I can if Mike is."

"He said he would."

Sunset brought an end to the filming day and the crew packed their gear and loaded the trucks. The caterers offered one last round of dessert and packed it in. Tom led the group to the main gate and watched as everyone left, noticing the last car in the gate in the morning didn't go out. He drove to the area the cars had been parked. Sure enough, a blue Ford Escort sat alone. Tom glanced around and noticed the guy walking near a barn.

"Hey, you!" he yelled at the dark figure. "Party's over. Time to head out."

The guy stopped and looked around. "Yeah, sorry!" he called out, waving his hand in acknowledgement. "I got turned around in the dark." He made a dash for his car and

SHARLEEN SCOTT

was out the gate before Tom could get a good look at him.

12

Dusk. Roy drove the miles from the MB Ranch in a simmering rage. If it wasn't for Tom Black, Roy would have his kid and be seeing Tennessee in his rearview mirror. He needed another plan now and didn't have one.

Tom Black would pay for this.

Several miles further, Roy saw the answer to one of his problems: Lefty's Tavern. He was dried out and needed a drink. He parked the borrowed Ford Escort between a Hummer and a Chevy pickup. Inside, the dance floor was scuffed, the tables thinly occupied, and the women reasonably attractive. After a few drinks, they'd all be supermodels. Behind the bar: a neon Budweiser sign and a bartender with his sleeves rolled up who looked like he knew how to build a beer. If a guy cared about atmosphere, Lefty's would do—well-seasoned without looking shabby and first-class country music on the juke. Roy didn't care about atmosphere. He wanted a beer. He stopped for a pack of Marlboros at the cig machine before walking in. The price made him choke, but he needed a smoke as much as the beer. A few guys sat hunched at the bar, nursing their favorite poison, probably praying for oblivion. Roy took a seat at the end of the bar. On the juke box: George Strait's "Amarillo by Morning." The bartender, a skinny dude with a comb-over, wandered his way.

"What's on tap?" Roy asked.

"Bud and Yazoo," the bartender said.

"Yazoo?" Roy snorted. "What the hell. Live dangerously, I always say. Gimme a Yazoo." After life in the can, it was a whole new world out here.

The bartender nodded and filled the order. While Roy waited, a pretty brunette sidled up and sat on the adjacent stool. She was friendly and stacked. His kind of woman. Tallie had a nice rack on her too, but she sure as hell wasn't friendly anymore. Uptight, hoity-toity rich girl is what she was.

"Did Otis get your drink order taken care of?" the waitress asked, looking him over with an appraising glance.

Roy smiled. Maybe he'd have a place to sleep tonight. "Under control, sweetheart, which is more than I can say about my heart when I look at you," he said, giving her the same appraising look. "You're one good-looking woman. But I'll bet everybody tells you that."

She laughed, flashing straight, white teeth. "A few, here and there. But it's something a girl never gets tired of hearing." The bartender set Roy's beer on the bar. Roy handed him a twenty. "Would you like something to eat with your beer?" she asked. "We make a great burger and fries. The pizza is real popular too. By the pan or slice."

"How about a burger with the works and you sit with me while I eat it?"

Otis brought Roy his change and gave the waitress a disapproving look. She straightened her spine and moved from the barstool. "I'll get your food order taken care of and check on you in a little bit." Roy grabbed her hand before she could leave.

"What's your name, pretty lady?" He glanced to the glaring bartender. "Just so I know who to tip later on."

"My name is Sherry, and I'm the only waitress on duty tonight."

He released her hand, and she wandered to the kitchen. The song now playing on the juke box: Trace Adkins' "Honky Tonk Badonkadonk." The way Sherry's hips swayed to the beat, Roy would bet money she was the one who'd dropped the coins in to hear it. Another patron slid onto the vacated stool next to Roy, dressed in Wranglers, scuffed cowboy boots, and a plaid shirt with a small Bible in the pocket. He held a shot glass in his hand, watching Sherry saunter across the room.

"Women," he said. "Bad news. Every one of them."

Roy glanced Sherry's direction with a frown. "What? Her? She doesn't seem so bad." She looked like a good lay to him. Who cared about the rest of it?

The newcomer took a sip of his whisky, savoring. "She'll break your heart. They all will."

Roy chuckled. "You struck out with her, didn't you?"

"No skin off my nose. Every last one of them is fickle and untrustworthy. They'll suck the life out of you and disappear with the plumber." He shook his head.

"The plumber?" Roy asked with a smile.

"Yup. The plumber. Evil buggers, if you ask me, sneaking in when a guy is out earning a living. He had all the time in the world to impress the missus with his pipe wrench." He shook his head. "I wish we'd never bought that house. All the plumbing was bad. I should've bought a newer one, and I might still have her."

Roy found truth in his statement, not the plumber, but the rest rang true. "I know what you mean. They don't do as they're told, argue all the time, and take off with the kid.

I hear you."

"Divorced, are you?"

Roy nodded. "Good riddance to her. You?"

The man nodded, forlorn. "Just got the papers yesterday. The Lord giveth and the Lord taketh away." He patted the Bible sticking out of his pocket. "Hey, Otis! Gimme another hit of this stuff." He slid his glass to the bartender. "It's gonna take a lot more than a couple shots to get me through tonight. Maybe the whole bottle."

Otis poured a refill. "No bottles for you. One at a time until I tell you you're done."

"What if my friend wants one too?" He tipped his head toward Roy.

"Then your friend can order for himself." Otis moved to the other end of the bar.

"Bastard," he said to the bartender's retreating back.

Roy chuckled. "So—"

"Phin is my name. Phineas is the full job but call me Phin. Can't tolerate that highbrow name."

Roy whistled and shook his head. "Can't blame you there. God-awful name if I ever heard one."

He leaned toward Roy. "My grandma was a movie fan, and she got all hung up on that *Round the World in Eighty Days* flick long before I was born. She thought David Niven was one hot little Englishman, so she talked my mama into saddling me with the name of his character." He frowned. "Got beat up in school a lot for it. Phin is what I prefer. Phin Mulberry."

Roy sipped his brew and didn't offer a name in return. No point to it.

Phin sighed and continued his rambling. "Yeah. The wife

took off with the best plumber Knoxville has ever seen. A pipe and faucet wizard. How does a guy compete with that?" Phin downed his whiskey and looked at his glass. Roy signaled the bartender to bring him another.

"I shouldn't," Phin said when Otis set the drink on the bar.

"Why not?" Roy asked. "It's not every day a guy gets rid of the old ball and chain." Roy tore open the Marlboros and tapped one out. "It's time for celebration. if you ask me."

"It's not that." Phin shook his head. "I got a job interview coming up and I shouldn't start drinking."

"When? Tomorrow?" Roy asked.

"No. Next week. But once I start on the booze, I can't stop." He picked up his glass and emptied it. "So anyway. That interview I was telling you about is over to the MB Ranch. You know the place?"

Roy lit his cigarette. "No, never heard of it. What kind of ranch is it?" He took a long drag and blew out the smoke. His mood was improving and it wasn't the nicotine.

"Cattle, bulls, that sort of thing. It's Clay Masterson's place. You know, the country singer. Real nice fella from what I heard. But it's his partner I have to deal with."

"You say that like he's tough to handle or something," Roy said.

"Just going by what I hear."

Sherry returned with Roy's burger and a ketchup bottle, leaning between Roy and Phin as she slid the plate in front of him. She looked from him to Phin and smiled. "So, are you boys related or something?"

Roy studied the drunk sitting by him. "No. Why?"

She laughed. "Cause if you had red hair, you'd pass as

brothers. It's kinda weird. Maybe you're shirttail relations or something. Around here, everybody seems to be related." She stepped away. "Anything else I can get you, just give me a shout."

After she left, Roy gave Phin another look. She could be on to something. "So Phin, buddy, what's the deal on this interview?"

Phin sipped his whiskey. "Well, I'll tell you. It's the dangedest thing and if I didn't need the job real bad, I don't know that I'd go through this."

"What's that?"

"This Tom Black fella wants a full resume. From a ranch hand. A resume. Can you believe it? I didn't even know what it was until I asked." He pointed at Roy, his finger weaving. "You know what I found out? There are services for that sort of thing. Folks who will type it all up and print it for you. So I hired one and they did a real nice job making me look good. It's a freaking work of art." He took another sip. "So then Black tells me to be honest on this resume because he checks it all out with a fine-toothed comb. Every detail."

"Why's that?"

"Cause of Clay Masterson, he says. He's gotta keep tight security because of him. I told him I didn't have any reason to lie to him. He says good, cause the guys he can trust are allowed to live in the ranch bunkhouse for free. A benefit, he calls it. That suits me fine. I like free," Phin said with a woeful chuckle. "The old lady cleaned me out, and I couldn't scrape up rent if I had to."

"So you know cattle and bulls?" Roy asked. "I worked for a stock contractor myself a few years back."

"Oh yeah." He pointed to himself and laughed. "Bulls R Us. That's why I drove from Knoxville for the interview. Black wants somebody who knows bulls. That would be me, all right. I've worked at a handful of ranches, like that Tim Rowe's place." He got a dreamy look in his eye. "He had a daughter who was something special. Roxanne was her name. This was back before the missus and I hooked up. Man, did I have a thing for Miss Roxanne. She had the prettiest blonde hair. But she was engaged already." He shrugged. "After that I worked for a big stock contractor named Gib Sanborn. You were in the business. Maybe you heard of him? Nice fella. Won all kinds of awards for being a good rodeo contractor."

Roy noticed Phin's glass was about empty and he waived to Otis for a refill. The bartender frowned.

"He's pretty well loaded," Otis said with concern.

"Don't worry," Roy said. "I'll take care of him."

Otis shrugged and filled the glass.

Several shots and a load of bullshit later, Phin listed heavily to one side like a sinking ship. "I gotta get going. Big day comin' up." When he tried to stand, his feet went out from under him. Roy caught him before he hit the floor. "Easy there, big fella. How about if I help you home?"

"Knoxville? It's a long drive."

"Not Knoxville. Where are you staying here in Nashville? I'll give you a lift."

Phin gave him a drunken smile. "That's real nice of you, friend. I have a room at the motel up the highway a ways. The Sunshine Inn or Sunbelt or some such thing. You know the one?"

Roy didn't have a clue but nodded anyway. "Yeah. I

know it. Let's get you home."

With Phin's limited assistance, Roy found his new friend's pickup in the parking lot: an eighties vintage Ford with oxidized red paint. Not pretty but functional. He poured Phin into the passenger seat and found the room key in the drunken man's pocket. The address was on the back of the fob. After a short drive, Roy found the place. It was seedy but Roy didn't plan on staying long. He parked at the far end of the lot, beneath the window of Phin's room, and looked over at his newfound friend.

"Yo, Phin." Roy poked Phin's shoulder. "Wake up. We're home."

Phin mumbled. Roy grimaced and resigned himself to carrying the guy to his room.

Roy half carried, half dragged him from the truck and tossed him on the unmade double bed. Phin groaned but didn't stir. Roy stood over him, panting. He wandered into the kitchenette for a drink of water, sitting on a pink plastic lawn chair to drink it. Phin moaned and rolled on his side. When Roy caught his breath, he found Phin's suitcase and rummaged through it, dumping clothes on the floor.

"Hey! What are you doing?" Phin rolled from the bed, landing on his knees. "Get out of my stuff! Hey!" He stood and made a staggering lunge. Roy stopped him easily, punching him in the stomach. Phin doubled over but regained enough balance to rush Roy again, smashing him into the wall. Roy grunted and shoved Phin off him.

"You damned thief!" Phin swayed, looking as if he would make another try. Roy had enough of this game. When Phin stepped toward him, Roy placed his boot in Phin's stomach and shoved him in the direction of the bed. He fell short, landing on the floor, his head cracking loudly against the bed frame. Roy stood over him, watching for further signs of a fight.

Phin didn't move. He didn't breathe either. When Roy nudged him with his boot, Phin's head lolled to the side, and his sightless eyes glazed.

"Must have cracked you good." He shrugged. "Oh well. It just makes it easier," he said. "I was wondering what I was going to do with you." He chuckled. "Problem solved." Roy turned from the body and continued rummaging through Phin's belongings, finding the resume. Phin was right. It was a freaking work of art. The interview date and time were even scribbled on the manila envelope. He placed it back in the suitcase and repacked the clothes. Next, he rolled Phin over and found his wallet. Inside: Phin's license, Social Security card, credit cards, some cash, and a picture of a woman Roy assumed was Phin's blood-sucking ex-wife. Not bad looking. The waitress at Lefty's was better though. He tucked the wallet in the suitcase. Another trip around the room and Roy had everything he needed: spare boots straight off Phin's feet, the Bible from his pocket, toiletries, and an alarm clock. Next to the clock he found a watch and tossed it in with the rest of the loot. He returned to Phin, studying him. Sherry was right. There was a slight resemblance. Roy wandered into the kitchen, found a paring knife, and sawed off a lock of Phin's hair. He wrapped it in plastic wrap and stuffed it in his pocket.

He grabbed a blanket and covered Phin, making sure the window shades were closed tight. He couldn't have anyone seeing the guy that way. He picked up the keys from the dresser and, using Phin's truck, made a quick trip to

Walmart. In the hair care aisle, he found Clairol Nice 'n Easy, natural reddish blonde. He pulled the sample of Phin's hair from his pocket and compared it with the photo on the box.

Perfect.

Hours later, his hair dyed, Roy tackled the job of Phin disposal. He wrapped the body in the bedspread, strapped it tight with a leather belt, and with a grunt, tossed him over his shoulder and carried him out into the night. The sun would rise soon and time was running out. Roy dumped the body in the truck bed, making sure Phin was wrapped tight and covered. He returned with the suitcase and extra clothes, which he laid in the front seat. After he cleared the room of Phin's belongings, Roy made a quick trip to the motel office. It was locked for the night, but there was a key drop slot in the door. Roy popped the key in and left.

The sun rose as Roy bid good-bye to his new friend. His final resting place: a middle school cafeteria dumpster, mixed in with leftover canned peaches and mashed potatoes.

Appropriate for a guy who left this world smashed.

13

Tom faced an impossible situation. Clay was performing on the Grand Ole Opry and Harlie invited the boys to sit with her, which meant Tom would spend the evening alone with Tallie. How would he survive it? Since Clay's bodyguards went along, he couldn't tell the boys to stay home. Cody was safe with Phil and Stuart. He needed to keep his distance so Tallie wasn't a temptation. A lot of things could happen in four long hours.

They ate dinner and cleared the dishes in silence. After, Tom announced he needed a shower and disappeared into his room. He stalled as long as possible before emerging in sweats and a T-shirt. Tallie was in her room, so he was safe in his recliner. While reading a Stephen King novel, he located a Chris Ledoux album on his iPod and slipped on the headphones with the volume as loud as he could stand it.

Tallie walked down the stairs past Tom and disappeared into the kitchen. His eyes almost bugged out of his head. Her pajamas, if the term applied, were so snug and tiny, she was nearly nude. Tight boy-style shorts barely covered her behind and the tank top with spaghetti straps fit so close he could make out every bump and luscious curve. His body did things he'd tried his damnedest to control. When she returned from the kitchen, he forced his eyes to the book. Tallie sat on the sofa, her back straight. He saw her lips move and knew she was talking to him, but he couldn't hear. When a sofa pillow hit him in the head, he admitted defeat and removed the headphones.

"What?"

"I want to talk to you."

"What about?" He almost swallowed his tongue when he looked at her. How could he talk to her when it felt like a bull rope tightened around his chest, constricting his breath?

She stared at him with unwavering blue eyes. "I want you to make love to me."

He thought he'd need to collect his jaw from the floor. "Can I take a shower first?"

"You already did."

"Oh, yeah." He let out an uncomfortable laugh and cleared his throat.

Tallie's eyes narrowed. "Oh, never mind." She jumped to her feet and stomped to the stairs.

"Tallie!" He rose from his chair, trying to untangle himself from the headphone cord before she was gone. He reached her as she scaled the stairs and grabbed her foot. "Wait a minute."

"Let me go," she said through clenched teeth. She kicked her foot. She sank to her knees, breathing hard. "Let...me...go."

He released her foot and sat at the bottom of the steps, elbows on knees and hands clasped, waiting to see if she would join him or run. With a surreptitious glance over his shoulder, he watched her silently debate what to do. "Will you sit and talk to me?"

She slid down the stairs to sit next to him, buried her face in her hands, and moaned. "Oh, now you want to talk to me."

"I think it's a good idea. What's going on?"

"Nothing, obviously." She scrubbed her hands over her face and huffed out a breath. "I'm a failure. I don't know what I'm doing. Maybe I need to read more. There must be an Idiot's Guide for this."

"An Idiot's Guide for what?"

"Holy cow." She groaned. "I'm so bad at this, you don't even have a clue what I'm trying to do."

She folded her arms across her chest, trying to hide the skimpy top, but didn't realize the pressure from her arms tormented him even more. Her breasts squished up like marshmallows in a bag. He gulped.

"Never mind," she said, shaking her head. "It was a bad idea. I should never—"

"What are you talking about?" Tom asked, dismayed to have missed some key point in the conversation while he'd been fantasizing about s'mores. He wondered if he had any chocolate bars. No, chocolate sauce would be better for what he had in mind.

"Do I have to spell it out?"

Tom looked at her vacantly.

She bit her lip and sighed. "I guess I do. Dang it, I'm trying to seduce you and am failing miserably. I thought you'd like these stupid pajamas and the way I walked across the room. I saw that in a movie and it worked for her. But it didn't work and you just sat there like a...a...neutered lump."

Tom flinched at the idea but remained silent. It was obvious she wasn't done yet, and he'd just look stupider than he already did if he opened his mouth. Clueless male. That was him.

"I don't know how to flirt or be sexy, so I thought I would tell you what I want, which apparently isn't what you want. Forget I brought it up." She twisted around to go up-stairs but Tom stopped her with a hand on her hip, turning her back to him.

He shook his head in disbelief. "She doesn't know how to be sexy, she says." He quaked with suppressed laughter. "Sweetheart, you don't need any books. If you haven't prac-ticed this, I'd say you have one heck of a natural talent. All you need to do is step into the room and I'm turned on. Knowing you and I share the same planet turns me on." He cupped her cheek with his hand and stared into her eyes. "You're an exciting woman. You've driven me insane for days. And this little outfit you're wearing tonight, oh man." He sucked in his breath and exhaled dramatically. "Trust me when I say you aren't a failure. Consider yourself a rous-ing success." He smiled. "No, correction. You are an arous-ing success."

"So, why are you backing off from me? Why did you apologize for kissing me? I started it."

He removed his hand. "I offered you a safe place to stay, and I didn't want you to think sleeping with me was a re-quirement. I want you to feel safe here."

"I do feel safe when I'm with you." She kissed the end of his nose. "You're such a good man to think that. But you're horrified I asked, aren't you? I saw the look on your face."

"Surprised, not horrified. No one has approached me that way before. Usually it's more, I don't know," he said with a shrug, "natural. It starts with some kissing and develops from there. Getting asked out of the blue is, well, the stuff performance anxiety is made of." Her face fell and he laughed. "What I'm trying to say is, for me, making love is a...a mood thing. We need to get the mood going first."

She brightened. "Okay—"

"But I don't think it's a good idea. I want you to feel secure here. You don't have to sleep with me—"

Tallie put a finger to his lips, silencing him. "Whoa, just a second, cowboy. Let's give those reins a pull and stop this horse. I might bake a pie out of appreciation. I might buy you a thank you card. But I would *not* sleep with you because I thought I had to. Is that what you were thinking? I'd be so grateful for your help I'd hop in bed with you?"

Now it was Tom's turn for embarrassment. Heat crawled up his neck, turning his tanned skin red. "Not exactly... Okay. Something like that. I didn't want you to think that was why I brought you here. I didn't want you to feel pressured." He shrugged. "I thought it was, you know, the polite thing to do...to give you some space."

"Polite?" She raised an eyebrow. "After I nearly tore your clothes off, you thought..." She gave him a strained smile. "Polite. Well, you certainly have been. I thought I'd done something to alienate you, and you were being courteous." Tallie bit her lip and sighed. "I applaud your politeness and good manners, Tom. I do. Your mother should be proud. I was raised by the most courteous and well-mannered woman in Arizona, so I understand the effort that goes into it."

Tom nodded. "See, that's what I was thinking...that you were used to something different, and here I was climbing all over you like I didn't have a scrap of self-control. I've been close to exploding every time you come near me," Tom said with relief. Finally, it was out in the open. His elephant-in-the-room good intentions had been exposed, and they could put this problem to rest. He'd continue to be frustrated and crabby, but now she'd know why. She could relax and feel secure, and he was glad to offer her that comfort. He leaned back, satisfied with the success of his plan. He wasn't as clueless as he thought.

Tallie looked at Tom, the object of her wildest desires, and frowned. Politeness had its place, no doubt about it, but so did passion. She didn't want a cold, civil relationship like her parents had. No, she wanted something better. Something more. Something that sizzled down to her toes. She wanted Tom and every decadent thing he represented. She wanted him to unleash that intensity and see where he could take her.

And he was polite. Good grief.

She fought to maintain her hurt look, but he seemed to be coming around. Success was within her grasp. Tallie laughed. "I'm so sorry."

"Why?"

"Because," she said, trying to contain her giggles, "I've been crafting sinister, diabolical plots against you, doing everything I could think of to get your attention. I thought you'd lost interest."

He shook his head and chuckled. "No. I've been taking a lot of cold showers and heading toward insanity."

She cupped her hand against his freshly shaved cheek and looked contrite. "I'm sorry."

"I doubt it," Tom said with a deep laugh.

He took her hand and pressed his lips to her palm. Tallie sighed. This sort of tenderness made her insides feel like sand melting into glass, molten hot and liquid. He moved from her palm to her fingertips, brushing his lips across them before giving her a look so hot, he scorched her.

"I've been interested since the moment I saw you. I've wanted you from the beginning." He stared into her blue eyes. "I want you now," he said in a deep, rough whisper that sent chills through her. "Right now."

She stared at him through long lashes and whispered, "So if I ask you to make love to me, you will? I've never made love, and I want to with you."

Tom frowned. "You were married and have a child. How can you say that?"

"I wouldn't call what Roy did making love. He had sex and I let him. If I didn't, I got beat up. Roy's a real romantic." She laid her head against Tom's shoulder and snuggled against his comfortable warmth. "He's going to kill me," she said. "I can't stay locked behind this fence forever. If they don't catch him soon, I have to return to my life and take my chances. Everything is in order with my attorney. My will is up-to-date, and there are instructions for Cody to go to one of my brothers in Arizona. It's important that Roy doesn't get him."

"Stop, Tallie—"

She leaned back and looked into his eyes, hoping he would understand. "Listen to me. I'm serious. I've always known Roy would finish the job."

"Tallie, I won't let him—"

"You don't know him, Tom. Taking Cody won't be enough for him. He won't be satisfied until I'm dead. Please promise me you'll help Cody get away from here after..."

"That won't be necessary, but if it makes you feel better, I promise I'll do everything I can for Cody." He put his arm around her and pulled her close. "But I also promise I won't let Roy anywhere near either of you. You'll be here to raise your son. That cop was right when he said this ranch is one of the most secure places in Nashville, and I'm the one who made it that way. We have state-of-the-art security equipment, electric fences, and round-the-clock security details. No one has ever come on this property that shouldn't be here." He tilted her chin with his finger. "I won't let anything happen to you or anyone else within these gates. You have my word on it."

"Okay," she whispered and leaned her head into his warm shoulder, relaxing into him. She sighed with contentment. "A few years ago, I made a list of all the things I wanted to do before Roy caught up with me and I've done the majority of them." She laughed. "Most of them were pretty silly, like eating rainbow ice cream and escargot." She wrinkled her nose. "Not at the same time. The rest included Cody, like hiking trips and special picnics. I've made scrapbooks of everything we've done and written stories about my family so he'll know them when he gets to Arizona. And when I met you," she continued, "I added a new item to the list. Something I thought I'd never have the chance to do."

"What?"

"I want to make love with a gentle man. I want to know what it's like to be touched by gentle hands." Before Tom could say anything, Tallie snaked her hand around his neck and kissed him, her lips hot and greedy. He groaned and moved his hand across her back, caressing, while she assaulted his mouth. "Take me to your bed, Tom. Make love to me." She laid her mouth on his again, delaying a response. She wanted him burning and unable to say no. He lay back on the stairs, taking her along. She sprawled across his body, feeling the heat rise from him as she continued her machinations on his mouth. There was no politeness in his grasping hands, no courtesy in his kiss. She stirred his passion as if it was soup and he quickly rose to the boiling point.

Tom groaned and broke the kiss. His fingers skimmed across her skin. "I suppose there isn't much point in fighting a determined woman."

"Not usually. And it would be good for me, you know." She licked her kiss-swollen lips, her confidence growing as his defenses crumbled.

"You mean, like therapy?"

"Something like that."

She noted a gleam in his eye when he said, "Are there studies to support your hypothesis that I should just give in?"

"Most certainly." She nodded with seriousness. "Probably even clinical trials."

"I'll be damned. I must have missed that issue of *Psychology Today*," Tom said, matching her serious tone. "If science demands it, we'd better get to it." He stood and held out his hand. "Let's go."

When Tallie walked into Tom's room, her nerves kicked into overdrive. Even though she wasn't afraid of him, her body tensed as he led her inside. She liked the look of the room and turned her attention to it instead of the man: the blue quilt covering the bed, the nightstand with a reading lamp, and an investment book with folded corners to mark interesting pages. His watch lay next to the book. The hardwood floor was cool on her feet in contrast with the warmth spreading through her body. He closed the bedroom door and looked at her. She backed against the door.

Tom tried to mask his concern.

Mood. They needed something to set the mood. Ambiance, too. None of this bright light and jarring silence stuff going on now. While Tallie propped up the door, or contemplated running—he wasn't sure which she was doing—Tom turned on the small bedside light and plugged the iPod into the stereo. He scanned the playlists for something soft and romantic.

Tom stepped toward her, turning off the ceiling light. She looked scared and it worried him. What if he wasn't what she needed? What if he wasn't gentle enough and frightened her? He'd never dealt with something like this before. Making love had always been instinctive for him. He just knew what to do. Now, he'd need to stop and consider if his actions would upset her. He looked into her pale-blue eyes and placed his hands gently on her neck, brushing his fingers across the fading bruises. "Are you okay?"

She stared at his lips, licking hers. "I'm good," she whispered. "How about you?"

He smiled. "I'm fine, thank you…now we have the pleasantries out of the way…may I…" She nodded, closed her eyes, and tilted her chin up, ready to be kissed. "Have this dance?"

She opened her eyes. "What?"

"Dance," he said with a soft laugh. "You know, two people, up close, moving in circles…" Bodies rubbing, breath mingling. So, why didn't he like dancing?

"I get that. I guess, if that's what you want to do."

"I promised you dinner and dancing," he said.

"We did eat."

"Okay then." He placed his hands on her hips. She wrapped her arms around his waist and leaned her head against him. Her shoulders relaxed as they swayed to the music. Tom slid his arms around her, holding her close, feeling the rise and fall of her breath as they turned in slow circles. She looked up into his eyes. His lips brushed hers, sweeping from side to side before capturing her mouth. He groaned, wanting more. There was no reason to hold back now. She wanted him too. He slid his hands across her shoulders and down her back. As he continued his kiss, he jerked her to him, holding her hips firm against him.

And then it hit him what he'd done. He'd been rough, exactly what she didn't need. He broke their embrace, backed up, and paced across the room. "This isn't going to work." He threw up his hands. "I can't do this."

Tallie looked at him with surprise. "You can't?"

"I can do that, it's just..." He exhaled. "I don't know if I can be what you need."

"I don't expect you to be any different than you are."

"I don't know if I can be gentle. I don't know if I am. No one has ever said 'ooo, baby, you were so gentle.' I just do what I do and everybody is happy."

"Everybody?" She bit her lip and smiled.

He scowled. "You know what I mean."

"I didn't mean to cause an anxiety attack, Tom. Come lay down with me, do what you do, and make me happy." She moved to the side of the bed and waited for him to follow. He didn't move. When she thought she'd need to retrieve him and prod him toward the bed, she felt his warm presence behind her, his work-calloused hands on her shoulders. She leaned into him, relishing the heat of his chest against her back.

"Changed your mind?" she asked. He gently squeezed her shoulders, massaging. The man's hands were as magical as his lips.

"Yeah. No guarantees but I'll do my best—"

She laughed and turned her face toward him. "I have a feeling, Tom, that you can do anything you set your mind to and do it exceptionally well."

"We'll see about that," he muttered under his breath. He placed his lips to the curve of her neck, slowly kissing his way to her shoulder. She shivered. With a hooked finger, he pulled aside the spaghetti strap of her top, first left, then right, and pulled down the scrap of stretchy fabric. Her breath caught when his tanned hands cupped her pale breasts, kneading gently.

"Tell me if I scare you," he whispered. "I'll stop if you want..."

"Don't—"

He stopped abruptly. "What?'

"I'm fine. Don't stop what you're doing. Just...don't bring him into this. I can't...not if I'm thinking about..." She turned in his arms. "I don't want to be a victim here. Not when I'm with you. He doesn't belong here."

"Okay," he whispered. "It's just us." He kissed her lips and cheeks, brushed his fingers through her curly hair. She pressed closer, molding her body to his. He bent for another kiss but stopped again. "Now, before we go any further with this—"

"Yes, I use birth control," she said dryly.

He smiled. "That's good. I always do anyway. But, what

I want to know—am I just a check mark on your list?" He looked at her with amusement. "Am I a means to an end, or do you kinda like me, just a little?"

"Well, there is the list. You did move to the top with lightning speed, outpacing polka dancing and accordion lessons." She ran her fingers across his cheek and smiled when he laughed. "But the main thing is that you make me so hot, I can't think straight." She rubbed her thumb across his lips. "I kinda like you a little, too."

His smile took on a self-satisfied gleam. "I can work with that. I kinda like you, too." He moved across the bed and relaxed against the pillows, extending his hand. She hesitated. With a determined nod, she lay next to him. He smiled and laid his hand on her waist, pulling her to him. Her shoulders were tense and he was sure she held her breath. That wouldn't do. Not unless he was kissing her. Tom tipped up her chin and nibbled her lips, teasing her with little tastes before capturing her lips in a slow seductive kiss that left her needing air. At least she wasn't holding her breath any longer. He rolled her to her back, continuing his kisses, going deep, retreating, teasing the tender spots on her neck while working his way to her breasts. He pushed the tank top from her middle, planning to work his way down. She grasped his hand, stopping him.

"What's wrong?"

"Turn off the light." She motioned to the bedside lamp.

"Why?" He skimmed his fingers across her arm.

Tallie frowned and looked away. "Because... Please just turn off the light." She moved his hand and replaced it with her own.

"Okay, but I want to know why."

Tallie squeezed her eyes tight and slowly moved her hands. "Look if you want, but it's ugly."

Tom slowly pulled the top, surprised to see a network of scars across her stomach and ribs. Curious, he slid her shorts down a bit and found similar scarring on her abdomen. He trailed one with his finger and she flinched. Despite his earlier assurance to not allow Roy in the room, he had to ask. "He did this?"

"Yes." She nodded. "In the accident...and after. I was smashed under the steering wheel. The paramedics were amazed Roy didn't succeed in killing me." She located a nasty scar on her ribcage. "This is where the bullet entered."

"Bullet? He shot you? You didn't tell me that before. You said the guy who stopped at the accident kept Roy from shooting."

"He did. The second time. He managed to squeeze off the first shot before that. I'm not sure what he thought he aimed for—my heart, I suppose—but the bullet ended up here. Roy's marksmanship is comparable to his skill as a lover. Nonexistent."

"Why—"

"Why didn't I tell you?" She shrugged and shook her head. "I don't know. Maybe I didn't want you to know my husband hated me enough to shoot me. I didn't want your pity." She gave him a steely look. "I don't want it now. So, have your look and I'll go." She started to move away but Tom stopped her.

"What are you doing?"

"Leaving."

"Why?"

"Because I saw the look on your face, Tom. You're disgusted. It's ugly and I know it is, so don't try to pretend otherwise."

"I'm not disgusted, Tallie. I'm pissed off he would do this to you. But I'm wondering, how did you expect to do this," he said, gesturing between them, "without me seeing the scars?"

"You were supposed to turn out the light when I asked. Now you've seen it, so I'll go." She moved to leave again.

"Tallie, stop. If you think I'd be turned off by a few scars, you're wrong." Tom pulled off his shirt, revealing his patchwork of scars and a moderate amount of dark chest hair. "If we had a competition," he said, "I'd be a contender. Bulls are not warm, fuzzy critters."

Tallie couldn't stop herself from inspecting the scars scattered across his wonderful body. She touched one and another, her wounds momentarily forgotten.

"My knee makes these look like beauty marks. Three surgeries worth."

Before she realized his intention, he slipped off his sweatpants and tossed them to the floor. She tried for nonchalance, touching a silver scar along his shoulder, tracing from end to end, as she tried to ignore how he now lay across the bed naked, at ease in nothing but skin. And it was attractive skin. Pretending she saw nude men everyday of her life, she concentrated on his torso. It wasn't as disconcerting as the rest of him. He was a gorgeous man, scars and all. "How did you get this one?"

"Cheyenne. A rank sucker named Kiss of Death scraped me against the chutes." He twisted to reveal marks on his back. She touched a jagged scar at the base of his neck. "Missoula." He turned back and laughed at the concern in her eyes. "Honey, in bull riding, it isn't if you get hurt, but when. It's part of it. A guy just hopes he isn't the one carried out on the board."

"I know. I've seen a lot of riders get hurt." She gave him a long look. "But not close up."

"There was an article written about me once that said I looked like a roadmap of the United States. I don't think it's that bad."

Tallie's brow creased as she rubbed her finger along a small scar on his nose. "It's not so bad." Bad enough, though, for her to shudder at the pain he'd endured to reach his goal. Type A to the core, Clay had said. The scars proved it. Tom Black had been dedicated to his sport. Broken bones, torn ligaments, concussions... She'd watched the competition where he nearly died. Devil's Spawn threw Tom forward, smashing his nose with its huge head. Kissing the bull, they called it. Despite the gushing blood, Tom held on as long as he could. As he lost consciousness, his hand hung up in the bull rope, trapping him in the well between the hooves and the horns. He was spun like a rag doll before falling beneath the bull's hooves. With one last spin, the bull's hoof had connected with his rider's head and a horn hooked his leg, smashing the knee. The phenomenal athlete, the rider slated to win by point accumulation and the oddsmakers, lay broken and bleeding in the dirt while bull fighters distracted the bull from his victim. Tallie had cried as they carried him away.

She raked her fingers through his hair, settling on the location of his head injury. "Las Vegas," she said softly. "World finals. The bull was named Devil's Spawn and he nearly killed you. I watched them carry you out on the board." A shared experience. Was this the reason she was so comfortable with Tom? She'd followed his career, had seen him climb to the top and lose it all in a moment. It was as if she'd always known him.

"Yeah, it was my turn to be carried out. I don't remember much about it. They say I was out of it for ten days or so and when I came to, I thought my head would explode." He laughed and shook his head. "Some days, I wished it had. But I survived. Like you did." Tom's eyes drifted to her middle, to the embarrassing marks. "Life scars everyone, Tallie. Some of us just wear them more openly than others." Tallie turned her head, unable to look at him looking at her.

He traced the scars across her ribs and stomach, bent and kissed the marred flesh. He wasn't revolted but angered she'd been hurt. When he was satisfied she wouldn't turn away from him, he laid his lips to hers, taking her mind from her fears. "You are so beautiful, Tallie," he said softly as he laid her back. "Everything about you is amazing to me."

Tallie was awed he could see her scars and consider her beautiful. She'd never felt beautiful before now. Ever. She'd been a scrawny teenager and a battered wife. No one had ever made her feel beautiful. As his hands roamed her body, her trepidation waned and she explored on her own, running her fingers across his scars, acknowledging another shared experience. They both nearly died but fought to come back. But he cut her musing short when he slipped off her pajama bottoms and shocked her with the intensity of his fingers' touch. She'd never experienced anything like it and was stunned as she climbed higher, all thoughts blurred by the incredible sensations.

He held her trembling body as she clung to him. When she relaxed, he feasted slowly across her skin, making her sigh and moan. A kiss here, a nibble there, and he surprised her when he rolled her over on her stomach and started again on her back. He kissed and touched everywhere, and she sighed when he rubbed the backs of her legs.

When nearly at the end of his endurance, he rolled her over and settled in comfortably. In her pale-blue eyes he saw heat, desire, and uncertainty. He kissed her as they slid together.

Tallie tensed, closed her eyes, and turned her head away from him, retreating into her mental safety zone. The place in her mind her ex-husband couldn't reach. She felt Tom moving, and all she could think of was Roy. In her mind, the man above her was Roy, and she tensed. She squeezed her eyes tight, held her breath, and tried to think of happy times, pretty things, and... A tear dripped from her eye and ran down her cheek.

Tom stopped. The woman beneath him was stiff as a steel rod and he was sure she was holding her breath again. He kissed the tear from her cheek and whispered, "Hey, sweetie. Open your eyes. Tallie honey, look at me. Please, look at me. We won't do this unless you do." She turned her head and looked at him with fear-filled eyes. "I am not him. I am not like him. You know that."

She exhaled with a shudder. "I know." She nodded. "I do. I know."

"We'll stop right here, if that's what you want."

She shook her head and tightened her legs around him. "No. I want you, Tom."

"Okay. Keep your eyes open and look at me. I want you

to know who is loving you. You don't need to be afraid. Don't retreat from me. Stay with me. I won't hurt you."

"I know." She locked her eyes on him, concentrating on the man looking into her eyes. He moved slowly, the intensity in his green eyes holding hers. He shifted, lifted her hips, and went deeper. She could tell holding back was difficult for him, but he kept his movements slow for her. She joined his rhythm, touched his shoulder muscles, his back, and her hands rested on his lean hips.

"Making love is beautiful, Tallie. Stay with me, honey. When two people care for each other, it is so beautiful." His voice caressed her fears, sending them away. She relaxed, only to tense again. She gasped and looked astonished. He smiled, watching her face as she crested, watched with joy as she fell. He let go and joined her, skidding and falling into bliss.

He lay there, pressing her into the bed, unable to move. His thoughts jumbled. He hadn't expected this depth of feeling. Tallie held him close, her fingers drawing circles on his back, her breath warm against his shoulder. Tom felt a fluttering in his chest and a catch in his throat. He rolled from her, pulling her along. Stunning feelings coursed through him. For years, sex had been a physical release, nothing more. But his heart was fully engaged now. How could it not be? He couldn't hold this woman without wanting her, without wanting to protect her and keep her safe. He'd known the first time he saw Tallie Peters she would be different and he'd been right. He kissed her, soft-lipped and reassuring.

She laid a hand across his heart, feeling its beat beneath her palm, steady and strong. Slowly, she moved her hand across his muscled body, stopping to cup his hip, feeling power in the fact she could. At least for this moment, his body belonged to her and she wanted to touch every bit of him. With Tom, she enjoyed a comfort level she'd never known. She buried her face against his chest and laughed. "I did it," she said. "I wasn't sure if I could."

"What?" he said, his voice lazy.

"This. When I decided to seduce you, I didn't stop to think about all this, the reality of this." She rubbed her hand along his thigh, raking the short black hair with her fingertips. "I nearly ran out the door a couple of times."

"I know."

She sucked air through her teeth and cringed. "It wasn't you. It's just...remembering. Then you talked to me and I forgot for a bit. It was wonderful, Tom. Thank you," she whispered.

Tom smiled a lazy, satiated smile. "You're welcome. I don't think I've ever been thanked before." He grabbed her butt and squeezed. "You aren't planning to run now, are you?"

"No. I'm good."

He surprised her with a quick roll resulting in his long body stretched on top of hers. "Good, because I'd thought, maybe, we might..." He raised an eyebrow and smiled.

Her breath caught. "Again?"

"Unless you don't want to. You were kind of tense the first time," he said. "I thought you might like to try again."

She bit her lip, contemplating. "Okay. If you think we should."

Tom nodded seriously. "Oh yeah. I think it's a mental health necessity. I've never heard of anyone being cured in one therapy session, and I'm not anywhere near done with you."

Hours later, they sat on the porch swing. The night air cooled with the disappearing sun. Frogs sang an evening chorus. Tom held Tallie's hand but released it when Clay and Harlie brought the boys home, deciding it best to keep the kids in the dark for a while. They were uncertain of their boys' reaction to this new situation. Tom knew Tallie feared Cody would be angry if a man touched her. Tom was trying to form a relationship with Michael and didn't want him to feel competition from Tallie. So they agreed to play it cool.

Not that it did a lot of good. Judging by the smile on Clay's face, he'd figured out what they'd been up to immediately.

"How was the show?" Tom called to the boys as they ran up the steps.

"Great. A lot of old twangy music, but Clay is cool," Michael said, eyeing Tom and Tallie sitting close before heading into the house with Cody on his heels.

"See, babe, I'm not the only one who thought some of that was twangy. But you were cool." Harlie grinned. Clay gave her a quick kiss.

"Just so you keep thinking that, I don't care what you say about the rest of them." Clay sat in a cedar deck chair and pulled Harlie into his lap. "You two have a nice evening without the kids?" Clay asked, making Tom squirm.

"Yeah, thanks for taking them." Tom gave Clay a *leave it alone* look.

"Watched some TV, I suppose. Ouch!" he cried out as Harlie kicked his leg.

"Sorry, love bug. I didn't realize that was you." Harlie gave him an innocent look that made him grin.

Red faced, Tallie jumped up from her chair. "If you want to stay, I'll make some coffee." She made a hasty departure into the house. Harlie followed a moment later.

After the women left, Clay turned to Tom with expectation in his eyes. "Well?"

"What?"

"You two."

"What about us?"

Clay laughed. "Buddy, I haven't seen you look this relaxed in ages. I was just wondering—"

"Don't," Tom said, glaring at Clay.

"Ah." Clay leaned back in his chair. "That's the way it is. I think it's great and it's about time, too." He chuckled at Tom's ticked-off glower. "I'm not going to tease you, Tom. But I will say it is pretty obvious to anyone who looks at you two that you're involved. You're trying awfully hard to look uninvolved."

Tom frowned. "We don't want the boys to know anything has changed. There are problems where both of them are concerned."

"I imagine there are, but even they are going to figure it out eventually."

"I suppose, but we'll deal with that when it happens."

Tallie filled the coffee pot and the soft gurgle of water filling the machine soothed her nerves. It was humiliating Clay already knew she and Tom had slept together. She hadn't had time to digest it herself yet. Apparently, she and Tom were throwing off signals any radar could pick up.

Low-flying pilots probably knew she'd slept with him. She assessed her clothing, making sure she hadn't omitted anything important, like her shirt, and was relieved everything was in place. Her lips were swollen, but here wasn't much she could do about that, and her body felt thoroughly and pleasantly used. After loading the filter and dumping coffee grounds in the machine, Tallie smiled to herself. Yes, she felt well-used and hoped for the chance to do it again soon. Tom was a wonderful lover. Passionate, considerate, and knowledgeable of a woman's needs. Hmmm. She hummed, remembering all the things they'd done that second time. She'd relaxed and enjoyed herself, not worried about what used to be, only thinking about here and now. Tom was her here and now. She flushed, thinking about how he'd caressed her with those work-worn hands, so tough and tender at the same time. And the way he whispered in her ear, encouraging her to join him, to fly with him, his already-low voice rough with passion...

"Can I give you a hand with anything?"

Startled from her fantasy, Tallie turned to find Harlie smiling in the kitchen doorway. She shook her head and crossed her arms tightly. "Uh, no, Harlie. I have it under control, thank you." How long had the woman been standing there? Long enough from the half smile she wore. It was a knowing smile, similar to Clay's. Tallie turned, opened the cupboard, and selected coffee mugs. "Thanks for taking the boys with you tonight. Cody hasn't seen a show like that before. I'll bet he was wide-eyed through the whole thing."

"He got a kick out of it and thought it was cool he knew one of the performers. Clay took them backstage and introduced them around."

Tallie picked up a dishrag and scrubbed the counter, trying not to look at Harlie. She was sure her cheeks blushed crimson. It was bad enough Tom's friends knew she'd slept with him, but getting caught fantasizing about it, too, was another thing altogether.

"Tallie," Harlie said softly. "Don't mind Clay. He and Tom have been needling each other since they were kids, babies even, from what Clay tells me. He loves Tom like a brother and doesn't mean anything by the teasing."

Tallie stopped in midscrub. "It's embarrassing for everyone to know." She turned a deeper shade of red. From the heat level registering in her cheeks, it must be just short of burgundy. "It should be private."

"I know what you mean. Try living in the Clay Masterson fishbowl for a while. The only time we have privacy is behind locked gates. Photographers follow him everywhere. But there are worse things."

"What could be worse?"

Harlie frowned. "Having Clay leave and know he was so angry, I'd never see him again. Everything worked out and we can look back now and laugh." She gave Tallie's hand an affectionate squeeze. "Maybe you will too. If he makes you happy, what does it matter what other people think?"

Tallie smiled. "I don't know if Tom is happy, but I know how he makes me feel. I've never had anything like this before. Tom is so...sweet and gentle." She smiled. "I've always daydreamed about romance. Bouquets of flowers, stolen kisses in quiet places. All that silly stuff."

Harlie nodded. "Clay brought me a bouquet of daisies once. Handpicked them even. He has a romantic soul."

Tallie sighed. "Handpicked daisies are romantic. Much

more than roses. Anyone can buy roses. If a man brought me sunflowers or some kind of wildflower, I'd melt." She sighed. "I want a man to sweep me off my feet." She touched the bruises on her neck. "Not knock me off of them."

"Well," Harlie said, "I can't vouch for Tom's romantic abilities, but I do know he is a wonderful guy who will go out of his way for someone he cares about."

Tallie nodded. "He's been wonderful to Cody and me, offering us a place to stay. I just hope..." She blushed. "Well, I hope he's happy, too."

"Clay says Tom held onto an impossible love for too long and it hurt him. He's been a walking shell for years, not allowing anyone to get close. Judging by the look on his face when he watched you leave the porch, I think those days are over."

14

Keeping their new relationship secret from the boys proved difficult, and Tom wondered if he and Tallie were doomed from the start. They had to be satisfied with a quick kiss now and then when the boys went out to play. He wanted a lot more and was sure she did, too. By nighttime, he had a plan, and if the boys would ever go to sleep, he'd try to implement it.

By eleven, he was certain the boys were asleep. Their room was dark and the chattering had ceased. Tom snuck by their room and gingerly opened Tallie's door.

"Tallie?" he whispered into the dark. When there wasn't an answer, he slipped off his clothes and tossed them into a pile on the floor. He lifted the sheet and climbed in bed with her, snuggling close. Tallie sighed in her sleep. He moved his hand across her hip and she woke with a start. Her scream was deafening.

"Tallie, it's okay, honey. Wake up. It's me, Tom." He tried to hush her, but the screaming continued until the hall light turned on and the bedroom door opened.

"What's wrong?" Cody asked from the door, visibly shaken by his mother's screams. Michael stood behind him, eyes narrowed.

Tallie looked at Tom with horror when she comprehended what she'd done. "I'm okay, guys. Just a bad dream."

"I heard her screaming and came up to see what was wrong," Tom said, trying to convince the boys. By the looks on their faces, he knew he'd failed.

"What happened to your pants?" Cody asked, obviously suspicious of Tom's explanation.

"I was in a hurry," he grumbled.

"Go back to bed, Cody. I'm fine." Tallie climbed from the bed and walked the boys down the hall. After making sure they were settled, she returned and leaned on the closed door. Her shoulders shook with amusement over Tom's discomfort.

"I'll go." Tom climbed from the bed and found his pants. "Can't do what I want in my own house anymore."

"I'm sorry. Let me know next time, and I'll stay awake." She gave him a kiss and a smile, and he left the room.

An hour later, Tom glanced up from the book he read and smiled when he saw Tallie sneaking in his bedroom door.

"Hi," he whispered. "What are you doing up?"

"Well," she said, sliding across the bed to him, "I thought you might have some ideas."

"I like the idea of you coming to see me. This may be the better way since I'm not likely to scream." He laid his book on the nightstand and took her in his arms. "At least not before I make love to you."

⟨≈⟩

Morning sun poured in the kitchen window, illuminating Tallie as she made a pot of coffee. She heard heavy footsteps behind her and smiled to herself: Tom. After she poured the water and turned on the coffeemaker, he stepped behind her and wrapped her in his embrace

"Sleep well last night?" he whispered.

"Very well. And you?" She leaned into him and he

brushed his lips on her neck.

"I wish you could stay with me longer. I'd love to wake up with you next to me." He nibbled her neck with his teeth.

"It would be lovely, but I'm not ready for the boys to know yet."

"I know—just wishful thinking."

Tallie contemplated turning and initiating a kiss when she heard running footsteps and felt something slam into Tom's back, squishing her between his body and the kitchen counter. She yelped with surprise.

"Get off of her!" Cody shrieked, pummeling the much larger man with his fists. "Leave her alone!"

"What the—!" Tom turned to fend off the hysterical boy's blows. "I'm not hurting her, Cody!" He tried to catch him but failed. Cody landed a solid punch to Tom's gut. "Damn it, Cody! I'm not hurting her."

"Don't touch her! You said she'd be safe here!" Tears ran down his face. "You said!"

"Cody!" Tallie said. "It's okay. He isn't hurting me. I'm fine." She moved to restrain him, but he let out an anguished cry and bolted for the door.

"I thought you were different, but you're just like him! You'll hurt her, just like him!" He threw a killing glare at Tom and shot from the house.

With a worried glance at Tom, Tallie took off after her son. She ran past the barns and corrals, catching him near the fishing pond. He leaned against a tree, crying out his fury, his shoulders shaking. She watched him, distressed over his pain, but decided not to indulge him. His father used his fists in anger and she wouldn't allow Cody to vent his rage the same way. He could talk it out the way other people did.

Tallie leaned against the tree. "You owe Tom an apology."

Cody shook his head violently. "No, I don't. He's hurting you. I don't owe him nothing."

"He's not hurting me. He's not like Roy." Tallie wondered just how badly his father had damaged Cody and what it would take for him to heal. He'd seen the worst Roy could do. He'd been in the car when it crashed, had heard the gunshot, and seen his father's gun pointed at Tallie's head, ready for the killing blast. Although Cody came away from the accident without physical injury, there were emotional scars. Like Tom said, life scars everyone—even innocent children.

Cody sniffled. "He touched you like Roy did when he made you cry. I know what comes next, Mom. He'll hit you and make you beg him to stop hitting you, just like Roy did."

Tallie closed her eyes, remembering Roy's abuse. She shook her head to clear the sticky, cobweb-like memories and opened her eyes. That was over and Tom was nothing like Roy. "No, Cody, Tom won't do that."

"I was there, Mom! I saw what Roy did to you, and Tom will be just like him. He has guns, too. Lots of them. I know—"

Tallie took her son by the shoulders. "Cody—"

He tried to pull away.

"Listen to me." Cody fought to turn away but Tallie held firm. "It's not the same," she said with force. "Tom is a good man. He's gentle and kind. I like him. He has guns because he handles the security on the ranch and he hunts.

Tom won't hurt me." When more tears trickled down Cody's cheeks, she put her arms around him and held him. "He's a good man, Cody." She heard the pickup tires crunching on the gravel driveway. It stopped and she heard footsteps coming near. When she saw the concern in Tom's eyes, she wanted to hold him too. He looked every bit as upset as Cody did.

"Is he okay?" Tom asked quietly.

She gave Cody a reassuring squeeze. "He's fine."

"Can I talk to him?"

"Is that okay, Cody?" Tallie asked.

Cody cast a reproving glare at Tom before nodding his head.

"I'll wait by the truck." Tallie released Cody and walked away.

Tom stepped past the boy to the pond bank, picked up a flat rock, and skimmed it across the water. Cody joined him near the water's edge, shoulders tensed as if ready to hit Tom again if necessary.

"Say what you want to say," Tom said.

"I don't want you touching her," Cody said. "I won't let you hurt her."

Tom skipped another rock and turned to Cody. "I would never hurt her."

"You were touching her like he did when he made her cry." Tears pooled in Cody's eyes again. He wiped them away with a rough sweep of his hand.

Tom tried to think of something to say to a boy who'd watched his mom get hurt when he was only five and too small to help her. Seeing the proof of how Roy mauled Tallie, Tom could understand Cody's rage and hoped he handled the situation right. If he didn't, Tom was sure it would be the end of him and Tallie. He knew how devoted Tallie was to her son. "I was touching her," Tom said. "But I wasn't hurting her. I like your mom and she likes me. Sometimes when grown-ups like each other, they touch." Tom picked up another rock and sent it bouncing across the water. Cody watched with interest. "I'm not like your dad."

"Roy. I don't call him Dad. He doesn't deserve it." Cody shoved his fists into his shorts pockets.

"Okay. I'm not like Roy. I don't use my fists on women and kids, never have. I won't hurt your mom or you. I can promise you that. Just like I promised your mom a safe place to stay. Me liking her doesn't make her any less safe."

Cody stared off across the pond. "Mike says you don't hit him."

"That's right."

"So I guess I have to believe Mom that you don't hurt her." Cody straightened his shoulders and stared into Tom's eyes with defiance. "If you ever try, you have to deal with me."

Tom had the urge to smile at the skinny boy struggling into manhood but refrained. "I'll keep that in mind, Cody. It's good you want to protect your mom. I want to protect her, too."

"Are you going to kill Roy?" Cody found a flat rock and tried to skip it like Tom had.

Tom picked up another rock and showed him how to hold it in his fingers. "I prefer to have the cops take care of Roy, but I'll do what's necessary to protect you and your mom." Tom watched with a smile as Cody successfully skipped his next rock. "Good job. Try this one. It's nice and flat." He handed him another rock.

"Mom said I have to apologize to you." He stared at the ground, holding the rock tight in his fist. "I'm sorry I hit you. You don't hate me, do you?" When he looked up, there was a hopeful gleam in his eyes.

"No, I don't hate you. Sometimes people do and say things when they're angry they wouldn't otherwise. I won't ever use my fists on you and I'd appreciate the same." Tom looked out over the water, listening to the gentle lap against the shore. A peaceful spot; it always calmed and soothed and it appeared to be working on Cody.

"It's okay with me if you want to hang out with Mom. She says you're a good guy and she likes you."

"Thanks, Cody. I'm glad to know you approve. Just so you know, if you see me holding your mom's hand, she's holding mine too." Tom handed Cody another rock and picked one for himself. "One more and we need to go eat breakfast. I'm starving."

"Me, too." Cody grinned as he let loose of his rock. It skipped four times, one more than Tom's. "I'm really hungry now."

They wandered to the truck, debating the menu choices for breakfast, and were back to normal by the time they reached Tallie.

"Pancakes," Cody said.

"I'm thinking waffles," Tom countered.

"What's the difference? They taste the same."

"Maybe so, but pancakes don't have those little dips for the syrup and butter to collect in."

"Hadn't thought of that," Cody said. "Okay, waffles.

Mike likes them, too."

Tallie smiled as they joined her. "Sounds like I'm cooking waffles for breakfast?"

Tom leaned in the driver's window while Cody went around to the passenger side.

"No," he said with a smile. "Cody and I are making waffles for you."

"I can't wait to see how that goes," she said with a smile. "You two are okay?" she asked before Cody opened the door.

"I think so. Now the question is, how will Michael take this?"

Tallie sighed. "You did well with this one. Maybe Michael won't mind."

They drove back to the house, where they found Michael waiting on the porch, shifting from one foot to the other.

"Where'd everybody go?" he asked as they climbed the porch steps.

"Cody was upset about something and we went to find him," Tom replied. "He's fine now. Cody and I are fixing waffles. Are you hungry?" Michael's eyes were troubled and Tom wondered if another eruption was imminent. He tried not to think badly of Jolie and the choices she made regarding Michael, but he wished for the effortless familiarity he could have with his son if he'd always known him. He'd like to throw his arm around Michael's shoulders and hug him as his dad had with him, but Michael wouldn't allow it and Tom wouldn't feel comfortable trying.

"What was Cody upset about?" Michael asked after Cody walked in the house with Tallie.

Tom debated before launching into his explanation. He'd

promised Michael the truth and now was the time to deliver. "He saw me kiss Tallie." He dropped the bomb and watched for a response.

"Oh." Michael shrugged, indifferent. "I wondered if he knew about that."

"What do you mean?"

"I saw you kiss her a couple of days ago. She didn't seem grossed out about it."

Tom laughed. "No, I don't think she's grossed out. Here I've been worried about what you'd think and you already knew."

Michael shrugged.

"So you don't care if Tallie and I are together?"

"Mom kissed Jason all the time. She liked it okay. No big deal," Michael said.

"Well, I guess I won't worry about it. Let's go eat." Tom opened the door, waiting for Michael to walk through.

Michael hesitated. "Tom?"

"Yeah?"

"Can I help with the waffles too?"

Tom grinned. "You bet. My waffle-building ability is limited and I can use all the help I can get."

After breakfast, Tom received a phone call from Lon announcing Gib Sanborn's arrival.

"He's here in the office and wants to see you. Says his schedule changed and he had to stop here a day early," Lon said.

"Shoot. I've got a guy coming in for an interview this morning, Lon. Looks like you'll have to talk to him. You know what you need. Just make sure to check him out good. Find out what you can and I'll look it over later. If I get done with Gib, I'll run in and talk to the guy myself." Tom hated to turn the responsibility over to Lon where hiring was concerned, but Gib was his best customer for the bulls and he didn't want to keep him waiting. He'd have to trust his foreman.

"If you don't make it, don't worry about it, Tom. I can handle it."

Tom disconnected the phone, grabbed his keys, and took off for the office.

Roy Peters took a last look in the mirror, making sure his makeover was complete. His blond hair was dyed red, his mustache had come in nice, and the glasses altered his appearance dramatically. The blond mustache concerned him, but he'd seen guys with red hair and blond mustaches and thought it would work. For the interview, he outfitted himself with Wranglers and a work shirt. He also wore Phin's worn cowboy hat and roughed-up boots. The small Bible rested in his shirt pocket. He drove to the MB Ranch in Phin's dilapidated Ford truck, rehearsing as he went, using Phin's resume as a script. On arrival, he was buzzed in the gate and directed to the office where Tom Black waited for him. Phin's papers in hand, he sauntered into the office.

Once inside, he didn't miss a detail, memorizing everything for future reference: the locations of the security monitors, the guns in the case, and the offices. He'd also noticed the relatively short distance between the office and a house he assumed was Tom Black's. The temptation was strong to leave now and make his way there, grab his kid, and run. But he'd been impatient once with Tallie and it cost him, so he cooled his craving, opened the office door, and began his charade.

"Mulberry?" a voice called from a back office.

"Yes, sir."

A balding head poked out the office door into the hall where Roy waited. "Come in. I'm Lon Taylor, ranch foreman. Tom Black has another meeting this morning, so I'll talk with you. Come on back." He waved him in, offering him the chair opposite the desk.

"Phineas Mulberry." Roy offered his hand to Lon. "But everybody calls me Phin. I can't stand that highbrow-sounding name." His eyes quickly scanned the office, noticing window locations and other details. "So, you need to hire?"

"We had a guy leave not too long ago and need to replace him. Where have you worked before?"

Roy handed the foreman Phin's resume.

"You worked for Tim Rowe? I'll be damned." Lon smiled. "I worked for Tim years ago. Heck of a guy. He had the prettiest daughter, but I imagine she's married and gone by now."

Roy tensed. "You mean Rosemary?"

Lon frowned. "No, that wasn't it. Gad, I can't remember..."

"Roseanne...Roxanne... Yeah, that's her name."

Lon nodded and smiled. "Yeah, that's her."

"I think she got engaged to someone, but I can't remember who." Roy watched Lon closely for any signs of disbelief and saw none. Slam dunk.

"No matter. Have you ever worked with bulls?" Lon asked.

"Yes, sir. I worked for a stock contractor when I was just

out of school, Gib Sanborn."

Lon leaned back in his chair and laughed. "Well, now, that's a coincidence. He's here today talking to Tom about buying Spitfire. We can wander out and have a chat with him." Lon reached for the ringing phone. "Excuse me a moment."

A sheen of sweat covered Roy's forehead. What would he do if they met? Chances were good Gib Sanborn would know he wasn't Phin. The resemblance wasn't that close. If Gib questioned his identity, all of his carefully laid plans would crumble to dust.

"Okay. We'll catch you later." Lon hung up the phone. "That was Tom. He's taking Gib up to Clay Masterson's house for lunch, so I guess we won't have a chance to talk to him." Lon leaned back in his chair, eyeing Roy closely. Roy could feel the sweat from his brow trickle down his face and was sure he'd done something to tip the man off.

"Usually Tom does the hiring, but since he's tied up today, it's my job. He'll want to run a check on you, but with your experience, I'll recommend he hire you. I can't see any reason not to. When can you start?"

"Tomorrow, if you need me."

"I could use you. Where are you living?" Lon asked, still eyeing Roy closely.

"A motel room for now, but Mr. Black mentioned a bunkhouse on the phone."

"We have a bunkhouse some of the guys like to stay in. You're welcome to use it if it suits you. Tom won't have you on security detail until he gets to know you, so you'll be on the day crew. Later on, he may add you to the night watch rotation."

"Why all the security?" Roy asked, feigning innocence.

"Several reasons. Clay Masterson is the main one. He lives in the big house near the front of the ranch. You wouldn't believe all the gooney people who want a glimpse of Clay. You'll see them standing around outside the fence with cameras, yelling at him. Some of the gals even blow kisses his way and try to throw things over the fence. Sometimes we find ladies panties stuck in the chain link. Plumb goofy, if you ask me," Lon said with a chuckle. "And the second reason is a friend of Tom's, Tallie Peters. Her ex-husband assaulted her and is trying to take her kid. We've stepped up the security because of them."

Roy nodded thoughtfully. "Some men are that way, I guess. Shameful, isn't?" Roy patted the Bible in his pocket the way Phin had at the bar.

"You got that right. Anyway, I have some things to get to," he said. "Be here at six tomorrow morning and I'll get you settled."

"I'll be here. Thank you, sir." Roy contained the urge to do a little dance on his way out. He just needed to make it through one more night in the city without getting picked up, and he'd be secure within the MB Ranch fence. It was the last place on earth the cops would think to look for him.

⁂

Tom finished his business with Gib on a high note. The stock contractor loved Spitfire and wanted the surly bull as soon as he could get him. Gib readily agreed to Tom's price and that put him into a fine mood. He talked with Lon afterward and was satisfied with his report of the interviewee. Tom made the necessary calls and found Mulberry's references impeccable. His former employers, including Gib, sang his praises and lamented that he'd moved on from their employ.

There was just one hitch. Lon offered Phin the bunkhouse before Tom had a chance to meet him. Tom had mentioned the bunkhouse over the phone as a possibility, but he never let a new hand in that fast. Rather than call and renege, Tom decided to meet Phin when he arrived first thing in the morning. With his glowing references, the guy should check out. For now, he considered the matter settled.

Tom had spent most of the day in the office and was getting stir-crazy staring at the walls. By midafternoon, he'd had enough and went to find Tallie and the boys. He liked the sound of that, Tallie and the boys. They were a family of sorts and the thought pleased him. He hadn't considered having a family for years, not since Jolie left. Now he had one plunked in his lap and was content with it. Clay was right. It was a tremendous feeling.

He walked to the corrals, hoping the boys weren't done with their riding lessons. Cody hadn't been on a horse before and Michael shrugged when asked. He shrugged about everything though. Ask him if the sky was blue and the kid would shrug. Tom wasn't sure if the kid was indifferent by nature or just putting on an act for his father's benefit. Time would tell.

As expected, Tallie leaned on the corral fence, shouting encouragement to the young riders and laughing at the trouble Cody had with his horse. Tom walked up behind her and placed his hands on her hips, pulling her against him.

"I was wondering if you'd be stuck inside all day." Despite the heat, Tallie snuggled against Tom. The boys continued riding around the corral, with Michael eyeing Tom and Tallie occasionally.

"Would you like to go for a ride? I'll saddle a couple of horses and we can take the boys out."

"How about one horse and I'll ride with you? I haven't been on horseback in years and I used an English saddle, not western."

"All right. I'll be back soon." Tom stepped away but turned back to give Tallie a kiss before leaving.

A short time later, Tom returned on a buckskin quarter horse.

"Would you boys like to go for a ride?" he asked to Cody's cheers and Michael's predictable shrug. Instead of growing closer to Michael, he drifted further away and Tom didn't know how to remedy the situation. "Rob, open the gate and let them out."

Tallie was about to give Tom her hand when Michael's mare shot from the corral, running wildly with the boy holding fast to her back.

"Shit!" Tom exclaimed. "Stay here. I'll go get him." He urged his horse to a gallop but couldn't catch Michael's runaway. He thought it odd Cornflower would bolt that way. Her docile nature was the main reason Michael rode her. He watched Michael closely as he neared him and realized he didn't hold on in fear. He urged Cornflower to run, turning occasionally to see if Tom followed.

Tom rode up beside Michael. "Slow down!"

"Yah!" Michael grinned and pushed Cornflower to go faster. He took a sharp right to Tom's house and slowed the mare so Tom could catch him.

"Get off of that horse right now!" Tom yelled as he

stopped near Michael and dismounted. "What did you think you were doing, riding like that? She could have broken a leg, and you could have been hurt."

"She didn't," Michael said as he slid from the saddle.

"That was irresponsible of you, Michael." Tom turned away, trying to curb his anger. This wasn't the way he wanted to be with his son. He turned around to see Michael kicking at the dirt with his tennis shoe, eyeing Tom. "Why didn't you tell me you could ride like that?" Tom's anger subsided and he had a hard time not smiling when Michael flashed a proud grin. "Your mom let you ride?"

"No, she didn't know about it. My friend Matt had horses and his dad let us ride them. I know what I'm doing." The belligerence returned to his voice.

"It would've been nice of you to let me know. You scared at least five years off me. I asked several times and you didn't say anything."

"I wanted to show you I could do it, that I can be a cowboy like you. Maybe you'd notice me, too," Michael said. His voice was low and edged with hurt.

"Notice you? You don't think I notice you?" It felt like a sack of concrete landed on him, flattening him to the ground. "I notice you all the time, Michael, but you've been so quiet. I thought you needed time to adjust and settle in. What should I do differently?"

Michael shoved his hands in his pockets and kicked at an imaginary rock with his toe. "You spend all your time with Tallie and Cody now." Michael's voice was so low, Tom could barely hear him. "Maybe we could go riding, just you and me."

"We can do that. I'm sorry. I didn't know you felt that

way."

Michael shrugged, obviously embarrassed to have his feelings exposed.

"Hop back up there. I imagine Cornflower has a few miles left in her today. We need to go by the corral and tell Tallie though. She'll be worried about you." Tom swung up on his mount and motioned for Michael to follow. The kid mounted in a flash. Tom laughed and shook his head.

"What?" Michael asked.

"You ride like you were born to it, like I did, and your grandpa. You've got some cowboy in you. Come on." Tom took off with Michael on his heels, riding fast but not reckless. As they rounded the barn and saw Tallie, they slowed their horses and stopped near her.

"How is he?" Tallie asked.

Tom leaned down. "He's fine. Heck of a rider."

"You sound proud, Tom." Tallie smiled at him.

"He's like me at his age. Do you mind if we go riding, just him and me? I'll explain later."

"Sure. I'll hang out here with Cody. He freaked out watching Michael, so I don't think he's ready for the open road yet."

"Maybe not," Tom agreed. "I'll be back in a bit."

Tom and Michael made several laps around the ranch before resting the horses near the pond's edge. They dropped onto the bank in the shade of a huge maple tree and relaxed while the horses drank their fill. Michael furrowed his brow.

"What's on your mind, Michael?"

"Nothing."

"Are you sure?" Tom picked up a small rock and tossed it in the water.

Michael took a breath. "You don't love my mom anymore, do you?"

Tom thought for a moment, looked out over the water, and tried to form an answer acceptable to an eleven-year-old. "I never stopped loving her, and even though she's gone, there is a part of me that still loves her. I always will."

"How can that be?" Michael picked up a small rock and dropped it in the water with a plunk.

"Even after she left, I loved her as much as I ever had, and I kept hoping she'd come back. There wasn't anyone else after her. And now that she's gone, I still love her, but in a different way." Tom pressed his hand over his heart. "I have a permanent spot for her right here, and I think about her sometimes. If I close my eyes and concentrate, I can hear her laugh in the back of my mind." A lump formed in his throat as he remembered the last time he'd heard her sweet laugh.

"But what about Tallie? How can you love Mom and like Tallie, too? Won't she take over Mom's spot?"

"When your mom died, I had to let go. I couldn't continue loving her the same way, like I did when I hoped she'd come back. I have to move on, make a life for you and me."

Michael looked at Tom with intense green eyes. "Why did Mom leave you?"

"What did she tell you?"

"She wouldn't say. Whenever I asked about you, she clammed up. I asked Grandma once. She said you disappointed Mom, but I don't understand what that means, and Grandma wouldn't explain it to me." Michael's eyes were filled with expectation.

Tom saw the need in the boy's eyes, the need to understand why the grown-ups in his life did what they did. "Disappointed, oh yeah. I disappointed her and myself, big-time. She didn't tell you anything at all?"

Michael shook his head.

"Well, kiddo, you won't ever be able to say that about me. I'll tell you anything you want to know. I can't imagine what it's been like for you to think you were alone in the world without any family. I need to get them all here to meet you soon, or maybe I'll take you to Montana for a visit so you can see where we're from. You look like your Grandpa Black. He's tall and black-haired like me. You've got some Irish, Scottish, and a little Crow in you from our side. Just a little from way back, maybe five generations or so."

The corner of Michael's mouth lifted into a half smile. "Indian or bird?"

Tom laughed. "Don't be thinking you can fly. There's a bit of Native in you. That's where you get those good-looking cheekbones that'll drive the girls crazy someday."

Michael put his fingers to his cheek and frowned.

Tom chuckled. "You can trust me on that one. They'll like you and you'll be happy about it." He blew out a breath. "But, that isn't what you need, is it?" Tom looked out over the water, remembering the good times with Jolie. There had been plenty of those before the accident. "Your mom was the prettiest girl I'd ever seen—strawberry-blonde hair and the sweetest smile—and I knew I had to have her for my own. After we started dating, I couldn't stand being away from her, but I had to travel to do my job. It took some convincing, but she agreed to travel with me to my competitions. We went all over the country in an old motor home—Vegas, Albuquerque, even New York. It was an ugly thing with worn-out green seats and a lumpy mattress, but she said she didn't care. She thought it was all great fun." He smiled at the memory. "I asked her to marry me the night before that bull tried to kill me. After the accident, I fell apart. My career was over, money was running low, and I was scared. I got depressed and started drinking. They explain alcohol abuse to you in school, don't they?" Michael nodded. "Well, I abused it pretty bad. Your mom tried to get me to stop, but the depression wouldn't let go and I couldn't stop. Jolie told me I'd done the one thing she wouldn't put up with—drinking. Your other grandpa, your mom's dad, was an alcoholic and Jolie grew up rough because of it. When I started drinking, I disappointed her. I wasn't who she thought I should be. I wasn't who I thought I should be either. When she found out she was pregnant with you, she left, and I never saw her again."

"How did you know about me?"

"Jason brought a video your mom made explaining everything. I'll show it to you sometime, if you like." He turned to look at Michael. "I'd have been there if I'd known about you. Please, believe me. You'd have known me if she'd told me about you."

"Do you hate her for it?"

"No, I understand her reasons. When she left, I couldn't make it through the day without getting drunk. She didn't want you growing up with that. But I straightened out. If she'd come back, she'd have seen I could be a father to you. I would've loved to watch you grow up. When Jason showed me the birth certificate with your little footprint, it tore me apart to know I'd missed so much of your life." Tom stared across the water, fighting the anger that came when he thought about all he'd missed: Michael's first steps, first words, seeing him ride a bike for the first time. The anger was aimed at Jolie in part but more and more at himself.

Michael nodded. "Sometimes I hated her for not telling me about you. I wanted to know where I came from. I don't look like Mom. I wanted to know who I was and she wouldn't tell me."

"It's my fault, not hers. If I had been a better person, she wouldn't have left. Don't hate your mom. She was wonderful. The best."

Michael nodded. "I think she was afraid I'd leave her to find you. She was afraid of being alone."

"What's done is done. We can't change the past. I hope I can make up for all the years we didn't have, Michael. But I have to tell you, there is a good possibility Tallie and Cody may be a part of our life."

"I know. Just don't forget about me."

"I won't." Tom smiled at Michael. They sat for a few minutes in companionable silence, listening to the warblers, watching mallards bob on the water. A trout jumped and splashed. Michael closed his eyes and smiled.

"What are you smiling about?" Tom asked.

Michael opened his eyes and gazed up at the passing clouds, a shadow of a smile on his lips. "I was just listening to Mom laugh."

15

It was 5:55 a.m. Tom squinted against the early morning sun, sipping hot coffee. He felt hungover but it wasn't booze giving the wrung-out feeling. It was Tallie and her midnight visits. He wasn't complaining but relishing the glorious fatigue that comes from making love to a beautiful woman through the night. She'd stayed to watch the sunrise, wrapped in his arms. He could get used to this real easy.

The air was pleasant. Mugginess would prevail soon, but for now, Tom enjoyed leaning on the porch post outside the office door. At 5:59 a.m. the gate buzzer in the office sounded. As instructed, Mulberry was at Tom's gate, not the main gate by Clay's. He could see a run-down truck waiting to enter and meandered into the office.

"Come straight in," Tom told him via intercom. "I'm at the office. You can't miss it." The gate swung open and the red Ford accelerated. Tom took a last gulp of the now-cooling coffee, set his mug on the railing, and waited until the truck pulled to a stop next to Tom's pickup. Mulberry seemed to hesitate before getting out. Nerves, maybe. No. He looked for something on the seat, sticking it in his breast pocket, before climbing from the truck cab. As the new employee walked to him, Tom saw the item in Mulberry's pocket was a small Bible. He supposed that was a good sign, a character reference of sorts. As the newcomer came near, Tom held out his hand.

"Tom Black."

Roy clasped Tom's hand. "Phineas Mulberry. It's good to meet you...sir."

Tom thought the handshake went on a heartbeat too long while Phineas gave him the same once-over Tom was giving him, like two bull elk preparing to lock antlers. From the odd look in the guy's eyes, he wasn't sure if he rated too high in ol' Phineas' estimation. Too bad. Tom's opinion was what mattered in this arena.

"Come in the office, Phineas—"

"Phin, sir, just Phin. I don't care for the other."

"Fine. Phin." Tom opened the office door and motioned for the new hire to follow. "I'll need your ID and social security card." Phin again hesitated. What was wrong with the guy? Jumpy, for some reason. Phin opened his wallet and handed over the requested items. While Tom made photocopies, Phin gazed out the window toward Tom's house.

"Nice place," Phin said. "Is it the foreman's house?"

Nosey bugger, Tom thought, but recanted the hasty assessment. Phin was new here and was showing interest, making conversation. He'd give a tour of the ranch in a few minutes anyway, so what was the big deal? Tallie. That's what. He was incredibly protective of her and didn't like this guy staring her way.

"No. That's my place. I'll show you around as soon as we're done here." He handed back the ID, glancing between the license photo and Phin's face. Phin was barefaced in the photo. No glasses. No glasses restriction listed either.

"Been wearing those glasses long?" Tom asked.

Phin tensed. "No, sir. Just developed astigmatism lately."

Tom nodded. That seemed reasonable enough. So why was he getting a weird vibe from the guy? Like a panther ready to pounce on him. Maybe Tom made him nervous. He smiled, trying to lighten the mood. "I'll take you around the ranch and show you the bunkhouse. I'll be honest with you, Phin. Lon jumped the gun offering you the bunkhouse so soon. When you and I talked before, I said it was something that could be available to you later on."

Phin narrowed his eyes.

"I'm not saying you can't be there. I am saying I'm not real comfortable with it so soon. I don't know you yet."

"Well, sir, I'll do my best to earn your trust. You won't regret it."

"I'm counting on that. Would you like a cup of coffee before we go?"

"I just had a cup with breakfast. But thank you for the kind offer...sir."

Tom frowned. Phin's constant use of "sir" was grating, especially considering the effort he put into the word, like he was choking on it. "Let's go."

As they drove the ranch, Tom tried to draw Phin out, get him to talk. Since Tom wasn't a great conversationalist himself, the effort was clunky and ineffective. Phin answered his questions but little more. What happened to the chatterbox he'd talked with on the phone last week? Tom shrugged it off, attributing it to nerves.

Tom pointed out the corrals, the bullpens, the hay barns, and equipment shed. He explained what Phin's duties would be, which included just about anything needing done.

"Low man on the totem pole sort of stuff at first," Tom said with a chuckle. "Lon will keep you busy."

"No problem, sir. Idle hands are the devil's workshop," Phin said with a serious nod.

"Yeah. I've heard that," Tom said and went on to explain the security situation, about Clay, Harlie, and Abby. He hesitated to elaborate on Tallie's situation, especially when Phin's eyes kept drifting back to Tom's house.

When Tom caught him staring again, Phin said, "I like the look of it. Very homey. My grandma had a similar house."

Okay. Phin was having a trip down memory lane. He couldn't fault the guy for that. Tom stopped the truck at the bunkhouse and led Phin inside. It was a basic structure with a community kitchen, living room, laundry, and bathroom. Three bedrooms. Only one was occupied at the moment. Phin would have his choice of the other bedrooms. "Housekeeping is your responsibility. This isn't the Sheraton so don't expect maid service. I'll warn you, Rob is a fussy roommate. Nothing pisses him off more than a dirty kitchen. Keep it clean or he'll want you out of here. Rob has been with me for years, so you can bet I listen to him."

Phin nodded. "Cleanliness is next to godliness, sir."

"Yeah. I've heard that."

The tour complete, Tom dropped Phin back at his truck and told him to get settled in the bunkhouse. Lon would find him there in a while and put him to work.

At home, he parked in his driveway, unable to shake the feeling that something was off about the guy. But why? Lon thought he was terrific. All his references checked out. His former employers loved him. Tom pulled his cell phone from his pocket and hit speed dial.

"Gib. Tom Black here. Sorry to call so early."

"Tom? Don't sweat the early hour. I rise with the sun. Is something wrong with my bull?"

"No. Nothing like that," Tom said. "I just wanted to ask you something...about this new guy I hired, Phineas Mulberry."

"Phin? I don't know that I can tell you any more than I did yesterday. He got along fine working for me."

Tom paused, not sure what he even wanted to ask. "Yeah, I know. But is there something, I don't know, a little weird about the guy?"

"How so?"

"I don't know. That's the problem. I get this odd feeling when I talk to him...like something isn't right. I can't put my finger on it though."

Gib chuckled. "Well, he is a handy one with the platitudes and scripture. That made a few of my guys leery around him at first. You know how cowboys are, kind of a rough-talking bunch among themselves. They worried Phin would take offense, but they warmed up when they realized his halo is a bit crooked."

Tom tensed at the mention of crooked haloes. "How so?"

"Our friend Phin likes to tie one on occasionally, but I've never known it to keep him from doing his work. He's a Saturday night hell-raiser. Stays dry the rest of the week."

"Nothing unusual there. Most of my guys like to hang out at Lefty's on occasion. I guess I'm just nitpicking." Tom laughed. "He's only been here an hour. I suppose I'd better give him a chance first."

"Maybe so," Gib said. "Despite his occasional boozing, Phin's a decent sort. Carries his Bible in his pocket everywhere he goes. Pats it occasionally. Not sure what that's about. Maybe just a habit."

"I noticed." He sighed. "Thanks, Gib. I appreciate the info." He disconnected the call and headed to the house.

Phin wore a crooked halo...just like Roy Peters.

No wonder the guy made him paranoid.

⚬⊸

Lon sent Roy to the barns and put him on the end of a shovel. From the shadows, Roy watched his family throughout the afternoon. There'd been a moment when he considered grabbing Cody from the corral, but Rob stuck close. Tallie, too. The way she turned her head, he wondered if she sensed his presence. He hoped she did.

When the boys finished riding, he followed them to the house and considered making the grab, but he changed his mind about snatching him in broad daylight. He'd wait until dark, when he could get away quicker and they couldn't follow as easily. Not now but soon.

Roy watched from behind a tree as Tallie moved around the kitchen making dinner. He made a mental note of everything she did and enjoyed it when she looked out the window, frowning. Roy chuckled to himself. Tallie could feel his eyes on her again. Good. He wanted her nervous. And when he took his kid, he wanted her scared. He wanted to bust her down a notch. She deserved it.

Tom came home and went straight to the kitchen, making sure the boys were upstairs before he put his arms around Tallie and kissed her. The way they were going at it, Roy wondered if they would do it in the kitchen while he watched. Anger flashed hot as he watched his ex-wife kiss another man with passion. She'd never been like that with him. If she had, maybe they wouldn't have had problems. To his thinking, their relationship had been normal, just like everybody else. Just like his parents before his dad moved to

Arizona.

Everything that happened was Tallie's fault and Roy laughed as he contemplated how sweet his revenge would be.

16

Two weeks had passed since Tallie's encounter with Roy. The police had no leads on Roy's whereabouts and Tom knew Tallie was growing restless. She missed her job and her freedom. Tom's nerves were also frayed as he checked with the police daily, only to hear the same tired refrain: There was no trace of Roy Peters anywhere.

Tallie confided to Tom that she thought the pressure had led to hallucinations. She had this creepy feeling of being watched, but when she turned around, she was alone. Even in the house, she had the feeling of eyes following her and that Roy was somewhere close by. Tom took what she said to heart and searched the neighborhood but found nothing out of the ordinary. He talked with neighbors to see if they'd seen any strangers or been missing anything that might indicate Roy was hiding in the area. Nothing turned up. His frustration mounted when Tallie talked about her need to return to work.

"No!" he argued again for what seemed like the hundredth time. "You can't leave until they find him."

"Tom, I can't hide here forever. For all we know, Roy may be gone, maybe back to Arizona to his dad's place. I can't keep sitting here." Tallie paced the living room floor. "I need to go back to work. Cody is who he wants, and if he's safe here on the ranch, why can't I go back to work?"

"And what's to stop him from grabbing you and demanding Cody? You've said yourself, the guy is unbalanced, and he won't stop until you're dead. Why wouldn't he go after you at work?" He held her arm to stop the pacing. She looked at him defiantly.

"You can't keep me prisoner here forever, Tom. I'll do what I want." She pulled her arm from his hand.

Tom sighed and admitted defeat. "You're right. I can't keep you here forever. It's your decision if you stay or leave." He turned from her and moved to the door. "I don't want anything to happen to either of you. Do what you want. Cody is welcome to stay as long as he needs to." Tom pushed open the screen door but stopped when Tallie spoke.

"Don't walk away, please."

Tom turned and looked at her; his heart wrenched at the distress in her eyes. "I'm not walking away. I thought we needed space to calm down." He walked back and took her in his arms. "I want you safe."

"I know." She clung to him. "I'm frustrated and scared."

"Me, too." He was frustrated that Roy was still free and Tallie couldn't lead a normal life, scared that she'd leave and he'd never see her again. He brushed his hand across her soft curls and spoke softly. "I know it isn't what you want, but there are a lot of things you could do here. I'll be in the office this morning. I'd love to have you hang out with me there. The boys like it when you watch them ride. Cowboys always want an audience to show off for, and Cody is a real ham." He kissed her temple. "Rob is getting the horses ready for them. He could saddle one for you too. Or Harlie might like some company. She'll probably go swimming with Abby soon."

She sighed and relaxed her shoulders. "I don't want to disturb you while you work. I already feel like a burden here."

Tom laughed. "If you are, you're the most enjoyable burden I've ever carried."

"Thanks. That's good to hear. Maybe I should take up knitting or something."

"I'd like to see that."

She looked up at him and smiled. "I'll watch the boys. Cody is doing well."

"He's a sharp kid and learns fast." Tom released her from his hug. Crisis averted. "I'll catch up with you when I'm done. Are you okay?"

"Yeah." She shrugged. "I'm fine."

After Tom left, Tallie straightened the living room, putting away Cody's shoes and the board game they played the night before. As she stood on tiptoes sliding the box back into the boys' closet, the phone rang. She reached it too late. Dial tone.

She held the phone a moment, hesitated, and dialed. Six-zero-two area code. Arizona.

"Kensington Corporation," an efficient female voice said.

"Lawrence Kensington, please."

"He's out of the office today. Would you care to leave a message on voicemail?"

Tallie wavered. "Yeah. Okay. That would be fine." The call was transferred. A male voice came on the line. Tallie leaned her head against the wall and closed her eyes, savoring the smooth timbre, the reassuring nature of the man. Like Tom, he'd always made her feel safe and cherished, too.

"This is Lawrence Kensington. I'm unable to take your call right now. Leave a message after the beep, and I'll call as soon as possible."

Tallie swallowed hard. "Um...oh, never mind," she whispered and disconnected the call. Happy birthday, Dad, had been on the tip of her tongue.

She wiped a tear from her cheek and walked into the hot sunshine, a lump forming in her throat. Maybe next year she wouldn't hang up before finishing the call. In eleven years, she hadn't managed it yet.

⟨∽⟩

He'd been watching her from his desk since she emerged from the house. The tank top, tight, low-cut jeans, and boots sabotaged his concentration. So much so that Tom couldn't get any work done and it annoyed him. When he couldn't focus any longer, he closed the file he worked on and shut down the computer. He was halfway out the door when Lon caught up with him.

"Tom! Wait a sec."

Tom sighed and turned to Lon with a smile. "Yeah. What's up?"

"If you're heading outside, could you do something for me?" he asked, and Tom nodded. "Could you tell Phin to go out to the south pasture and help with those busted sprinklers? I'm on my way to town for parts, and it'll save me time if I don't have to find him."

"Sure. No problem," Tom said. He moved aside to allow Lon out the door ahead of him. Last he'd seen of Phin, he was mucking out the barn near the corral. Tom wandered that way. As he neared the barn door, he saw Phin staring straight at Tallie. Tom had a strange urge to punch the guy. It was a fierce, territorial impulse and one he couldn't remember feeling before.

"Must be love," he muttered to himself. As he watched his new hired hand, Phin knelt to his knee, eyes trained on Tallie, studying her like a butterfly under glass. Tom didn't like the look on the guy's face and planned to have a discussion with him about what part of the ranch was off-limits to the employees. Namely, Tallie. Before Tom reached him, Phin closed his eyes and bowed his head. Tom stopped. After a moment, Phin opened his eyes and looked Tom's direction.

"Sorry, sir. I was just giving thanks for this wonderful opportunity you've given me here on your ranch."

"No problem," Tom said. "Sorry to interrupt. Lon needs you out in the south pasture. Follow this driveway beyond the pond and turn right. You'll see the guys out that way." After Phin left, Tom blew out a breath. This compulsion to break people into pieces on Tallie's behalf was becoming a habit with him. He walked into the hot sun, quietly stepping behind where she leaned on the shed watching the boys ride their horses. He grabbed her hand and pulled her around the corner into the cool shadows. She squealed with surprise.

Greedy lips captured hers, startling her. She started to fight, pushing against his chest, but laughed instead when her eyes adjusted to the darkness and Tom's handsome face came into focus. She'd chew him out later for scaring her, but for now, she'd enjoy his kiss.

"Come with me for a minute. I want to show you something." Humor sparkled in his green eyes. He took her hand and led her down the driveway to a metal building. Taking keys from his pocket, he looked around before unlocking the door. The air inside was refreshing and cool, the hum of the air conditioner the only sound in the dark interior. Tom felt along the wall for a light switch and illuminated the room.

"What is that?"

"Clay's tour bus. Ever seen one?" He pulled her toward the door.

"No. Should we be in here?" she whispered, feeling like a kid sneaking into a movie theatre.

"Sure. I have to take care of the thing, so I'm in here all the time. Come on." He opened the coach door and hit a light switch on his way up the steps.

"Why is it so cool in here?"

"We keep it in a climate-controlled building to protect Clay's investment. Can't just park it in a shed and let the birds nest on it."

Tallie walked around, awed by the large living room, full kitchen, entertainment center, and huge TV. When she stepped in the bedroom door, Tom put his arms around her and she smiled.

"Wanted to show me a tour bus, did you?" She turned in his arms.

"Wanted to make love to you in a tour bus. I've been watching you all morning. I was going nuts thinking I'd have to wait until tonight, when I was blasted by a stroke of genius." He kissed her, stunning her with heat and impatience. "This bus was begging to be used." He smiled. "So am I." He kissed her again, unhurried and deep until her eyes rolled back in her head. The man could kiss—no doubt about it. Slow-motion paradise. His lips trailed down her neck, leaving a warm trail. He pulled the strap of her top down with his finger and moved his warm mouth slowly across her skin before returning to look into her eyes.

"I don't have to wait until midnight, do I?" he asked, his breath ragged.

"No," she said with limited breath. "Don't you dare stop."

He pushed her shirt up, revealing she wore nothing underneath. As he pulled the shirt over her head, he captured her hands and held them over her head and feasted on her neck and breasts. Tallie breathed heavily as he tormented her, making her moan as he bit and nibbled. He assaulted her lips again, continuing to hold her hands as his other hand toyed with her full breast, making her whimper, before trailing down her stomach to unfasten her jeans. Finding success, he plunged his hand into her pants. She jerked against him as he played, not letting her touch him, but making her feel everything. She didn't fight his strength, had no desire to do so, and he held her effortlessly.

She cried out as he sent her over the edge. He watched her face as she climbed and fell, reveling in the sensation of her as her body arched against him. When she was weak and limp, he released her hands and held her.

"Dear god," she muttered, gasping for breath. "And you aren't done, are you?" He shook his head and gave her a mischievous smile.

"That's just round one, honey." He tenderly kissed her lips, the heat starting to build again, but he slowed down so she could briefly regain her senses. While she caught her breath, he helped her kick off her boots before slowly lowering her jeans, planting hot kisses on her flat stomach, running his hands slowly over her hips, kissing and touching.

"What about the bed?" she asked. "I don't think I can stand up." She sucked in her breath as he kissed across her stomach, his breath leaving a warm trail.

"Not yet." Tom kicked off his boots and unzipped his jeans. "Chapter Six, page one-fifty. Modified. You need to stand up for that one."

"What are you talking about?"

"The book you told me about. The one my sister left in the guest room. You said that chapter was particularly interesting."

"You read it?"

He grinned.

"Um...I didn't mean..." She blushed. "I was just using that to tease you. You don't have to..."

"Too late. I'm not sure if I can manage all the acrobatics in the other chapters with my knee difficulty, but I'll give this one my best shot." He gave her a once-over, estimating. "Shouldn't be a problem. If I can lift a hay bale, I figure I can lift you without my knee giving out."

She lifted a brow. "I'm sure I weigh substantially less than a hay bale."

He laughed. "Glad to hear it." Before she could object or offer commentary, he kissed her long and hard. His hands moved across her bare skin, making her shiver. His breathing was harsh, his movements determined as he lifted her, wrapping her legs around his hips. She looked into his eyes as they joined, both moaning at the contact. He held her tight, his fingers digging into her hips as he ground into her, hard and fast against the wall. She gasped, encouraging him to keep going until she could stand it no longer. She called out, her body quivering and shaking. Tom let go and their passions united as they plunged over the edge.

Tom took the few necessary steps and dropped them to

the bed. They lay panting.

"Dear god," she said again, staring at the ceiling.

"Ditto." He fought to regain his breath, thinking every time with Tallie was better than the time before. He rolled onto his side, gently skimming his fingers along her hip, admiring her curves, the delicate dip between hip and tummy and her soft skin. He turned her to her side, saw marks on her hips where his hands had been, and was stricken with guilt.

"I hurt you, Tallie. I'm so sorry." He scooted close against her, holding her. "I didn't mean to hurt you."

"You didn't hurt me." She kissed his nose and smiled.

"You'll have bruises. I shouldn't have been so rough."

"I'm fine." She laughed. "You don't hear me complaining, do you?"

"No."

"Baby, that was the best I've ever experienced, and I don't mind a few fingerprints, as long as they're yours." Tallie propped herself up on her elbow, looking into his eyes. "You have been so careful and tender, making sure I wasn't scared. I wondered when that finely tuned control of yours would explode. It just did and I enjoyed it a lot. Sometimes it's fun to lose control."

Tom smiled and pulled her down to him for a kiss. "I'm glad you feel that way, because I'm planning to see you again at midnight."

"I'm counting on it."

17

"Eww! Gross! Fast-forward it!" Michael held his throat and gagged. "Hurry, I'm getting sick!"

Tom laughed and pushed the button on the remote control. "You guys said you wanted to watch this."

"You didn't tell us there was so much gross stuff." From a pile of pillows on the floor, Cody added his two cents with disgust. "It's disturbing!"

"Hey, if I can watch all the bloody war scenes, you guys can watch the love scenes." Tallie argued as she watched Tom fast-forward the movie. "We could watch the Disney movie I wanted."

"Yuck. We should have watched *Terminator 4* or *X-Men*," Michael commented from his spot in the recliner, laid back with his legs thrown over the arm.

"Give it a rest, guys. *Pearl Harbor* is a good compromise. Tallie gets her love story. We men get blood, guts, and war. Shut up or I'll let Tallie put on *Pinocchio*." Tom winked at Tallie.

"You're evil!" Michael exclaimed in mock horror.

"I like *Pinocchio*." Tallie pouted into Tom's shoulder.

"I did, too, when I was five," Michael said, and Tallie blew a raspberry at him. "Hey, I get in trouble for that."

"Tallie can blow raspberries at anyone she wants." Tom squeezed her and thought about the great time they were having together. Like a family, complete with arguments and teasing. Tom snuggled in tighter with Tallie, enjoying the fact he could lay on the sofa with her draped across him while watching a movie and the boys didn't care. As if sensing his thoughts, Tallie looked up at him and smiled. Tom ran his fingers through her hair and kissed her, jumping when a pillow hit him in the head.

"Isn't it bad enough that we have to see that gross stuff on TV?" Michael gagged.

Tom smiled and grabbed the pillow from the floor. "Thanks." He held the pillow up and kissed Tallie behind it. He was tempted to tell her he loved her—the mood was right to whisper it in her ear. But something held him back. A memory of the other woman he'd told about his love and how he'd disappointed her and destroyed everything. No, he'd keep it to himself, and if he messed up what they had, it might not hurt her so much.

"What's wrong?" she whispered.

"Nothing. What's right is a better question."

"And?"

"At the moment, everything."

◦◦◦

Tom drifted in a dream. Determined hands rubbed his skin, soft breasts pressed against his bare back, teeth nibbled his shoulder blade. His first thought: Jolie. He was a little ticked off she'd returned, but as he woke, he shook off that goofy idea. The hands stroking his body were definitely real, not a ghostly dream. He'd made love with Tallie earlier and she'd returned to her room. Must have changed her mind, he thought with a contented sigh.

"Mmm, Tallie honey, that feels nice." He snuggled against her warm body, contemplating a roll toward her.

"You stupid idiot!" An enraged voice shrieked before she

placed her feet on his butt and shoved him from his bed to the floor. He landed hard, tangled in the sheet. "Will you ever get my name right?"

"What the hell?" he yelled, unable to see in the dark what had hit him. Whatever or whoever it was had a kick like an irate mule. Maybe Jolie was back and brought an angry friend. In the dark, the voice seemed incorporeal, and considering his earlier experience, the idea wasn't so farfetched.

"Who is Tallie honey?" the phantom voice shrieked again. The light in the stairway turned on, illuminating Tom naked on the floor, blinking furiously in the bright light. Sherry was on her knees, hands on hips, in the middle of his bed, also naked. Two saucer-eyed boys watched with Tallie in the hall. Her back was ramrod straight, hands clasped tight, and her troubled blue eyes darted between Tom and Sherry.

"I am," Tallie said quietly.

"Sherry? What are you doing here?" He blocked the light from his eyes with his hand. As soon as his eyes adjusted, he saw the boys staring at the naked woman in his bed.

"Get back to bed you two. NOW!" he said, harsher than necessary, but the situation was just so unbelievable. The boys ran up the stairs. "Tallie, honey, it's not what you think."

"I don't know what I think yet, Tom." She frowned and walked upstairs.

Tom heard her bedroom door close and thought it wasn't likely to open for him anytime soon. He stood and wrapped the sheet around his hips, glaring at the exposed woman in his bed. "Put some clothes on, will you? My son will probably be damaged for life."

"Your son?"

"Yes, my son." He waved his hand toward the stairs. "My girlfriend and her son, too. What are you doing here? I told you last time you were here it was over."

Sherry pouted and climbed from the bed. "I thought I'd give you a second chance." She hunted for her clothes and, finding them, stepped into her panties and jeans.

"I don't want a second chance. I thought it was pretty clear." He paced across the floor, holding the sheet.

"I love you, Tom."

"So you said. And I told you how I felt about it. I don't love you. I'm in love with someone else. I'm sorry." Tom instantly regretted his harsh tone when she appeared upset. "I'm sorry, Sherry," he said softly. "You're a terrific woman, and you deserve a man who can love you the way you should be loved. I could go through the motions, but it wouldn't be real."

Sherry straightened her spine and snorted. "Is it the woman upstairs?" She found her shoes and slid them on her feet. "

"Yes, that's Tallie." He retrieved Sherry's purse from the floor and, after she'd slipped on her shirt, handed it to her. "You'd better be going. How did you get in here anyway?"

"Rob opened the gate and you gave me this." She swung a key in front of his face.

Tom took it and tossed it on his nightstand. He'd forgotten to take her name off the security list and felt like the idiot she thought him. The gate situation was easy enough to remedy in the morning, but he wondered how he'd fix things with Tallie.

He pulled on a pair of shorts and locked the door after Sherry departed. He looked upstairs, contemplating his best course of action. Go up now and try to explain or let it sit until morning. He'd meet the problem head on. But when he reached Tallie's door, it was locked. He rested his head on the doorframe before turning and going downstairs to his room.

Restless and unable to sleep, Roy walked the dark ranch roads, the problem of grabbing Cody plaguing him. Tom, Tallie, and Rob took turns hanging out with the boys so they were never alone, and Roy was nervous about the possibility of detection if he didn't get out soon. It was only a matter of time and Tallie would see him. He doubted his Phin facade would fool her.

He needed to snatch Cody and run.

As the road turned, he wandered near Tom's place and saw a startling sight that had his senses humming: a hot brunette stomping from the house. If he walked a little faster, he might intercept her.

"What's a pretty thing like you doing out here alone this time of night?" he said.

She let out a startled cry at the voice in the dark but calmed when Roy stepped into the light. "My plans for the evening fell apart, so I'm heading home." She narrowed her eyes and looked at him closer. "Hey, I know you. You were at Lefty's, drinking whisky with that blond guy." She laughed. "He looked like your twin."

Roy smiled, cocky. He had her fooled. "Sherry, right?"

"Right. You have a good memory." She glared at Tom's house. "Better than some, anyway. You're Phin, right?"

He nodded. "Right. You have a good memory too."

She smiled. "For the right people. What are you doing walking around?" She leaned on her car and looked him over as he walked closer.

"I'm part of the security team tonight." He lied. "But I'm done. How about you and me head over to the bunkhouse and open up a bottle of Jack I've been saving for a special occasion?" His gaze wandered her body. She smiled, enjoying the attention. "It doesn't get any more special than this."

She glared at Tom's locked door. "Why not? Hop in. I'll drive my car over." She climbed in the driver's seat and started the engine.

Roy folded his long legs into the Toyota and she drove to the bunkhouse, parking at the dark end where Roy suggested. He didn't want anyone seeing her car, and he was pretty sure the security cameras didn't reach the area.

Roy had the bunkhouse to himself for the night since Rob had security duty. He'd be alone until morning, plenty of time to enjoy this morsel of sexy femininity. While Roy went to his room for the whisky, Sherry settled on the couch in the large communal living room and flicked on the TV with the remote.

Bottle in hand, he wandered into the kitchen for glasses and returned to find Sherry watching an old black-and-white movie. "Here you go." He handed her a glass and threw back his own in one gulp before dropping on the couch next to her. He refilled his glass several times, enjoying the burn down his throat. He refilled Sherry's glass and noticed her getting tipsy enough to giggle when he ran his hand along her leg. He'd never had a problem getting women. There was something about the way he looked that turned them on, and pretty little Sherry followed suit.

She laid her head back on the couch, allowing Roy to touch her without complaint. They'd consumed most of the bottle, and he was sure she felt as good as he did. He kissed her while his hands roamed. She shivered. He laid her back on the couch, his weight pressing her down. His breathing quickened as he pushed up her shirt.

"That feels so good, baby." Sherry moaned.

"It does." He moaned. "My heartbeat goes out of control when I look at you, pretty lady."

Sherry opened her eyes and placed a restraining hand on Roy's chest. "Wait a sec. What did you just say?" She tried to push him away. "That's what the blond guy said to me at Lefty's." She narrowed her eyes and looked at him with suspicion. "You aren't Phin."

Roy grinned. "Sure I am. Nothing wrong with stealing a guy's pickup lines, is there?"

"Nothing wrong with it except you two weren't sitting together when he said it. You aren't Phin." She reached up to Roy's hair, frowning. "You dyed it. What's going on?"

"Nothing you need to be concerned with," he said. He leaned and tried to kiss her again.

She pushed against his chest. "No. I don't like this. I don't know what kind of game you're playing, but I don't want any part of it. Does Tom know who you are?"

Roy tensed. "Sure. He knows."

She snorted. "I doubt it. If he did, your butt would be on the highway, not sitting in his bunkhouse. Let me up."

He shook his head. "No. I like you right where you are." He kissed her hard. She tried to twist away but he held her down. "Knock it off, Tallie."

"Tallie?" she sputtered. "Is that what you called me? That's the second time tonight someone called me Tallie. This is just too weird for me." She tried to push him off, but he held her down. "Let me go! I don't want to be part of your creepy little fantasy. I'm going home."

"Shut up." He held her down and kissed her hard as she fought to get away.

"Damn it! Let me up!"

Roy sat back on his knees. "I said shut up!"

Her eyes were wide now. Her breathing came in gasps. She was afraid. Good. He liked it that way.

"Let me up, please. I need to go home." She wiggled feebly beneath him.

"You aren't going anywhere until I say so." He lay on top of her and kissed her again.

"Stop, please. I want to leave."

"You aren't going anywhere. Just lay back and enjoy it." He pushed at her clothes.

She started to cry. "Please...no," she whispered, shaking her head.

Her terrified sobs only pushed him further. "Knock it off," he growled

Sherry twisted from under him, trying to get away, but Roy caught her around the waist. "Where do you think you're going?" He laughed as she fought, kicking and screaming. When his grip failed, she lurched forward, but he caught her again. They fell hard to the floor, the rough landing knocking the breath from her, but she continued to fight. She managed to wedge her knee between his legs but lacked the mobility to send it home with any force. With desperate fists flailing, she landed a few good punches before

CAUGHT IN THE SPIN

Roy belted her hard on the side of her head. Panting from the exertion, Roy waited for her next attack, but Sherry didn't move.

18

Tallie woke from a restless night to find the boys rummaging through the cupboards for cereal. No sign of Tom anywhere. During the night, she'd made the decision to presume what Tom said was true. It wasn't what she thought. It would break her heart if it was.

She helped the boys with their Cheerios and made a pot of coffee. Another pass by Tom's room confirmed it was empty. She sat at the table, a steaming cup of coffee in hand. The boys fidgeted. She knew they all wondered the same thing, but she didn't know what to tell them.

"Tallie?" Michael said, staring into his cereal bowl.

"Yes?"

"Who was that lady in Tom's room last night? You know the one..." He turned scarlet.

"I know who you mean, Michael, and I don't know who she is." Tallie shrugged her shoulders, trying to add an air of insignificance to the episode.

"I don't get it." Cody let out a frustrated huff. "I thought he liked you, Mom."

Tallie flushed. She'd thought the same, but when she reflected on how their relationship began, it was she who chased him. Maybe he'd been involved with this other woman then and Tallie was fooling herself.

"Finish your breakfast, guys. Maybe Rob will saddle the horses for you this morning, or you could go fishing." She tried to change the subject.

"Fishing," Michael said.

"Yeah, fishing. My butt hurts from all that riding. Maybe Rob will take us out in the boat?" Cody added with a grin, forgetting Tom and the naked woman.

"Yeah! Let's go."

"Brush your teeth first," Tallie called after them. She sat at the kitchen table, going through the motions of reading the paper, but on reaching the back page, she couldn't remember a word. She didn't want to believe Tom had no feelings for her. She wanted to talk to him and have him explain so they could move on.

Or end it.

Tom avoided the house all day. He didn't usually dodge confrontation this way, but he didn't know what to say to her. How do you explain a naked woman in your bed in the middle of the night to the woman who just left the same bed? He spent the day working in the office and hung out with the crew while they made fence repairs. He was starved by dinnertime but decided to wait until evening to go in the house. The last thing he wanted was to face all three of them over dinner. The explanation he gave Tallie wouldn't be G-rated for the boys.

He felt like a criminal, slinking in the kitchen door and hoping to grab something to eat on the way to his room. Bath water ran upstairs and he assumed it was Tallie. He filled a plate with the spaghetti she'd made for dinner and snuck into his room to eat. He hoped she didn't see him. Luck was with him. He finished his meal, had a quick shower, and was on his way out the front door when he heard footsteps on the stairs.

"Tom," she said softly, looking at him with those iridescent blue eyes. "Can I talk to you?"

He hesitated, shifting his eyes from her. "I have some things to take care of. Later, okay?" He glanced at her and was sure he saw disgust, or at least disappointment, in her eyes. What's new about that? Eventually, he disappointed everyone. Usually, he disappointed himself most of all.

"Okay," she said with a resigned nod. "When you have time."

Tom was out the door and in his truck before she could change his mind.

Fluorescent lights illuminated a collection of restored cars in Clay's shop. A '56 T-Bird, a '62 Corvette, and at least a dozen others filled the building, all shiny as the day they stood on the showroom floor. Tom walked past them, stopping in the corner near a '65 Mustang convertible in need of repairs. He flicked on the stereo, Hank Jr. and his rowdy friends playing loud, and surveyed the work to be done. He was elbow deep in the engine when he heard footsteps behind him.

"Are you here to help or gawk?" Tom asked.

"I guess I could give you a hand." Clay set a pop can on the tool chest and peered under the hood with a frown creasing his brow.

"Harlie saw the light on out here and was worried," Clay said. Tom looked up at him. "What's going on?"

"Nothing I can't handle."

"Well, if that was true, you'd be home handling it, not here playing grease monkey." Clay's blue eyes pierced his gaze, making Tom squirm. "Maybe I can help."

"I don't know what you can do. I can't figure out what I

can do." Tom reached to the stereo and lowered the volume.

"Give it a shot. Maybe we'll get lucky."

Tom sighed. "Last night I had the damnedest thing happen and I'm still not sure what to do." He paced across the floor. "I was sleeping and I woke up to a woman's hands on me, real friendly. I said something, thinking it was Tallie, and found myself mule kicked on my butt to the floor. When the light came on in the hall, I realized it wasn't Tallie, but Sherry."

Clay grinned.

"It's not funny, Clay!"

"Sorry," he snickered. "But I have this image in my head of your naked ass hitting the floor. I'm assuming the naked part anyway, since you omitted that amusing detail."

"Well, here's another image for you," Tom added irritably. "Sherry was also in the buff, sitting in the middle of my bed, with Tallie, Cody, and Michael looking in the door."

"What was she doing there? I thought you'd ended things."

"We had. She said she wanted to give me a second chance. I told her to get her clothes on and go home. But the damage was done. Tallie was upstairs behind a locked door. She wouldn't talk to me."

"You forgot to change the gate list," Clay said.

"Yeah, I forgot. I never expected her to come back." Tom ran his hands through his black hair. "I just don't know what to do to fix this."

"Talk to her."

"I can't even look at her!" Tom said. "Every time I try, I see the disappointment in her eyes, like I've failed her." He resumed his pacing, rubbing his hand across the back of his neck.

"I think you'll find that Tallie has a great capacity for understanding. Women are amazing that way. Give her a try. If you explain what happened, she'll understand. You'll never know how she feels unless you go home and talk to her."

"And how do I explain this thing to the boys? The woman was stark naked in the middle of my bed!"

Clay grinned again. "Hmm, two eleven-year-old boys saw a large-breasted, naked woman. I wouldn't worry about that one. In a couple of years, they'll appreciate the memory and thank you for it." He laughed. "In a day or so, they'll forget all about it, especially if you and Tallie treat it like the nothing it is."

Tom stopped pacing and smiled. "I guess that's possible."

"Of course it is. Man," Clay said, looking wistful, "can you imagine seeing a naked woman up close at eleven? I'd have given anything for that. We had to wait until we were thirteen." Clay laughed. "Remember that?"

Tom wasn't in the mood for an excursion down memory lane, but he couldn't help but laugh. "Yeah. If we hadn't run fast, Barney Cole would have knocked the stuffing out of us for watching his wife skinny-dipping. She wasn't bad for an old lady."

"Old? She was only about forty, if that," Clay said.

"At thirteen, everybody over thirty is old, especially when we were supposed to be looking at her daughter." Tom chuckled and shook his head at the memory. He and Clay were always up to something as kids and were in trouble for it half the time. Sobering, he sighed with resignation. "I'll talk to Tallie."

"Good. My work here is done." He slapped Tom on the shoulder, picked up his pop can, and turned to leave. "I have a worried woman at home and she's always real snugly when she's worried. Thanks, pal, I owe you one." Clay winked and sauntered out the door.

Tallie was finishing the evening dishes when the phone rang. She wiped her hands and grabbed it.

"Tallie? Clay. I need a favor. Well, I need you to do a favor for Tom."

Tallie leaned against the kitchen counter. "The way Tom's behaving, I don't know why I should do him any favors. I don't even know where he is."

"That's just it. He's here beating himself up over something concerning you and he says he can't talk to you about it. Tom's real good at that. He rips himself up regularly over stuff, takes blame for things he shouldn't. He needs to talk to you and clear this up before he bashes himself senseless."

Tallie liked the idea of Tom bashed senseless but wanted the joy of doing it herself.

"Will you come up here and talk to him?"

"I don't know if it will do any good, Clay. He hid from me all day and when I tried to talk to him tonight, he ran out as fast as he could." Tallie pushed away from the counter and paced across the kitchen floor.

"He'll talk to you if I have to lock the shop door to keep him in there. He locked me in a closet once and I'd consider it a privilege to return the favor." Clay laughed. "I'm not going to tell you much about this, other than to say it isn't what you're probably thinking, and Tom is more or less an innocent bystander. Will you talk to him? You can drop the boys at the house and we'll entertain them."

"Innocent bystander, huh?" Tallie wasn't sure how innocent he could be, but she'd let him explain. "Okay. I'll talk to him. Tom's lucky to have a friend like you."

"Yeah, well, he's a major maintenance project most of the time." Clay laughed.

"But you care about him," Tallie said.

"Yeah." Clay sounded uncomfortable at the admission. "He's always been there, like a brother, since we were two years old. We look after each other, always have. He needs to talk to you, Tallie, or he'll continue to beat himself up over this and there isn't any reason for it."

"Okay, I'll bring the boys over. Thanks, Clay." She hung up and walked into the living room where the boys watched a *SpongeBob SquarePants* cartoon.

"I need to go out for a few minutes, guys. Grab your shoes and I'll drop you off at Clay's for a while." Tallie waited for the groans that usually accompanied an interrupted TV show.

"Cool! Harlie has lots of ice cream." Michael jumped from his chair and grabbed his shoes. Cody was right behind him. Grateful for the ease of that, Tallie grabbed her car keys and shooed the boys out the door. The next task required greater effort.

Clay directed her to the shop and took the boys to the house where Harlie was making chocolate milkshakes. Tallie opened the shop door with caution. Brantley Gilbert's "Bottom's Up" blasted from the stereo along with the tapping of tools under the hood of an old Mustang convertible.

Tom called out from under the hood. "Come back to kick

my butt again?"

"I was hoping it wouldn't come to that," Tallie said as she walked up beside the car, her cowboy boots thunking on the concrete.

Tom glanced up and frowned. "Oh. I thought you were Clay."

"He's in the house drinking milkshakes with the boys." She stuffed her hands in her jeans pockets and shifted her feet.

"So this is his doing?" Clearly ticked off, Tom reached back and shut off the stereo.

"He called and asked me to come up and talk to you." She crossed her arms and frowned.

"Did he tell you all about it?" he said, obviously irritated.

"No. He said you were beating yourself up for nothing. You're lucky to have a friend like him."

"That's what he tells me. I suppose he's right since he keeps me from being the king of self-destructive behavior." Tom leaned his hands on the car but didn't come out from under the hood. "I'm not sure where to start."

"Then I will. I know this relationship started because I kept throwing myself at you, so if—"

"Wait a minute." Tom interrupted. "If you were throwing yourself at me, I was doing a whole lot of catching. Is this what's been going through your mind? That I was involved with someone else and you at the same time?"

"I didn't know what to think. And when you avoided me and wouldn't talk to me, my imagination ran wild." Tallie turned and paced.

"I wanted to talk to you last night."

"I know." She looked at him. "I heard you come upstairs, but I wasn't sure what to do at that point. I thought it would be better to talk in the morning."

Tom let out a sigh. "And by morning, I'd lost my nerve. Look, Tallie, it's not what you're thinking." Now it was his turn to pace while she leaned on the car. "Her name is Sherry Price and we were involved for a few months. I hadn't seen her since the day I met you. She'd stomped out of here the morning you came to see Clay and I haven't seen her since."

"You had an argument or something?"

"She was mad because she said..." He frowned. "She said she was in love with me and when I couldn't return it, she got mad. It pretty well ended the relationship right there as far as I was concerned. She was going in a direction I couldn't follow."

"So, why?"

"Why did she crawl into my bed in the middle of the night?" Tallie nodded and he continued. "Because that was pretty much the nature of our so-called relationship. Sometimes I like to go out with the guys to a local bar. I don't drink, just have a pop or something, but it's fun to hang out with the crew. Sherry is a waitress at the place. We went out a few times, had some laughs, and she started coming over after her shift ended, usually in the middle of the night." Tom grimaced. "Do you see why I didn't want to explain this to you?"

Tallie nodded slowly.

"It's not something I'm proud of. Anyway, last night she decided to 'give me a second chance,' as she put it. I didn't want a second chance. I know it sounds cold, but I'd forgotten about her already."

"So you were surprised to find her there?" Tallie asked.

"I thought it was you coming back, which I thought was a fine idea, by the way. But Sherry didn't appreciate it when I called her Tallie."

"Tallie honey," she corrected, fighting to keep a straight face.

"Right. Anyway, last time she was here, I accidentally called her Shelly, which pissed her off. Last night I called her Tallie and she kicked me to the floor. You turned on the lights, I'm naked on the floor, she's naked in the bed, and there are three sets of eyes looking at me like I'm cheating scum. Four sets of eyes if you count Sherry." He rubbed the back of his neck and winced. "And the look on your face cut right through me. I couldn't talk to you. I couldn't even look at you without seeing the disappointment in your eyes."

"So after we went upstairs, she went home?"

He nodded. "Yeah. I told her it was over the last time she was here. I'm with you now, and I don't want to see anyone else, Tallie. I think you and I have a great thing going." He stood still, watching her for a reaction.

"The boys were asking about her this morning. I didn't know what to say."

"Clay told me that in a few years, they'd be thanking me for their first look at a large-breasted, naked woman up close." He smiled when Tallie laughed. "Do you believe me when I tell you I'm not interested in her anymore?" He stepped to her.

"I believe you, Tom." She looked up at him. "I'm sorry I didn't give you a chance—"

"Don't apologize." He took her in his arms and held her

close. "You have nothing to be sorry about. I'm sorry I didn't talk to you earlier."

"I should have let you in last night."

"How about if we say we were both wrong and call it good?" He tipped her chin up. "All I know is that I haven't thought of anyone but you since the day I looked from the haystack and saw those gorgeous legs of yours."

She smiled.

"And our first kiss sealed the deal." He lowered his lips to hers and kissed her slowly. "And I sink deeper and deeper every time I kiss you." He proved it by kissing her again. "Are we okay?"

"Yeah." She sighed. "But we'd better stop this. I may have consented to the tour bus, but I'm not extroverted enough for the backseat of an old Mustang."

"Darn." He chuckled. "That's okay if we still have our date at midnight."

"I'll be there." She hugged him tight. "I need to get the boys. Harlie is probably getting tired."

Tom grabbed his cell phone and dialed. "Clay, you conniving son of a bitch." He winked at Tallie. "I know...you were just trying to help. Thanks for that and for keeping the boys. You can send them out here. They can crawl around in your cars while I clean up my tools." Tom disconnected the call. "One quick kiss before the thundering herd arrives?" He took her face in his hands and kissed her. "Midnight is too far away," he said with a sigh when the boys ran in the door.

"Wow! This is so cool! Are these all Clay's?" Michael asked.

"He buys them and we fix them. Hey, guys, there's a

couple of neat motorcycles you need to see back here. Come on." Tom led Tallie and the boys to the bikes and they swarmed over them. As he held her tight and watched them, she thought it was good to be back to normal.

19

Pancakes, eggs, hot coffee, and a delicious woman sitting across the table from him. Tom wasn't sure how he'd landed in this lucky spot, but he was smart enough to be thankful he was in it. The boys had eaten and ran from the kitchen, yakking about Rob teaching them to shoot with a bow and arrow on the far side of the pond. Tom debated getting Tallie back into bed for a few minutes. Well, maybe more than a few minutes. The boys would be busy for hours. Still in her robe, she concentrated on the morning paper, her finger absently twirling a pale blonde curl by her ear. He doubted she had much on beneath the robe, and it would only take a second to have her undressed and where he wanted her. The suggestion floated across his tongue when he heard his front screen door slap against the frame and cowboy boots clunk across the living room. Tom leaned back in his chair with a sigh and gave Clay a dirty look when he stepped in the kitchen.

"Mornin'," Clay said. "Got a cocklebur in an uncomfortable spot, Tom? That's a nasty-looking face for this early in the day." He looked from Tom to Tallie and grinned. "Am I interrupting something?"

Tallie looked up from the newspaper and glanced at Tom with a confused frown. "I don't think so. We were just finishing breakfast. There's coffee if you want some."

Clay wandered to the coffeemaker, poured a cup, and dumped in a spoon of sugar.

Tom tried to loosen his scowl but didn't feel as if he'd been successful. It wasn't often he and Tallie had time alone during the day and now Masterson interrupted his plans. "What's up?" he asked with irritated briskness. If he could get Clay out the door quickly, he would grab Tallie and make a run for the bedroom.

Clay hooked a chair with his foot, spun it around, and straddled it, his elbows leaning comfortably on the back. Obviously, he wasn't going anywhere soon. He looked thoughtful and thoroughly engrossed in the steam rising from his coffee. Something was definitely bothering him.

"Well?" Tom asked.

"The kid got drunk," Clay said.

"Jax?" Tom shrugged. "So? He's a big boy, Clay. You've got to quit thinking of him as a little kid—"

"He got stinking drunk three days ago. He's been on a bender and it has me concerned." Clay sipped his coffee and gave Tom a *you should understand what I'm saying* look.

Tom did have a bit of experience with benders. His lasted two years. "He's young, Clay. Guys his age do stuff like that. It doesn't mean..." He didn't finish. It didn't mean Jax would follow Tom's path to alcoholism, and he thought Clay was getting a little paranoid. "He's probably just partying with his friends. He'll be all right."

Clay shook his head slowly. "It's more serious than that, Tom. He's kinda screwed up right now. When he came home, he started talking and kept me up most of the night before he passed out."

"What was he talking about?"

"About what caused him to leave Angel Beach two years ago. I don't know that I should talk about it. He was pretty drunk and I doubt he'll remember telling me all the details." He paused and sipped his coffee. "What I will say is that Jax was engaged. There was a big misunderstanding and the girl dumped him. The whole situation was pretty ugly."

Tom shrugged again. Been there. Done that. He'd been engaged and got dumped too. And turned into an alcoholic over it. Well, crap. He blew out his breath and wondered what this had to do with him, other than the fact that he'd lived through this exact scenario. "He was what, seventeen or eighteen at the time? What could have been so bad? Kids that age break up all the time."

Clay rubbed his chin, obviously debating what to say next. "True," he said. "But most of them don't sleep with their fiancé's sister. Like I said, it was an ugly situation."

Tom choked on the coffee he'd just gulped. Okay, so it wasn't been there, done that.

Tallie shifted her eyes and cleared her throat. "Where exactly was the misunderstanding? Did he or didn't he sleep with her sister?"

"He did."

"So…" Tallie shook her head, obviously bewildered.

"He says he was tricked and it's a long story."

"And you believe him?" Tom asked.

"Yeah. I do." Clay nodded. "Anyway, something happened with a woman he's been seeing, and it stirred up all his anger over this other deal, and the kid went on a three-day bender. When he sobered up, I told him I thought it would be good if he got away for a while and offered him an airline ticket wherever he wants to go."

"Where does he want to go?" Tom asked.

Clay laughed. "Home. I offer him a ticket to anywhere—a

friend included in the deal—and he wants to go to Oregon. One of his buddies is home for a couple of weeks before college starts up and he wants to hang with his friend. I was thinking he'd want to go to one of those French beaches with all the nude women or something, and he picks Oregon, where people wear parkas to the beach. Go figure." He sipped his coffee. "So, I need one of the guys to run him to the airport."

"When?"

"Now. His flight leaves in about three hours."

Tom looked at Tallie and blew out a breath. "I'll take him."

"One of the guys can do it," Clay said.

"No. I'll take him. It'll give me a chance to talk to him." He smiled. "The dangers of alcohol and all that stuff."

Clay nodded. "That might not be a bad idea. You can use some of that psychology on him too. Straighten him out."

Tallie looked at Tom. "Use what?"

Clay smiled. "Didn't Tom tell you about that?"

Tallie shrugged. "What?"

Tom kicked at Clay's chair leg. "Shut up, Clay," he said with a laugh.

Clay shifted his chair out of kicking range and ignored Tom. "That he took all kinds of psychology classes in college. As far as I know, he's the only bull rider with a business major and a psych minor. No animal husbandry degrees for him." Clay started to laugh. "We weren't sure what he was going to do with it. Maybe lay those bulls out on a couch after he beat them and ask, 'And how did that make you feel?'" Clay set his coffee down, laughing so hard he snorted.

Even though he'd heard it all many times before, Tom couldn't help but join him.

"No, I know," Clay continued, "maybe he was planning to have encounter groups in the locker room so everyone could discuss their pre-ride anxiety—"

"No, that's not right and you know it," Tom said with a laugh. "When you took off for Nashville, I figured you'd need to have your head worked over once in a while. Pound it down to a normal size." He looked at Tallie. "And I haven't been successful yet."

Tallie looked from one to the other. "As superstitious as cowboys are, you could have therapy sessions to break them of their rabbit's-foot habit or that yellow-shirt superstition." Tom rolled his eyes and Tallie laughed. "And what's up with the hat on the bed, anyway?"

"Okay, okay," Tom said with a smile. "Enough already. I'll talk to Jax." He gave Clay a pointed stare. "No psychoanalysis mumbo jumbo though." He glanced across at Tallie and frowned. "I hate to leave you here alone."

Tallie laughed. "I'm not exactly alone. There is your crew, Clay, Harlie, the boys, and the small matter of a high-voltage fence, security cameras, and your arsenal of weapons in the bedroom. I'll be fine."

"Do you have any experience with firearms?" Tom asked. He wasn't surprised when she shook her head. "The guns won't do you any good. Don't touch them until I can show you the right way to use a gun."

Tallie shook her head and smiled. "Darn. There goes my morning entertainment. Go to the airport, fusspot. I'll be fine."

Tom reluctantly agreed and walked Clay to the door. "Tell Jax I'll be up to the house for him in about half an hour." He glanced at Tallie standing in the kitchen doorway. "I have something I need to do before I take off."

After Clay left, Tom took Tallie in his arms.

"Psychology, huh?" she said.

"Yeah. It was just something that interested me at the time. The inner workings of the human psyche and all that garbage." He leaned in for a kiss. "What makes people tick."

"So." She interrupted his progress, his lips paused directly over hers. "When you said I needed therapy for my problem, you were drawing on your academic experience?"

Tom smiled. "Something like that. And I'm thinking," he said, his lips hovered over hers, ready to connect, "that you are in serious need of another session."

"And you think you're qualified to handle it?" She smiled.

He pecked her lips with his and swung her up into his arms. "The doctor is in, baby."

A mechanical problem delayed Jax's flight until late afternoon. By evening, the flight hadn't been cleared for takeoff and was rescheduled again. Tom had planned to run Jax to the airport and return as soon as possible. Tallie sent the boys to bed, a storm was kicking up, and Tom wasn't back. The phone beside her bed rang and she grabbed it.

"It'll be a while yet," Tom said. "The weather service issued a tornado warning and we've been advised to sit tight until things calm down. So," he said with a sigh, "I guess I'm stuck here."

Tallie had listened to the increasing wind for hours;

branches scraped ominously against the house. "Maybe they'll reschedule for tomorrow?"

"Maybe, but I'm still stuck until we know for sure. Bring the dogs in the house and turn on the radio—"

"I know—"

"Get the boys and take them to my room. You'll want to be on the lower floor and stay away—"

"I know. Stay away from the windows." Tallie smiled to herself over Tom's concern. The need to take care of everyone was deeply embedded in him and she found it endearing. "I've been through this before."

"I know you have," he said. "But I can't be there, and I want to make sure you and the boys are okay. There's an emergency kit in the storage room off the kitchen with some flashlights and a small radio, just in case the power goes out. Let's see, what else? Oh...the bottled water is in the storage room too. If the power goes out, the pump goes with it. Make sure the doors are locked tight and I'll be there as quick as I can."

Tom disconnected the call and Tallie headed upstairs to the boys' room. She'd always hated wind. As a kid, a storm engulfed the Phoenix valley before she had time to get inside. She'd huddled under a tree as the violent wind pulled roofing from the neighbor's house, sending it crashing around her. Now, the wind rattled the bedroom window and brought back her childhood fear. But with two boys and a couple of dogs to worry about, she couldn't give in to it.

She roused the boys and shuttled them downstairs to Tom's room, tucking them into his large bed; the dogs nestled against their feet. After a particularly nasty gust rattled the windows, she made a sojourn around the house, closing shades and checking locks. Confident everything was secured, she grabbed a blanket and curled into a ball on the sofa, the TV tuned to the local news.

An hour later, a door slammed, waking Tallie from an unplanned nap. Before the noise could wake the boys, she slipped on her shoes and went in search of the annoyance. The lights flickered, making her heart race. She threw open the front door dead bolt, bracing against the onslaught of moving air when she opened the door. Finding the screen firmly latched, she slammed the door and locked it.

The lights flickered again.

Before she reached the back door, the lights wavered one last time, leaving her bathed in eerie darkness. With no television noise to compete, the wind's howl took on an unearthly wail. She stood still, listening, waiting for her eyes to adjust to the newborn blackness. No security lights shone in the windows. It was inky and terrifying. With tentative steps and a reassuring hand on the wall, she made her way to the back door; the wall became a braille map. When she reached the door, she felt around for the dead bolt, threw it open, and turned the knob. The wind cascaded over her and knocked her to the floor. The screen door flailed and slapped against its frame. Branches and leaves flew into her face. Fear of getting smashed by the door left her immobile, debating if it was that important. Tom could buy another door if this one tore loose from its hinges. A smashed hand would take time to mend.

But the noise would wake the boys.

Tallie blew out her breath and lunged for the swinging door, crying out when it smacked her sensitive fingertips. She lunged again and caught the handle, pulling it against a strong gust and blast of rain in her face. The handle, slick with rain, slipped from her hand, banging against the house. Before she could catch it again, Clay's border collie Clyde was at her side, a low growl emanating from his throat.

"Yeah, I know," she said to the dog. "You'd think we were in Kansas, wouldn't you, Toto? Get back now." She tried to push the dog with her foot but Clyde resisted, growling into the dark. "It's just wind, puppy. Come back." Tallie caught the screen door again and pulled it closed. But before she could drop the hook into the latch, Clyde pushed against it, running into the yard howling and snarling. Tallie peered out, unable to see what had upset the dog. Lightning flashed, momentarily blinding her. A few seconds later, another burst of lightning illuminated the yard, and Tallie saw a man standing in the rain. Her first thought was Tom but another flash of light proved her wrong. This man had red hair, not black, and Clyde was trying to tear him to pieces.

Tallie didn't want to leave the dog in the yard, but she needed a flashlight. Clyde continued his attack, his angry snarls and yips muted by the deluge. Leaving the door swinging in the wind, Tallie made her way to the storage room. Clyde was still going crazy, and she needed to see what was happening. Her breath came in fearful gasps as she felt along the hallway wall. Blood pounded in her ears. She found the kitchen doorway and made her way by memory to the storage room door. If she didn't hurry, the man could be seriously injured. Another lightning flash illuminated the room, and she saw the box of supplies with a flashlight on top. She grabbed it, tested for batteries, and was relieved when a beam of light sprang from the metal tube. Tom was superbly dependable. She found that an attractive feature in a man. With the precious flashlight, she made her way to the door in time to see Clyde lunge for the man's arm. He swung out, hitting the insistent dog. Clyde landed on his side with a yelp but was instantly on his feet and prowling, ready for another assault. Tallie couldn't believe the normally mild-mannered dog attacked this way. Who was this guy and why would the dog attack?

"Clyde!" she called, trying to get the dog's attention. She aimed the light into the yard but it was absorbed by the heavy rainfall. She couldn't see the man's face, but judging by the way he held his hand, she knew Clyde had hurt him.

"Stupid dog!" the man yelled as he kicked at Clyde.

Tallie froze. That voice was familiar but it couldn't be. Not Roy. Not here.

In the next flash of lightning, the yard was empty. He was gone. If it was Roy, she knew he wouldn't go far. He'd watch and wait for his best opportunity. She called to Clyde, who reluctantly limped in the door, stopping on the threshold to sniff the air. Tallie pulled him in, made a grab for the screen door, caught and latched it. She locked the dead bolt with shaking hands.

The power was out, the electric fence was off, and Roy was out there. Tallie ran to Tom's bedroom with the dog on her heels, slammed the door, and grabbed Tom's rifle from the wall rack. She doubted it was loaded, but it would make a good club. When she was a kid, her dad had offered to teach her to shoot and she'd refused. Idiot. Tom was right. She didn't even know how to load the gun. Now she'd probably be a dead idiot.

Lightning flashed and Tallie saw a shadow on the window shade. It was Roy, and she didn't know how to load the gun. On the bed, Cody stirred, sitting up.

"Mom? What's going on?"

"Shhh. Don't talk."

"Why?"

"Someone's out there. You and Michael need to get in the bathroom. Now. Close the door behind you." She yanked her son's hand. "Go."

Cody nudged Michael, waking him. He whispered Tallie's instructions. The boys jumped from the bed and crawled to the bathroom. She heard the click of the door and released the breath she held. At least the boys were safe. The wind tossed rain at the house. Tallie wasn't sure if she heard footsteps in the maelstrom or not, but with the rifle in her hand, she was prepared for whatever came her way. The shadow moved across the window shade again. Clyde tensed, growling, but he didn't move. Cookie whimpered. Tallie had heard dogs sensed things about people. Apparently, Clyde had a good handle on the stench of evil. Roy reeked of it.

Tallie took up a defensive position, her back against the wall beside the door. If Roy came in, she'd bust his head open. If he climbed through the window, she'd see him. Tense, she waited, watching and listening. The wind began to falter and die down. Tallie heard voices outside. Men's voices. Oh no. Now there were two of them. Roy had help. Her fear mounted, roaring through her system. This was it. This was where she would die. She heard the front door open and heavy footsteps moved across the room. She waited, her hands gripping the rifle stock like a club. This time, she would go down fighting. She wouldn't sit there, waiting for Roy to execute her like before. No, this time she would fight. The bedroom door swung open and the man stepped in. Tallie let out a banshee scream and swung the rifle. The man dodged, dropping to the floor. Tallie swung the rifle back, preparing to pound her assailant's head, when a strong hand grasped her ankle and pulled her foot out from under her. She hit the floor with a thud, her breath knocked from her lungs. She was going to die now.

"Damn it, Tallie! You could have killed me!"

Tallie lay immobilized, gasping for breath. When she was able to fill her lungs with precious air, she whispered, "Tom?"

"Yes," he said, his voice sharp. "Who'd you think—"

"I thought you were Roy. I'm sorry." She laughed, nearly hysterical. She'd thought this was her day to die. "The boys," she said between gasps for air. "The boys are in the bathroom."

She heard Tom search for and locate the flashlight. He opened the bathroom door and said, "It's okay. You can come out now." Tom left the room and returned a moment later with a glowing lantern. The boys were in his bed, snuggled under the blue quilt. He helped Tallie up from the floor, hugging her to him. She'd stopped laughing and now her body shook.

"It's okay. I'm back. You're okay," he soothed. "The storm is blowing over. We'll be all right."

"But he's out there."

Tom rubbed his hand across her hair. "No, he isn't. It's okay."

"But I saw—"

"I know. You saw a man, but it wasn't Roy Peters."

Later, Tom and Tallie held each other close, safe in a

double sleeping bag on Tom's bedroom floor. He'd changed into sweatpants and a well-worn T-shirt. She wore an old chamois shirt from Tom's closet, soft from years of wear. His reassuring scent permeated the fabric. The boys slept in the bed, an occasional mumble emitting from one or the other.

"So," Tom whispered, "the tornadoes didn't materialize, the wind died down, and they cleared Jax's flight. He's on his way to Portland. Now, tell me what happened here. Why did you try to split my skull?"

Tallie explained about the screen door and the dog rushing into the yard to attack a man. "He yelled at Clyde and sounded just like Roy. It was dark and raining and I couldn't see well, but I was sure it was Roy. I got Clyde to come in the house, and we came in here. I saw the man's shadow outside the window and grabbed your rifle thinking I could use it as a club. I'm sorry I hit you."

"You just nicked my arm."

"Did you see Roy out there? We should've called the police," she said, her voice shaking.

"Like I said before, it wasn't Roy."

"But I heard him, Tom. I heard his voice. It was Roy. Clyde bit his hand and he yelled at him."

"It was the new guy, Mulberry. He might preach at you, but he's harmless enough. I talked to him when I came in. He said he was checking the house to make sure you were okay. He showed me where Clyde nipped him, so I know it was him you saw. It's okay. He's part of the crew."

"Oh." She sighed with relief. "I'm so glad. I thought for sure it was Roy."

"Just Mulberry doing his job. Nothing to worry about." Tom yawned and pulled her close. "Nothing at all."

20

"Tom, this is Sally. There's a sheriff's detective at the gate who wants to talk to all of us. Says his name is…just a sec…who are you again?" Tom heard Sally ask. "He says his name is Fleming and he wants to talk to us ASAP."

Tom paused from the contract he read, puzzled about Sally's call. "All of us? What does it have to do with you?" If it concerned Roy Peters, it shouldn't involve Clay's housekeeper.

"I don't know, but he's quite insistent about talking to Clay and Harlie too."

"Let him in. I'll be up to the house right away." He disconnected the call and leaned back in his office chair. All of them? It made no sense. Blowing out a breath, he grabbed his hat and left the office.

In Clay's kitchen, they gathered around the table, drinking coffee. Clay, Harlie, Sally, and the detective looked up as Tom walked in. Introductions made, Tom tossed his hat on the kitchen counter and sat down.

"Should I have brought Tallie?" he asked.

"I'll start with this group." Detective Fleming glanced around the table, apparently assessing the people seated there.

"Is this about Roy Peters?" Tom asked to break the silence.

"I don't believe so. We're aware of the situation from Nashville Metro PD, but I don't know of a connection." He looked around again. "Early this morning a woman's body was found in a car near here. The vehicle was in the trees about a quarter mile south of your main gate. Last night's storm tore the branches away, and the mail carrier found it this morning."

"The poor woman," Harlie said, moving her hand to hold Clay's. "Do you know who she is?"

"The ID in her purse and the name on the car registration matches. Do any of you know Sherry Price?"

Clay gaped at Tom. The detective also turned his attention to Tom.

"Sherry?" Tom sat up straight as a wave of shock rippled through him. "Are you sure?"

Detective Fleming nodded slowly. "Yes, sir. A family member has made a positive identification. I take it you knew her?"

"Yes. We were seeing each other for a while several months back." Tom couldn't believe Sherry was dead. "What happened? Was another vehicle involved?"

The detective stared at Tom. "Possibly you can tell me?"

"How would I know? I wasn't with her." Tom blinked as understanding hit him. "It was a car accident, wasn't it?"

The detective removed a notebook from his pocket and scribbled. "When was the last time you saw her, Mr. Black?"

Tom was sure the color drained from his face. Apparently, Sherry's death wasn't an accident, and this detective was looking at him like a suspect. "A couple nights ago. She showed up at the house."

"What time?"

"I don't know for sure. I'd been asleep."

"Asleep?"

Tom glanced around the table at his friends, uncomfortable about the way the detective zeroed in on him like he'd done something wrong. "She woke me in the middle of the night. We talked for a few minutes and she left."

"What did you talk about?"

"Nothing much. I told her to go home," Tom said.

"It must have been important for her to want to talk to you in the middle of the night. Can you tell me what happened?"

Tom frowned. How many times would he have to repeat this embarrassing story? And should he ask for a lawyer? He hadn't done anything except send her home. "I was asleep and when I woke up, she was in my bed," he said. "Conversation wasn't why she was there."

"Was that a normal occurrence?" Fleming asked, writing on his pad.

"It had been for a while. We were involved for a couple of months. She'd come by after work at Lefty's. I ended the relationship last month. She wanted to start things up again." The detective looked at him and Tom continued. "I thought she was Tallie—I called her Tallie—and that made her angry."

"So you fought with her?"

Tom frowned at how easily his words could be twisted into something ugly. "No, I didn't, but she was angry."

"What happened next?"

"Like I said, she was angry that I called her Tallie."

"Who is Tallie?"

"Tallie Peters. My girlfriend. She and her son are staying with me until Roy Peters is caught," Tom said. "Sherry got mad and yelled at me because I called her Tallie. Then she shoved me out of bed onto the floor. Tallie and the boys heard the commotion and came downstairs."

"So, three other people can place her in your home that night?"

"Yes. My son, Michael, Tallie, and her son, Cody. After that, Sherry got dressed. I walked her to the door and locked it behind her."

"Did you see her get in her car?"

Tom thought for a moment and shook his head. "No, I didn't see her get into it. I went upstairs to talk with Tallie and went back to bed."

"But you were the last person to see her alive," the detective commented.

"She was fine when she left my house," Tom said, locking eyes with the detective. "She walked out the door on her own two feet."

Fleming nodded. "We'll need to get fingerprints from everyone on the ranch."

Tom felt the detective watching to see if that bothered Tom. It didn't. He knew he had nothing to hide. "Mine are on file at your office with my weapons permit, but I'll do it again if you need it. I can set you up in the office and run everybody in to you."

"So, Detective," Clay said, leaning forward, "Sherry's death wasn't an accident?"

Fleming let out a slow breath. "It wasn't an accident. Miss Price was murdered, possibly the night she was on your property, but I won't know for sure until we get the coroner's report back. There are several clear prints inside the vehicle."

"Would you like to look at the surveillance records?" Tom asked. "The cameras may have picked up something useful that night."

"Yes, sir. That was my next question. I'll call my office and have them send a fingerprint tech and meet you at your office." He stood and walked to the door. "Thanks for your cooperation, folks." He stepped toward the door.

Tom stopped him. "Detective?"

"Yes?"

"What happened to her?"

The detective stared at Tom, obviously debating how much information to give. "She was raped and strangled." He stepped out, closing the door behind him.

Clay ran a hand through his hair. "You think Roy Peters could have something to do with this?"

Tom rubbed the back of his neck and shrugged. "The guy is nuts. I wouldn't put it past him. Poor Sherry. She didn't deserve that." Tom frowned, feeling sick that he'd sent her out into the night. "I'd better go and set the office up for the detective." He rushed out, stopping near Fleming's vehicle.

"If you want to follow me, I'll run you over to the office and show you where things are. I'm pretty sure Rob was on duty that night, so I'll round him up for you to talk to."

"I appreciate it," the detective replied.

"Can I ask you something?"

Fleming nodded.

"Am I suspect or something? That felt like an interrogation in there."

"Just procedure, Mr. Black. Until we get a clearer picture, we cover all the bases. At the moment, you are a person of interest in the investigation." He started his vehicle. "That's all I can tell you at the moment."

Lon was in the office. After a brief explanation, Tom left him with the detective searching the surveillance records from that evening. Tom excused himself to find Rob and the other employees. He drove near the pond and saw Rob in the boat with the boys, baiting hooks and laughing at something Michael told him. He pulled the truck to a stop near the boat dock and honked to get Rob's attention, waving him to shore. The lanky cowboy waved acknowledgement to Tom's summons and started the boat's motor. Tom could hear the boys' groans as they neared the dock. Tom grabbed the rope Rob threw and tied it to a post.

"Sorry to interrupt your fun, guys, but something has come up, and I need Rob at the office."

"Ah, man!" Michael groaned. "Can we sit in the boat?"

"No." Tom shook his head. "I need you two to head back to the house. I'll explain later. Get your gear put away."

"But—" Cody started to argue.

"Just do as you're told. I'll explain when I get to the house. Get to it." Tom returned to his truck with Rob following. "I'll meet you at the office, Rob. Could you round up the crew on your way in? I'll go around the south end if you'll go the other way and check the bunkhouse. I need everybody at the office."

"What's up?" Rob asked, frowning.

"A sheriff's detective says they found Sherry Price's car shoved in the trees down the road. She was in it, raped and strangled. They want everybody's fingerprints."

Rob's eyes went wide. "Do they think it was the night

she was here?"

"Looks like it."

He whistled and scratched his head. "Well, I let her in the gate and watched her go back out a few hours later," Rob said.

"A few hours later? She was only at my house a few minutes. Are you sure?" Tom questioned Rob's memory, sure he was mistaken.

"I'm positive. I was heating my dinner in the microwave when she came in. That took a few minutes. I ate it and took a drive around the ranch. When I got back to the office, I listened to a radio program and watched her drive out the gate."

"She was at my place for maybe ten to fifteen minutes, tops. Did you see her car anywhere other than my house?"

Rob shook his head. "No, and that's weird. I didn't see her car by your place or anywhere else. But I saw her drive in and out."

"We'd better talk to Detective Fleming and take a look at the video for that time frame. She must have seen someone else after she left my house. I'll meet you at the office in a few minutes."

⁣⁣⁣⁣⁣⁣⁣⁣⁣⁣⁣⁣⁣◦⦿◦

Afternoon sun trickled through his bedroom blinds, highlighting Roy's flexing fingers. He could feel her neck in his hands if he thought about it, feel it as he applied the pressure. He'd felt powerful, like he could do anything, control life and death. It was better this time. Phin was an accident but not Sherry. He'd wanted to kill her before she could run to Tom Black and ruin everything. So he did. Bursting with confidence, he'd thought he could grab the kid and take care of Tallie too. Black had taken that guy to the airport last night and Tallie was home alone for the first time. The storm had provided the perfect opportunity and he could have grabbed them.

If it hadn't been for that dog attacking him, he'd have been long gone before anyone realized he was even there. By the time he shook off the animal, Tom was back and saw him in the yard. Luckily, the guy bought his do-gooder speech about checking on Tallie and the boys for him. He'd had enough of this waiting bullshit now. It was time to make his move and grab the kid, and if he could get his hands on Tallie, so much the better.

Luck was with him when he'd disposed of Sherry's body. He hadn't heard a word about her, so he was in the clear on that one. Just like Phin. As far as he knew, his body hadn't surfaced either. He laughed. Who would suspect a Bible thumper like him anyway? Around here, he was just a no-body with a shit scooper. He lounged on his bunk and laughed at his success.

"Hey, Phin!" Rob called from the living room. "They want us in the office."

Roy stood and leaned on the bedroom doorframe. "Why?"

"Detective wants to talk to everybody and take some fingerprints." Rob grabbed a glass from the cupboard and filled it with water.

Roy's stomach muscles clenched. "Why?"

"Found a woman's body down the road. They're checking everybody in the neighborhood. Come on." Rob downed the water. "They're ready for us."

"I'll be right there after I make a pit stop," Roy called to

Rob and walked to the bathroom. He closed the door, leaning against it. Sweat beaded on his brow. It was time to grab the kid. As soon as they took his prints, he was finished and back in prison—for life this time.

He stayed in the bathroom for a few minutes, making a plan. If all the hands were at the office for fingerprinting, Tom would be there too. Roy ran into his room and grabbed his belongings—shirts, socks, a lighter, and cigs—and threw them in a bag. He tossed the Bible in the trash can. He'd ransacked the office during the storm and grabbed a few extra items: money from the petty-cash box and an extra cell phone. He left the bunkhouse, looking around before jumping in his pickup. After a roundabout route through the ranch, he turned the truck off and let it glide into the driveway behind Tom's house. Adrenaline pumped loudly in his ears as he made his way to the kitchen door, walking tightly against the wall. Careful not to bang the back door, he stepped in, listening for Cody. At the sound of footsteps upstairs, he dashed across the living room and into a bedroom. Roy looked around, noted a rifle hanging on a wall rack and a handgun nearby. As he moved in the direction of the door, a screen slammed. Roy melted into the shadows.

"Tom?" He heard Tallie's voice.

"Yeah. Where are you?" Tom called as he walked across the living room.

"Upstairs, in the boys' room."

"Are they here?" Tom asked, climbing the stairs.

"No. Should they be?"

Roy could hear their voices but couldn't make out the continuing conversation. He had what he needed. Cody was outside somewhere. He grabbed the handgun and stuffed it in his shirt. Next, he pulled the rifle from the rack and opened dresser drawers, searching until he located the ammo. He grabbed what he could and quietly retraced his steps to his pickup. Holding his breath, he started the truck and drove from the house.

⁊

Tom's office crawled with activity when he and Tallie arrived. Ranch hands leaned against the walls, sat on desks, and sipped cans of pop. None seemed concerned about the fingerprinting and interviews. Tom was glad, since he hadn't convinced Tallie she wasn't needed there. She followed him into the office.

"How's it going?" Tom asked Rob, who had taken Lon's place at the computer.

"Fine, I guess. I told the detective everything I told you, and we're looking over the surveillance video now." He nodded at the monitor. "They're about halfway through the guys out there. Stop right there." Rob pointed at the picture. "That's the car going out the gate. Four twenty-five a.m."

"What time did she drive in?" Tom asked.

"Two twelve a.m.," Fleming answered.

"She was at my house until two thirty at the latest. Any sign of her on the other cameras?" Tom asked. "Take a look at number seven. It shows the area around the barns and bunkhouse." Rob moved the cursor and clicked on another file. "See, right there." Tom pointed at the Toyota driving past the camera. "Two thirty-five a.m. Look at the passenger seat. Is there someone with her?" Tom squinted at the picture. "Stop and enlarge it." Rob complied. "See, right there." Tom pointed. "There's a shadow and it looks like an

elbow sticking out the passenger window. Let it run again."
They watched the car move from sight. Another file showed
an unidentifiable man walking around the ranch at that
time. The next revealed her car near the gate.

Tom pointed to another file. "This one should show who
was in the car when it went through the gate, maybe clear
enough to make out a face." They watched as the car came
into view. "Enlarge the picture." Tom directed. "That isn't
Sherry driving."

"Do you know who he is?" Fleming studied the image of
a large man behind the wheel of the car.

Rob leaned forward for a better look at the red-haired
man. "Looks like that new guy, Phin."

"Is he here? What's his last name?" the detective asked.

"Phin Mulberry." Rob looked out the door at the group
of cowboys and said, "Is Phin out there?"

"No," a chorus of voices responded before going back to
their conversations.

Tallie gripped Tom's hand. "Enlarge the picture again.
The face. Enlarge the face!"

Tom looked at her, alarmed by her tone. "Do what she
says, Rob."

He complied, enlarging Phin's face until it filled the
screen. Tallie gasped.

"What's wrong?"

"Roy," she whispered. "That's Roy."

Tom shook his head. "No, honey. I told you before.
That's the new guy. Phin Mulberry."

"I don't care what he called himself." She pointed to the
screen. "That's Roy Peters."

Tom felt the room pitch. "You're sure?"

She nodded. "No doubt about it."

Tom wanted to kick something. His own butt was a good start. "How could I have been so stupid? The son of a bitch has been here the whole time! Lon!" He leaned out the office door and yelled. "Has Phin been in for fingerprinting?"

Lon looked over the list of employees and shook his head. "Not yet."

"Shit!" Tom muttered. "That's Roy Peters, Tallie's ex-husband. He's been here under our noses for weeks. Detective, I'll bet if you check Roy Peters' fingerprints, they'll match those in the car. We need to find him, fast." Tom whistled a two-fingered screech to get the attention of the men. His stomach churned at the thought of the massive error he'd made in hiring Phin and ignoring Tallie's instincts and his own. "Listen up!" he yelled as he walked to the center of the room. "Everybody, fan out across the ranch. We need to find Phin Mulberry. Since he didn't come in for fingerprinting, he's probably trying to leave. Call me on my cell phone when you find him." He ran for the door with Tallie close behind.

Tom gunned the truck engine, spinning gravel. The boys should be at the house. Horrible thoughts crossed his mind of what he'd find when he got there. He parked in front, jumping out as fast as he could, and ran into the house. Tallie right on his heels.

"Michael! Cody! Are you here?" he yelled as he ran through the house. They searched upstairs and down.

"They aren't here, Tom."

"I told them to come to the house when I talked to Rob over two hours ago." Tom's stomach twisted again.

"We have to find them. Right now." She ran for the door

with Tom close behind.

They jumped in the truck and made a methodical search of the ranch on their way to the pond. When Tom saw the scattered fishing gear on the dock, he knew Roy had them.

Tallie jumped from the truck and walked slowly down the boat dock, dropping to her knees by the gear. She looked at the haphazard pile, the carelessly tossed tackle boxes. One pole lay on the dock, the other in the water.

"He has them," she said, her calm demeanor clearly covering rising hysteria. "He took Michael, too."

Tom stood next to her, surveying the fishing gear and the water. "We don't know that for sure."

"Michael would have run home to tell you if he was able to. He wouldn't let anyone hurt or take Cody without telling you." Tallie covered her face with her hands.

Tom hesitated before speaking. "We don't know anything for sure, Tallie. We'll tell Detective Fleming about the fishing gear and check in with the guys. Maybe someone found something." He held out his hand to help her up.

They were quiet as they drove the ranch, making a pretense of looking for the boys, but Tom knew they wouldn't find them. He hoped to see two smiling boys run from behind a barn, laughing about the joke they'd played on everyone, but all remained quiet. Tom called Harlie to see if the boys wandered their direction and was disappointed. They hadn't seen them all morning.

When Tom and Tallie arrived at the office, Rob had an image of a red Ford pickup on the security monitor.

"Tom," Rob said, "I think you've got a big problem."

21

Roy drove for an hour, careful not to speed or otherwise draw attention to the truck. Most likely, the state police had been alerted by now and a speeding infraction could land him back in prison. After leaving the Nashville area, he pulled a cell phone from his bag and made a call.

"Wally? It's Roy."

"Roy? Hells bells, I thought you were still in the joint. When did you get out?" a surprised voice replied.

"It's a long story, cousin, and I don't have time right now. I need to know if Uncle Fletcher still has that place on the lake."

"You mean the fishing shack? Yeah, it's mine now. He left it to me when he died a couple years ago, but nobody's been up there in at least five years. Why do you need to know about that?" Wally Peters asked.

"I need you to meet me up there." Roy slowed the truck as a patrol car drove by.

"When?"

"Now."

"Now? I can't run out there to go fishing at the drop of a hat. I've got work to do."

"I don't want to go fishing, Wally. I got a problem, and I need your help. Will you meet me there?" he said with just enough desperation in his voice to do the trick.

Wally sighed. "I guess if you need help, I'll get up there as soon as I can."

"Thanks, Wally. Can you stop and pick up some groceries along the way? Some hamburger stuff, milk, bread, eggs, and maybe some breakfast cereal like Frosted Flakes. A handful of candy bars would be good. I need some Band-Aids and ointment too. I got a bite on my hand that needs tending."

"What trouble you in, Roy?"

"I'll explain when I see you. Get me a tank of propane for the stove and some of those cheap prepaid phones from the gas station while you're there. Don't forget the groceries. Paper plates and stuff too. Oh, and maybe some blankets, toilet paper, and stuff like that. Towels."

"Roy, I can't afford to get mixed up in your trouble. Lucy and I are talking about getting married, and I don't want to mess that up."

"What you can't afford is to miss out on the deal I got going. That little honey of yours just might appreciate the cash I'll drop on you when this is all done." Roy glanced over Cody's head at Michael. The cash cow. He'd been thinking as he drove and figured out how the brat could help him out. If Tom Black wanted his kid back, it was going to cost him.

"What kind of deal?"

"Get to the cabin and I'll fill you in." Roy disconnected the call and smiled. He knew his cousin couldn't resist the lure of easy money. No Peters could. It was in the genes.

In the early evening, Roy pulled the truck to a stop in front of a dilapidated cabin and smiled at the perfection of it. An old shack nestled sweetly among the trees was the last place anyone would look for him. He doubted his family even remembered the old place. He eased the truck deeper into the trees near the side of the building and cut the engine.

Cody squirmed in his seat. "I need the bathroom."

"We'll get there soon enough. I'm laying down the rules first. If either of you try to run, you're dead. Simple enough to remember, don't you think?" He opened the door and stepped from the truck, motioning with his head for the boys to follow. "Outhouse is right over there in those trees. You can go one at a time and I'll be watching you." As Michael climbed from the truck, Roy grabbed his T-shirt collar and held him while Cody ran to the outhouse. When Cody returned, he allowed Michael to go but held Cody, pulling him to the cabin.

A breeze drifted across the lake, slapping small waves on the shore and rustling tree branches, giving the illusion of calm. Roy kicked open the cabin door and a cloud of dust billowed and settled to the floor. Cody coughed and fanned the air.

"It's about the same as the outhouse," Cody grumbled.

"It's grubby but it's home. Get in there and sit down while I get your friend."

Roy shoved Cody toward a tattered sofa, which raised an even larger dust cloud when he fell to the cushions. Cody sneezed.

Roy deposited Michael in the cabin and walked out to greet his newly arrived cousin. Wally Peters was a large man with a full beard and dark hair hanging from under a green John Deere cap. When he climbed from his vintage International truck, he huffed from the effort of moving his sizeable gut.

"Did you get the groceries?" Roy leaned on the pickup.

"What? No hello, cousin—thanks for coming?"

"Yeah, yeah. Thanks. Did you get the groceries?"

"You owe me some money." Wally grabbed a grocery bag and handed it to him. "What in the hell are you doing, Roy?"

"Nice to see you, too, Wally." Roy grinned.

"Ain't nothing funny about this, cousin. On the way here I saw one of those message signs on the highway that said Child Amber Alert. Tune to local media. So I did."

"And what does that have to do with me?" Roy shrugged.

"Let me see." Wally took off his cap and ran his hand through his hair. "According to the radio, two boys were kidnapped from the Masterson-Black Ranch this morning by a guy in an old red Ford pickup truck." His gaze landed on Roy's truck nestled in the brush. "One of them was named Michael Black Morgan and the other is named Cody Peters. Sound familiar? You call me out of the blue to meet you up here in the middle of goddamned nowhere and tell me to bring Frosted Flakes and candy bars. Are you going to try and tell me you don't have those boys? I may be a lot of things, Roy, but stupid ain't one of them."

"So what if I do? Cody's my kid. They can't call that kidnapping."

"Does the term 'noncustodial parent' ring any bells with you? That's what they're calling you, and they say it's a felony, dimwit. What about the other one? You ain't related to him. What did you take him for?" Wally glanced at the cabin where two boys looked out the dirty window.

"I didn't plan to, but he latched onto Cody like an octopus and wouldn't let go. So I threw them both in."

"And that's going to get you sent back to prison, shit for brains. You stole a kid from Clay Masterson's ranch. You don't mess with famous people like him. How dense can you be?" Wally thunked Roy on the forehead with his palm. Roy slapped his hand away and glared.

"I didn't bring you here for a lecture. I need help, and you're the only one I can trust to do it." A slow smile crossed Roy's face. "And I got a plan to make us a whole lot of money."

"What?"

"Ransom for that black-haired kid. I figure he's worth a million or two." Roy grinned.

Wally whistled. "His family has that kind of money?"

"I don't know about his old man, but the guy is pals with Clay Masterson, and you know how much money that guy must have. A million is pocket change to him."

"I don't know about this, Roy." Wally frowned. "I can't be getting involved in one of your messes. I have plans of my own."

"Just help me get these burgers fixed and we'll talk about it later. Come meet my boy." Roy grabbed another bag and walked to the cabin. Wally grabbed the others and followed him.

As the door opened, Cody and Michael ran toward a bed shoved against a wall.

"Set that stuff on the counter, Wally. I need to clean this kitchen before we eat. Cody," he called. "This is my cousin, Wally."

Cody stared at the large man.

Wally nodded at him. "Hey, Cody. What's your friend's name?"

Cody swallowed. "Michael."

"You guys hungry?" Wally asked.

Both nodded but didn't speak. "We'll get burgers cooked for you." He turned and walked to Roy in the kitchen area. "You got those boys scared witless, Roy. What's the matter with you?"

"They'll get over it. Tallie wouldn't let me have the kid, so I had to take him." Roy dug through the cupboards for a skillet.

"There's a good reason for that. You tried to kill her. Or did you forget that little fact?" Wally was knocked off balance when Roy lunged at him, grabbed his shirt at the collar, and shoved him against the counter.

"He's my kid!" Roy tightened his grip on Wally. "Mine!"

"Cousin," Wally said quietly. "You have five seconds to get your hands off me. The way I see things, you'd better be treating me real nice, because I'm the only help you got here."

Roy released him and stepped back, holding up his hands. "Let's get this food fixed and those boys to bed. You and I can talk outside later."

The meal was eaten in silence. The boys ate fast and left the table. Wally finished and brought in clean blankets and pillows from the truck and made the kids' bed. When they crawled in and looked sleepy, Wally signaled toward the door for Roy to follow.

The two men sat on a log at water's edge, listening to the night sounds and staring into hazy dusk.

"I don't like what you're doing here, Roy."

"Don't suppose you do."

"But I won't talk you into taking them back, will I?"

"Nope. I'm going to see it through. I'm calling Tom Black in the morning to let him know what it will take for him to get his kid back. When I have the money, me and Cody will take off."

"What makes you think you'll get away with it?"

"I have a plan. He tried to hide my kid from me, so I'm going to enjoy myself for a time, playing with the bastard's head. And if Tallie works up a good sweat over it, that's good, too." Roy grinned.

"You're nuts." Wally sighed and shook his head.

"I need your help, Wally. They'll be watching for my truck. Did you bring the phones?"

"Yeah. Charged and ready to use."

"Good. After I make a call tomorrow, I'll ditch the one I got. Damned thing could be a homing beacon." His prison education had been thorough in many areas and cell phones were a biggie. "I'll need you to stay with the boys for a bit."

"What for?"

"I need your truck, too."

"I thought you needed to hide out? If you take my truck—"

"I'll stick to the back roads."

Wally scowled, looking confused.

"I gotta take Black's cell phone for a ride, Wally. Throw off the scent. Understand? I'll make my call and get rid of the thing. They'll think I'm somewhere else. So, you'll be back with my stuff?"

Wally nodded. "Yeah. I'll help you, but only because I don't want anything happening to those boys. Give me a list of what you need, and I'll be back tomorrow."

Roy slung his arm around Wally's neck and grinned.

"And cousin? Just so you know...if I come back and those boys are gone, I will hunt you down."

Evening shadows crawled across the cabin floor; angry male voices coasted in the window on a cool breeze. Michael and Cody lay in their hastily made bed, unable to sleep.

"Cody? Are you asleep?" Michael whispered.

"No," Cody whispered. "Are you scared?"

Michael hesitated. "Are you?"

"Yeah. I remember what he was like before he went to prison. When he says he'll kill us, he means it. He'll kill us dead, for sure. He shot Mom once and would have killed her if he could have. Just do what he tells you, Mike. Don't piss him off." Cody turned in the dark toward Michael. "I'm scared."

"Me, too. What do you think he's going to do with me?" Michael asked, his voice shaking.

"I don't know. Money, maybe? I saw a show on TV about kidnapping. Maybe he'll make Tom pay for you."

"Maybe he'll just kill me." The knot in Michael's stomach clenched tighter.

"Don't give him a reason to do anything. What do you think of Wally?"

"I don't think he's crazy like Roy. There's something in his eyes when he looks at us. Maybe he'll help us get away."

"Somebody's gotta help us. No way we can do it by ourselves," Cody said. "I looked around out there and it's nothin' but trees...and maybe some bears." He gulped. "I don't want to be bear food."

Footsteps clunked on the front step and Michael tensed. "Shh, Cody. He's coming back." He closed his eyes, pretending to sleep.

Roy walked in, taking time to pump water into a glass. He knocked it back in a swallow and wandered toward the boys' bed. Even with his eyes closed, Michael knew Roy was there from the stench of stale cigarette smoke and the rasp of his breathing. Fear kept him physically immobile but the smoke smell tickled Michael's nose. He wondered how long it would take for a guy to die of lung cancer. Too long, he figured, to do him and Cody any good. What does the guy want? Would he kill him now? He tried to stay still. One wiggle and Roy would know he was awake. He wished the guy would go away, far away. But he didn't. Roy stood there, humming. Michael recognized the song from the radio and his stomach knotted tighter. Cody was right about Roy's plan.

Michael heard Roy chuckle and sensed him turn away from the bed and head to his own. As he walked away, he sang a line from Steve Miller's "Take the Money and Run."

22

"I understand why he took Cody, but why Michael?" Tom paced the living room floor, his agitation growing. With his stomach churning and his fists clenched, he was certain he'd have no problem throttling Roy Peters with his bare hands. He itched for the chance. Tallie sat on the sofa, toying with a thread on her denim shorts. Harlie was nearby, ready to offer comfort if Tallie broke down. Clay leaned on the kitchen doorframe, a coffee mug in hand. The television was tuned to a local channel, the boys' abduction the top story. Tom's attention was drawn to the picture of Michael and Cody on the screen.

"We stepped up security last year for a reason, Tom," Clay said.

A commercial interrupted the news coverage. Tom looked at Clay. "I know. You were afraid someone would try to do something to your family. So? This isn't your family. It's mine."

Clay shrugged. "He's after ransom, plain and simple."

"Ransom? That would be an obvious reason if it were your kid or if I had any money, which I don't." Tom resumed his pacing.

"I do," Clay said.

"But I don't! Not enough to interest anyone, anyway."

"Roy spent time on my property. He knows who I am. He's probably heard the speculation of my net worth. Most likely, he's figured out you're my best friend and if you need money, I'll give it to you in a heartbeat."

Tom dropped into his recliner, frustrated at the situation he found himself in: inside the well with his hand caught in the rope, and Clay was jumping in the arena to save him again.

"I don't want you bailing me out, Clay."

"The offer stands, nonetheless. Kick that pride of yours in the butt and take the money if you need it. Whatever it takes to get Michael back, it's yours." Clay looked at Tallie. "Cody, too."

Tallie blinked, looking like a she'd come into the sunlight from a fogbank. "Thank you," she said. "I'll pay you back. Every penny."

Clay shook his head. "No," he said. "Tom always says I have more money than I know what to do with and he's right. You know all that speculation of my net worth? It's inaccurate. I'm worth a heck of a lot more than that. So if I have to buy those boys back, I will. Then we'll let the cops have at him."

"No point in arguing with him, Tom, and you know it," Harlie said. "Once he sets his mind on something, he's about as pigheaded as a man can be."

Clay winked at Harlie. "Determined sounds better than pigheaded."

"You are pigheaded," Tom said, "and I appreciate it. At least we have something to bargain with." Tom heard footsteps and glanced out the door to see Detective Frank Jeffers, the lead detective on the abduction case, climbing the steps. Frank worked in concert with a team of four others, including Detective Fleming, the murder investigation detective. Clay opened the screen door and Jeffers walked in.

Tom noted worry lines etched his already-creased forehead.

The detective nodded to the assembled group, dropped into an offered chair, and blew out a breath. "You know," he said, "I'd hoped my last two months on this job would be easy ones, and now we've got a murder and a double kidnapping," he said with a frown. "I'm wishing as much as you folks that they didn't both involve you." He reached in his pocket, pulled out an antacid roll, and popped one in his mouth. "Any contact from Peters?"

"No," Tom said. "Do you have any news yet?"

"Nothing conclusive. Since we issued the statewide Amber Alert, the eight-hundred number is getting a load of activity. So far, we've received hundreds of leads and we're working through them. I figure that two-hour head start gave Peters a chance to find a hidey-hole though. We've been to his old house and the other places you've suggested, but nothing yet. We'll keep on it."

"What do you think the chances are of finding them?" Tom asked. He'd worked the odds out himself and didn't feel good about the probability of locating the boys in time. Roy wanted Cody; Michael was a problem. Tom wanted them found before Roy decided to rid himself of the problem.

"Since we know who we're looking for, that increases our odds. Eventually, he'll make a mistake and someone will recognize him, or someone who knows him will feel guilty and turn him in," Detective Jeffers said. "But on the flip side, if he murdered Sherry Price as we believe, he has more reason to keep hidden. Most likely, he'll have to find someone to help him, so we're concentrating on people he knows at the moment."

"And if he murdered Sherry," Tom said, speculating, "he's even more unbalanced than we thought, and that places Michael in even greater danger."

"It does," the detective said with a sigh. "I hope he'll contact you soon so we know what he's after."

"You can add theft to his list of charges," Tom said. "A rifle, handgun, and ammo for both are missing from my bedroom. I just noticed it a while ago. It was all there this morning."

"Crazy and armed. Hell of a combination." Jeffers clicked his pen. "I'll get the word out."

"What about the Feds?" Tom asked. "Shouldn't the FBI be in on this?"

"They are," he said with a nod. "As soon as Fleming called in the report, the Child Abduction Response Team went into action. CART includes local, state, and federal agencies. We've also had calls from local law enforcement across the state offering their assistance. We've got a flood of volunteers pinning up posters, canvassing neighborhoods, and asking questions. Hundreds of them and they keep showing up. We're doing everything possible to find the boys fast." He stood, moved toward the door, but turned back. "The number of reporters and satellite trucks at your gate is growing. I've given some progress reports and made announcements. Some of the reporters have asked if they can talk to you, too."

Tom looked at Tallie. She shook her head. "Not me. If Roy sees me, I'll just make him mad. There's no telling what he'll do."

"I could have the same problem," Tom said. "Roy hasn't demanded ransom yet, and I'm thinking that taking Michael is a personal stab at me. What do you think, Detective?"

He shrugged. "You may be right. But you might want to consider it anyway. The more publicity we get, the better our chances that someone will come forward with information."

"I'll do it," Clay said.

Tom nodded. "That's a good idea. If you do it, the story gets bigger. Might as well use that name of yours to get some attention."

"I agree," Jeffers said. "But it isn't just his name drawing attention to this."

"What do you mean?" Tom asked.

"We're getting a lot of calls on the tip line about Clay Masterson, but we're also getting some asking if you're the bull rider. Are you?"

Tom frowned. "I was, but it was a long time ago."

Detective Jeffers smiled. "Some of these folks have long memories and they want to help. It wouldn't hurt to have you both on the news."

Clay and Tom exchanged a glance. "All right. If it'll help," Tom said. "When?"

The detective glanced at his watch. "It's late. Let's get it done first thing in the morning. It'll give the media something to chew on throughout the day. Call me immediately if Peters contacts you or if you think of anything else that may be helpful." He nodded to the group and stepped out into the night, stopping at the threshold. "There's one more piece to this puzzle we haven't tackled in-depth yet."

"What's that?" Tom asked.

"What happened to the real Phin Mulberry? Nobody has seen him since he took off from Lefty's. The bartender recognized Roy from the photo we're circulating and came forward. He said Phin Mulberry was drinking with a blond guy and they left together. The car Roy borrowed from his neighbor was left in the parking lot. If a body turns up, we could possibly have another murder to pin on him. Get some sleep, folks." He departed, the screen slapping behind him.

"It is late." Tom studied his tired friends who had been with him and Tallie since the boys' kidnapping was discovered that afternoon. "You two should go home. If Roy calls, I'll let you know."

"We can stay longer," Harlie said.

Tom stood, favoring his bad knee, and walked to the sofa where she sat, holding out a hand to help her up. "Pregnant women need their rest, Harlie. We already have two kids to worry about. Let's not make it three. Go home and get some sleep." He pulled her to her feet and hugged her. "Thanks for being here."

"I wish we could do more to help, Tom," she said, returning the hug.

"I know. Take her home, Clay. I'll talk with you later."

Clay put his arm around Tom and squeezed his shoulder. "We'll get them back. Whatever it takes. I'm thinking of offering a reward. We'll talk about it in the morning." Clay released him and slid his arm around Harlie. "Get some rest, both of you," Clay ordered as he walked out the door.

Tom held his hand out to Tallie. "Come on. Lay down with me for a while." Tallie had that glazed expression again and Tom worried she was back inside herself, inside that safe place she retreated to. She knew firsthand what Roy Peters was capable of, and he knew it had her terrified. "Sitting here isn't going to help anyone, honey. We'll hear the phone if anyone calls. Come on," he said softly.

Tallie reluctantly put her hand in his and allowed him to lead her to his room. Looking lost, Tallie stood near the bed, waiting for Tom. Not bothering to remove clothes, he lay down and pulled her into his arms.

"We'll get them back, Tallie. Whatever it takes, we'll get them back."

23

Tallie watched a dust mote wend its way across an early morning sunbeam. She imagined a voice screaming to be noticed, like in *Horton Hears a Who*. She sighed. It was Cody's favorite story when he was three. She lay on Tom's bed, her back turned to him, exhausted from a night of pacing and worry. She felt every minute of missed sleep. Tom sat on the edge, stroking her arm, attempting to comfort her. Nothing short of hearing Cody and Michael yelling "We are here!" would console her now. Only wrapping her arms around those boys would ease her anxiety.

"Is the detective back?" she asked, her voice flat.

"Yes, and he wants to ask you a few more questions about Roy. About his family and where they live. They want to try more places, talk to more people. Can you get up?"

"So there isn't any news this morning?"

"No. Jeffers said his department, the state police, FBI, and hundreds of volunteers searched throughout the night but came up empty. Clay and I will talk to the reporters. See what we can stir up."

Tallie rolled toward him. "I'd better get up and figure out something I can do, too." She crawled from the bed, deciding she needed to snap out of it. Tom's son was missing as well as hers, and it wasn't fair to expect him to shoulder the burden. She took his hand and squeezed as they walked to the kitchen.

CAUGHT IN THE SPIN

The detective sipped his coffee and nodded as Tallie entered the room with Tom.

"Morning, Miss Peters," he said as she sat down. "I was wondering if we could talk about Roy's family again. The information you gave earlier was a good start, but we need to dig deeper." He flipped opened a notebook and glanced at the annotations. "You said his dad was in Arizona last you heard and his mother died. He hasn't any siblings. What about cousins, aunts, or uncles? Any friends you know about?"

Tallie accepted the buttered bagel and cup of coffee Tom handed her. She absently sipped.

"I think most of his family is in Tennessee, but I met only a few of them. His dad has a bunch of brothers and sisters. His mother had a sister, I think, but I didn't meet her. Roy wasn't close to his family. When his parents divorced, his dad took him to Phoenix, and I don't think he came here to visit often." Tallie shrugged, knowing her vague response wasn't helpful. "When we moved here, his mom was ill and didn't talk much. I took care of her and Roy worked nights at a gas station." She frowned as she thought.

"Can you think of any names?" he prodded.

"I do remember a cousin named Penny coming to visit Roy's mom. Penny Marble. She lives in Greenbrier, or she did ten years ago. He has a lot of cousins on his dad's side. There's Freddy and Burt Peters, brothers who lived in Nashville. Chester Peters, but I think he moved somewhere, Chattanooga maybe. We did see Wally Peters occasionally. He and Roy were close when they were kids. Since Roy's been in prison, I haven't thought about any of these people at all. I hope this gives you a place to start though."

"Yes, it does. We'll see if we can locate these people." He made notes in the pad. "Can you recall if anyone in the family lived in a remote place where he could hide? Like a farm?"

Tallie shook her head. "I wish I knew, but we just didn't have much to do with his family and if he had friends, they didn't come around the house. But I'll think about it today and call you."

"More coffee?" Tom asked as he refilled his cup.

"No thanks, Tom," the detective said. "If you and Clay are ready, I'll take you out to the reporters to make a statement."

Tom nodded. "I'll call Clay and get cleaned up." He ran his hand through his hair. His cell phone rang and he grabbed it from the charger on the counter. "Tom Black." He listened and frowned. "Who is this...Why...Tallie...Is this Roy Peters?" Tom waved for the detective to move closer and pushed the speaker button. Roy's voice came through loud and clear.

"Hell, you're a whole lot sharper than I been giving you credit for, *sir*." Roy emphasized the word even more than before, laughing. "I expected you to call me Phin. For a while anyway."

"Where are the boys? We know you have them," Tom said. Tallie moved from her chair and was at his side. Tom held up his hand, indicating she shouldn't speak.

"They're doing just fine...for now. But if you try to play any games with me, the situation could change superfast."

"What do you want?" Tom's body tensed. "Money? Just name it and I'll see what I can do."

"Well, now. I'm still thinking on that. I'll be in touch,

sir."

"Let me talk to them," Tom said. "Peters!" Tom was immobile for a moment, the nerve in his neck jumping. He disconnected the call and tossed the phone on the table. "Damn him, why won't he say what he wants?" Tom sat and rubbed a shaking hand through his already-disheveled hair. When he settled himself, he picked up the phone and checked caller ID. "Son of a bitch.

"What's the number, Tom?" Detective Jeffers asked.

With a rueful laugh, Tom shook his head. "Mine. He's using the cell phone I gave him when he started working here. He could be anywhere. I should cancel the cell service."

"No," Tallie said. "If you do that, he might stop calling. We can't risk it."

"You're right." Tom closed his eyes.

When he opened them, Tallie saw the worry he'd been trying to hide.

"I just want to talk to the boys, make sure they're okay."

Tallie stepped to him and wrapped her arms around his neck.

"He's had enough time to..." He stopped without completing the thought out loud, but Tallie knew what he was thinking. He was afraid his son could already be dead.

"What should we do, Detective?" she asked.

"We can track the cell phone. The service provider can check to see what cell tower he's close to. Cells send out a ping to surrounding towers. We might find out the area he's in. For now, stay close to your phone. He's playing with you." The detective stood and rotated his shoulders. "I'll get on these names and see if we can stir up his family. Contact me as soon as he calls again. Also, I need the info on that cell phone he's using. We can check to see if he's made any other calls since yesterday. If he's staying in one place, we may still be able to trace him."

Tom grabbed a piece of scratch paper from a drawer and jotted the number down. After tucking the note in his pocket, Frank Jeffers left the kitchen.

When they were alone, Tom looked at Tallie. "Michael and I were just starting to know each other..."

"Don't go there. We'll get him back. Both of them, alive and unharmed." She held him tight. Tom had been her rock through all her problems and now he needed her strength. "Let's fix some breakfast. Then, you and Clay can talk to the reporters and I'll get on the Internet to see what I can find out about Roy's family. I'll search the phone listings and see if I can come up with some addresses and phone numbers." She unwrapped herself from his arms and opened the refrigerator door. "Eggs and bacon?"

After breakfast, Tom swung by Clay's place and picked him up for the short drive to the front gate and their appointment with the TV news crews. As they drew closer, sweat collected between Tom's shoulder blades. He hadn't been in front of a camera in more than a dozen years. Not since the night before the World Finals—the night before the accident. He'd been cocky and full of himself then. A far cry from how he felt today.

Clay was cool and calm. He made his living facing thousands of fans a night and Tom was glad he was by his side. Brothers. They'd been shoring each other up since toddlerhood and today was just another mile in the road. As they neared the gate, Clay frowned and exhaled loudly.

Tom heard him and glanced his way. "What?"

"This." He indicated the mass of reporters. "I hate this."

"I know it's a mess and all, but once the boys are found—"

"Nah, I don't mean that. I mean interviews. I can't stand interviews. All the poking and prodding they do. I hate it." Lines furrowed his brow. "They ask such personal questions...stuff that's none of their business...stuff that's nobody's business...I hate it."

"Why did you volunteer for this?" Tom said. "I'm not forcing you to do it."

"I'm doing it because you need me to do it."

Tom stopped the truck and removed the keys from the ignition. "You don't have to—"

Clay laughed. "Yeah, I do. Remember Cheyenne?"

"What about it?"

"That pretty little reporter sashayed up to you and asked you about bull riding and you froze up. You'd think she was asking you for the meaning of life or something."

Tom smiled. "Oh yeah. That. I was having a bad day and couldn't get my mind wrapped around the question."

"Right. And what are you having today?"

Tom rolled his eyes and half smiled. "The worst possible day of my life. I get your point."

Clay climbed from the pickup and groaned.

"Thanks, Clay. I owe you big-time for this."

Clay leaned in. "You don't owe me a thing, Tommy. It's me who owes you."

Tom opened his mouth to object.

"You know what I'm talking about. I intruded on your life. You didn't have to accept me as your brother but you did. We're family because you allowed it to happen. I'll always owe you for that."

Clay slammed the truck door and pushed a few buttons on the control panel. The gate crept open. Tom watched him, admiring the way he approached the crowd. The superstar had arrived and no one there would know Clay didn't want to talk to them. They were putty in the hands of a master performer. Tom climbed from the truck, straightened his spine, and followed him through the gate.

Detective Jeffers took his place with Clay and Tom, forcing the reporters to take a step back. "This isn't a celebrity feeding frenzy," he reminded them. "This is a crime investigation and these gentlemen are to be treated with respect."

After some discussion, Clay stepped forward, took a paper from his pocket, and read his prepared statement. "I want to thank everyone for coming out today. As Detective Jeffers said earlier, we've had a lot of leads to follow, but so far, none have led to the boys' return. Roy Peters has been in contact with Tom and Tallie, so we know without a doubt he has them. If anyone has information regarding the whereabouts of Roy Peters, Michael Black Morgan, or Cody Peters, please contact the sheriff's department as soon as possible. I am offering a reward of fifty thousand dollars for *solid* information leading us to the boys."

Clay stepped aside before anyone could ask questions. Tom took his place. "Thanks for coming, folks. I'm Tom Black, Michael's father. I just want to say thanks to all the volunteers who came out to help. It means a lot to Tallie and me." Tom looked straight into the camera. "Michael and Cody, if you can hear me, I want you to know we are doing everything we can to find you. You'll be home soon."

His voice cracked. "I promise." From the corner of his eye, Tom caught a glimpse of something...someone. A woman with strawberry-blonde hair. He turned his head and stared at where she'd been. A shiver ran down his spine. Tom panned the assembled crowd, but she was gone. He turned from the camera, muttered "Thank you," and headed to his truck.

"You okay?" Clay asked when he caught up.

Tom swallowed hard and shook his head. "No," he whispered. "I'm—" He caught himself and reconsidered what he was about to say. "I'm fine. It's just like Cheyenne all over again. I froze. That's all."

Clay frowned and held out his hand. "Give me the keys."

Tom complied with the request. "Go ahead and take the truck to your place. I'll come by for it later. I feel like walking."

Clay gave him a long, considering look. "All right. I suppose the walk will do you some good."

Tom walked the ranch, passing the barns, hay stacks, and machine sheds, ending up at the far side of the pond sitting on a rock. No box turtles today, just a few mallards and an occasional trout. His cell phone rang. Caller ID: Jason Gardner. Tom let it go to voicemail. Jason wasn't someone he could talk to right now. He imagined how the conversation would go and wasn't up to it.

The dock was visible from his rock perch. The boat was still tied to the piling. It hadn't moved since the boys climbed from it. When the deputies arrived to assist Detective Jeffers, they'd collected the fishing gear from the dock and lifted fingerprints. When the boys came home, Tom planned to take them shopping for new gear. They'd make an afternoon of it. When they came home, not if, he kept telling himself. When.

His cell rang again. Caller ID: The Black B Ranch, Montana. Dad. He considered letting voicemail do its thing again but answered anyway. It would save him from making the call later.

"When were you planning to call us?" Sheldon Black said, his voice gruff. "We shouldn't hear about our grandson's kidnapping on CNN. You should have called last night."

In his mind, Tom could see his dad pacing in front of the panoramic office windows facing the mountains, black hair with salt-and-pepper temples, and frowning like the dickens. Tom squeezed his eyes tight and pinched the bridge of his nose. A dull ache indicated a headache coming on. "And tell you what, Dad? That I screwed up again?"

"Tom—"

"I mean it. What could I say?"

Sheldon was silent a moment. "You're blaming yourself for this?" He sighed. "Of course you are. Thomas Michael, when are you going to stop knocking yourself around for things outside your control?"

"I hired the guy, Dad. I gave him the perfect hiding place right under my nose."

"So you made a mistake. Nobody's perfect and you'll kill yourself aiming for it."

"I know I'm not perfect. Never said I was or wanted to be." Tom stared off across the water. "I'm just trying to be the man I think I should be and I keep falling short."

"The problem is, you've set the bar so high you can't possibly live up to it," he said. "Nobody could." Sheldon's voice warmed. "But you come closer than anyone else could. You're a fine man, and your mom and I have always been proud of you."

Tom snorted. "Not sure why. Maybe you need to set your bar a little higher."

Sheldon laughed. "We'd be proud no matter what you do. And since you always give two hundred percent to everything you do, it's pretty easy. We have three of the best kids a family could have," he said. Tom knew he referred to Tom, his sister, and Clay, the foster son. They never called Clay that though. He was just the other son to them. "From what I can see, you stepped up to the plate when it was required of you. When you found out about Michael, you didn't hesitate to take on the responsibility—"

Tom frowned. "Anyone would've done the same."

"Some would. Some wouldn't. But you did. You always have."

Tom knew he meant Clay's father, who abandoned his two-year-old son. There was a guy who not only didn't step up to the plate, he couldn't even find it. Things changed between Clay and his dad two years ago, but they were still finding their way to a solid father-son relationship.

"It's always been in your nature to take care of everybody around you, to try to protect them. You tried with Jolie, promising to take her away from the life she had and give her a better one. It's why the accident was so tough on you. You couldn't take care of her the way you'd promised."

"There was more to it than that—"

"I suppose there was, but it was a factor. You wanted to protect her from all the bad things in life."

"And I became one of them."

Sheldon ignored that comment. "And you did the same sort of thing with Clay when you were just a tyke. You were like his bodyguard—even when you guys were little squirts."

"I was?"

Sheldon's chuckle was a calming sound to Tom. "I suppose you were too little to remember when Hunt Masterson came back and took Clay away. You boys were four. You were so upset that the stranger took your brother away. We couldn't convince you he wasn't your brother and we'd just been caring for him until his dad came back. You got your slingshot and were going to get that guy for taking Clay."

Tom smiled. He did remember that. He wanted to whack that guy between the eyes.

"Clay came back. Dumped on our doorstep like an unwanted puppy, confused over what was going on. The man who said to call him daddy was gone again. You took little Clay by the hand and led him into the kitchen. You got him a towel to wipe his eyes and told him nobody was ever taking your brother away again. You'd protect him. And all these years later, you're still doing your best to keep him and everyone around you safe."

Tom felt a lump in his throat. "Yeah, well, Clay's done his share for me, too. He's offered to put up ransom for the boys."

"I thought he would. He understands family and his heart is always in the right place. Yours is too. I'm confident you did what you could to keep the whole lot of them out of harm's way. Sometimes, things go awry and there's nothing you can do about it."

"Shit happens, right?" Tom said.

"Right."

"Michael is a great kid, Dad. I wish you could meet him."

"I will. He'll be home soon. From the looks of things on TV, you have just about everybody in Tennessee looking for them. Somebody is bound to trip over them soon. Would you like us to come? Your mom has been checking on airline tickets, ready to fly when you give us the word."

Tom smiled. He could see his mother with her bags packed, ready to go. "As much as I'd love to have you here, I think it's better if you don't. It's a madhouse with all the cops crawling around and the reporters at the gate. We're accosted for interviews when we try to leave. Besides, Tallie is already stressed out. I think meeting her future in-laws right now would be too much for her."

"Oh? Future in-laws are we?"

"I hope so. But...I don't know. Everything is such a mess now." Tom checked his watch. "I gotta go, Dad. This is the number Roy Peters has been calling. I don't want to miss him. I'm glad you called."

"We love you and are here if you need us, Tommy. You know that."

"Yeah. I know. Love you, too."

The call disconnected, Tom stared across the pond, wondering if he would ever have the chance to say those words to his son. And no matter what his dad said, he knew who was to blame for this.

Tom Black.

24

Evening shadows crawled through the room when Tallie finished her Internet search. She'd amassed a large list of names and addresses for the sheriff's department and felt she'd contributed something, rather than sit helplessly waiting. Roy hadn't called again and when Tom tried to dial the cell phone number, it wasn't in service. There was nothing to do but wait for the next call. Frank Jeffers returned and Tom went over their research with him while Tallie showered. She needed to relax, so Tom offered to handle it. Jeffers brought others from the CART team and Tom spent the evening hashing out possibilities. But until Roy called, it was all conjecture and amounted to nothing but frustration.

The officers departed after consuming enough coffee to wire them tight for the remainder of the evening. Tom cleared the mugs from the table. Tension caused his hands to shake and he nearly dropped the mugs in the sink. Murky dusk filled the evening sky. A hint of sunset visible through the kitchen window beckoned Tom into the dimming light. He needed out of the house for a few minutes. Since Roy's call earlier in the day, his anger built steadily, inch by inch, until it consumed him. The unproductive session with the cops didn't help.

After a glance at his bedroom door, Tom wandered into the muggy night. A cricket and frog concerto blended with his boot steps on the porch, and moths darted around the porch light in chaotic flight. Tom paused on the top step, debating whether to sit or walk the ranch, choosing to walk.

The amphibian chorus faded, and his boots crunching the gravel filled the void. A horse whinnied; a dog barked. Normal, he thought, and continued on, passing barns and pole buildings stacked with hay. After a moment, it occurred to him he possibly retraced Sherry's last steps. He stopped. She'd wanted him to love her and he didn't. Couldn't. He felt bad about it but there wasn't much he could have done to change it. His heart had been waiting for Tallie and knew her immediately as the woman meant for him. He let out a held breath and walked again, hands stuffed in his pockets, shoulders slumped, eyes trained on dark shadows. Had Roy waited for Sherry in these dark holes, like a mountain lion hunting his prey? Or had Sherry helped him by flirting, making his attack easier? She'd been a flirt. All the guys at Lefty's had wanted Sherry to wait on them because she was a tease. And now she was dead.

Detective Fleming's investigation proved she'd been in the bunkhouse. Two whiskey glasses, one with Sherry's prints, were found. Other evidence proved she'd died there, on the floor. Raped and strangled. Roy hadn't been gentle about either. Tom shuddered. He'd never understood such brutality.

He walked by the bunkhouse, now draped in crime tape, but didn't pause long. It bothered him and would for some time. Maybe he'd bulldoze the thing when this was over. The driveway turned right near the building's end, straightening before bending again near Clay's place. A soft voice interrupted the quiet. A woman. He twisted around, thinking it could be her again. Or now, would he see Sherry too? He heard the voice again and relaxed. Not unearthly after all. Clay and Harlie sat on the porch, his arm wrapped round her shoulders, her head resting against him. She looked into her husband's eyes and Clay kissed her. Tom remained in the shadows, not wanting to intrude.

It could have been Harlie crumpled and broken by Roy's sadistic hands. It could have been Abby kidnapped for ransom, or Clay murdered to satisfy some sick impulse. No one knew why Roy had murdered Sherry. Most likely, anyone he'd encountered that night could have been his victim. Sherry was the unlucky winner, in the wrong place at the wrong time. And Tom lived with the guilt he'd sent her straight to the guy who murdered her.

Tom moved away. He needed to get back to the house. Roy was long gone, but Tom still felt uncomfortable leaving Tallie alone. If she woke, he should be there. He rounded the end of Clay's shop and took a shortcut between it and the machine shed, emerging under a blinding fluorescent security light. When his eyes adjusted, he covered the distance to the house.

After locking all the doors, he wandered to his bedroom. When he opened the door, he was greeted with a lovely sight that left him weak in the knees: Tallie, asleep on his bed. He was amazed by the effect she had on him. He'd been falling in love since the day he saw her and knew he'd found the woman to replace Jolie in his heart. It scared him because he was sure it couldn't last. Not now. She'd placed her trust in him and he'd failed. He'd failed them all: Tallie, Cody, Michael, and Jolie.

Tom braced his hands against the doorframe as living room light spilled in, highlighting the lovely woman. She'd never looked more appealing. With a sigh, he stepped from the door and removed his shirt. He tossed it to a chair, slipped off his boots, jeans, and socks. He lay on the bed, keeping to his side of the large mattress, with his hands folded behind his head and eyes on the ceiling. He wondered what the boys were doing tonight. Had Roy fed them? Was Michael still alive? Would he ever know what happened to his son? Worry knotted his stomach. Shame followed closely. MB Ranch security was his responsibility, and for twelve years he'd kept Clay safe and unmolested by his more fervent fans. And now Tom's inattention had placed two innocent kids at risk. With Roy hiding safely under Tom's nose, everyone on the ranch had been endangered. Poor Sherry paid the ultimate price.

He sat on the edge of the bed, ready to get up again. Tallie stirred and rolled to her back. With a stretch, she opened her eyes and located Tom. He glanced her way but didn't speak.

"Are you leaving?" she asked.

"I need antacid." Tom grimaced and placed a hand on his stomach. He moved to stand but Tallie reached for him.

"Don't." He pulled his arm from her hand.

She sat up. "What's wrong, Tom? Did Roy call?"

"No."

She tried to move closer but he stopped her with a frown over his shoulder. "Did the detective leave? Did he have anything new?"

"Yes, he left. No, nothing new."

"What—"

"I just want...I just need to be left alone, okay?" He wanted to move away but was already on the edge of the mattress. He didn't want to be comforted or touched. He didn't deserve either. Not from Tallie. Not from anyone.

Tallie moved closer. "Talk to me," she whispered. "I know you're upset about all this. So am I. But if we lean on each other..." She tried to take his hand. He pulled it away. "I know what you're feeling—"

"Do you?"

"Yes, I—"

"How many promises have you made lately that you haven't kept? How many people have you let down?"

"Tom—"

He stood. "None. That's how many. But I rack 'em up like pool balls just to knock 'em around. I promised Cody I would protect you from Roy. I didn't, did I? I also promised Cody I'd keep him safe. Look where he is. I promised Michael I'd take care of him. Blew that one too. It's my job to keep Clay, Harlie, and Abby safe. I hired Roy and put them at risk. I always handle the hiring myself, but I was busy and delegated the job. I had a bad feeling about this new guy, but I shrugged it off because I was too distracted to bother with it. I trusted other people's opinions when my instincts said I shouldn't." He looked at Tallie. "I thought there was something wrong, but I didn't follow through. You told me you saw him in my yard, and I didn't take it seriously."

"There was no way for you to know," Tallie said. "It isn't your fault."

"You don't understand," he said, his frustration mounting. "Clay's security is my number-one responsibility. It tops everything else—the ranch, the bull operation, everything. And I messed up. No one has come on this ranch in twelve years without me personally checking them out and when the stakes were high, I screwed up. When I should have been more vigilant, I was less."

"You did what you could," she whispered.

Tom gave a derisive snort and left the room, returning a moment later with the antacid bottle. He downed a gulp and slammed the bottle on the nightstand. Tallie watched, staring with those haunting blue eyes that condemned his actions as ineffective even though she said otherwise. If Cody didn't come back, he knew who Tallie would blame. He dropped to the edge of the bed and worked a kink from his knee. Tallie again tried to comfort and he shook her off. "I need some sleep," he said.

Without another word, he lay on his side, his back turned to Tallie. He couldn't face those eyes tonight.

Tallie stared at Tom's bare back, biting her lip. Okay, if he wanted solitude, he could have it. In his self-deprecating mood, she couldn't talk to him anyway. Where he got the idea she wouldn't understand his feelings, she couldn't fathom. She scooted across the bed and made her way from the room, stopping briefly at the bedroom door to see if Tom would ask her to stay. He didn't.

Sleep was out of the question now. Her nap had done its job; Tallie was wide awake and tense. She remembered seeing a box of hot chocolate in the cupboard and thought fixing a cup would occupy her for a few minutes and keep her from dwelling on Tom's assertion he had the entire emotional trauma locked up. Tallie also carried enough guilt and remorse to debilitate her. But Tom had it worked around to where this whole problem was his fault. Well, she had news for him—there was plenty of guilt to go around. While the water heated in the microwave, Tallie gazed out the window into the inky dark. Cody was out there somewhere, alone and unprotected, with only Michael to share his fear. She hoped Michael was still with him. Inwardly, she worried about Michael most. She knew Roy too well, knew his sadistic streak intimately, and wouldn't be surprised if he did something to Michael just for the fun of it, such as dump him off on a lonely highway in the middle of the night. The ding of the microwave brought her attention back. She scooped two large heaps of powered chocolate into the steaming water and stirred.

She went upstairs thinking she would read in her room for a while. The door to Michael's room was ajar and the sight of young boys' clothes thrown in a haphazard pile made her pause midstep. Roy took the kids from the boat dock wearing shabby play clothes with worn knees. It was doubtful he'd buy clean clothes, and the boys would look like strays, not the sharp-looking kids in the photo Tom gave the detective. There was only one picture of the two of them, taken the day they'd shopped for boots and hats. Tallie had bought a disposable camera at the grocery store and insisted on snapping photos. The boys groaned initially, but when encouraged by Tom, both hammed it up for the camera. That picture was printed in the paper, front page, above the fold. Detective Fleming said kidnapping cases took precedence. This proved it.

The clothing pile bothered her. It had been in the same place for days, reminding Tallie how long the boys had been gone. She set her mug on the dresser and scooped the pile into her arms, depositing it in the bathroom hamper. Next, she straightened the bedding on Michael's upper bunk, but when it was time to fix Cody's bed, she sat on it instead, fingering the mussed sheets. Where was he? Was he terrified? Of course he was, she chided herself. Just thinking about Roy always sent Cody into a spasm of fear. He'd experienced his father's unbalanced fury often enough. The poor kid never knew when Roy would snap. One minute they played catch in the yard, the next, Cody cowered from his father, screaming for Tallie. She always ran to help, only to become the bully's target. But if it kept Roy from hurting his son, Tallie stepped in. She would do it now if she could, but she feared the situation was well beyond the stage where she could distract Roy that way again. He wanted his son. He wanted Tallie dead. Or that was the original plan anyway. Now, he had his son, and Tallie doubted she was of interest to him any longer.

She curled her body around the wad of Cody's blankets. A lump under the bedding drew her attention, and she reached in to investigate, thinking it a pair of discarded socks. It wasn't anything as innocuous as that—but an item to sear her heart: Cody's teddy bear. He'd had the bear since he was a baby and was given the gift by Roy's grandmother. Nana, they all called her. Tallie hadn't known Cody packed it or even paid attention to the old bear any longer. He hadn't seen Nana since the divorce, and the fact he kept the bear said what she'd meant to him. But there it was, safely hidden beneath his covers where he could seek comfort from his beloved friend without Michael knowing. Tallie hugged the bear with its worn fur and dangling threads and held back tears. She needed to be strong for Cody. Tears wouldn't do.

Her thoughts drifted as she snuggled the bear, back to

the conversation with Tom. She'd been intent on comforting him and hadn't processed his words, but now, alone in the dark, his meaning hit her. A distraction kept him from doing his job properly, he'd said. And just what had the distraction been? Her. Instead of concentrating on important things, he'd frittered away his time with Tallie. He blamed her.

Still hugging the bear, she crawled from the lower bunk and went to her own room. Silver moonlight streamed through the window, highlighting the suitcases propped in the corner. She grabbed one, dropped it to the bed, and left it lying open while she removed clothing from the drawers. She dropped the armload into the suitcase and returned for more. The pile grew into a disorganized heap before Tallie slowed for a break. With the bear clutched to her chest, she leaned against the window frame.

"Tallie? I heard a noise..."

She glanced from the moonlit landscape to see Tom standing in the doorway, his eyes locked on her packed suitcases.

"I'm sorry—"

"Don't be. You're right." She swallowed and turned to stare out the window. "I should have followed my first instinct and left Nashville before Roy was released. I have a little money saved, enough for Cody and me to live on for a few months. If we'd left, none of this would have happened." She clutched the bear tighter, needing the connection with her son.

"What are you talking about?"

"Blame. You're right to blame me. I shouldn't have come here. I shouldn't have dumped my problems on you. If I'd taken Cody and run like I planned, Roy wouldn't have followed me here. Michael would be okay. Sherry would be alive. And you could concentrate on what is important to you."

"Tallie, I don't—"

She turned from the window. "Sure you do. You said you were distracted from your job. Who was distracting you? Me. Because of me, everyone was at risk here. If I wasn't here, you could have focused on your job, keeping your friends safe. You'd still have your son."

He stepped toward her. "No, Tal—"

"Yes. And how dare you try to claim a monopoly on broken promises. I made a promise over five years ago and I couldn't keep it. After the accident, I promised Cody that I'd never allow his father to hurt him. I promised he would never see Roy again. Mothers are supposed to keep their promises. It's part of what we do." She tried to control her anger but couldn't. "I failed. So don't you get all self-righteous and try to say YOU are the only one to make important promises, because I've made them too. And I've failed just as badly."

Tom looked stricken, as if she'd punched him. "That's not—"

"It's what you said. You said I hadn't made any promises." She swallowed hard. "It doesn't matter," she said. "I need to go and you can get on with what's important without me bothering you. It wasn't my idea to come here anyway."

"What are you talking about?" Tom ran his fingers through his hair. "I didn't mean you were distracting me."

Tallie brushed past him, heading to the bed and the open

suitcases. She was leaving and that was that. She didn't care what he had to say. Not now. "It sure sounded like it to me." She laid the bear on the nightstand and stuffed clothing into the corners of the suitcase.

"You can't leave."

"Watch me."

Tom moved, trying to block her from closing the suitcase. "I don't want you to go."

She huffed her breath and went around him. "Just leave me alone. I respected you when you wanted to be alone. Now I request the same." She looked him square in the face.

"No." He held his ground. "You have this screwed up and I want to explain."

"News flash, Tom. I don't care." She continued packing until Tom's silence forced her to look at him, into his wounded eyes. It was a lie. She cared too much. Her anger dissolved and her lip quivered. She turned away, unable to look at him.

"Neither of us is at our best right now," he said. "We're both saying things we don't mean. I know I did. Let's not fight each other and give Roy what he wants. If he knew we were at each other's throats, he'd think he won. For the record, I was distracted but not the way you think." Tom moved to the bed, moving a suitcase to the floor. He sat on the edge, working his knee. "The day Roy came, posing as Phin Mulberry, I was supposed to talk with him but at the last minute, Gib Sanborn came. Gib is my best customer for the bulls, so I let Lon talk to Phin. Lon is a trusting guy, and he thought Phin was okay and recommended I hire him. After Gib left, I made a couple of calls and checked his references. They seemed okay. Exemplary, even. The first time

I met the guy, there was something about him that made me uncomfortable, but I let him stay in the bunkhouse anyway. I blame myself for this mess. Not you. When you needed help, I offered you a safe place, and I compromised your safety with my carelessness. I gave Roy the perfect hiding place."

"But if I hadn't called you in the first place, none of this would have happened."

"No, it would probably have turned out differently. Cody could still be gone and you could be dead."

"But instead, Michael is gone too, and poor Sherry is dead."

"Sherry here when she shouldn't have been was my fault, too. I should have taken her name off the security list and I forgot. Clay reminded me to do it and I didn't. If I had done what I was supposed to do, Rob would've turned her away at the gate and she'd be alive now. It's my guilt to bear, not yours." Tom lay back on the bed and scrubbed his hands over his face. "Clay was at risk and I have that guilt too. His safety is a top priority for me."

"So you keep saying." At Tom's mention of Clay and his overwhelming responsibility, a twinge of jealousy jabbed her. Clay and his family would always come first. Big hotshot star that he was, she supposed he deserved it. Guys like him always seemed to get the best everyone had to offer, including their friends' undying loyalty. "Why?" she said, sure she sounded peevish. "Why do you personally have to devote so much to his security? There is a huge fence, a full crew. Just how many crazy fans does the man have?" She paced to the window and turned back. "You seem to do everything around here, take the responsibility for everything. There must be other people—"

Tom narrowed his eyes and looked at her in the silver light. "I suppose there are. But I'm the only one who owes his life to Clay. I wouldn't be here now if it weren't for him. I owe him everything."

"And now he expects you to devote your life to him because he brought you to Nashville to run his ranch after the accident?"

Tom frowned. "He doesn't expect a damned thing from me. I take care of things around here because I want to. Because I feel I owe him."

"But you don't have a life of your own, Tom. You take care of them all the time—"

"Until you, Michael, and Cody came along, I didn't need a life of my own," he said. "I didn't have anybody else to worry about. Just me, and that's been pretty darned lonely." He paused. "Clay bringing me to Nashville did save me but it wasn't the only thing. About a year and half after the accident, I hit rock bottom. I had a friend from high school who was a heavy drinker and he kept me supplied with booze. As long as Bobby was around, I thought I was doing okay, but all he did was worsen the problem. Nobody could get me to stop, not Jolie, not my parents. As a last resort, Mom called Clay and asked him to come." Tom stared at the ceiling, obviously reliving that day. "I was passed out and when I came to, I was sitting in a cold shower and Clay was holding me down, trying to sober me up. He said it was an intervention. I argued with him, said I didn't need his nose stuck in my business. He said he had every right to keep his brother from killing himself—that's what we are— brothers."

"He thought the booze would kill you?"

"The booze may have initially saved my life. When Clay found me, I was passed out on my bed with a pistol in my hand."

"You tried to kill yourself?"

Tom shrugged. "I guess so. I don't even remember it. I passed out before I could pull the trigger. If I'd come to and found the gun again, I may have finished the job."

"Or not. Maybe you would've reconsidered it," she offered optimistically.

He shook his head. "I'd have ended it." Tom paused. "So, after he finished drowning me in the shower, Clay took me to the hospital. I'd fallen a few days before that and tore the knee again. Clay paid for the surgery and got me back on my feet. He bought this place and here we are, business partners. When I say I owe him my life, I mean it."

Tallie bit her lip, feeling foolish for her jealousy. She moved to the bed and lay down next to him, her arm across his chest. Tom pulled her to him and held her, his face close to hers.

"I'm glad he saved you," she whispered.

"Yeah. Me, too." He placed a kiss on her nose. "Please don't leave. Guilt I can bear. You leaving, I can't. Please don't leave." Tom planted tender kisses on her cheeks. "Stay with me. You said we need to lean on each other. I know I need you."

She closed her eyes, enjoying the feel of his lips on her cheeks.

"I'm sorry," he murmured. "I was angry with myself, not you. I shouldn't have taken it out on you."

Tallie wrapped her arms around him, nuzzled her face to

his neck, and let out a long, drawn-out sob. She'd tried to be tough, but now the dam was irreparably damaged and tears gushed from her eyes. Tom rolled, taking her with him to hold tight in his arms. His fingers smoothed her hair, his lips caressed her temple. Tallie's shoulders shook, her body trembled. He didn't interrupt with useless words. The flood of emotion released, she was quiet, save for the occasional sniffle, clinging to Tom as if he was a lifeline.

"It's good to get it out once in a while. Bottling it up doesn't do you any good," he whispered. "I did that for years and look where it got me." He brushed his fingers through her hair and she relaxed against him. "I don't think alcoholism would suit you."

She sniffed and laughed. "Probably not. I doubt it suited you either."

"No. But you do." He sighed and caressed her back. "We'll get them back."

"How can you be so sure?"

"Because Roy will slip up. He's unbalanced and will do something impulsive to tip someone off. That's what Detective Jeffers said. We'll have them back soon."

She felt his tension and rubbed her hand soothingly across his chest, her foot along his shin. He relaxed but quickly tensed again when she spoke. "I love you, Tom." He lay still, not saying anything. Tallie bit her lip, assuming she had her response. She relaxed her hold on him. "Well..."

Tom lifted his head and looked into her pale-blue eyes. "Shh." He pressed his finger to her lips. "Let's not talk about that."

"Oh." She frowned and tried to roll away. "I guess I know where we stand now." Tears threatened again but Tallie didn't want him to see, didn't want him to know how deeply she wanted his love. Tom stopped her from moving away and placed his hand on her cheek.

"It's not that way, Tallie. It's just...it's not the right time to talk about it. It's not the right time for any of this."

"Why? If it's what I feel, why can't I tell you? Unless you don't feel anything for me." She almost held her breath, afraid to have him confirm her greatest fear.

"I have feelings for you, strong feelings." He looked into her eyes.

"Then why?"

"Because we're caught in an unreal situation and it's causing our emotions to run wild. Our boys have been kidnapped and are in danger. Maybe we're clinging together because of that stress and fear. Maybe it's something more."

"Tom—"

"I just don't think it's the right time to talk about it. When I hear those words said to me, I want to know they're from the heart." He brushed his fingers through her hair. "I'll warn you, Tallie, when I fall, I fall hard, and I couldn't bear it if you realize later it was just the situation."

Tallie saw fear and insecurity in his eyes and loved him even more. Tom Black, her rock-solid hero, was afraid she wouldn't love him. He needed her to love him.

"I disagree, but I'll do as you ask after I say one last thing." Tallie rested her palm on his unshaven cheek. "I know my heart now and I don't believe for a second I'm clinging to you because of this horrific situation. You're a comfort to me and it's possible I'd fall apart without you. My love for you is real and it's yours when you're ready to take it."

"You say that now," he said, "but I don't think we should talk about it until the boys are home safe and we get back to our normal lives. Then, we can step back and make sure we aren't reacting to this mess we're in."

"Okay." She smiled and gave in, knowing her feelings wouldn't change.

25

Tallie woke early with tormenting thoughts jabbing her like a sharp stick. Where was Cody? Was he getting enough to eat? Was Roy hurting him? And as much as she worried about her son, she worried about Michael more. When would Roy decide the extra boy was more of a problem than he was worth?

Had he already?

She rolled from Tom's embrace and crawled from the bed. She had a plan and would discuss it with Tom when he woke. Walking softly, she wandered into the bathroom to dress and prepare for the day. She combed her lengthening hair and looked at herself in the mirror, wondering if this ordeal had aged her. Tallie felt at least twice her twenty-nine years, maybe more.

She found her way through the house in the gray of early morning, stopping in the kitchen to make coffee and break-fast. If Tom agreed to her plan, they'd need a hearty meal to get them on their way. As the coffee perked, she pulled the cord on the window blind, inviting a stream of sunshine in. She daydreamed, staring out the window, thinking ahead to the time their boys would be home and Tom would be forced to confront his feelings for her. She knew he had them but wondered if he was afraid for her to see. The memory of the previous night's conversation returned, and she contem-plated if Tom still retained his love for Michael's mother. He said when he fell, he fell hard, and she knew he referred to

Michael's mom, the impossible love he'd held too long. Maybe he hadn't come to terms with her death and couldn't commit to another woman yet. Maybe he never would. Tallie frowned and rubbed her temples. Was she competing with a ghost?

The coffeemaker gurgled. Tallie snapped back to the present and prepared breakfast. When the eggs and toast were ready, she covered the plates with lids and went to wake him.

Opening the bedroom door, she saw a sight that had her longing to crawl back to bed and never leave. Tom Black, asleep, innocently uncovered in bed. As if there was anything innocent about Tom.

"Hey," she whispered as she ran her hand across his back.

"Hmm?"

"Time to wake up, sleepyhead," Tallie said quietly, her hand moved from his back, lingering briefly before trailing her fingers down his leg. When he didn't move, she smacked him on the butt and made him groan. "Wake up, Tom. We have things to do today."

Tom chuckled, his voice heavy with sleep. "You keep doing what you're doing back there and I can guarantee what you'll be doing today, honey." He rolled and caught her in his arms.

"I want to help look for the boys. I'm tired of sitting around waiting for Roy to call."

"Come again?" He blinked, obviously trying to wake up.

"I can't sit here hoping Roy will call. He called on the cell phone before, so chances are, he'll do that again. Why do we have to sit here waiting?"

He sat up, stretched, and yawned. "What do you have in

mind?"

"Get dressed and come to the kitchen. I'll tell you while we have breakfast." She stood to leave.

Tom stretched again, frowned, and apparently tried to focus on the clock. "What time is it?"

"Time to get off our butts and get our boys home."

He found Tallie in the kitchen setting the table with the efficiency of a marine drill instructor, not even acknowledging Tom's arrival. He poured a cup of coffee and sat at the table, looking at Tallie with admiration. Last night she'd been nearly destroyed by the actions of her ex-husband and today she was ready to fight. "What's your plan?" he asked.

She sat at the table. "I'm done sitting around. I know Roy better than his family does and it's time to educate them. So far the sheriff's department can't get any information from his relatives, and knowing the Peters' family, they never will. Chances are good one of them knows something, and they think they're helping poor Roy get his kid away from the evil ex-wife." She sipped her coffee. "I want to visit them and tell them just what a louse they're protecting."

"You don't think the detectives have tried that already?"

"I have information and ammunition they don't have." Tallie pulled up her shirt to reveal her scars. "They can't show tangible proof of what Roy is capable of. I can." She lowered her shirt. "I plan to inform them of everything that creep did to me and my son. I've always had the impression Roy's family thought he was wrongfully imprisoned, and I intend to make them see the truth. And maybe when I'm done, whoever knows where he is will start talking."

Tom sipped his coffee. "Jeffers might not like it if we start questioning people."

"Why not?" she countered. "He's already talked to the people I want to talk to, and he should be appreciative if we come up with something."

Tom thought about it and couldn't see any reason not to talk to Roy's family. He doubted he could stop Tallie anyway. She was back in determined-woman mode.

Tom shrugged. "Okay. We'll sneak out the livestock gate after breakfast."

Freddy Peters' home sat on the back half of an overgrown lot strewn with old pickups, a camper, and other leftovers of no use to anyone. Freddy needed a shave, shower, and a fresh shirt. He leaned on the doorframe, squinting into the sun.

"Jeez, Tallie." He moaned. "I haven't seen or heard from Roy since they locked him up, and I'm getting tired of being bugged about it. I work nights and don't appreciate being woke up all the time."

"I need some help, Freddy," Tallie said. "He has my son."

"The kid belongs to him, too," Freddy said.

"His kid is terrified of him and doesn't want to see him. I'm scared for him and need to get him back."

"Not my problem and from what I understand, a father taking his kid isn't a crime."

Tom shifted closer to Tallie. "See, Freddy," he said, his voice deceptively calm. "It is a crime to kidnap my child. If you know something, you'd better be sharing it real quick."

Freddy straightened and clenched his fists. "I don't know anything."

"That much is obvious or you'd be willing to help." Tallie sighed. "Roy tried to kill me. That's why he went to prison." She lifted her shirt to expose her scarred midriff. "This is what your beloved cousin is capable of, Freddy. He did this to me." She lowered her shirt after Freddy looked and turned away. "He beat his son when he was only five years old and that's why I was leaving him. That's why he tried to kill me. As soon as they released him, he threatened us again." She pointed to the faded bruise on her neck. "He did this to me."

Tom added, "The cops are ninety-nine percent sure he killed a friend of mine a few days before the kidnapping, and they're still looking for the guy Roy impersonated to get on my ranch. They're starting to call him a psychopath," he said. "So, if you know where he is, you'd better be spilling it or you could be considered an accessory to murder, kidnapping, and whatever crime Roy committed against Phin Mulberry. He has my son, Michael, and we're worried he'll be Roy's next victim."

Freddy ran a hand through his hair. "Shit!" he muttered. "You gotta believe me, Tallie. I don't know where he is. I haven't heard from him. But if I do, I'll let you know. I swear it."

Tom reached into his pocket and handed him a business card. "Call the cell number if you hear anything."

"Thanks, Freddy. We appreciate anything you come up with." Tallie and Tom returned to the pickup as Freddy closed his door.

"Do you believe him?" Tom asked as he opened the truck door for her.

"For some reason, I do. He and Roy weren't close that I

know of, so he probably doesn't know anything. But if someone slips up around him, I think we can count on Freddy to call with the information."

Tom slid into the driver's seat. "Where to next?"

Tallie closed her eyes and let out a frustrated sigh. Three stops without success and she was getting down. She opened her eyes and said with determination, "Nana's."

"Roy's grandmother? Would she tell you anything?" Tom drove onto the street.

"His grandmother on his mother's side. If she knows anything, she'll talk to me." Tallie took a sip from the water bottle in the cup holder and returned it. "Nana didn't approve of her daughter's choice of husband and didn't think much of her grandson when he started treating me poorly."

"What is she going to know?"

Tallie smiled. "Probably not much, but I want to see her. After the unproductive morning we've had, I just want to see her."

⚮

Nana's home had always reminded Tallie of a dollhouse, with its brightly painted shutters, peaked roof, and gingerbread trim, just as the woman who dwelled within had always been the perfect grandma. There was usually a hug, a cup of coffee with cookies, and a good dose of conversation at Nana's kitchen table if a person had a moment to sit. Tallie hadn't seen Roy's grandmother since the divorce and she wondered about the reception she'd receive.

Clasping Tom's hand, she pressed the button to the ancient doorbell. After a moment, a voice called, "Coming, coming. Don't be gettin' your knickers in a twist. I'm coming!"

CAUGHT IN THE SPIN

Tallie held her breath. The door opened and she stared into a shocked face. Fearing rejection, Tallie remained still, gazing into soft brown eyes set in a wrinkled face surrounded by gray curls. Not quite Tallie's height, Nana looked up into Tallie's face and let out a squeal of delight.

"Oh oh oh!" she cried out happily. "My darling has come to visit. Come here and give me a hug!" Nana pushed open the screen door and pulled Tallie into a bear hug, nearly knocking the breath from her.

"Where have you been, child? I've missed you terribly." Nana released Tallie from her grip and looked into her face with obvious love. "Come in, come in. Can't leave y'all standing on the step all day." Taking Tallie by the hand, she led her into a small living room. "Can you stay for a while? Have a seat, have a seat," she said with excitement. "You too, son." She waved Tom into the room and motioned to a bright, flowered sofa. He took a seat on one end, and Tallie sat next to him.

Nana sat in a rocking chair. "Why haven't I seen you, Tallie?"

"Well..." Tallie squirmed under the woman's intense stare, glancing around the room that hadn't changed in five years. Knickknacks and doilies covered every surface. "Since I divorced Roy, I didn't think his family would want me around anymore."

"Now that's the silliest thing I've ever heard, Tallie Peters. You divorced that idiot grandson of mine. You didn't divorce me."

Tallie laughed. "I'm sorry. I should have come to see you. I just didn't think...how have you been?"

"Just fine and better now that you're here." She gave

Tom a glance. "Are you planning to introduce your friend?"

"Oh, sorry again. Nana, this is Tom Black. Tom, this is Nana, or I should say, Bea Gilkey. Cody's great-grandma."

Tom stood and leaned near the woman with hand out-stretched. "Nice to meet you, Mrs. Gilkey."

She squeezed his hand and gave him a friendly smile. "There'll be no Mrs. Gilkey around here. Call me Nana. Everybody does."

"Nice to meet you, Nana." Tom smiled in return. He sat back in his seat, taking Tallie's hand in his.

"I put a pot of coffee on before you came. Maybe you'd give me a hand in the kitchen, Tallie dear?" Nana stood, straightening a kink from her back, reminding Tallie how Nana was getting older. Tallie followed her to the doorway.

"We'll be right back, Tom," Tallie said. She entered the kitchen, and Nana scooped her into another hug.

"Don't you dare stay away so long again," she scolded and released her.

"I won't. I promise." Tallie went to the cupboard and found the coffee mugs in the place she remembered. Nana collected the cream and sugar for the table.

"He's a pretty one, isn't he?" Nana commented, directing Tallie to set the mugs on the table.

Tallie smiled. "I don't know if he'd like being called pretty, but he is easy on the eyes."

"You love him, don't you?" Nana asked, making Tallie blush. "I can see it. Is he good to you?"

"He's wonderful. Very gentle and sweet. He's a good man."

"I'm glad. You deserve something good for a change. Go get your man, honey. We'll have coffee at the table." She shooed her from the room.

Tallie called Tom into the kitchen, and they sat sipping hot coffee and nibbling gingersnaps at the round, cozy table. The room had a homey feel with its white lace curtains and glass-fronted cabinets. The floor was pink vinyl. Brightly colored floral prints adorned the walls. Tallie had spent many hours in this kitchen talking girl talk with Nana while Cody played with Hot Wheels on the floor. She sipped her coffee and her gaze landed on a newspaper at the side of the table. She picked up a front page emblazoned with the full-color photo of Michael and Cody in their new cowboy hats.

"From the look of him, I'd say that would be your boy, Tom?" Nana asked.

"Yes, ma'am," Tom said with a frown.

"Is that why you're here, Tallie? Are you hoping I might be able to help with your trouble?"

"We're desperate for any information. You've been following the news stories?" Nana nodded. "So you know Roy has them? He's only called once and didn't say much. He wouldn't let Tom talk to the boys and won't say what he wants. The sheriff's department hasn't come up with anything yet, so we're visiting Roy's relatives and hoping someone will talk to us."

"Oh, honey, I wish I knew something to tell you. I haven't talked to Roy in a long, long time. Have any of those Peters told you anything?"

"No." Tallie frowned.

"I'm not surprised they won't talk to you. They always were a tight bunch. Fought like cats and dogs among themselves most of the time but loyal when there's trouble. When my Leticia was having problems with Roy's daddy, they all closed ranks on her and acted like she was the bad one when it was that lousy Leland Peters who was beating her up."

Tallie raised her brows. "Like father, like son. Roy said he didn't know what caused his parents' breakup, and Lettie didn't want to talk about it when she was so sick."

"Leland used his fists on her like it was some sort of sport for him. She tired of it and begged him for a divorce. The only way he'd agree was if she'd give him custody of Roy." Nana sighed. "My poor daughter didn't have half the backbone you have, Tallie. She was scared for her son but tired of getting knocked around. So she let him have his way, thinking she'd still see Roy sometimes. Leland packed up and moved to Arizona and she hardly saw the boy for years." Nana sipped her coffee. "We never did know for sure if he abused Roy."

"He may have," Tallie offered. "Roy never said as much, but there was something in his eyes when he looked at Leland. He hated him. When we lived with him, they fought a lot, but Roy was bigger than his father by then."

Nana continued. "When Lettie got sick, she wanted to see Roy. I was darned surprised when the boy moved back here with you. I thought there was hope for him if he could marry a peach like you." Nana reached for Tallie's hand and squeezed. "But I was wrong. He has too much of his daddy in him."

"I was never sure what went wrong." Tallie shrugged. "We were young and didn't know what we were doing, but I thought we got along fine. When his mom died, Roy changed overnight."

Nana frowned. "I have a good idea from things he said to his mom. Probably shouldn't tell tales, but he talked to her some before you married him. He was excited and called to brag about it."

"What did he say?" Tallie said quietly.

Nana's frown deepened. "I shouldn't tell you this." She paused but Tallie encouraged her to continue. "Well, he told his mama that he'd found the golden goose. He was marrying himself a little rich girl from Scottsdale, high society and all that. He said you'd be getting a hefty trust fund when you turned twenty-one and he'd be in the money."

"Oh." Tallie winced. "That's all I was? A trust fund? That clears things up a bit." She let out a little laugh. "Funny thing was, when I chose to marry Roy, my mother took away the trust fund. She said if I married that low-life boy, I was on my own. I guess it made him mad when he figured it out. I thought he loved me, and I gave up two million dollars to be with him and have my baby." She sipped her coffee and tried to conceal the hurt. "Stupid, huh?"

Tom reached over and squeezed her hand. "No. It's admirable, Tallie. You could have had a life of pampered luxury but you chose your son. I've said it before and I'll say it again. Everything about you amazes me."

Tears welled in her eyes when she looked at Tom. How did she get lucky enough to find this man? Tallie wiped her eyes and shrugged off his compliments before she started to blubber. "Do you have any ideas that may help us, Nana?"

Nana sniffed and wiped her nose with a hanky. "Have you talked to Wally Peters yet? He and Roy were close before Roy moved to Arizona, and I heard he spent some time with him after you two came back."

"No, not yet," Tom said. "Maybe we'll go there next. Should we be heading out, Tallie?"

Tallie nodded. "Yes. Thanks for the coffee and the comfort, Nana." Tallie stood to leave, picking up coffee cups to put in the sink.

"Leave that for me, honey. You have more important things to do."

Nana walked with them to Tom's truck, tapping Tom on the shoulder while Tallie climbed in the driver's door.

"Take good care of her, Tom. She needs to be treated right for a change."

"I will," he said and climbed into the pickup cab. "Call us if you hear anything." He handed her his card.

As nice as the visit had been, it drove home to Tallie the futility of their search. No one knew anything, and if they did, they weren't talking.

26

Three days without a TV, his Nintendo DS, video games, or pizza. Michael wondered if he'd go as crazy as the nutcase who kept threatening to shoot him. There was nothing to do but watch spiders run across the wall, count the boards in the ceiling, and try not to tick off the creep. It was easy if a kid sat still and didn't breathe.

"Think he'll stay outside for a while?" Michael asked Cody. They sat on the bed, leaning against the wall, staring off into space. "Why doesn't he call Tom or something?"

"I dunno. He says he has a plan. Wants to play with Tom's head." Cody answered lazily, his eyes fixed on a dust speck floating across the room.

"You think Roy's smart enough to play with Tom's head?" Michael snickered. "Don't know if Wally's much better."

Cody smiled at that. "Maybe there's a deck of cards around here. You know how to play poker?" Cody jumped up and went into the kitchen area. Michael followed and watched while Cody dug through the drawers, tossing aside old clothespins, matchsticks, and dull pencils.

The door flew open, startling the boys. "What the hell you doing?" Roy stomped into the cabin and grabbed both by their collars. "I told you to sit still over there."

"We're just looking for cards. We're bored." Cody yelped as Roy drug him across the room and tossed him on the bed. Michael followed in a jumble of arms and legs, stirring up a cloud of dust when he landed.

"Why don't you call my dad and let me out of here? He'll give you money if that's what you want." Michael spat the words at him.

"Maybe I've already talked to your precious papa. Maybe he doesn't think you're worth two cents," Roy said.

Michael had his own doubts Tom would come through for him. He didn't know him and he lay awake at night wondering. But to hear Roy say it out loud was just too much. "You're a liar!" Michael screeched and flung himself at Roy, fists flying. He managed to connect a few punches before Roy subdued and shoved him. Michael landed on the floor, his head connecting with a thud.

"Stupid little shit!" Roy said. "You try that again and I'll pound you into the floor."

Cody stared at Roy with horror. When Roy spun on his heel and left the cabin, Cody let out the breath he held and jumped to the floor, kneeling next to his friend. Shoulders shaking, Cody could see Michael trying not to cry, and failing.

"Mike? You okay?" Cody whispered, watching over his shoulder for his father to return.

"My head...hurts." He let out a sob. "He's lying. I know he is." Michael curled into a ball. "He's a lying, ugly creep."

"Roy always lies. It's all he knows how to do. But he doesn't know Tom like we do. Come on. I'll help you up on the bed." Cody helped Michael up and gasped when he saw the welt on the side of the other boy's head. "Your lip is bleeding. I'll get you some water."

"No!" Michael warned. "If you go over there, he'll hurt

you too."

"Don't care," Cody said with bravado. "I'm getting you some water." Cody inched his way to the kitchen, watching for Roy out the window. Luckily, the pump was primed and the cup filled quickly. He grabbed a clean paper towel and snuck back to Michael. When he peeked out the window, he saw Roy pacing at the lake edge.

⌾⌾

The ring of his cell phone took Tom by surprise. Caller ID: unavailable. If it was Roy, he'd changed phones. Tom slowed the truck and stopped on the highway's shoulder.

"Is it him?" Tallie asked.

"I don't know." He turned off the truck and answered the call. "Tom Black."

"You know, Tom old buddy, that is one mouthy kid you've got there. I may have to teach him some manners before I'm done with him." Roy's voice was agitated.

Cold fear crawled down Tom's back. An agitated Roy Peters was even more dangerous than usual. "You harm one hair on his head, Roy, and I'll see you pay for it."

Roy laughed. "I'll bet you'd try. He seems to have an awful lot of faith in his daddy, so we'll have to see if you deserve it."

"What do you want, Roy?"

"I've been giving that a lot of thought since you and I chatted before. Originally, I'd have been happy with a million bucks, but since I've had to deal with that smart-mouthed brat of yours, I'm upping it to two million. He keeps it up and I'll make it three. But for now, I'll say two."

Was it a coincidence he demanded the amount of Tallie's lost trust fund? Tom closed his eyes and fought to control his anger. "Fine, it's yours. Two million for both boys." He'd call Clay ASAP and set it up.

Roy laughed. "I think you misunderstood something there, buddy. That's two million for your kid. There's no dealing on Cody. He stays with me."

Tom wasn't surprised, but he swore under his breath anyway. "How about another million for Cody? You can go to Mexico or something and live like a king."

"Nope. No deal on Cody. He's mine. He stays with me. We're one happy little family, my boy and me."

Tom looked at Tallie's stricken face. "I want to talk to them."

"Not a good time, Tom. They're busy right now."

"You'll have your money, but I want proof they're okay first. Let me talk to them."

"Hello! We must have a bad connection!" Roy tapped his phone on something. "I said no."

Tom took a deep breath. "I just want to talk to them. I..." He closed his eyes as images of his son went through his mind. The son Jolie had entrusted into his care. "I'll tell him to behave for you. Just let me talk to him."

"Nope, but I got an idea." Roy laughed. "You want proof? There's a rest stop on Highway Twenty-Four, southbound lane. Be there at four o'clock sharp this afternoon. Alone. No cops. No Tallie. Just you."

"Why can't Tallie be there? Cody is her son."

"Not anymore. She might as well forget about him, because Cody has been liberated from her wimp-creating clutches. Now, do as you're told, Tom, or you won't be seeing your brat again either."

"What am I supposed to do when I get there? I can't

have the money that fast."

"We'll talk about the money later. You want proof your kid is okay. I'm giving it to you. Be there at four." Roy disconnected the call.

Tom tossed the phone on the dash. "That psychotic son of a bitch! I'm supposed to go to some rest area on Highway Twenty-Four, and he'll give me proof the boys are okay."

"Let's go."

"I can't take you. He said I have to go alone."

Tallie's anger spiked. "Like hell you're going alone. He has my son too."

Tom turned to face her. "Tallie, honey, listen to me." She opened her mouth to argue. "No, baby, listen." He placed a finger gently to her lips. "Roy isn't dealing with a full deck. He wants to play with me for a while and if I don't do exactly what he says, he'll hurt my son. He wants your son, so the danger of Roy hurting him isn't as great. But for some sick reason, Roy is getting off on tormenting me. We have to play his game and pay the ransom for Michael."

"What about ransom for Cody?" she asked quietly.

"He says there no deal on Cody, so we'll have to try and find them and get them back."

Tallie took a deep breath and played absently with the seat belt. "Okay. We'll play his game for now. Do you think there's time to talk to Wally before you go?"

Tom checked his watch: 1:00 p.m. "I'd better not risk it. I'll run you home, and we can talk to Clay about the money."

As they drove, Tom debated calling Detective Jeffers but didn't. He knew Frank Jeffers would want to send deputies along and that would only provoke Roy. Tom was dealing with a lunatic, and he wasn't giving him any excuses to hurt his child.

As far as Tom could tell, Roy didn't need any excuses for anything he did.

27

Heavy interstate traffic flew by at teeth-rattling speed. Tom sat, waiting for the right moment. He found what he hoped was the correct rest area and loitered at the edge of the off-ramp until 4:00 p.m. on the dot, not wanting to arrive too early or too late. Not having Tallie along to distract him, his mind wandered to unpleasant thoughts. Somehow, he had to make this right; somehow, he had to get the boys back unharmed.

He had no idea what he'd find in the rest area, and from his location on the highway, he couldn't see through the trees. At the appointed time, he inched his truck down the off-ramp and crept into the rest area, scanning for sign of the boys.

Cody stood on the sidewalk near the end of the parking strip: grubby, obviously tired, and visibly apprehensive. Tom eased his pickup into a space twenty feet from Cody, afraid to get too close and have Roy do something. He surveyed the area before climbing from the truck, leaving the door open for a quick retreat if needed. He watched the trees behind Cody, glancing at the restrooms and the Dumpster at the end of the sidewalk. Roy could be hiding anywhere. With caution, he walked around the front of the truck, noticing the nervous look on Cody's face as he neared him.

Cody raised his hands as if to push Tom away. "Stop! Don't come any closer. Roy said I'd be in big trouble if I let you come near me."

Tom raised his hands and made a show of stepping back.

"I knew you'd come," Cody said in a happy burst. A smile covered his grimy face. "Mike was afraid you wouldn't, but I knew you would."

"Of course I came. We've been working with the cops to find where he's keeping you." Tom tried to sound reassuring. "Where are Roy and Michael, Cody?" he asked quietly as he examined the area.

"He left Mike behind and I don't know where Roy is. He dumped me off and drove out. He told me to stand here and talk to you. I'm supposed to tell you we're okay. He said you wanted proof or you wouldn't give him the money." Cody stood as if glue held him in place.

"Are you okay? Is Michael okay?" Tom wondered if he could grab Cody and run with him.

"I'm okay. Roy..." Cody swallowed hard and frowned. "Roy shoved Mike this morning and gave him a headache. But he's better now."

Tom clenched his teeth and took a deep, calming breath. "Is he feeding you? Does he let you wash or anything?"

"We're eating okay. Lots of hamburgers and cereal, but he feeds us. No bath though." Cody's eyes shifted. "We want to swim in the lake but Roy won't let us. The cabin is dusty and we have to wash in a bucket."

"What lake?"

"I don't know." Cody's eyes shifted again. "I never saw the name and Roy didn't say."

"What else can you tell me, Cody?" Tom prodded quietly.

Cody shook his head nervously. "Nothing. I'm just supposed to tell you we're okay. If I tell you anything else he says he'll kill Mike. If you come after us, he'll shoot Mike."

"Shit," Tom muttered. "Can you tell me if anyone is helping him?" Cody fidgeted and looked around, making Tom wonder how close Roy was to them. Rather than speak, Cody nodded.

"Who?"

Cody shook his head, clearly afraid to say more.

"Is he close enough to hear us?"

"I don't know."

Tom fought the temptation to grab the boy and run, refraining out of fear for his own son. And he knew that was what Roy wanted. He wanted Tom to fight with his instinct to snatch Tallie's son. He was making him choose his own son over Tallie's. "What would happen if you got in my truck?"

Cody's eyes went silver-dollar wide. "No. I can't." He shook his head. "If I'm not here when he gets back, he'll kill Mike. I can't let him do that. And, and Mike's scared. I can't leave him alone."

"Well," Tom said in exasperation, "what am I supposed to do now? Leave you standing here by yourself when I go?"

Cody dug into his pocket and removed a mangled piece of paper, holding it out to Tom.

"Roy said to give you this. It's your instructions. He says you have to follow it exactly or..." Cody swallowed hard. "Or Mike's dead." Tom took the few steps necessary to take the paper from Cody's dirty fingers. "He says you have thirty minutes from the time I give you that to do what it says."

Tom read the note: Drive back toward Nashville until you see a grocery store from the highway. Pull into the parking lot. "And do what?"

"I don't know, but you have to go. Now!" Cody backed away from Tom.

Tom hesitated, wanting to grab the kid and run.

"Hurry, Tom," Cody pleaded. "He's going to kill him. Go, now."

Tom thought his heart would blast out of his chest as he watched the scared kid back away, tears sprouting from his eyes and running down his dirt-streaked face. Leaving him in the parking lot would tear Tom to pieces and Roy knew it.

"Go!" Cody screamed and continued to back away.

"Okay, I'll do what he says, but we're going to find you guys. I promise. Tell Michael—" What, he thought—I love him? "Tell Michael I'll have him home soon. He can count on me." Tom dashed to his truck, keeping his eyes on Cody. He climbed in and drove away, watching in the rearview mirror for any sign of Roy. He saw only a scared kid standing alone.

Back on the interstate, he drove until he saw the first grocery store and hoped it was the right one. He parked his truck near the center of the lot. After a few frustrating minutes, Tom's cell phone rang.

"Tom Black," he said abruptly.

"You aren't such a noble guy after all," Roy said.

"What's that supposed to mean?"

"I kinda wondered if a true-blue hero type like you would grab the boy to make his little woman happy. How's Tallie going to feel when you tell her you chose your boy over hers? Not too happy, I'll bet."

"You know I had no choice but to leave him there. You

have Cody scared to death that you'll kill Michael. There was no choice."

"Oh, there was a choice and you made it." Roy laughed. "Now I got a question for you. What does the sign in the far left window of that grocery store say?"

Tom looked at the store, bewildered by the request. He watched an elderly couple walk in the door so he could see the sign. "Ground beef, three forty-nine a pound."

"Bingo. You just proved you can follow instructions. We can get down to business now, and you'd better do exactly as I say because Cody's fears are real. If you mess with me, I will kill your kid. He's a pain in the ass, and I don't like him. Maybe it's because he looks just like the guy who's banging my ex-wife."

Suspicions confirmed. Michael's kidnapping was a personal attack on Tom. For what it was worth, he now knew for sure. "What do you want me to do?"

"We'll start talking money. Two million transferred into my account. I'll call you with the account number." The phone went dead.

Tom dropped his head to the steering wheel, which was gripped in his fists. His rage threatened to blow him apart. He wanted to shout his frustrations but internalized his anger to use on Roy when he caught up with him. Roy Peters was playing games with the wrong guy and he would pay for it.

But right now, there was work to do. Cody mentioned a cabin and a lake, so he had a place to search. He started the truck and pulled back out on the interstate, returning to the rest stop. As anticipated, Cody was gone. Back on the highway, he called the sheriff's department and reported to Jeffers.

When he drove into Clay's driveway, he saw Tallie standing there. He turned off the truck and sat for a moment, wondering how to explain what happened and how he justified leaving her son.

She walked to the truck as he got out and closed the door. She reached for him.

"Don't." He shook his head and waved her away. "Not until I tell you what happened." The weight of his decision hit him when he saw her face. She trusted him. He leaned on the truck door. "I talked to Cody."

"On the phone?"

"He was there. I talked to him."

"What happened?" she sputtered as she looked in the empty truck. "Where is he?"

Tom felt limp and was glad for the truck holding him up. "He was in the rest area when I drove in. He said Roy told him to stand there and talk to me, tell me they were okay so I'd give him the money. I wanted to grab him and run, but Cody panicked and backed away. He said if he wasn't there when Roy came back...he'd...he'd kill Michael."

"Oh, Tom." She stifled a cry with her hand.

"I asked him what would happen if he got in my truck, and he said Michael would die. I wanted to grab him for you. I debated it and almost did it anyway, but Cody told me Roy had already hurt Michael this morning, and I backed off because I was afraid he'd do it again." He looked at Tallie with pleading eyes, silently begging her to understand his position. He'd had no choice.

"How did Cody look? Is he healthy?"

"He says Roy is feeding them lots of hamburgers and cereal, so they aren't hungry. Other than Michael getting hit today, he says they're okay." He watched for a sign indicating she understood his decision. "Tallie." He sighed. "I'm sorry. I wanted to grab him, but Roy didn't leave me a choice. He would have killed my son."

"Do you think I want you to sacrifice Michael for Cody?"

"I don't know what you're thinking. All I know is, leaving Cody there tore me apart. He was so scared, but I couldn't do anything. Roy knew exactly what he was doing."

Tallie took the necessary steps to reach him and wrapped her arms around him. "He left you no choice. I understand that. As much as I would love to see Cody sitting in your truck, I couldn't live with the idea that it caused Roy to harm Michael."

He wrapped his arms around her and sighed.

"On a positive note, if there can be one, Cody gave me as much of a clue as he could."

Tallie looked up at him. "A clue? What kind?"

"He said Roy wouldn't let them swim in the lake," Tom said. "The cabin is real dirty, and they wanted to wash. I called Detective Jeffers and relayed that, and he's getting deputies into the area with boats as soon as possible. The problem is, there are hundreds of miles of shoreline and it could take some time. But Cody also told me someone is helping Roy. He couldn't say who, but there is someone."

"Do you think it's one of his relatives?"

"I can't say for sure, but I have a feeling Wally Peters is our best bet from the number of times his name has been mentioned. I want to talk to him."

"I'm going with you. If you're kicking some Peters butt tonight, I want to help."

A chain saw's buzz filled the evening air; short bursts and long hums indicated Wally's location. Tallie remembered other times she'd been to this house sitting among the trees, recalled the layout, and found the woodpile with ease. Wally glanced up and stiffened at the sight of his guests.

Wally removed his safety glasses and laid aside the chain saw as they came closer. The way his eyes darted from Tom to Tallie indicated guilt.

"Hi, Wally. Do you remember me?" Tallie asked. She walked to the woodpile and stopped near Wally.

"Yeah, Tallie, it hasn't been that long. Nice to see you," he said as if he were visiting with an old friend over afternoon tea.

"This is Tom Black," she said.

Wally nodded. "Nice to meet you. What can I do for you, Tallie?"

"Where's Roy?"

"How would I know?" he said with a scowl. "I haven't talked to him in years. I already told the cops that. Why do you think I'd know?"

"Because," Tom said, "your name keeps popping up in every conversation we have."

"I have no idea where he is." Sweat beaded on Wally's forehead.

"You know he kidnapped our boys?" Tallie said.

"I heard," he said with a nod.

"I'm scared for them, Wally. If you have any ideas, we'd appreciate the help. I'm afraid he's going to hurt them." Tallie's stomach twisted at the thought.

"He wouldn't hurt them, Tallie."

"What makes you say that? Have you forgotten he tried to kill me and take Cody when I tried to leave him?"

Wally frowned. "No, I—"

"Did you know he beat me up regularly when we were married, beat his little boy? Did this to me?" She pulled up her shirt, baring her scarred midriff again. "If you know anything, how can you protect a man who can do this to his wife?"

"I don't know anything!" Wally said with gritted teeth.

Tom stepped forward. "Do you also know that before he took our boys, he murdered a friend of mine, brutally raped her, and left her body to rot in her car? He stole the identity of a man who hasn't been seen since Roy had a beer with him in a bar."

Wally's eyes shifted and he sweated profusely.

"How can you protect a man capable of that?" Tom asked.

"I'm not protecting him!" He backed up a step. "I don't know anything."

Tallie glared at him. "I think you do. If you change your mind, call us. Our sons' lives depend on it."

Tom handed Wally a card. "We'll be waiting to hear from you." They walked back to the truck, not speaking until Tom had driven several blocks.

"He knows something, doesn't he?" Tallie asked.

"I think so. I don't think he sweats like that from cutting wood. But other than beating the crap out of him, I don't know how we'd get him to talk." Tom chuckled. "Beating the crap out of him would feel good after what his cousin did to me today."

"I think I'd enjoy seeing you stomp him," she said. "I

might even help." She'd never had the urge to commit vio-
lence before, but where lying Peters were concerned, she felt
a change of heart coming on. Cowboy boots were called
shitkickers for a reason, and she had a new pair to break in.
She reached for Tom's hand and held it. "What now?"

"Wally needs watching."

"We can use my car. He wouldn't recognize it."

"We?" Tom asked.

"Of course, we. Do you think I'm letting you sit here by
yourself all night?" She didn't wait for an answer. "I'm
wondering, if we shook him up, would he run to Roy tonight
and tell him? If he did, we could follow him."

The corner of his mouth quirked into a smile. "Maybe.
Let's get your car and come back. At least we'll feel like
we're doing something."

They returned with sandwiches and a thermos of coffee.
From a vantage point down the street, they watched Wally's
house for hours, waiting for him to leave, and they were
sorely disappointed when he didn't. On edge, Tallie watched
as he cut wood, stacked it, and cut more wood. After dark,
Wally packed his chain saw in its case and went in the
house. Discouraged, Tom and Tallie called it a night and
went home.

28

Michael woke to the annoying stab of a mattress spring poking straight into his butt. He wiggled in an unsuccessful effort to dislodge it. He'd started the day before with a split lip and pounding head and ended it with sore wrists and ankles. A spring in his rear wasn't so bad. He rubbed at the marks left by the duct tape Roy used to hold his wrists the day before. Not wanting to take him along while Cody talked to Tom, Roy bound his hands and feet and locked him a dark closet. He'd huddled in the corner of the dank space, hoping the scratching noises he heard were tree branches and not mice. He'd nearly cried with relief when Cody and Roy returned and released him from his scary prison.

Roy's mood was unusually good last night. He joked with an unresponsive Cody and needled Michael about the fun he'd had tormenting Tom. Michael felt hope when he heard that Tom was at the appointed meeting place and was pissed off at the treatment he received from Roy. His dad deserved better than that.

When Roy went outdoors for his evening smoke break and phone calls, Cody filled Michael in on the meeting with Tom. Mike's heart filled at the thought of his dad sending a message to him via Cody, telling him he'd find him, that he could count on him. Michael hoped he could but wasn't sure. He'd started believing his dad was as cool as Cody thought. His dad. He'd begun thinking of Tom as his dad a lot more during this nightmare. Not once in several days had he thought of him as Tom. Just Dad.

Michael heard Roy moving around in the kitchen but didn't dare look. He'd already learned not to draw Roy's attention. Sometimes the creep needed a reason to smack him, other times not.

He stiffened when he heard Roy's boots coming in the direction of the bed but didn't move until Roy kicked the bed frame.

"Get up, both of you. We have things to do today."

Cody stirred but didn't wake. Roy pulled the blanket from him. "Get up! We're getting out of here today."

At that, Cody sat up. "What? Where are we going?" Cody rubbed the sleepiness from his eyes.

"You and I are heading out later today. I'm calling Black about the money. As soon as he takes care of it, we're leaving."

"What about Mike?"

"Haven't decided on that yet. He'll know soon enough." Roy turned and walked to the kitchen.

Mike wondered what the slimy jerk was going to do with him.

Following their usual morning routine, Mike and Cody visited the outhouse one by one, washed in the bucket in the sink, and were served Frosted Flakes for breakfast. They ate in silence. Mike kept his eyes down, afraid to attract Roy's attention. The guy was wound up tight as a baseball's innards.

"After you eat, I want you to settle down over there by the bed until I tell you otherwise," Roy ordered before he grabbed a new cell phone and walked out the door.

The day promised to be warm, nearly perfect. Roy dialed Tom's cell number and saw only dollar signs.

"It's time, Tom ol' boy," he said in greeting.

"For what, Roy?" Tom said.

"Money. Moolah. Dinero. Today's the day. Cough up the dough and you'll get your boy back." Roy leaned on a tree, enjoying the exchange.

"What do I have to do?"

"Transfer two million dollars into my account. I'll text the number. After I've confirmed the money is there, I'll let you know where your kid is. Easy enough, don't you think?"

"What about Cody?"

"My boy is none of your concern. Tell Tallie to just forget about him. He's no longer her son."

"I'll pass on your message. You'll have your money today."

"Good boy, Tom. I'll be in touch."

Time was running out. If Roy wanted the money, he intended to bolt, and their chances of finding both boys dwindled to zero. Tom was walking to the office when Roy called but detoured to his truck and drove to Clay's instead.

Stepping into the sun-splashed kitchen, he found Clay, Harlie, and Abby eating breakfast and was stabbed with jealousy. He wanted this. Just once, couldn't he have what everyone else took for granted? No, life had a way of kicking Tom in the teeth every time happiness landed in his sights. His hand was always stuck in the damned rope while the bull spun him around.

"Morning, Tom. Have some breakfast," Clay called from

the table, waving at a chair.

"I don't have much of an appetite this morning." Tom leaned heavily on the back of a chair, feeling worn and edgy. "Roy called."

"Money?" Clay asked.

Tom nodded. "Two million transferred into his account. After he verifies it's there, he'll call and let me know where Michael is. Or so he says."

"What about Cody?" Harlie asked.

"He still says there's no deal on Cody. He's taking him, and that's going to kill Tallie." He stood straight, rubbing his hand on his stiff neck. He hadn't slept well. "I have a feeling Wally Peters knows something, so I'm going to keep tabs on him again today. Maybe he'll slip up."

"I'll call and get the money taken care of first thing. Don't worry about that," Clay said.

"Thanks. I don't know what I'd do..."

"Don't, Tom," Clay said. "Get Michael back. We don't need to worry about anything else right now."

Tom nodded. "I need to stop in the office and talk to Tallie. If I'm following Wally around today, I may talk her into staying home. Maybe she could hang out with you, Harlie?"

Harlie nodded, sending her brown curls into a bounce. "Of course she can, if she'd like to."

He blew out a breath. "Maybe I'll just go and not tell her. She was sleeping when I left. Would you run up to the house in a while and talk to her, Harlie? I don't want her in the middle of what I'm doing today."

Harlie nodded. "Sure."

"I'll call you later. Thanks, both of you." He walked over

to Abby and kissed the top of her head and headed out the door.

His office was a disaster and Tom cringed at the mile-high mess on his desk. The guys accused him of perfection-ism where his office was concerned, but right now, he didn't care. He walked by the desk and opened the wall safe. Dig-ging around, he found a set of keys and opened the office gun cabinet on the opposite wall and selected a rifle and several boxes of ammo. A handgun would be a nice addition, but Roy had his.

He hoped the guns wouldn't be necessary, but if Wally led him to Roy, Tom would defend himself if necessary. Re-turning the keys to the safe, he glanced at the pile of bills on his desk. The cell phone bill lay on top. The detective men-tioned the check on Roy's cell phone calls turned up nega-tive. Needing confirmation, he tore open the master bill containing individual listings for each of the company's cell phones. He flipped through the pages until he found Roy's. The bill went up to and included the first two days that Roy had the boys. Disappointed, he saw Roy hadn't called any-one but Tom.

As he folded the bill, he noticed a listing for another cell phone, an extra phone he hadn't issued to anyone. He glanced toward the counter holding the chargers and saw the extra phone was gone and there were three calls to the same number on the bill.

He grabbed the phone book, looked up Wally Peters, and almost whooped with joy when the number listed for Roy's cousin matched the number on the bill. The bastard was in on it. Tom stuffed the phone bill in his pocket and snuck out the livestock gate, heading for Wally's house again. It was time to take matters into his hands and there was no way they were carrying Tom Black out on the board this time.

Tom parked his pickup in Wally's driveway. The trip into the city had seemed long—too long—when all Tom wanted was to pound Wally Peters. He had to calm himself, try not to give Wally an edge by losing control. He thought back to his bull riding days and the methods he used to prepare for competition. Then as now, he needed a clear head to take control of the situation as best he could and not let the beast win. By the time he turned off the ignition, his adrenaline was pumping. His mind was focused. Swing open the gate. He was ready to ride.

Tom stalked up the sidewalk and pounded the door with his fist. Wally answered, looking apprehensive when he recognized Tom.

"I'm done talking to you," Wally stated as he backed away from the door.

Tom stepped in. "For the sake of accuracy, you're done lying to me." Tom moved closer.

"Get out of my house! I've got nothing to say to you, Black."

"You have plenty to say to me, Peters!" Tom shoved Wally into the wall, satisfied with the loud sheetrock crack from Wally's weight.

"Now look, I don't know anything about Roy—" Wally was cut off by Tom's fist connecting with his jaw. Wally attempted to dodge further assault by feigning left but tripped on the hall rug, landing on the floor with a thud.

Tom stood over him, fists clenched, breathing hard.

"I know you've talked to Roy at least three times. The first time within two hours of the kidnapping. I have a copy of his cell phone bill, so don't try bullshitting your way out of it. Tell me where they are."

"I don't know."

Tom placed his boot on Wally's throat and applied pressure.

Wally gagged and tried to push Tom's boot away. "Okay, okay! Let me up, and I'll talk to you."

Tom hesitated, tempted to increase the pressure and squash Wally like a stinkbug. "You try anything, Wally, and you'll regret it." Tom removed his foot from Wally's neck and backed up enough for him to stand.

"It's not like you think," Wally said. He wiped blood from his split lip and rubbed his throat, watching Tom carefully.

"Wally, what I'm thinking will have you in prison for years. If there's a different version, I'm interested in hearing it. You know where they are?"

"Yes."

"Why are you protecting that scum? You know what he is. How can you cover for him?"

"I'm not protecting him. I've been keeping him from hurting those boys." He licked at his bloodied lip. "I've been taking food to them and trying to keep Roy calmed down." Wally leaned on the wall, obviously waiting for Tom to belt him again.

"Why not tell the cops where they are and keep yourself out of it?"

"Because I know Roy. You go in there with a bunch of

cops and he'll kill those kids just out of spite. He's lost whatever sanity he had and he didn't have much to start with. I've been trying to figure out a way to get them out of there, but he's always close by."

"Do you know what his plans are?" Tom wasn't sure why he believed Wally now after he'd lied so many times, but he did.

"Not for sure. He wants the money so he can take off with Cody. I don't know what he's planning to do with Michael. He won't say."

"Roy is planning something today. He called this morning wanting the money transferred. After he's confirmed the transfer, he said he'd tell me where I can find Michael. I want to find them before that and get both boys back. Will you help me, Wally? Or do I call the cops now and turn you in as an accessory to kidnapping?"

"I'll help you." Wally took a deep breath. "I didn't want to lie to you and Tallie. You have to understand the situation I'm in here. I know how crazy Roy is and it won't take much for him to snap."

"Where is he?"

"I inherited a cabin when my dad died. Just a ramshackle old thing, but Roy remembered staying there when we were kids. He's been there the whole time. I talked to him last night and he's expecting me there later today. If I drive in first, he won't be alarmed."

Tom considered it. "Why should I trust you? Maybe you'll drive in there and warn him I'm behind you."

"You can trust me because I've been trying to help those boys all along. Do you want to follow me in?"

"I guess I don't have a choice. What time is he expecting

you?"

"Whenever I get there."

"Let's go before Roy gets any ideas about leaving."

Wally headed out the back door as Tom departed the front, stopping when he saw a thoroughly pissed-off blonde leaning against his truck, her arms folded tight across her heaving chest. He scowled. "What are you doing here?"

"Going wherever you are and don't you dare try to stop me," Tallie said. With a glare, she opened the truck door, slid in, and fastened her seat belt.

Tom shook his head. He knew there wasn't any point in arguing with her when she had that determined look on her face.

A soft breeze ruffled Tom's black hair, sending loose strands into his eyes. Absently, he pushed it aside. Hidden in the trees, he watched the cabin through a pair of binoculars, hoping for glimpses of the boys. Occasionally, he detected movement through the front window but otherwise, it was quiet. Wally returned from a brief scouting mission around the cabin yard, shaking his head when Tom questioned him. "Nothing has changed," he said. "I didn't want to get close enough to alert Roy yet, so I can't tell you for sure where the boys are. I heard him talking to Michael. That's all."

Tallie stepped up to Tom's elbow. "Are we calling the cops now?"

Both men answered in unison. "No."

With an exasperated sigh, she paced away, returning with a glower on her face. "If you won't, I will." She pointed a finger toward the cabin. "That's my son in there—"

"And mine," Tom added. "We talked about this on the way here, Tallie. If we go in there with cops, Roy will go nuts. I won't risk it."

"And I have no say in this?"

Tom gave her a long look. "Not really."

Tallie growled under her breath and stomped off, muttering. "Damned cowboys and rednecks playing hero. Think they can go in there on their own and not get killed. Yee frigging haw." She threw herself against Tom's truck, folding her arms across her chest.

Ignoring her, Wally continued. "Here's what I'll do, Tom." He lifted his ball cap and ran shaky fingers through his sweaty hair. "I'll drive in there and park off to the side where I always do. Roy usually comes out to talk to me so the boys don't hear. I'll keep him talking out there as long as I can." He lowered his voice and glanced at Tallie leaning against the truck. "While I got him occupied, you get around to the back door. There aren't any windows back there so he won't see you."

"Any chance it'll be locked?"

"No. Daddy never kept anything of value here so he didn't bother with locks. You should be able to get in easy." Wally took a breath. "That door opens between the kitchen and sleep area like this." With a stick, he scratched a map in the dirt, indicating the kitchen area, sleep area, doors, and windows. "He's been keeping the boys in the sleep corner and hardly lets them move. So, after you're in the door, go to your right. They should be right there." He looked at his cousin's ex-wife. "Tallie, for God's sake, don't let Roy know you're here. He's been in a real state over you and if he knows you're here, he'll do something just to spite you. If you value those kids' lives, stay with the truck and keep quiet. Right now, he's about as stable as Jell-O in a heat wave."

"What if Roy doesn't come out?" Tom asked. "We need a contingency plan."

"Got one," Wally said with a nod. "If he don't come out, I go inside and see what's what. He usually lets the boys go to the outhouse one at a time. I'll try to get the boys to ask for a bathroom trip. I'll offer to go along and maybe he'll let 'em both go. You can grab 'em and get 'em in the truck."

Tom frowned. "That isn't much of a plan."

"It's all I got." Wally dug keys from his pocket. "I'll head in there." He disappeared through the trees. A moment later, he drove his pickup past Tom and Tallie, nervous sweat dripping from his temples. Tom watched until he parked, and turned to Tallie. Her earlier anger had melted into fear. Tom wrapped his arms around her.

"It'll be okay. We'll get them," he said. "Do as Wally says. Stay right here. Don't let Roy know you're here."

She bit her lip and nodded. "Don't do anything rash, Tom. Please, be careful." She wrapped her arms tight around his neck and squeezed him to her.

"I'll be all right. Keep the shotgun handy. You know how to use it now, but it's better if you don't have to." He released his grip and stepped away, grabbing the rifle from the gun rack. Tom left Tallie near the truck, hoping she'd do as she was told and stay there. He worked his way through the trees and underbrush, moving and stopping until he'd found a good vantage point to watch Wally. Roy didn't follow his regular pattern and stayed in the cabin after his cousin's arrival. Wally waited but had to dump Plan A. Tom watched as Wally hefted his bulk from the truck and made his way inside, hitching his pants as he walked.

⌘

"So, Roy, what's your plan for today?' Wally asked. He sat at the rickety table, sipping a pop, eyeing Roy across the table.

"I just need to make a call and I'm out of here."

"Where are you heading?"

"You think I'd tell you?" Roy laughed. "I'm not telling anybody. Just disappearing like smoke." He made a waving gesture with his hands. "Just me and Cody."

Wally glanced around, his eyes landing on Michael. "Where is Cody? Outhouse?"

"Never you mind," Roy said with a grin. "That part of things is firmly under control."

"What about Michael? Are you giving him back?" Wally looked again at the boy sitting on the bed, his dark eyes as wide as twin full moons. Roy followed Wally's gaze and contemplated the question.

"You know, Tom Black doesn't deserve to get that kid back, and I don't want to take him with me. Could be the little sucker will have an accident before I take off." He grinned.

"You're planning to kill him?" Wally asked, horrified.

"What do you care? He ain't your kid." Roy looked at his cousin.

"No, you're right. I don't care." Wally fidgeted when Roy's gaze intensified.

"You're acting kinda funny, Wally. You didn't tell anybody where to find me, did you?"

Wally shifted in his seat and swallowed hard. "No. Who

would I tell?"

"You always had the hots for Tallie. Maybe you think she'll take a look at you if you save her kid? Maybe you think you'll get a turn at her when ol' Tom is done with her?"

Sweat dripped down Wally's brow. "I don't know what you're talking about, Roy. She's a nice woman, but I never had the hots for her. She was your wife."

"Damn right she was! A damned useless wife who was supposed to have two million dollars." Roy rose from his chair, pacing the kitchen like a caged lion. "I'm taking Cody. That will hurt her more than anything else I could do. I tried everything, and she just pointed that hoity-toity chin in the air and looked at me like she didn't think I was good enough for her! Taking Cody will squash her, and I'm going to enjoy knowing I did it." Roy continued pacing, stopping by the sink with his back to Wally. He chuckled. "And someday, I'll come back and take care of her."

Wally stood and walked to Roy. "I'm not letting you hurt those boys, Roy. You're done playing games with them."

Roy sneered. "What do you think you can do about it?"

"I'm taking them back to their parents."

Roy gripped the counter with both hands. "It's not gonna happen, Wally."

Wally shifted his weight from one foot to the other. "It has to happen, Roy. If you hurt that boy, the cops will never stop looking for you." Wally swallowed. "And...and they say you murdered a woman. I told them I didn't think you did it but they say there's proof you did. And...and maybe some guy, too."

Roy looked over his shoulder and his glare froze Wally speechless. "Nice of you to defend me, cousin. Real nice of you." He laughed. "A damned waste of breath though."

"Tell me you didn't do it. You didn't kill her."

Roy grinned. "If it will make you happy, I will." The sun shone brightly through the window, highlighting Roy's flexing hands, opening and closing. "But it would be a lie." He chuckled. "It was her fault, you know. If she hadn't figured out who I was, I could have let her go. But she'd have told Black I was there and I couldn't let her do that. Could I?"

Wally shook his head, sending rivulets of sweat down his neck.

"And the other one was just an accident. No fun at all." He chuckled again. "You sure seem buggy, Wally. Like you've got something...or someone...to hide."

"No. Nothing of the sort."

"You told the cops, didn't you?"

"No—"

"You did. I can tell."

Wally backed up a step. "I didn't. But it's only a matter of time until they figure it out. So...I'm taking that boy, and I'm getting out of here."

Roy reached into the sink and swung around to face an astonished Wally with a paring knife in his hand. "Like hell you are." The knife blade flashed in the sunlight before Roy buried it deep in Wally's chest.

Wally stumbled, looking at Roy with bewilderment. "Jesus Christ, Roy!" he sputtered before falling to the floor, the knife blade planted firmly in his chest. Wally lay on his back, gasping for breath as Roy stepped over him. Wally felt cold as the life slowly drained from his body.

CAUGHT IN THE SPIN

"Too bad you won't be meeting him where you're going, cousin," Wally heard Roy say with moderate interest. "I doubt there's a Peters yet who made it to heaven, and I don't see you starting a new trend."

29

"I got a feeling, Mikey boy," Roy said, "that my cousin wasn't particularly honest with me."

Mike watched Roy walk across the cabin to where Mike sat, cowboy boots thunking on the dry plank floor. He stopped in front of the nervous boy.

"I got a feeling we may have company soon. But that's okay. The more the merrier." Roy laughed and walked around the cabin, glancing out the windows. "Not yet, but those cops will be coming. It'll be fun, won't it, Mikey?" He chuckled and looked over his shoulder at Michael. "What do you think? Should I go out or let them come in after us? We need a plan. Just you and me. Like Butch and Sundance."

Michael looked at him with fear-filled eyes, unable to answer for the duct tape on his mouth. He wiggled his hands, also held with duct tape and secured to the bedpost. His feet were numb from the pressure of the tape around his ankles. He was so scared he was sure he'd pee his pants. Cody was nowhere in sight.

Roy ambled to him, pistol in his hand, cocked and ready to fire. "I didn't hear you, Mikey. Should we let them come to us? Maybe your papa will be the first one I shoot. Right between the eyes. Would you like that, Mikey?" Roy rubbed his hair with the pistol. Michael flinched.

"It'll be just like on TV, won't it? They'll expect me to give myself up." Roy laughed. "Not goddamned likely! No siree." He walked to the window, pointed the pistol, and pulled the trigger. "Just like that! I'll shoot him dead." Roy did a little dance, spinning in circles, and returned to the window again. "They'll be coming. I know it." Again, he pointed the revolver out the window, aiming at a tree. "There's a big fat one, right there. See him, Mikey? A big ol' deputy with his belly hanging over his belt. The fat bastard thinks he can get me before I get him." He pulled the trigger and cackled with glee as a shot rang out. "That damned cop thinks he's John Wayne or something. Come out with your hands up, Pilgrim." Roy jumped in front of the window and fired again, hopping from view when imaginary deputies returned his fire. "They're here, Mikey. I knew it." He glanced at Wally's prone body. "Dipshit led 'em right to me." Roy sauntered over to Wally and kicked his prone cousin in the leg. He looked from Wally's body to Michael, a spark in his eye. With a grin, Roy swung around and kicked the gas line; the pungent aroma quickly filled the air.

Michael wiggled his hands, trying to get free from the bedpost. He had a good idea what Roy had in mind. Cody had been gone from the cabin for hours, and Roy kept making comments about killing people. Michael knew he was next and from what he remembered about gas, he knew what was coming. Kaboom! Watching Roy closely, he shifted his hands when Roy turned away, twisting and turning, hoping to slacken the tape enough to slip his hands free. Even a kid could see Roy was slipping into la-la land. The shooting was one-sided. No cops returned fire. Michael panicked, not sure if he could get free before the nutcase did something to the kid he hated. Roy walked to Michael and pulled a matchbox from his pocket, making a big production of removing a match. With a snigger, he touched the match to the striker but didn't pull it across.

"Boom!" Roy laughed when Michael jumped. "Scared you, didn't I?" He stuffed the matches back in his pocket and returned to the window. "That," he said, "will be my grand finale. Hold on to your hat. It'll be showtime soon." The assault from the window continued with Roy laughing after each round. Panic was not an option, Michael decided. Studying the tape, he figured he could wiggle his hands and work the tape free from the post and slide his hands up and over. The thick odor of propane burned his eyes and his head hurt. Soon, he wouldn't be able to breathe and he doubted the cops were even coming. Despite Cody's message from Tom, Michael doubted his dad was coming either. Not in time, anyway. He wiggled his hands and felt a surge of optimism when the tape pulled away. He kept his eyes on Roy, moving his wrists only when Roy turned away. If he could get free, maybe he could get out that door. And then what? Run like a crazy man. That's what.

Roy jumped in front of the window, took a shot, and jumped back before the imaginary deputies could return fire. Over and over he followed the pattern. When a voice called out, Roy grinned.

"Roy!"

Roy chuckled. "Well, I'll be damned," he said quietly. "The cavalry has arrived."

⁂

She couldn't sit still. The truck was a stifling hot oven she needed to escape. The wait was interminable, the tension building as the seconds ticked by. When Tom didn't return, she had to take action, to help. If she didn't act quickly, her opportunity would vanish. Tallie needed to do something only she could do. Supply a distraction only she could provide. How many times had she thwarted Roy's attacks on Cody by throwing herself into the middle and allowing her son to escape? One more time for old time's sake. Quietly, she moved from the truck, sneaking behind the trees. From what she could see, the plan had fallen apart. Wally was inside and hadn't reemerged. She watched Tom, hunkered down behind the trees, obviously debating his next move. From what Tallie could see, Tom needed a distraction to get in the back door. For some reason, Roy was shooting his pistol from the front window and yelling at the trees. He'd snapped and the boys were in even bigger danger. Roy poked the gun barrel in and out of the window like a kid playing peekaboo. An ill-placed step snapped a twig and Tallie held her breath. Roy moved to the window again and pulled the trigger, hitting a tree near her hiding place. When he retreated, Tallie resumed her trek, weaving between the trees. When she reached a break in the foliage, she stepped out and walked purposefully into the cabin yard, yelling to get Roy's attention.

"Roy! I want to talk to you!" she called.

Roy looked out the window and smiled. "Do you now? Just what do we have to talk about?"

"A trade," she said.

"You don't have anything I want. Now go on back to your boyfriend and skedaddle on out of here. The boys and I have some business to finish."

She stood still, shoulders thrown back, chin held high.

"Go on now, Tallie. Get moving. Don't make me hurt you."

"Not until I make my offer." She took a breath and tried

to steady her shaking hands. It was pointless. They shook like windblown leaves no matter how she tried to control them. "I've been thinking, Roy. About us."

"Us?" he said with a sneer. "There's no us anymore, not since you tried to take off with my boy."

"But there could be. An us, I mean." She took a step closer, stirring the dirt beneath her boots. "Like I said, I've been thinking about you and how things used to be. We were good together once. We could be that way again."

"What about Black? I thought you two were pretty hot and heavy. What's he gonna think of this offer of yours? It might hurt his tender little feelings."

"Him?" She shrugged. "He isn't anything to me, just something to do for a while. I was lonely and he was there. You know how it is." A knot formed in her stomach. "It's always been you I loved, Roy. You were the first, and a girl doesn't get over her first love easily. If I'd known you were getting out of prison, I'd have picked you up. We could have gone somewhere together. Just like it used to be."

Roy laughed. "You expect me to believe that? I saw you with Black. You were all over him."

"It was an act, Roy. I needed help and he was there. But now I see I was wrong. I shouldn't have run from you."

"Damned right. A wife belongs with her husband. A boy belongs with his father," Roy said with conviction. "It's the natural order of things."

"I agree. That's why I want to propose a trade," she said with a gulp. "Me for Michael. I'll come in there and you'll let Michael go."

"Nah, this is bullshit. You're trying to play with my head."

CAUGHT IN THE SPIN

Tallie froze when the gun barrel slinked out the window, trained on her. "No, I'm not. A boy should be with his father. You said it yourself. Let Michael go so he can be with his father. I'll go with you, wherever you want me to go. We'll be a family again, you, me, and Cody. Just like old times." Sweat beaded and trickled down her neck. She didn't dare wipe it away for fear he'd pull the trigger. "Please, Roy. I've missed you. Let me come in."

⚜

From his perch beneath the underbrush, Tom debated his next move. Wally's plan had disintegrated. Last he'd seen of him, he'd walked in the cabin and disappeared. Now he wondered if Wally was setting him up. If he opened the back door, would he find the two of them waiting for him, or was one of the bullets Roy's final gift to Wally?

Using the front door was guaranteed suicide while Roy played shooting gallery. Tom considered the sniper approach, hiding behind a tree and taking Roy out through the open window. The problem there: He might hit one of the boys. He could go in the back door and try to shoot Roy, but again, he might hit Cody or Michael. He wouldn't risk it. He needed a way to get the gun away from Roy and subdue him. During the next barrage, Tom crawled from his hiding place and worked toward the cabin. Halfway to the door, he heard a voice that froze him.

Tallie.

He could hear her voice and Roy's retorts. He backed up a few steps and saw her in the cabin yard, head held high. She was the bravest woman he'd ever met and at that moment, she was the most stubborn. The truck was the safest place for her, and there she was staring down a rifle barrel.

His heart pounded while he pondered his choices: rush Tallie and get her away from Roy's line of fire, or continue to the back door and use Tallie as the diversion she intended. He doubted he could do anything before Roy pulled the trigger. His only option was the back door and disarming Roy.

And if he failed, Tallie would die, just like she said she would. There was only one thing to do and he couldn't fail.

Not this time.

Tom moved to the cabin wall, flattening his back against it. Although covered in grime, the window offered a view of the interior scene. Roy stood at the side of the front window, occasionally shouting at Tallie. Michael sat on the bed with tape across his mouth and around his ankles. He wiggled his wrists while keeping a close watch on Roy. When he succeeded in freeing his wrist from the bedpost, he held his hands near the post, giving the illusion he was still taped. The conversation out front increased, keeping Roy occupied. Tom couldn't delay any longer. If Michael freed his ankles, he'd most likely make a run for it and Roy would gun him down. Tom worked his way around the cabin and climbed the steps. As he reached for the doorknob, the shooting began again. His heart pounded with fear for Tallie. She was in Roy's sights, possibly dead already. He couldn't give in to the panic ripping through him. He couldn't get to Tallie to help her but he could possibly save Michael and Cody.

The door swung open partway on squeaky hinges, the noise muffled by the gunshots. Tom flattened his back against the wall, trying to gauge Roy's location. Propane fumes burned his eyes and blurred his vision. His breath came in hard gasps. Every instinct told him to get away fast, but he stumbled in, hoping to get to Michael and Cody.

CAUGHT IN THE SPIN

As Tom pushed the door open, a dark flash barreled into him, pushing him backward down the cabin steps. Tom stumbled. There was a deafening roar and searing heat scorched his face before everything went dark.

30

Tom drifted in a haze, wading in and out of a gelatinous fog. Jolie meandered through his mind, her sweet voice whispered in his ear, her hand held in his. She wasn't gone. She was here again, with him, whispering encouragement for him to get up and walk again. He reached for her, wanting to touch her, but his hand grabbed air.

He tried to move and couldn't. It couldn't be happening again. With effort, he tried to shift his legs, but they were weighed down. Paralyzed. This time he truly was paralyzed. Was that why she was here?

"Jolie?" he whispered, reaching for her. "Jolie?" He heard a sharp gasp and shook his muddled head. An explosion. Not a bull riding wreck. That was before. His head hurt. Why couldn't he move his legs? He could feel them but couldn't move them. A groan emanated from deep inside him. Jolie was gone and shouldn't be here now. They'd said their good-byes, and he needed to get on with his life. "Jolie..." The haze lifted, and Tom understood where he was and what had happened. The warm hand holding his hadn't been Jolie's.

Tom opened his eyes, squinting against the sunshine. It felt as if his eyebrows had been singed from his face. The cabin was now a pile of burning rubble. He watched as the last remaining wall crumbled, sending debris through the air like jagged rain. Tears filled his burning eyes. The boys couldn't have survived but he had to look anyway.

But he couldn't move his legs.

He shifted to his elbow and looked around. "Oh, no," he said when he realized the weight on his legs wasn't cabin wreckage but his son. Tom sat up, moving Michael to the ground next to him. He felt for a pulse on his neck. It was there. "Michael. Wake up, please." He checked for injuries and found only small scrapes on his hands and singed hair on the back of his head. Most likely he suffered from carbon monoxide poisoning or had been rendered unconscious by the blast. Duct tape still held his mouth shut. With shaking hands, Tom peeled the tape from his son's mouth, but the boy remained limp and unmoving. Tom drew him into his arms and held him tight, willing him to wake up and be okay. "Come on, Michael. You're breathing. You'll be okay. You will. Come on." He rubbed his hand across Michael's cheek, his fingers through his dusty hair. Michael's eyes fluttered and he moaned.

"Dad?"

Tears filled Tom's eyes. "Yeah."

Michael smiled weakly and clung to his father. Silent tears dripped down his cheeks, turning to sobs that soaked Tom's shirt. Tom held him as he cried. When Michael's shaking subsided, he looked at Tom.

"I knew you'd come. Roy said you wouldn't, but I knew you would." He smiled as he wiped the tears from his face, leaving dark streaks. "Roy's nothing but a big fat liar."

"Of course I came, Michael. You're my son and I love you. I would do anything to get you back. Anything."

Michael wiped his dripping nose with his hand and smiled. "I love you too, Dad." Tom grabbed him in his arms and held him again. Movement caught his eye. Tallie, arms hugged tight around her middle and tears streaming down her face as she stared at the cabin wreckage.

"Tallie, honey," Tom said. "Come here." He held his hand to her.

She shook her head. "I can't find him anywhere." She crumpled to the ground, sobbing. Tom released Michael from his grasp, scrambled to her side, and wrapped his arms around her. Her body shook with grief.

"I can't find Cody," she cried. "I've looked all over."

Tom tightened his hold on her, afraid she might launch herself into the burning debris to find Cody.

Michael looked around, frowning. "Where is Cody?"

Tom looked at the destroyed cabin and felt sick. "Michael, I'm afraid Cody is...gone."

"I know that. But where?" Michael looked into the trees, as if he would see his friend there.

"Wasn't he in the cabin with you?" Tom asked with a frown.

Michael shook his head. "No. Roy took him somewhere this morning. I haven't seen him since breakfast." He got to his feet, wobbled a little, and looked around.

"He wasn't in the cabin when it blew up?" Tallie asked.

"No."

Tom jumped to his feet. "Come on. We need to look."

The three fanned out, searching the cabin area, the woodshed, and the outhouse but couldn't find a trace of the missing boy. They dismantled the woodpile and looked in the brush. When Tom heard a strange sound, he held up his hand. "Shhhh. I hear something." Again he heard a methodical thumping, different from the crackle of the cabin fire.

Tom cocked his head, listening, trying to figure out where

the thumping came from. "Keep looking. He's somewhere close." They extended the search to the area further from the cabin, locating Roy's red truck parked in a thicket on a slope beyond the yard. The banging grew louder as they walked nearer. The first to reach the truck door, Tom yanked it open to find Cody bound and gagged with duct tape, lying in the seat, kicking the door.

"Cody!" Tom said with relief. "I didn't think we'd ever find you." He reached in and pulled the boy up, frantically picking the edges of the tape covering his mouth. When he'd removed it, Tom pulled the boy from the truck and set him under a tree. Tallie wrapped her arms around Cody, tears flooding her eyes.

"Are you okay?" she asked as she patted him, looking for injuries. Tom handed her a pocket knife, and she sliced through the duct tape binding his wrists and ankles.

"Yeah," he croaked. "Can I have some water? Roy had bottles in the truck. I could see them but couldn't get to them."

Tom ran to the truck, returning with the water.

When Cody finished his drink, Tallie grabbed him into a hug.

"Are you really okay?" She leaned back, looking him over and grimacing at the tape marks and bruises left by his father. Cody nodded. Tallie wiped tears from her eyes. Michael plopped down next to his friend.

"Mike!" Cody croaked. "Are you okay?"

"Yeah. The cabin blew up." Michael stated, his voice lacking emotion. "Roy's dead."

Cody looked thoughtful for a moment. "Good."

When Tom finished removing the tape from Cody's ankles, he helped the boy to his feet and half carried him to his pickup. Tom called the sheriff's department with the news the boys were found. Seated comfortably in the backseat, the boys related their story from the first moments of the kidnapping to the gas explosion that killed Roy.

"Why were you in the truck, Cody?" Tom asked.

"Roy said the money was in the bank and we were taking off. He didn't say where." Cody rubbed his red wrists. "He said he didn't want me running, so he taped me up and stuck me in that hot old truck. I thought I was going to roast to death."

"What did he plan to do with Michael?" Tom asked.

"I don't know, but he wasn't going with us. Roy said all kinds of mean stuff, like he'd like to kill Mike just because you made him mad. He talked about tying Mike up in the cabin and starting a fire. I'm glad he's okay. I was really scared when I heard that explosion."

"It looks like there was a gas leak," Tom said.

Michael shook his head. "It wasn't a leak, Dad. Roy kicked the pipe loose and said he was gonna blow me up when it was time to go." He glanced toward the burning cabin. "Roy is dead, right?"

Tom nodded. "I don't see how he could have survived the explosion."

Cody frowned. "Mike did."

Tom squeezed Michael's shoulder. "He's dead. You don't have to worry about him again."

⊙≋⊙

It was late afternoon when Tom pulled the pickup to a stop in front of his house. From the front seat, he nudged Michael and Cody awake. Cody opened the truck door and fell into his mother's waiting arms. She held her hand out to Michael, and Tom was pleased she pulled his son into her hug as well. He knew how much Michael needed it.

"I can't believe you're home," she said as she held them. "Both of you, safe." She hugged the boys again. "I'll bet you guys are hungry. Sally said on the phone she put a pizza in the oven. She's probably in the kitchen if you want to go on ahead."

"Yeah!" the boys said in unison and they headed into the house.

"We'll be there in a minute," she called after them. "Wash your hands."

Tom climbed from the truck, slammed the door, and walked to her, laughing that she would tell two filthy boys to wash their hands. It would take sandblasting to get the grime off them. He wanted nothing more than to wrap his arms around her and hold her. The ordeal had taken a lot out of her. Him, too. She'd held up well under the detective's questioning and the reporters. Word had gotten out about the boys' rescue, and when they emerged from the cabin road, a flood of news vans blocked their path. On the drive back, Tallie was quiet. Tired, he supposed.

Now she looked at him warily and he wasn't sure why. He attempted to hold her and she stepped back, frowning. He shrugged and gave her a questioning look.

"Problem?"

She looked at him as if trying to figure something out. "No. I'm okay. It's just..." She struggled for words and gave up, leaning her face into his chest. "I was so scared." Her breath came in gasps. "I was trying to talk to Roy...trying to make some kind of deal and hoping to give you time to get inside, and the cabin exploded. The force of it knocked me down but I got up and I ran as fast as I could...and when I got there, you were on the ground and Michael was lying across you, looking like he wasn't breathing. And you started calling out..." She swallowed. "You called out...and appeared to be in horrible pain." She shook as he held her. "I couldn't find Cody, and I was so scared for the boys, for you. I couldn't bear losing any of you."

"I know," he whispered. "I felt the same way when I heard you talking to Roy. That was the craziest thing you could possibly do, Tallie." He swallowed hard. "When I heard the shots...I thought he'd..." Tears welled up in his eyes. He couldn't bear the thought of losing any of them either. "Damn, you're going to make me cry or something." He squeezed her tight. "The boys are home, and we're going to be okay."

31

"No!" Michael screamed. "No! Don't shoot! Don't shoot! Ahhhh!" He thrashed from side to side, kicking his sheets over the side of the bed. "No!" he screamed again. "Don't kill him! You can't kill my dad! No!" He screamed louder. Tom ran in the room, reaching for the terrified boy who rolled frantically in the upper bunk, trying to keep him from landing on the floor.

"Michael, it's just a dream. Wake up," he whispered, not wanting to startle him. "It's just a dream, Michael. Wake up. I'm okay."

Michael woke with a start, reaching for Tom's arm. "He was here. He was going to kill you. Roy was back. He had a gun." He looked at Tom with terror-filled eyes. "He said he was going to shoot you between the eyes. I had to stop him, but my hands were taped together." His breathing came in gasps and his green eyes were wild. He held up his hands, feeling his wrists for the tape he thought was still there.

Tom placed his hand on Michael's shoulder and squeezed gently. "It was just a dream, Michael, just another dream. Roy's gone and he can't come back to hurt you. Never again."

"Is he okay?" Cody asked from the bottom bunk. "Maybe we should trade bunks so he can sleep with the dogs."

"He's fine, Cody, just another dream. Do you want to trade with him?" he asked Michael. "Cookie and Clyde could keep you company." Michael nodded and crawled from his bed and into the other vacated by Cody. Cookie and Clyde took their places around his feet.

"Dad? Will you stay?"

"Sure. Lie down and go back to sleep." Tom reached over and ran his hand over Michael's hair. "I'll be right here." He sat on the floor, leaning on the bed, listening to the boys breathe as they drifted to sleep, and wondered when the nightmares would end. Cody was spared the nocturnal terrors Michael had suffered the past three nights. But Cody experienced a different fear than Michael: fear of not seeing his mother again, fear of his father's abuse, and the fear of seeing his friend hurt. But Michael was made to believe he'd die. Roy had made a sick game of tormenting the boy with his mortality, and if he wasn't threatening Michael, he was threatening Tom. A boy who recently lost his mother to an early death had a difficult time dealing with the possible loss of his father, too. Tom spent the past three nights sitting with him, trying to ward off the terrors, and supposed he'd be here quite a few more. The dreams had lessened in number since the first night, but they still came ferociously.

Michael stirred, feeling over the side of the bed for Tom. "Dad?" he whispered.

"I'm here. Go back to sleep."

"I need to know something..." Michael blew out his breath. "You're going to think I'm nuts but...do you believe in...ghosts?"

Tom froze. "A lot of people do," he said vaguely. "Why?"

"Because...um..." He blew out his breath again. "She was there."

"Who?" The hair on the back of Tom's neck stood up and a shiver cruised along his spine.

"Mom. She was there."

"In your dream? You dreamed of her, right?" Tom tensed.

"No. In the cabin. She was in the cabin. I couldn't see her, but she was there." Michael's voice shook. "She talked to me. More than once." He paused. "When Roy took Cody to talk to you, he stuck me in the closet. I was scared and she...Mom...talked to me. She said I was going to be okay."

Tom swallowed hard. "You know, it could be that you wanted her there, so you imagined it. Or maybe you fell asleep and dreamed of her?"

He took a deep breath. "No. I don't think so, because...it happened again. When Roy was shooting out the window, I was picking at the tape, trying to get it off my wrists. He kicked the gas line and the smell was getting bad. I was feeling icky and thought I was going to pass out, and she talked to me again."

"You're sure it wasn't the gas fumes making you hear things? Tallie was out front talking to Roy. Maybe you heard Tallie and thought it was Mom." Tom's heart was pounding.

"No. I know Mom's voice. It was her. She told me you were waiting for me and to run. The cabin was going to blow up. She yelled at me to run fast and get out. Right now. I had just got the tape off my ankles, so I jumped up and ran. When I got to the door, the cabin blew up. If I hadn't listened..." Michael's hand shook where he laid it on Tom's shoulder, gripping his father's shirt tight in his fist. Tom reached up and held it.

"Then," Michael continued. "When I was laying there with you, she talked to me again."

"Tallie was there, Michael. Are you sure it wasn't Tallie talking to you?" Tom suggested again. "Tallie was talking to me, asking if I was okay."

"No. It was Mom. I saw her."

Tom squeezed his hand. "Saw her?"

"Yeah. She looked real pretty, just like she used to before she got sick. Her hair was long," Michael said. "She told me I was okay, and I had to wake up. She kept saying, 'Come on, Mike. Wake up. Dad needs you.'" Michael rolled to his back and scooted his head toward Tom. "She said some stuff about you. She said she had to come back to help because you shouldn't be alone. She felt bad that she'd left you alone before and she wanted me to be with you now."

"I do need you. But are you sure you weren't dreaming?" A thrum of excitement ran through his veins. They couldn't both have dreamed her. Was this the proof he'd been looking for? He smiled. Houdini hadn't figured out how to come back. Had Jolie? He wasn't ready to concede yet. "Maybe she's so deeply embedded in our hearts that we think we hear and see her when we need to."

"It seemed so real."

Tom evaded the question a moment longer. "If it's true, does it scare you or bother you that she came back?"

"No. I think it's cool. I got to say good-bye this time." He sniffed and Tom could tell he was trying to hold back tears. "When she...went before, I was asleep, and I didn't get to say good-bye. I think maybe it's why she came back. So, do you believe in ghosts, Dad?"

Tom was silent a moment, remembering his own good-bye with Jolie and how it had allowed him to get on with his life. Was it for real? He didn't know, but he was willing to keep an open mind if it helped Michael heal. "Yeah, Michael. I think I do."

He drifted to sleep and was awakened by a soft hand caressing his cheek. Tallie. He was grateful she'd come, as his backside was protesting his uncomfortable choice of sleeping arrangements. She helped him to his feet, put her arm around his waist, and they wandered to his room.

Tom slept with Tallie in his arms, thinking he needed to marry this woman and never let her go. Jolie was right. He shouldn't be alone anymore.

32

Tom walked around with a smile on his face most of the morning. Loving Tallie in the early hours had put a skip in his step he hadn't had for a while. She awakened him with gentle, arousing caresses, turning him inside out. Able to relax together for the first time, they unleashed their passions and made love with an abandon neither had allowed before. He'd wanted to stay in bed with her all day, but duty called and he spent the morning in the office sorting the accumulated mess.

Now, he stood on the porch watching her shove clothing in her car and realized she'd been saying good-bye. Had she already decided she didn't love him, that it was the situation driving her emotions after all? While he thought of loving her forever, marrying her, she thought about leaving him.

He stood stoically, his face an expressionless mask. He thought he saw a flicker of emotion cross her face when she saw him, but then it was gone.

"Leaving?"

She nodded. "Yeah. It's time to go home. I need to get back to work."

He frowned as he nodded. "Need help with anything else?"

"I just need to get Cody and I'm ready to go."

"I'll get him." He walked into the house and up the stairs. "Cody, your mom is ready to go." He looked in Michael's room and saw two long-faced boys. Cody dragged his feet as he left the room.

"Why?" Michael asked.

"I don't know, Michael. It's her decision." With that, he went downstairs to say good-bye. Tallie stood in the driver's door, ready to climb in, but paused to look at him as he walked toward her.

"Do you have enough gas to get back to town?" he asked, even though it wasn't what he wanted to say. He wanted to beg her not to go, but his wounded pride held tight rein and he couldn't say the words. He wouldn't humiliate himself when she made her position clear. She didn't want him.

"I'm fine, thanks." She looked at him as if the last month hadn't happened, as if they hadn't just made love that morning. The air was thick with tension but neither broke it.

"Thanks for letting us stay with you. I appreciate everything you did for us," she said.

"Glad I could help."

"Well." She gave him one last uncomfortable look, climbed into the car, and pulled the door closed. The engine roared to life. She stared at him. "Give me a call sometime, okay?"

Sometime? That was a classic kiss-off if he ever heard one. "Yeah, sure." He nodded as she backed her car into the drive and pulled away. He waited, hoping she would turn around, but all he saw were taillights as she drove out the gate.

33

"Rob!" Tom yelled out the office door. "Why isn't that fence fixed down on the south corner? Get your butt moving!"

"I'm going. I'm going. Just wanted to drink a pop first." Rob muttered under his breath as he walked out the door.

"Ernie!" Tom yelled again. "Get in here. Now!"

"What?" A thin young man in dusty Wranglers peeked in from the outer office as Clay walked in. Ernie glanced at him and poked his head in Tom's door. "Clay's here. I'm heading out to help Rob."

"Good. Get going." Tom leaned back in his chair. Clay sauntered in and made himself at home in the opposite chair. Leaning back, he swung his boots up on the corner of Tom's desk and smiled at the glower he received.

"Piss-poor mood you're in, Tom. What did poor ol' Ernie do to deserve that verbal pounding?"

"I'm fine, and he's slacking off." Tom scowled. "What do you want? I don't have time for your bullshit today."

"But you're getting it anyway. You've been spitting fire for two weeks now. Why don't you go see her? I'm sure your employees would appreciate it. I know I would."

Tom glared. "She left. I'm not going to see her."

"I talked to Harv today." Clay took off his hat, ran his fingers through his sandy-blond hair, and replaced the hat.

"So? You talk to Harv every day."

"Well, today was different. He wanted to know what

we'd done to Tallie. He says he sent a perfectly good employee out here and we returned her in one heck of a bad mood. She's been grouchy, touchy, and absentminded. Sounds like someone else I know."

"She made her choice."

Clay shrugged. "Doesn't matter anyway. He said a couple of days ago her mood improved considerably when a guy picked her up for lunch—a tall, blond, hunky-looking guy. She seemed real happy to see him. Squealed when she hugged him. Remember when she met you? She squealed then too." He frowned. "She didn't squeal when she met me. What do you suppose that means?" Clay looked around the office nonchalantly.

Tom's jaw tensed. "So? She's not my problem anymore."

"Are you trying to say you don't feel anything for her? It doesn't bother you that she's seeing someone else?"

He scowled. "Why are you doing this, Clay? You know how I feel about her. Why torture me with this crap? She left. I've been there before. End of story."

"Did you talk to her before she left? Did you tell her how you feel?"

"I didn't get the chance. She packed up and left darned fast."

Clay shook his head and frowned. "So you're letting some other guy move in on her because you didn't talk fast enough? Man, I'd be in there fighting for her. Unless she isn't worth it." Clay shrugged.

Tom scowled. "She's worth it. I just didn't think she wanted to hear what I had to say."

"If it was me, I'd tell her and let her decide." He dropped his feet to the floor. "I gotta go." He rose from his chair and headed to the door. "You love her, go talk to her. If you don't love her, no big deal, right? I guess I can handle another twelve years of nursing your broken heart, but I'd prefer not." He stopped, looking thoughtful.

"If you do go, take some flowers," he said with a nod. "Harlie gets all gooey over daisies and stuff like that. I picked her some volunteer violets from the yard the other day and made her cry. You'd think I grew them for her, not just found them." He shrugged. "With Harlie, it might be hormones. I never know for sure."

Tom blew out a breath. "I suppose I could stop in town for some roses or something."

Clay shook his head. "Not roses. I have it on good authority Tallie isn't impressed with roses. Too cliché. Pick her some sunflowers or some kind of wildflowers, and she'll be all over you."

"How do you know that?"

Clay laughed. "I wish I could say I have the inside track to the female mind but I don't. She told Harlie. Do what you will with the information, but I'll tell you," he said and winked, "a smart man would be down by the pond picking flowers."

Tom frowned at Clay's departing back. She left. Why should he have to make the next move? But he did and he'd known it before Clay jabbed him with the idea.

He sat at his desk for a while, unable to concentrate. Tallie and a new guy. Goddamn. The jerk probably had an account at the florist's shop and gave her flowers every day. Tom closed the office and walked home. Michael lounged on the porch swing with the dogs; his flexing foot moved the swing back and forth. Cookie and Clyde thumped their tails when he walked up and sat next to his son.

"What's up?" he asked.

"Bored."

"There's lots of stuff to do around here. Want to go fishing?" Michael shook his head. "We could saddle up the horses." Michael shook his head. "I could massacre you in one of those video games." Tom smiled.

Michael snorted and continued to stare off into space. "When's Tallie coming back?"

Gad. It was coming at him from all sides. Tom blew out another breath. "I don't think she is."

"Did you disappoint her like you did Mom?"

Ouch. Tom frowned and sighed. "Different situation this time but same result. She left."

"Why?"

"I'm not positive, but I think it's because I didn't say what she wanted to hear."

"Do you know what she wants to hear?"

"I thought I did."

"Why not say it?" Michael said with exasperation. "I thought you liked her. You were doing all that kissing and stuff and you said it didn't gross her out. Make her come back."

"No, it didn't gross her out. She likes kissing." The corner of Tom's mouth lifted into a smile. In a couple of years, Michael would know how difficult all this male/female stuff was. Love was a dangerous obstacle course and only the lucky ones survived undamaged. "But I can't make her come back if she doesn't want to."

"She likes you."

"I thought so." He remembered when she said she loved

him. If he hadn't been such a coward, he'd have told her how he felt then. But he played it safe to protect himself. He was such an idiot.

"Then why don't you go ask her to marry us?" Michael looked up at Tom.

"Us?"

"Yeah. Us. That's what Jason said when he wanted Mom to marry him. He said it was like marrying both of us because we're a package deal. Can't have one without the other."

"You want a wicked stepmother, do you?" Tom smiled and ruffled Michael's hair. He needed a haircut before school started. It hung down his neck in a shimmering black wave.

"Nothing wicked about Tallie. She's neat. And Cody would be my brother. Like you and Clay. Brothers but not really."

"I thought about marrying her. Having her around all the time would be nice. You think I should?"

"Don't get mad, but you've been grumpy since she left."

The kid was right. Grumpy was putting a polite spin of his insufferable behavior.

"I'll go to Harlie's and play with Abby in the pool if you want to go see her." He leaned toward Tom like a knowing conspirator. "I know guys like privacy for mushy stuff like that."

Tom laughed. "Got it all figured out, don't you?" He smiled at his son. "Clay said the same thing about my grumpy mood. Sorry."

"Should I get my swimming suit?" Michael asked, making Tom laugh again.

"Doesn't sound like I have much choice since the pack of

you are ganging up on me. I need to get cleaned up first, and I'll drop you off at Clay and Harlie's. Tallie should be home from work by then. Go find your swimsuit, Michael."

Michael jumped up from the swing and ran to the door, turning back before going in. "Hey, Dad?"

"What?"

"You can call me Mike if you want." He paused for a moment before running in the house

Tom watched him go, a lump forming in his throat.

⁓

Two hours later, Tom parked in front of Tallie's duplex and sat staring at the front door. His hands were sweaty and his stomach did a flip-flop. He'd done this once before with Jolie, but he'd been younger and hadn't had the experience of a mutilated heart. He'd also had a lot more confidence. Steeling his nerves, he grabbed the bouquet of sunflowers from the seat and walked to the door. He rang the bell and waited for what seemed like an eternity.

The door opened. A man looked out at him and Tom suddenly felt foolish holding a bunch of flowers. The guy was tall, had blond curly hair, and looked Tom square in the eye with his pale-blue eyes. Apparently, Tallie wanted the exact opposite of him.

"Hello." The man glanced at the sunflowers like Tom was a Hare Krishna looking for donations at the airport. "What can I do for you?"

"I just stopped by to see Tallie, but I can come back later." He turned to leave.

"She's here. Just a second. Hey, Tal, you have company!" he called into the kitchen. "Want to come in?"

"No, that's okay," Tom said as Tallie came into view,

drying her hands on a dish towel. Their eyes met.

"Tom, hi," she said.

"You're busy. I'll come back another time." He looked from her to his blond replacement and turned to leave.

"I'm not busy. Come in." She invited him, her eyes never leaving his face.

"This is Tom?" A smile lit the blond man's face. "Tallie, sweetheart, maybe you should introduce me."

Tom tensed and glowered at the man. Sweetheart?

Tallie put her arm around the man's waist, and he wrapped his arm around her shoulder. "Right. Tom, this is Tanner Kensington, my brother. My twin brother."

Tom's eyes went wide. "Oh, your brother." He quickly retracted the urge to pummel the guy for touching Tallie. He wondered if he should kill Clay for that bit of deception but held out his hand to shake with Tanner. "Tom Black. Nice to meet you." What a relief. Her brother.

"Nice to meet you, too. We used to watch you ride bulls way back when. I was surprised to find out Tallie knew you." He gave Tom an easy smile complete with Tallie's dimples.

"Come in out of the heat, Tom." Tallie took his hand and pulled him in the door.

"I'm surprised to meet you, too. Tallie said she hadn't seen her family in years."

Tanner frowned and looked at Tallie apologetically. "That's true. I haven't seen her since we were in high school. We kept tabs on her after she married Roy, but when she moved here, we lost track of her. Our mother forbade any of us from seeing her, and when we were older, we couldn't find her. I wouldn't have found her now if Cody hadn't been kidnapped from Clay Masterson's ranch. It was a huge story and we heard about it in Phoenix. Sis runs in an impressive circle these days." He looked lovingly at his sister. "As soon as we heard she was here, Dad sent me to find her and here I am, trying to talk her into moving back to Arizona."

"Oh?" Tom didn't like the sound of that.

"Not successfully. She seems to like Nashville for some reason." He smiled. "If it's okay with you, Tallie, I promised Cody I'd take him out for a chili dog and video games."

"He'll love it. Cody!" she called. "Uncle Tan wants to take you out for a chili dog."

"Sweet!" Cody said as he ran from his room, stopping when he saw Tom. "Tom! I have an uncle. Isn't that cool?" Cody grinned as his uncle wrapped an arm around his neck and rubbed his head.

"Yeah, that's cool," Tom said with a smile.

"Come on, Cody. Let's get something to eat and play some video games. We'll be back in say, three hours or so." Tanner winked at Tallie. "See you later. Nice meeting you, Tom. Come on, munchkin." Tanner steered Cody out the door, leaving Tallie and Tom to stare at each other.

"Uh, hmm. Hi," Tallie said.

"Hi," he said quietly. "Twins, huh? I should have seen the resemblance sooner."

"Oh, well." She shrugged. "Where's Michael?"

"Swimming at Clay's." He stuffed his hands in his pockets, tense now that Tanner and Cody left them alone.

"Is he still having nightmares?"

"Not for the past week. He's doing better. I spent a few more nights sleeping on his bedroom floor and it seemed to help."

"You're a good dad, Tom." She crossed her arms across her middle and took a breath.

Tom smiled at her compliment. "Thanks, I'm trying. He told me today I could call him Mike."

Tallie smiled, revealing adorable dimples. "That's wonderful. It means he's letting down his guard, doesn't it?"

"Yeah, I hope so." Tom frowned again and decided he'd had enough chitchat. "Help me out, Tallie. I don't know what to say. Something went wrong and you left. Why? What happened?" He searched her face for an answer.

She bit her lip. "A couple of things." She gave him a long look. "Would you like a pop or something?"

Tom shook his head and waited, a little worried about what she would say. Apparently, it was more serious than he thought if she thought he needed a beverage first. No quick "I love you" would cure this.

She took a deep breath and rubbed her hand behind her neck. "Well," she said, walking away from him, stopping near the front window. "After the cabin exploded, I told you I ran around to where I'd last seen you."

"Yes."

"When I got there, you and Michael were laid out on the ground and I couldn't find Cody."

"Right. You told me all this—"

"I was sure Cody had been in the cabin and was...gone. But you were still there, even though you looked like you were dead. I knelt down next to you to see if you were breathing, and you were. I started talking to you, begging you to wake up and be okay, urging you to get up...you tossed around and moaned and then...then you called out...a name."

Tom felt a sinking feeling in his gut. "A name?"

She looked at him and nodded. "Yes. Multiple times, in fact."

"What name?" he asked, although he knew. He remembered.

"Well, it wasn't mine. You called for Jolie, over and over." She bit her lip. "I know how you loved her, and hearing you call out for her reminded me of things you've said. Clues, I guess you could call them. When I put them all together, I realized there wasn't much of a chance for us."

Tom frowned. "What kind of clues? I don't know what you're talking about."

"Oh, things like, you'd told me when you fall, you fall hard, and I know you were talking about her. When I said I loved you and you couldn't say it back, I know it was because of her. You stopped seeing Sherry because she wanted something from you that you couldn't give her. I decided I didn't want to spend the rest of my life competing with Jolie's ghost, and I couldn't stick around until you decided to end things with me. I also have Cody to think about. He was already getting attached to you, and I thought it would be difficult for him if things went the way I thought they would."

Tom stiffened at her choice of words—Jolie's ghost—and let out the breath he'd been holding. "I'm not sure what to say." What could he say? Where could he even start? She had a laundry list of complaints against him. Valid complaints.

"It's okay." She headed toward the kitchen. "How about that pop?"

"Wait a sec. It's not okay." He grabbed her arm as she

moved by. "I want to explain some things to you. Please."
She stopped but wouldn't look at him. "There is a logical
explanation for this. I told you about my accident. It wasn't
just my knee but a head injury, too. I was out of it for several weeks. They said I was thrashing around so bad I was
restrained to keep from hurting myself more. I would kind of
wake up once in a while and Jolie would be there, talking to
me, whispering encouraging things in my ear. When I woke
up enough to know what was going on, I thought I was paralyzed. I couldn't move my arms or legs because of the re-
straints. It scared the hell out of me. Jolie...she was always
there. After the cabin exploded, my mind was gummed up
from the gas fumes and it seemed like it was all happening
again. Exactly the same way. I couldn't move my legs and
there was a voice whispering in my ear. I was just confused
for a minute, Tallie." He paused. "I did love her and probably held on longer than I should have. But she's gone and
can't ever come back. She'll always be the mother of my
son, and I'll always be grateful to her for giving Michael to
me. But I've grieved for her and made my peace with her
memory. She isn't an issue any longer, not the way you
think anyway. Not for me." He let go of her arm. "When I
told you I fall hard, I meant it. I do. I have, for you. When I
said we needed to wait to discuss love and all that, it was
because I was already so much in love with you I couldn't
stand the idea that you wouldn't love me back. And I did
end things with Sherry because I didn't love her. The night
she came to see me, I told her that again. I told her I was in
love with someone else. I was talking about you, not Jolie."
He paused and took a breath. "Is there anything else?"

"There is." She gave him a level stare and Tom felt like

they were back to square one. "I left, mostly because of my doubts. I didn't think you would ever move on from Jolie's memory and commit to a relationship with me. But, I also left for you...because you said you needed time after the boys were home to figure things out. You said we needed to get back to our normal lives to make sure what we felt wasn't just a reaction to our situation. I gave you what you said you wanted. I came back to my normal life and gave you time."

"You could have stayed with me."

"I came to your house because I needed a safe place. The threat was gone. I needed to come home, clean up the mess, and get back to work. Cody needs to start school in a few weeks. My life is here." The agitation in her voice increased as she spoke.

"So that's it? No matter what I say, it's over?"

"I don't want to end this. No. But Tom...you didn't even ask me to stay. I had no choice but to come home."

Tom stared, dumbfounded. "You were already there. I didn't think I needed to ask you to stay. I thought you understood—" He exhaled and ran his hand through his black hair. No, she hadn't. He'd thrown out enough mixed signals to confuse Tallie for decades to come. "If I ask you to come back now, would you?"

"Have you had enough time to think about what you want, Tom? Is this just a reaction to the situation we were in or is it more? Are you able to put Jolie in the past?"

"Yes. I can. I have. I told her it was over and I didn't want her to come back anymore." Tom clenched his jaw tight. Oh man, did he say that?

"You told her?" Tallie frowned. "When did you tell her

this? I thought she left you—"

Tom interrupted, waving his hand. "It's a long story. I'll tell you about it later." He paced away and came back. "It's so much more than a simple reaction to a situation. At least it is for me. Help me fix this, Tallie. I love you, but I don't know what to do. What can I do?"

"Tell me again," she whispered.

"What?"

"Tell me how you feel."

"I love you, Tallie. I'm miserable without you. Don't push me away."

"That's a good start." She smiled her dimpled smile. "I love you, and all I've wanted was for you to love me. I wanted to hear you say those words and know you meant them." She walked to him, placed her hands on his cheeks, and kissed him. His arms went around her and he returned the kiss, long and sweet. He held her tight, relieved to hold her again.

"I've missed you so much, Tallie."

"I've missed you too," she whispered. "Take me to bed, do what you do, and make me happy, Tom."

"I like that idea but hold on a second." He released her from his hug. "I got myself in trouble with you because I didn't talk fast enough, and I'm not done talking yet. When I'm done, we'll get to that." He took a deep breath and pulled her hands to his lips and kissed her fingers. "I want to spend the rest of my life with you. I want to help you raise your son, have you help me raise mine, and maybe we could have a few more kids that would be ours together." He swallowed hard. "I'm just a busted up old cowboy, and I'm not usually good at stuff like this. I'm not smooth. Snappy lyrics and love songs are Clay's thing, not mine." He paused. "I don't have a ring yet, and if I get down on my knee to propose, I won't be able to get back up. So I'm just asking, plain and simple. Will you marry me, Tallie?"

She sniffed. "What does Mike think?"

Tom smiled and added one more item to his list of reasons he loved her. "He asked me today if I was ever going to ask you to marry us."

"Us?" she laughed even though she was clearly close to tears.

"That's what I said. He explained it to me that we are a package deal. You can't marry just me. You would be marrying both of us."

"I guess I need to clarify this proposal before accepting." She gave him a teasing smile. "Are you asking us, Cody and me, to marry you?"

"Right. One package deal marrying the other. If you need to check with him, I guess I can wait." He bit his lip to hold back a smile.

"I have it on good authority Cody would approve, so on behalf of both of us, I accept your proposal. Yes, I'll marry you." Tears flooded her eyes. She sniffed and laughed as he took her in his arms and held her.

"But I want you to move back now. I want you with me now. The boys can start school together. We can start being a family. Will you?"

"Yes." She smiled through her tears. "Now, are you done talking? For a guy who doesn't like to talk, you sure chatter a lot." She wrapped her arms around his neck and kissed him. She grabbed his hand and pulled him into the bedroom. "Then, when you get your breath back," she said with a knowing smile, "you can tell me that long story about how you told Jolie not to come back. Considering the look on your face when you said that, I think it'll be one heck of a good story."

Tom laughed. "I like how you organize your priorities. First things first." He took her in his arms and they fell on the bed together. "There is one thing I need to know before I tell you the story."

"What?"

"Do you believe in ghosts?"

The end

Also from Sharleen Scott
and
Out West Press

Tangles

While faced with the challenge of his mother's escalating Alzheimer's disease, Logan McKinnon discovers her secret journals that leave him questioning everything he knows about his family. With no one left to ask, Logan must find the man in the journals to discover a truth he may not want to know.

Caught in Cross Seas
Book one in the CAUGHT series

When country music superstar Clay Masterson finds his supposedly dead father, he wants to do two things: buy dear ol' dad a beer to thank him for being a great father for the ten minutes he spent at it, and kick his dad's sorry butt to Montana to face an eighteen-year-old murder charge. Harlie Cates will try to stop him.

Happily ever after could be a problem for them.

Caught in Make-Believe
Book three in the CAUGHT series
Coming soon

ABOUT THE AUTHOR

Sharleen Scott lives in the foothills of the Cascade Mountains in the beautiful Pacific Northwest with her husband, Brett, two kids, and two spoiled cats.

You can visit her at
www.sharleenscott.com
www.facebook.com/outwestpress
www.instagram.com/sharleenscott305
Also on Goodreads and Pinterest.

SHARLEEN SCOTT

If you enjoyed this book,
please leave a review at Amazon.com.

Made in the USA
Coppell, TX
02 March 2021

51100078R10239